Ritual Abuse – Winter

Spiritual Warfare

Lynda L. Irons

Irons Quill

Scripture taken from the NEW AMERICAN STANDARD BIBLE ®, Copyright © 1960, 1962, 1963, 1968, 1971, 1972, 1975, 1977, 1995 by the Lockman Foundation. Used by permission.

All rights reserved. Except for brief quotes, no portion of this book may be reproduced, stored in a retrieval system, or transmitted in any form – electronic, mechanical, photocopy, recording, scanning, or other means without prior approval from and/or crediting this author. Contact the author at ironsquillreader@gmail.com. Questions and comments are welcome.

This is a work of fiction that is loosely based on some actual experiences from the author's life. Names, characters, places, and incidents that resemble that of any actual persons, living or dead, businesses, locales, churches, events, and so on, are purely coincidental and are the product of the author's wild imagination.

This story is not for everyone. It contains some very disturbing information. Unfortunately, while this is purely fictional, it depicts the tormented lives of far too many ritual abuse survivors who live in unsuspecting communities. The representative characters give voice to these amazing survivors in a way that only hints at the horrors that they experienced day in and day out. This narrative is not meant to be sensational, rather to raise awareness that these people exist and desperately need the help of the Church.

WARNING: If you are a Satanic or Witchcraft Ritual Abuse survivor, please be aware that reading some portions of this book could trigger any unresolved programming or issues.

Table of Contents

	Page
Key Characters from <u>Ritual Abuse – Autumn</u>	6
Chapter 1 Thursday, November 2	8
Chapter 2 Friday, November 3	43
Chapter 3 Saturday, November 4, Demon Revels	69
Chapter 4 Sunday, November 5, Full Moon	81
Chapter 5 Tuesday, November 7	102
Chapter 6 Friday, November 10	111
Chapter 7 Tuesday, November 21	135
Chapter 8 Thursday, December 21, Winter Solstice	163
Chapter 9 Sunday, December 24, Demon Revels	185
Chapter 10 Friday, January 5	200
Chapter 11 Sunday, January 21	220
Chapter 12 Thursday, January 25	235
Chapter 13 Monday, February 5	255
Chapter 14 Friday, February 9	276
Chapter 15 Sunday, February 11, Last Quarter Moon	302
Chapter 16 Friday, February 16	328
Chapter 17 Sunday, February 18	350
Chapter 18 Wednesday, February 21, Ash Wednesday	369
Chapter 19 Friday, February 23	382
Chapter 20 Sunday, February 25	402
Chapter 21 Monday, March 5	421
Chapter 22 Sunday, March 11	436
Chapter 23 Saturday, March 17, St. Patrick's Day	451
Other Books By This Author	460

Key Characters from Ritual Abuse – Autumn

This is the second in a four-book series. Ritual Abuse – Spring and Ritual Abuse – Summer follow this one. The following are some of the key characters that were introduced in the first book, Ritual Abuse – Autumn:

Abigail Steele, a widow and counselor, started her life over after the deaths of her husband and three sons by purchasing a small ten-acre farm in a remote area of the county.

Carrie Sue Wagner was born to Satanist parents, Ron and Susan. She had been programmed and fragmented into multiple personalities by the intentional torment she sustained both at home and at rituals. She has been seeing Abigail Steele for counseling.

F. Amy Bolton is another SRA survivor but she was not quite sure if she was willing to leave the cult. She has also been seeing Abigail Steele for counseling.

Prinz, the regional master, had risen to power over the decades. He was reputed to be over a century old.

Daggett and Darod are area masters and subject to Prinz until they can overthrow him.

Zorroz and Herrak are local masters reigning under Daggett and Darod respectively. Carrie Sue falls under Daggett's jurisdiction while Amy falls under Darod's. These men and many others are pillars in their local communities as professionals, businessmen, family men, and even church goers.

Gary and Cindy McCord are good friends of Abigail Steele and the parents of Traci and Bryan. Cindy and Abigail are prayer partners and they all attend the

Baptist church in Springfield where Daniel Spalding is the pastor.

Lee Norris, Gary's cousin, recently made a decision to sell his ranch in Montana and move back east to be near his extended family.

Earl and Jan Milner are Abigail's elderly neighbors to her north.

David and Martha York are her elderly neighbors to the south.

1

Thursday, November 2, 2006

The fire threw heat and light in irregular bursts and flickers that gave the five-sided rock a sinister glow. It was shortly after midnight and even though Prinz was the highest-ranking master in this region, his natural and supernatural instincts were telling him that this was not going to be a good night.

Not only had his king not shown up for any of the previous four nights of rituals and revels, his own masters were becoming tentative and weak. Perhaps they, too, were losing their physical and spiritual faculties; perhaps they were losing their fear of him as well. They had nothing to lose.

Prinz was loath to admit his own decline in the last year. Oh, how he had schemed and fought for this position decade after decade for over a century. Once again, he cursed that woman, that servant of the Great Enemy, and once again he renewed his resolve to make her life miserable and to ruin her reputation if he could not kill her.

Killing her dog, cutting her brake lines, leaving threats on her phone, having her tailed, sending in his programmed women for counseling, and invading her home were mild harassments compared to the things he was planning. He had never come up against this kind of opposition before. He certainly did not want to acknowledge the disquiet in his cold soul.

Looking at Daggett, his highest-ranking master in this area, and at what was left of this mockery of All Saints Day, at this satanic high holy day, he ordered

Daggett to see what the commotion was down the lane. "What's taking Zorroz so long getting back up here?" he growled his demand. Zorroz was the local master and this was his home territory and usual ritual site.

Daggett did not want to admit that he was shaken by the presence of Prinz. Bowing with due respect, he turned and walked rapidly with as much dignity as he could muster back toward the barn where Zorroz was supposed to have retrieved Carrie Sue Wagner, bound and hooded, gagged and drugged, to the epicenter of the festivities. The bone-chilling wind increased and noisy eddies of crisp leaves stirred, as if a phantom were walking beside him, adding to his uneasiness.

By the dim light of the nearly half moon Daggett saw several people gathered around a robed form who was on his knees. As he drew closer, Daggett heard gasping and rasping coming from the distressed man. Realizing that it was Zorroz, his sense of foreboding rose as rapidly as if he had been assaulted himself. Regaining his composure, he questioned no one in particular, "What's going on here? Where's Carrion?" He used Carrie Sue Wagner's cult name.

Zorroz gathered his strength and staggered to his feet still clutching his throat, breathing ragged breaths, trying to clear his drowning vocal cords. He gasped unintelligible words, frantically pointing back toward the barn and the road beyond it. Apparently, some of his sheriff's instincts had not left him and he registered the glimpse of Carry Sue backing away and moving in that direction.

Daggett quickly barked orders at the two guards and the three others who had been drawn to the unusual commotion. Not one of them was accustomed to any irregularities in the rituals. It was not that long ago that Carrion's brother had temporarily escaped, but he paid dearly for that with his life. Now, not only had Carrion escaped, but she had apparently summoned supernatural powers of some kind to overcome a man with the strength and stature of Zorroz.

The men immediately responded and set out like bloodhounds down the trail that led past the barn and merged with the rutted gravel driveway that was now jammed with the van and four-wheelers, cars and pickup trucks. One of the men shed his dark robe, leaped into his truck, got the big diesel engine roaring with the headlights probing into the woods. He turned around to head to the road. "I'll cut her off so she can't get to that farm!" They knew Abigail Steele's property, indeed, several of them had visited the place in the not so distant past.

With David in executive control, Carrie Sue made good time running down the driveway. Staying in the shadows of the overhanging trees as much as possible, she had to dart into the woods several times and lay low since some of the Satanists were still arriving on four-wheelers or in their vehicles. She was grateful for the clouds which obscured the moonlight, but it forced her to move much slower in order to avoid obstacles and minimize excessive noise. She never realized just how much noise one crisp leaf could make and now she found herself having to shuffle through wind-swept piles along her dimly lit route.

Unfamiliar with the terrain, David, nevertheless, had a general idea of the direction of Abigail Steele's farm. The internal leaders had a brief meeting with Carrie Sue and decided that they should try to stay off of the main road. Cutting through the thick woods, risking a possible encounter with obstacles, fences or animals, they arbitrarily picked a point before the old farmhouse and turned north, hoping that they were going roughly parallel to the curvy, hilly road that would eventually lead them to Abigail's farm about a mile away.

Carrie Sue had led a fairly sedentary lifestyle. This morning's walk to her brother's abandoned car, about a mile in the opposite direction from Abigail's farm, was one of the longest hikes she had ever made in her sheltered life. Despite David being in executive control and others switching in to spell him, they were soon winded as they desperately scurried on, stumbling and slipping on what appeared to be a narrow animal trail.

Topping a fairly steep grade, they did not anticipate the unexpectedly precipitous angle as the trail abruptly plunged downward. Thrown off stride, David's foot struck a protruding root and they sprawled noisily. They grunted as the impact briefly knocked the breath out of them, snapping twigs as loudly and easily as the metatarsals in Carrie Sue's left foot snapped.

Immediately, her trackers began to shout gleefully to one another, having heard the unnatural sounds that were picked up and sent reverberating through the mostly still night.

"This way!"

"We've got her now!"

Converging near the source of the sounds, they were somewhat perplexed that they could not pick up her natural trail or her spiritual scent as they had come to expect when pursuing their prey. Tonight, they were more afraid of Prinz, Daggett, and Zorroz for failure to capture Carrion than they were of the woman who took Zorroz down.

Carrie Sue could hear her pursuers rapidly closing the distance that David and the others had worked so hard to build. Scrambling to their feet, having no time to assess any damage, they limped and lurched further down the trail, crying out to God, "Oh, God, please strengthen us! God, help us run faster! God! Please! We need to get to Abigail's house." Their desperate pleas turned to angry prayers when they seemed to be getting more tired and weak with each step. "God, are You on their side?" she accused the One she had so recently dared to trust.

Lungs screaming, pain from the injured foot finally registering, hearing her pursuers' accelerated footsteps closing in on her, Carrie Sue hobbled off the path just as the moon slipped behind a cloud. She found herself next to a large oak tree and sagged against it, bitterly resigning herself to recapture.

It was just a matter of time.

Prinz was furious; more furious than usual. "What do you mean, she got away?" *How could a woman who was supposed to have been drugged, bound, and guarded escape from someone like Zorroz?* Even though his hooded robe completely hid his dark features, he glowered at those who were unfortunate enough to be within eyesight causing them to cringe and shrink back with alarm as they sensed more than saw his fury. He began to utter curses as he strode through the crowd looking more ominous than ever.

"She will pay," he screamed, not knowing himself if he meant Carrie Sue Wagner or Abigail Steele.

The intimidating driver of the noisy diesel truck roared up and down York Creek Road several times until he was satisfied that his presence would keep Carrion off of the road and in the woods where she would be more easily captured. He unwittingly let her know just how close she was to the road. He soon found a place to back his truck onto the edge of the road on the far side of York Creek and waited smugly. He did not want to risk rousing the occupants of the farm next to Abigail Steele. Taking his vigil there at the creek, he waited for her to come to him, that is, if she even made it this far.

Two sets of heavy footsteps pounded down the trail going slower than they wanted to because of the sudden loss of moonlight. They moved cautiously past the large oak tree and down the narrow trail toward York Creek.

Carrie Sue held her breath as they neared and was just beginning to calm down now that they passed. She was astounded that they had missed her. *Oh, God, You did that, didn't You? You put a cloud in front of the moon. You did answer my prayer to keep anyone from tracking me.* Carrie Sue could not stop the tears of gratitude from seeping from her weary eyes. As encouraged as she was, she knew that she could not just march out of there; she would have to be as wise as a serpent if she were to survive this night.

Once she was certain that they were far enough away, she slid down to the base of the oak and tried to assess the damage to her left foot. It was throbbing and beginning to swell so she dared not remove her tennis shoe lest she would not be able to put it back on. *Oh, Lord, I need wisdom. I can't stay here. I can't move far or fast. Help!* She leaned against the trunk of the solid oak with her eyes closed and waited for what seemed like an hour.

The sound of a vehicle startled her. She realized that it was on York Creek Road and it confirmed that she apparently was not very far away from the road. That gave her a measure of hope. Maybe she was closer to Abigail's farm than she thought. *Think! God, help me think.* Maybe she could escape. Maybe.

The trees and foliage displayed a dappled pattern of light as the moon emerged from behind the cloud. One of the beams settled on a sturdy branch that was about five feet long. A thought formed in her head and she carefully scooted toward the fallen branch. That was when she realized just how badly she had scraped the palms of her hands in the fall. *I've been through worse.*

She paused and listened for a moment before trying to regain her feet using the stout branch for balance. She was pleased to discover that, despite the severe pain that shot up her shin from just behind her toes, she could tolerate putting her heel down, enabling her to hobble using the branch for support.

Not daring to return to the narrow trail, she began to pick her way gingerly and carefully through the brush and wild berry canes that grew in the woods, startling herself whenever she disturbed crisp leaves or stepped on a brittle stick or brushed against a brittle shrub or small tree. Foot throbbing, hands smarting, she pushed through the pain and continued to follow the fall of the land, always heading downhill and yet not entirely sure that she was not walking in circles. She believed; she hoped that she would end up either at the road or down by the creek.

Prinz had to save face somehow. Everyone except for the five men which he had dispatched to recapture Carrion were gathered to worship their king. He called Zorroz to the center of the gathering and looked deeply into his eyes. "Zorroz, do you believe that you shall be made whole?"

Zorroz croaked his response. "Yes, master, I do. I believe. Help me."

Prinz put the tips of his fingers on the swollen throat and uttered, "Be healed in the name of Lucifer!"

Immediately, the astounded Zorroz felt the swelling go down. The bruising disappeared and he was able to speak clearly. "Praise be to the king and to you, a most worthy servant of the king!"

Gasps could be heard throughout the gathering. Chanting began and the somber mood at the ritual shifted dramatically.

"Yes, indeed, we shall do greater works than these."

Prinz felt exonerated and saw the respect and awe in his followers. Carrie Sue had evaded tonight's destiny for now, but the ever resourceful, ever insatiable, ever brutal one pointed to a tiny girl child whose glazed eyes widened with terror. The group began to sway and chant as one. Rhythms were beaten on primitive instruments, and the dark night began to reverberate with familiar revelry that would continue for several more hours.

Once again Urdang and the other demons wheeled and circled around the gathering like blood-thirsty vultures waiting to pounce on their prey. They were thoroughly mystified that they were unable to pounce on Carrie Sue tonight and were displeased by their ineffectiveness in directing her pursuers to her.

By three o'clock in the morning the festivities were completed, vile curses were sent out, and Prinz was somewhat satisfied and satiated by the lingering taste of blood in his mouth. Daggett began to feel more at ease as the furniture and instruments were taken to the van which would then transport them to the storage place in the windowless building for the next ritual. The participants dutifully cleared away all evidence of their presence including the cremated remains of the honored child.

Zorroz was not entirely sure of his fate. Either he was being esteemed by Prinz and deemed valuable enough to save or else he was being set up for his downfall. He would have to tread even more carefully than he had in the past. It was, after all, a dog-eat-dog world and he trusted no one.

Carrie Sue had been fleeing for her life for over three hours now. Most of that time she was hobbled by what she assumed was a broken or severely sprained foot. She estimated that she might be more than half way to Abigail's farmhouse, but she had not yet come to York Creek. She intentionally stayed away from the road, especially now that the ritual participants were driving home. *Are they still after me?* Carrie Sue continued to hear noises in the woods, but she was not entirely sure if the unfamiliar sounds were from humans or from nocturnal animals or because of the wind.

After briefly considering whether or not she should find some place to wait out the night, her internal leadership group thought it would be best to keep on moving. After all, she was wearing only a lightweight sweatshirt over her regular clothes and it was in the forties. It was even colder with winds; she could freeze to death. *Wouldn't that be ironic – survive all the tortures of Satanism and then succumb to hypothermia.* Carrie Sue broke into a wry smile and carefully continued to put one foot in front of the other.

The man in the diesel-powered pickup truck got out and wandered back along the edge of the field next to the creek. He moved stealthily, stopping frequently, listening for any sounds that Carrion might make. One of the other trackers had headed away from the road and was checking the back trails in case she had gone that way. The other two men went back up the trail that they had come down after checking with the man in the pickup. The fifth man patrolled the road. She had to be out there.

They would find her and she would pay dearly.

Carrie Sue's foot pain was excruciating after taking an unexpectedly hard step. *Oh, Lord Jesus, help!* On the next step, ground crumbled under her foot and she was suddenly hurtling down a steep incline head first. Instinctively tucking and rolling, covering her head with her arms, she came to rest in the bottom of a ditch.

A muddy ditch.

She was sure that anyone in the vicinity could hear that crash. She was scared. She was hurt. And she was mad. *God, I just asked for help and now I'm in a ditch, I'm wet, and I'm a sitting duck. Just whose side are You on, anyway?* She nearly sobbed as she was wracked with fresh waves of pain from her foot, hands, and now her left shoulder and back. She was scratched and bruised, weary and worn.

The man who was patrolling the road heard the noise behind him and headed toward the sound at the same time that the other men did. It also alerted the Rottweiler who got off of the front porch of her owner's house and trotted down the long driveway toward the road. Toward the ditch.

The moon emerged once again from behind the cloud and shone like a beacon on the five-foot-deep ditch. Carrie Sue assessed her situation. She cautiously looked around her and saw that there was a large pipe a few feet in front of her. Above it was stone work and metal bars which indicated a driveway. Alarmed by the sound of her trackers' muffled exchanges; she instinctively scooted forward through the damp ditch and slid into the culvert. She was grateful that its dirt-filled bottom was relatively dry and, more importantly, it muted any sound that she might have made had she been moving on cold, bare metal.

Suddenly, the Rottweiler broke into a series of warning barks and howls as she neared the edge of her domain. Carrie Sue's heart stopped momentarily and then beat so loudly that she thought that the sound of it would echo out of either end of the pipe. The man on the road froze as did the other four men. They were aware of the property near their ritual host's farm and knew of the dog. The five men retreated to the pickup truck where they discussed the situation quietly.

"False alarm," one of the men said, "that old dog's probably just chasing a coon."

"It could be her, we need to check it out," another cautioned.

"Naw, if it was her, the dog would still be going nuts," the first one opined.

"How long are we going to do this?" a third one voiced his weariness.

"Do you want to be the one to tell Prinz that we let her get away?" the pickup driver asked.

"She must be holed up in the woods somewhere. We might have to wait for daybreak."

The pickup driver assumed control. "We still have a couple hours. You," he pointed to the first man, "keep patrolling the road. You three split up and search for hiding places. She's out there somewhere. I'll keep a watch on this end. We know which way she's going. Eventually, she'll have to come this way. You flush her out and I'll be here to nab her."

Carrie Sue began to shiver in the metal pipe. She was not entirely sure if it was because of the cold or the fear. When the Rottweiler was satisfied that she had effectively chased the intruders from her territory and was about to head back up to the porch, the breeze shifted slightly and she caught a new scent.

She followed it down into the ditch.

Abigail stirred in her sleep and rolled over before coming fully awake. Aware that it was getting chilly in the house, she slipped out from under her comforter and made her way to the wood stove. She opened the damper so the smoke would not back into the living room and then slowly opened the metal door, peering into the orange-red bed of embers. She had learned to add wood to the fire practically in her sleep. Smaller round logs were nestled into the embers and then a wedge of oak was placed on top of them. Closing the door, she used the bathroom and noted the time – four-thirty in the morning. It was pitch black outside.

Walking back into the living room, she adjusted the damper and then crawled back into bed and began to pray. "Oh, Lord, Carrie Sue is out there cold and alone. Abba, Father, please send help from Your sanctuary. Put her in a safe place and keep her warm. Guard her from harm...."

Abigail prayed until she drifted off to sleep again clinging to her hope in God. She did not want to think about what the cult would have done to her friend. If she survived, she would have been tortured beyond imagination, her mind fragmented and reprogrammed, her life once again dismantled by their malevolence. If she was sacrificed, her body would never be found. There would be no evidence; and, with Sheriff Bynum being one of them, an investigation would be farcical.

The Rottweiler sniffed and snuffled and then began to whine a high-pitched query as she edged closer to the terrified and barely breathing Carrie Sue. Imminent danger from the dog had caused a child personality to switch into executive control causing David, Titus, and Ichabod great frustration. They were protectors; they should have executive control to deal with the dog.

"God," they cried out in frustration, "can't we catch a lousy break tonight?"

The dog, sensing a weak and helpless little one, responded maternally. She smelled the drying blood from numerous scratches and abrasions. She smelled the fear and sensed the vulnerability coming from this intruder. Deliberately and cautiously inching forward, releasing a muffled woof, nosing the hands that were covering the vulnerable face, the Rottweiler opened her vice-grip jaws and licked the cold, blood-flecked flesh as if she were comforting one of her own pups.

The child personality, Leah, was about three years old. Her presence was triggered by the appearance of the dog because she had been programmed during a ritual in which Carrie Sue was introduced to bestiality by a cult-trained, demonized dog. Resigned to her fate, she expected the same kind of torment tonight and was totally bewildered by the nurturing care and warmth coming from the dog.

The Rottweiler crawled further into the culvert and lay down next to Leah's huddled form with a paw over her shoulder, breathing warm puffs into her face, occasionally licking her face or hands, and worriedly nudging her as she would have done for one of her own distressed pups.

Beginning to relax and breathe more normally, Leah stopped shivering and dared to open her eyes in the dim light to look at the large dog. She could only see a silhouette of this canine that seemed to be guarding her while keeping her warm.

The male protectors breathed a sigh of relief and began to wonder if perhaps, God had over-ridden their prayers for strength. They would have challenged the dog and lost that battle for sure. *I wonder if this is what Paul meant when he said, 'when I am weak, then I am strong?'* They apologized to God for their anger and decided that it would be best for Leah to remain in executive control until God let them know what their next move should be.

They found out sooner than they anticipated. The Rottweiler suddenly lifted her head and was at full attention. She scrambled to her feet and walked stiff-legged to the end of the culvert hearing, smelling, and seeing things with her keen senses. A rumbling growl erupted from deep within her chest and she charged out of the culvert barking ferociously at something or someone nearby.

The abrupt change in the situation caused an abrupt switch in executive control. As the vulnerable Leah retreated to her internal place, David, the protector, was once again able to assume control of Carrie Sue's body and crawled back up the culvert the way they had come in. He miraculously found their walking stick and grabbed it as he crawled as quickly as he could up the side of the ditch and onto the wide shoulder of the road. By that time, the Rottweiler was dashing down the road and chasing a man who was hollering for help.

Taking full advantage of this development, David painfully crawled onto the pavement and used the stick to stand up. Looking both ways, he reoriented himself and crossed the road at an angle that brought them a few painstaking steps closer to Abigail's farm. David could make out some of the buildings that belonged to Abigail's neighbor about a quarter of a mile ahead. He knew that the creek, named for the York's, meandered just on this side of their farmstead.

We know where some of those guys are, but they don't know where we are. And we need to keep it that way. Titus, David, Carrie Sue, and Ichabod strategized with the speed of thought. They concluded that it would be too risky to just walk down the highway or in front of the York's house because of the dog and the men. An alternative would be to cross the road and duck into the woods on this side of the creek. They could then cross the creek and walk behind the York's place, approaching Abigail's house through Buster's pasture. It would mean twice the distance, cold water and mud, but it seemed to be the only safe route.

Painstakingly lowering himself to the ground and flattening the grasses as he slid down the incline that led into the woods, David began what they hoped was the last leg of their journey. They were grateful for the short rest in the culvert and had no idea of the time. It was still very dark. After what seemed to be at least an hour, David stumbled upon another narrow trail, wide enough for a deer or a horse, that seemed to be heading at an angle toward the creek; at least it was heading away from the road and somewhat downhill.

Sunrise was 6:18. Abigail's eyes blinked open before her mind was fully oriented. Once it was, the jarring thoughts of the last couple of days cascaded over her like a bucket of cold water and fully awakened her. Flinging back the covers, flipping her legs over the edge of the bed, she hastily dressed and began her morning routine. Adding logs to the glowing bed of coals in the woodstove, she moved through the kitchen and donned her boots and coat before heading down to take care of Buster. He would be surprised at the early breakfast today.

As usual, he was at the far end of the pasture and as usual he stampeded toward the tack room where he reared up, pawing the air before dropping down near Abigail and prancing around her much like a puppy.

"Hey, boy," Abigail said softly, "I'm going to give you a little bit now, but we might be going for a ride pretty soon so I'll give you some more later." She patted him on the rump and walked quickly back up to the fence, slid through and rushed over the cold dew-drenched grass. *Carrie Sue must be freezing! If she was still alive.*

If.

Returning to the house with prayers continually on her lips and in her thoughts, she promptly opened the refrigerator and grabbed a bar of Colby-Jack cheese, slicing a thick slab to eat. She did not want to stop for breakfast, but knew that she would need some protein. "Oh, Lord," she prayed her daily declaration, "this is the day that You have made and I will, yes, I *will* rejoice and be glad in it."

Abigail had determined to pray that prayer every day since that fateful night just over ten years ago when her husband and three sons had been killed – and now she seriously wondered about the possibility that they had been murdered by the very cult that was trying to kill Carrie Sue and herself!

Shuddering involuntarily, she remembered the day Carrie Sue's brother had come into this house intent upon killing her. Even worse, Sheriff Bynum had come to arrest the man. *Ugh! He was in my house!* Her eyes moistened as she remembered that they poisoned her dog barely a month ago. Oh, how she missed Dude. Shaking off the intruding thoughts, she began to form a plan to see if she could find Carrie Sue. It might just be an exercise in futility, but if she truly believed God's Word, then no weapon formed against her would prosper. That verse was embroidered and hanging in her bedroom for a reason.

"Lord, You said that no weapon formed against us would prosper. I do believe it. I pray that Carrie Sue will have avoided all attacks against her from humans and demons, from critters and the elements. Lord, guide my steps as I look for her today."

Grabbing her truck keys, thinking about her plan as she shut the door behind her, Abigail scrambled down the front porch steps and walked briskly over to her truck. She looked hopefully into Carrie Sue's car, but it was just as empty as it was yesterday. Abigail still felt more than a little responsible for Carrie Sue's apparent abduction. *If only I had taken that walk with her.*

Carrie Sue had spent all those nights with Abigail just so that this very thing would not have happened. October twenty-eight was the beginning of those five nights and she was supposed to have gone home this morning. *Was it just yesterday that this nightmare began?*

Abigail backed out of her parking place and then made her way down the curvy driveway and out to the road. She turned to the right and drove slowly along the frontage of her property with the windows down despite the chill in the air. After scanning the York's property, she turned her attention to the left side of the road and was startled to see a full-sized black pickup truck backed onto the field near the creek. It looked familiar. She racked her brain to remember where she had seen it before. Slowing as she approached it, she faced forward but looked out of the corners of her eyes and saw the two men in the front seat. The driver was Max Berryman. Max Berryman, the son of the owner of the biggest car dealership in the county! Max Berryman, also a member of Springfield First Baptist Church!

And he was looking right at her.

Abigail feigned interest in something that might have been on the seat next to her and turned her head away, hoping that he would have thought that she did not pay attention to his unusual presence. It did not work. She could hear the noisy diesel engine roaring to life behind her so she reflexively hit the gas. Rounding the sharp bend in the road, praying for protection, she abruptly applied her brakes and ducked into a driveway on the right-hand side of the road.

She was relieved to see that the driveway curled back the way she came with a thick area of shrubs and trees concealing both the driveway and the house. Coming to an abrupt stop, turning off the headlights, putting it in park so her brake lights would not show, she prayed that Max would continue down the road. She had Walther with her, but she certainly did not want to shoot anyone – even in self-defense.

The big diesel roared up the road not long after that and did keep going. Hurriedly putting the truck in reverse, she quickly drove home. Parking the truck in its usual place, she ran into the house and headed straight for the phone.

Cindy was waiting for her call and answered it immediately. "Did Carrie Sue come home yet?" Cindy and Gary had been apprised of the situation and they were praying.

"No! Is Gary home?" Abigail asked breathlessly. "I just drove down the road and Max Berryman and some other guy were waiting in his truck down by the field. He chased me after I drove by..."

"He what?" Cindy interrupted.

"I don't have time to explain," Abigail said urgently, "is Gary there? I need some help here. If they're still down there, that means Carrie Sue is still out there somewhere. I just know it."

"Wait," Cindy said and called out, "Gary! Abigail needs to talk to you."

Abigail waited an interminably long minute and finally heard Gary's voice. "What's going on?"

"I just got back from driving down the road. Max Berryman and some other guy were in his truck at the corner of the field by the creek. Gary, I think they're still looking for Carrie Sue. I think she might have escaped. I want to get on Buster and go find her..."

"Whoa, hold on there," Gary stopped her. "First of all, don't you leave your house until we get there. We don't need to lose you, too."

"Okay, but hurry," Abigail said impatiently, "can I at least get Buster saddled up and ready to go?"

"Take Walther with you," Gary cautioned.

"No sooner done than said," Abigail responded. *I do have some horse sense.* She really was grateful for Gary's protective big brotherly ways.

"Okay," he said, "my cousin, Lee, came in yesterday with four of his horses. Wait a sec while I check with him. He's in the kitchen."

Abigail remembered that she had agreed to keep Lee's horses temporarily until he could find a suitable place to board them. They had met about a month ago on that fateful Sunday when they found Dude dead. Mixed emotions battled within Abigail vying for her attention. No one had pursued a relationship with her since Darryl and the boys had died; perhaps because she gave off a "not interested" aura. But this man was interesting and she was feeling lonely; alone.

"Ab." Gary brought her back to the present. "We're on our way with the horses. We should be there in less than an hour."

"Okay." Abigail sighed in relief. "Thanks. Hurry!"

Ignoring the early hour, Abigail also called Pastor Spalding and her neighbors to the north. Earl and Jan Milner were prayer warriors as well as friends. She filled them in on the latest and they promised to keep a watchful eye out. Earl was a sharpshooter from World War II and had taught Abigail to shoot. He said he would make sure no suspicious vehicles came up the driveway while they were out on the horses.

Traffic on the road increased as people headed to their jobs. Carrie Sue could hear the loud pickup truck as it roared up the road toward the farm that contained the ritual site. She wondered if that meant that the search was called off or if it was a ruse to get her to come out to the road. Or maybe it was some other truck with a loud diesel engine. She was still closer to the road than she was to the far end of Abigail's little farm. She was grateful the dim light of morning allowed her to see better and move a bit faster. She had stumbled and fallen several times in the dark since she started this leg of her journey and was beyond fatigued.

The creek was visible through the brush and trees and she was hoping that the trail would lead to an easy crossing. The last thing she wanted to do was to wade through a cold creek but she kept putting one foot in front of the other praying as she went. David was exhausted so Titus and Ichabod also took turns taking executive control and feeling the pain of what they were all convinced was a broken foot.

Lee and Gary moved quickly and efficiently toward the back of Gary's garage. He and Cindy lived on a two-acre piece of property that was at the edge of Kingston, a small town about seven miles from Abigail's ten acre mini-farm. Lee's four mares were tethered and grazing near the back of the property. Lee expertly caught and led two of them toward the horse trailer that was still hitched to his pickup truck in anticipation of moving the horses to Abigail's farm sometime later that day. Saddles and tack were stored in the front compartment of the trailer.

"Hey, it'll just take an extra minute to get all four of them in here," Lee said.

"Go for it," Gary called back. He finished securing the first two horses while Lee went back for the other two and quickly secured them as well.

Twenty-three minutes from the time that Gary said good-bye to Abigail they were on the road. Neither of them said much other than discussing directions to Abigail's farm. Once they were through Kingston, they had five miles of the curving, hilly Kingston Road to navigate before it intersected with York Creek Road.

Steaming up the first grade in the big diesel, pulling over two tons of horse flesh plus a trailer, they picked up some speed on the downhill grade. Lee drove the unfamiliar curves carefully, and finally, with Gary's instruction, he slowed down for the turn into Abigail's driveway. They bumped and creaked their way slowly up the gravel driveway and saw Abigail holding Buster in the back yard once they made the final curve. The horses had endured a long trip from Montana, spent the night in an unfamiliar place, and now they were being asked to take the men for a ride.

Buster was a good horse, but unfamiliar sights and sounds could spook him. The rattles and squeaks of the truck and trailer were unfamiliar. Abigail spoke softly to him and kept him under control. Alert ears twitched like radar beacons, nostrils flared, nose lifted, Buster was on full alert and excited by the presence of the other horses. He was a gelding, but he did not know what that meant.

"Hey, Gary," Lee instructed as he opened the back door of the trailer, "open up that front compartment and grab that dark brown bridle and the black one. And grab a couple sets of reins." Each horse had her own bit and bridle but he used the saddles on any of the horses.

"Gotcha," Gary replied and quickly found what he needed in the neatly packed compartment. He brought them to Lee who deftly slipped off one halter and slipped the bridle and bit on Sparkles. He clipped the reins onto the rings and tied them to a bar on the trailer. Sparkles was a well-trained horse, but even well-trained horses could act up in situations like this.

He took the next set from Gary who went back to the compartment, "Any special blankets or saddles?"

"No," Lee said, "just grab a couple."

Gary was a mechanic and very strong. He had no trouble tucking a blanket under each arm and carrying a large saddle in each hand. Walking over to Lee, he moved his arm so that Lee could remove the blanket, shake it a little and throw it over Sparkles' back. He did the same with the saddle. By that time Gary had begun to saddle the other horse.

"That's Misty," Lee said, "she's a little spunky, but she's strong."

Untying the reins, Lee handed Sparkles to Gary. They both mounted up. Abigail was already on Buster and walked him slowly toward Sparkles and Misty. They were all on high alert, but their riders did not have time to let them socialize.

"Abigail," Gary said, "why don't you fill us in on what you think is going on."

"Sure," Abigail said pointing in a southeasterly direction through her stand of woods, "I went down the road early this morning and drove past Max Berryman parked by the creek. There was another guy in there with him, but I couldn't tell who he was. They took off after me, but I ducked into a driveway and they blew by me. I came back home and called you. I have a very strong feeling that Carrie Sue somehow got away from them and that's why they're still hanging around here."

"Where do you think she is?" Lee asked.

"Well, I've been thinking and praying about this," Abigail pointed higher and a little further to the left, "the farm with the ritual rock is about a mile or so down that way and across the road. I think that Carrie Sue would have tried to get to the road and follow it down to my house. But I heard that truck going up and down the road a couple of times during the night so I think she was forced to walk through the woods."

Gary picked up on her idea. "I think, then, that we should go down the road and look for signs. She might have left a footprint or something if she got far enough to cross it."

"I think this would be a good time to pray," Lee added, looking at both Abigail and Gary.

"Great idea," Abigail said. *Wow, I like this guy.* She quickly tucked that thought away and focused on the prayers as they took turns.

They prayed with their eyes open, looking through the woods as they walked their horses, hoping to see Carrie Sue come walking up through the trees.

Abigail led the way through the front yard and down to the road. They decided that Gary and Abigail should ride on the far side of the road and Lee should take the near side since he was more experienced with looking for signs.

Walking slower than any of them wanted to, pausing when a vehicle came down the road, they moved onto the shoulder whenever they could to avoid spooking horses or drivers. At York Creek, Lee crossed to Abigail and Gary's side of the road. They could plainly see the tire tracks of the full-sized pickup truck that had spun out of there not that long ago. They also noticed several sets of footprints coming and going from the truck.

"I can't tell for sure without taking a bit of time to study this area," Lee said thoughtfully, "but there were definitely more than two guys here last night." He briefly eyed the fields with the creek running next to it. *Lord, this would be some nice land.* He tucked that thought away and focused on the task at hand.

Abigail's heart sank. *How could her city-slicker friend not only navigate her way through these woods, but also be able to evade several men?*

"Let's keep going," Gary said.

They turned their horses and resumed their search along the road. A couple hundred feet beyond York Creek the shoulder dropped off steeply. Lee called out, "I think we might have something here."

Abigail and Gary crossed the road and looked as he pointed to the flattened roadside grasses that were just wide enough for a woman to have made if she were to slide down on her bottom rather than take the steep incline on her feet.

"I guess if it was dark and steep, I'd slide down, too," Gary said.

"Let's go, then." Abigail was hopeful once again.

They gave the horses their heads as they went down the slope leaning back in their saddles. Lee took the lead and began to pick his way through the tangled underbrush. He could see a footprint once in a while, but he was briefly mystified by the odd indentations he found as well.

Turning back toward Abigail and Gary behind her, he said, "I have her footprints, they're very fresh and it looks like she's limping badly."

"Oh, dear." Abigail was in anguish for her friend, but her hopes were rising. Oh, how she wanted to kick Buster in the sides and gallop to Carrie Sue's rescue. But of course, that would not be wise. They were still uncertain about the whereabouts of the men who may well be tracking Carrie Sue or waiting to ambush them.

Soon Lee came upon the narrow trail and they were able to pick up the pace. They were steadily heading toward the creek and the prints were even fresher.

"Abigail, call out for Carrie Sue, she'll recognize your voice," Lee instructed as he turned in the saddle.

"Carrie Sue! Where are you?"

Carrie Sue could not believe her ears. She had heard the noises behind her and was certain that the men would soon find her so she stopped and leaned against the next large tree just off the trail, resigning herself to a final disappointment. Beyond exhausted, broken and bruised, cold and wet, her despair flamed into hope as she recognized the voice of her friend.

"Over here! I'm over here!" Carrie Sue sagged to the base of the tree and began to weep with relief. Could this nightmare of a night actually be over?

Lee spurred Misty and quickly covered the ground to Carrie Sue. Abigail and Gary were right behind him. Lee had already dismounted like a rodeo rider and was assessing Carrie Sue's condition. He appraised her black eye and swollen left ankle and foot and asked, "Is there anything else besides your eye and foot?"

Carrie Sue could not speak, she merely held out her skinned, blood-crusted palms.

Abigail dismounted, dropped Buster's reins and ran over to Carrie Sue, weeping with relief. "Oh, my, you must be freezing." Quickly shedding her coat, she helped Carrie Sue get into it.

"Gary, you hand her to me. I'll ride behind her." He did not want to take a chance of her passing out at this point and falling off of the horse. Lee was already on Misty by the time Gary had picked up the shivering woman. In no time, Carrie Sue was securely in the saddle while Lee sat partially on the blanket and partially on Misty's rump.

Abigail took the lead. "There's a crossing up ahead a little bit; we can go through the back gate." Urging Buster into a brisk walk down the trail, they soon came to the place in the creek where it had a firm bottom that was wide and shallow. Emerging from the cold creek, zigzagging through the stand of woods that bordered it, they came to the edge of the large field that lay between Abigail's property and the Blue River bottoms.

"I'm going on ahead to get the gate opened," Abigail shouted over her shoulder as she gave Buster a nudge with her heels.

Gary stayed behind with Lee who did not want to further traumatize the quivering woman by galloping. Soon they came to the gate and headed up the trail toward the tack room and the house beyond it. Abigail waited for them to enter and closed the gate behind them before remounting and loping up the hill. Buster was bewildered when Abigail urged him to continue up to the house where she dismounted and let the reins fall to the ground. He might wander back to his feed bowl, or he might get acquainted with the mares, or he might just decide to munch on the good grass that was left in the back yard.

Lee handed Carrie Sue down to Gary and then dismounted by sliding backward off of Misty's rump. He then took her reins and grabbed up Sparkle's reins as well, leading them back to the trailer where Sassy and Lady were impatiently waiting. The occasional metallic stomp of a shoed hoof reverberated through the trailer. It would take him less than thirty minutes to lightly groom them and lead them to Buster's pasture. Offloading Sassy and Lady, he led them to the pasture as well.

Buster had already wandered down to the tack room and was awaiting Abigail's attention. He stamped and nickered nervously when Lee approached but quieted quickly with his reassuring manners and low voice. Lee gave Buster a small scoop of sweet feed and then dished out four more scoops spaced far enough apart that if any two horses had their hind legs toward one another, they would not be able to kick each other. Horses zealously guard their sweet feed. After taking care of all the horses, Lee strode quickly toward the house, securing the gate behind him.

Meanwhile, Abigail had the house open and told Gary to put Carrie Sue on her bed in the back bedroom.

"No," Carrie Sue protested weakly, "I'm filthy."

"Everything's washable. Let's get you taken care of and worry about that later," Abigail soothed.

Gary gently laid her down on the bed. Meanwhile, Abigail darted into the kitchen and grabbed a bottle of water from the refrigerator. Looking for a quick and nutritious snack, she also picked up a granola bar and brought them to Carrie Sue who rapidly sucked down most of the water.

"How did you hurt your foot?" the always analytical Gary asked. "Do you think it's broken or sprained?"

"I smashed it really hard against something that was sticking up in the trail. I heard something crunch so I think it's probably broken." Carrie Sue gratefully bit into the granola bar and tried not to inhale it.

"We should get you to the ER and get these injuries taken care of," Gary said.

The thought struck terror in Carrie Sue and she turned even paler. She just wanted to be in a safe place and any place out there seemed unsafe to her at the moment. Where were the men? If she fell into their clutches once, it could happen again.

Fortunately, the water and food were beginning to revive Carrie Sue a little bit and her mildly acerbic humor came through. "What would I tell them? Oh, I smashed my head on my brother's car and the next thing I knew, I was being taken to a ritual, but I punched out the sheriff before I escaped and tripped and fell in the dark."

Abigail and Gary looked at each other. Carrie Sue had a valid point. Her injuries and the torn, muddy clothing would raise a lot of suspicious questions. It was obvious that she had been through an ordeal. How would she explain the older shiner and a more recent fracture plus the scratches and abrasions? The medical people were not fools. More importantly, what if there was a cult plant in the hospital?

Lee had joined them after securing his horses. "It sounds like we need to have another prayer session."

"Good idea," Abigail said, "Why don't you start us; we'll pray as the Spirit leads."

When they had finished praying they looked at each other expectantly. At last Abigail spoke. "Here's what I'm thinking," she paused and looked at Carrie Sue, "I think you definitely need to get that foot X-rayed but I also think that it's important not to raise any questions. I mean, we don't want anyone calling Sheriff Bynum or anything. Do you think that you're up to getting into the shower?"

"Well," Carrie Sue said, making another attempt at humor, "it's been broken all night and I've walked on it all night; what's another hour?"

"What about security?" Gary asked. "Do you think you two will be okay? I mean, they've obviously had this place staked out all night. If they think Carrie Sue is here, don't you think they'll come after her again? What if they follow you?"

Lee was looking a little bewildered as he tried to follow their concerns. *Just what kind of a situation have I gotten myself into here?* He resolved to ask Gary more about it later.

"Gary," Abigail tilted her head and exhaled slightly, "no weapon formed against us will prosper. Period. They might get a nice shot in once in a while, but they won't win. We won't be careless, but I refuse to spend my life being intimidated."

"Okay," he said, "I'm just saying ..."

"Thanks," Abigail said looking at both Gary and then Lee, "I really appreciate it, I mean, I really, really needed you guys. This would have been impossible without your help."

"Well then," Gary said, "how about if we hang out here until Carrie Sue is ready to go to the ER and then

Lee can take me back home so maybe I can get a little work in today."

"Oh, my." Abigail startled. "What time is it?"

"It's getting close to nine," he replied.

"It seems later than that for some reason," Abigail mused and then looked at Carrie Sue. "I've got an old pair of crutches upstairs, let me get them for you so you can get going. Do you want to eat something now or later?" Her mind was racing with thoughts of all the things that needed to be done.

"I'd rather get cleaned up first, but I think I need help with that shoe." Carrie Sue looked at her left foot.

Lee stepped forward. "I worked with the rescue squad back in Montana, let me do that."

Carrie Sue nodded her assent. She felt both relief and apprehension. She would not have to get the shoe off by herself, but she knew that it would really throb regardless of who helped her.

"Lee, do you want me to unhitch the horse trailer while you do that?" Gary asked.

"Good idea, thanks, the keys are in the truck," Lee responded. He had already approached the bed and knelt down in preparation for removing the shoe from Carrie Sue's bruised and badly swollen left foot.

Abigail went upstairs to get the crutches. Locating them in the back of the closet of the bedroom that took up the north half of the upper floor, Abigail grabbed them and headed back down the stairs, stopping in the utility room to wipe them down. She estimated that Carrie Sue would need for them to be about a notch shorter and proceeded to press the metal stoppers to make the adjustments on each crutch. By the time she returned to the bedroom, Lee had removed the shoe, peeled off the soggy sock, and elevated Carrie Sue's foot on the extra pillow.

"Ouch! That's a lot of bruising," Abigail observed sympathetically. "Can you move your toes?"

"I don't even want to move my pinky let alone my toes," Carrie Sue said apprehensively, "I'm afraid of how much it'll hurt."

"Don't then," Lee cautioned, "I think that's a pretty good indication that you have some significant damage there. You're probably right about fractures."

"Are you ready to try to get to the shower with the crutches?" Abigail asked.

"No sense in delaying the inevitable," Carrie Sue sighed. "Actually, a hot shower sounds pretty good. I might drain your water heater."

"Do whatever helps, just remember that heat and having the leg down will increase the swelling."

"Oh, yeah."

"Here, let me move your left leg," Lee said looking her in the eyes, "I'll take good care of it. Start by dropping your right leg over the edge." Turning to Abigail, he said, "You help her sit up."

Carrie Sue grunted as she grabbed Abigail's forearm but between the three of them she was soon sitting at the edge of the bed. "Ooh, I'm a little light-headed."

"That's to be expected," Lee said reassuringly as he carefully lowered her foot to the floor, "give yourself a minute. You've been through quite an ordeal."

Taking in Lee's calming presence, Abigail mentally reviewed what she knew about the man from his last visit and she found herself wanting to know even more about him. She was both tantalized and terrified. She had not considered a relationship that could possibly lead to something significant since she was widowed ten years ago. No, she would not allow such thoughts to surface.

Until today, that is.

"I think I'm ready," Carrie Sue warbled. "I used crutches once in high school after I sprained my ankle real bad." She reached for the hand grips and scooted forward. Abigail steadied her on one side and Lee steadied her on the other.

"Good job," Abigail said encouragingly.

"Well, it's a whole lot easier than that old stick I was using. That was a God-thing. I'll have to tell you about it later." Carrie Sue advanced the crutches and took a tentative hop but by the time she got to the bathroom she was using the crutches proficiently.

"What clothes do you want me to get for you?" Abigail asked.

"Probably those boot-cut jeans and whatever shirt is handy," Carrie Sue replied and then added a little self-consciously, "Um, grab some clean undies, too."

"Gotcha covered," Abigail said as she retreated to the bedroom to find the items that were already packed in Carrie Sue's suitcase. *She was supposed to have gone home all safe and sound.* Abigail berated herself again. *I shouldn't have taken that ride on Buster.* After delivering the clothing to the bathroom, Abigail went into the kitchen and began to scramble eggs and fry bacon, put out fruit and the last of the blueberry muffins for her unexpected guests.

It took Carrie Sue some time, but her extreme modesty would not allow her to ask for help in getting dressed. It was beyond wonderful to wash away the external filth of last night's adventure as well as internal feelings of contamination after having been handled by the cult. She was relieved that most of the abrasions on her hands and knees were superficial. Coming into the kitchen, inhaling the aromas deeply, Carrie Sue began to weep tears of relief, tears of gratitude, tears of joy, tears of everything.

Gary pulled the chair out for Carrie Sue and she sat down gratefully and then exclaimed, "I think I could eat every bit of this myself!"

Lee pulled out an extra chair and insisted that Carrie Sue prop the injured leg on it. "Can you stand an ice pack? It'll help with pain and swelling." She nodded her assent and he found the ice pack in the freezer.

During the meal, they discussed the situation and decided that Abigail would drive Carrie Sue to the local hospital in Springfield. Lee would drive Gary back to the McCord's house so Gary could get to work. Lee gave Abigail his cell phone number in case she needed anything. He was planning to spend the day looking for a place to live. She reciprocated and told him to call if he needed help with directions.

A typical wait in an emergency room is about four to six hours if the illness or injury was not life-threatening. Carrie Sue's was not. Carrie Sue got registered, settled in the waiting room in a wheelchair, and passed the time talking in hushed tones using vague references to the events of the night while paging aimlessly through dog-eared magazines.

"Carrie Sue Wagner?" a uniformed woman called.

2

Friday, November 3

Reflecting on today's upcoming appointment with her counselor, F. Amy Bolton felt internal tugs pulling her in several directions. Viewing herself as independent and tough, she thought at one time that she could play both sides against the middle and not get burned. Now, she was not quite so sure. She was going to have to choose one side or the other and go whole-heartedly with that choice.

After last Friday's session with Abigail, she was beginning to comprehend that there was so much more to her own internal system than she had ever imagined. Her system resembled a prison complex and *she* was beginning to feel like an inmate.

She realized that at least one of the subterranean levels comprised of deeply wounded personalities and headed by the diabolical commandant, Nicholai, was way out of her league and outnumbered the Head Honcho's upper level personalities. There was no ruling them; indeed, she was beginning to comprehend that they had been controlling her far more than she would like to admit.

Amy realized that she was also losing time more than she wanted to admit. She was finding herself in strange places and not knowing how or why she was there. Items were mysteriously disappearing from her possessions and other things were just as mysteriously showing up. Perhaps Abigail was right and the other personalities were very busy when she was not in executive control. What were they doing? And more importantly, just how much of that missing time was devoted to Satanism?

Amy mentally reviewed the recent changes and information that had been emerging in the last month or so. Head Warden had defected from being cult-loyal to being God-loyal. Most of the guards on his surface prison level had also defected. Their prisoners – many wounded and broken personalities – had been healed and integrated before the last series of rituals and were then replaced by all the newly-created, demonized, and programmed personalities. Zuard, the captured and now defected former subterranean spy, had told Head Warden quite a bit about his sector, but no one knew for sure just how many levels there were or how extensive the tunnels and mazes were.

There was a monumental battle raging internally. Why? What was at stake? Why was the devil and the cult so invested in controlling her? *I'm just a nobody; a pizza delivery girl.* Abigail said that she, the host Amy, was not even the original core person and that the core was probably an infant hidden deep inside and guarded by the cult-loyal ones. Just what was she supposed to do with that?

Amy's head hurt. She often got headaches when she thought about her internal world. She did not always realize just how much switching was going on in her mind as various parts were alerted and triggered by the thoughts and activities in which she engaged.

Switching from personality to personality brought physical pain that she processed as a headache. Abigail called it a switching headache. She got them a lot when she was in session with Abigail. Maybe it was time to get serious about the healing.

Abigail had been up for an hour and had already stoked up the fire in the woodstove. Anxious to see how Buster was doing with Lee's mares, she dressed in layers and put on gloves before slipping out into the frosty morning. As she crossed the white tipped grass, she scanned the woods and the pasture. It was a habit; a good habit that she had developed since she started getting the threatening phone calls which escalated lately to the cutting of her brake lines, the poisoning of her dog, the break-in by Carrie Sue's brother, and more. And she always took Walther with her. She patted the appendix holster that lay inside her belt.

Buster and the mares were at the far end of the pasture. They seemed to be getting along peacefully. Buster noticed Abigail and gave a piercing whinny, startling the mares. Ears flattening, they tensed up as Buster began his morning gallop up to the tack room. They went through their usual drill with him rearing up, pawing the air, and prancing around Abigail as he awaited his morning feed.

The curious mares cautiously followed him up the trail next to the woods in a magnificent parade. *Lee sure has some pretty horses.* Bringing up his name brought a slight adrenaline rush which Abigail tried to stifle as she busied herself with the task at hand.

"I don't know your name yet, pretty girl, but I bet you want some sweet feed, too." Abigail addressed the leader. She would find out later that it was Misty. Hens are not the only animals that have pecking orders. Misty had established herself as the leader of this herd.

They were a still little skittish, but they would warm up to Abigail in time.

After pouring Buster's sweet feed into his bowl, she filled a bucket and dumped four piles on the ground. "Okay, ladies, breakfast is served," Abigail said while returning the bucket and then locking up the tack room. Thumping Buster on his side as she walked past him, she then detoured around the mares. Horses are very protective of their feed and she did not want to risk getting kicked. They did not know that she was not fond of sweet feed – or hay for that matter.

About the time she slid through the fence she heard the sound of a diesel truck coming up the driveway. Thinking that it was Max Berryman who had chased her yesterday morning in his big black diesel, she instinctively darted to her right and took cover behind the shed. Pulling Walther out of the holster, quickly chambering a bullet, Abigail moved to the back corner where she could observe Max and, God forbid, shoot him if he made a move to abduct Carrie Sue.

Commanding herself to breathe slowly, gripping the weapon firmly with left hand over right, index finger safely outside of the trigger guard, she waited with Walther pointed to the ground as the midnight blue truck pulled past her truck and Carrie Sue's car. The driver turned off the ignition, slowly opened the door, and casually got out.

Abigail collapsed against the shed with relief and let out a long breath. "Lee!" Abigail shouted.

Lee scanned the area and finally located Abigail coming from behind the shed. "Hey," he greeted her, "what are you doing back there?"

"Uh," Abigail hesitated as she walked toward him holstering Walther, "I thought maybe you were Max Berryman going after Carrie Sue so I was going to shoot you."

Lee's eyes widened as he realized that she was dead serious. "I am so sorry, Abigail," he said, realizing his gaffe. "I should have called first. Are you all right?"

"Yeah, I'm fine," Abigail replied with a shake of her head and a smile, "and, really, no need to apologize. I'm sorry for upsetting you. Your truck looked black from that angle and with the diesel ... well, I just kind of assumed the worst. Yesterday was crazy and I kind of remember you saying you'd be by in the morning to tend to the horses. I'm just glad it was you and not Max." Abigail walked to her own truck and lowered the tail gate. She removed the magazine and then ejected the bullet from the chamber into the bed of the truck, retrieved it, and reloaded it.

"Yeah," he agreed with a smile as he watched her put the magazine back into the pistol using a practiced slap with the heel of her hand, "me, too."

"I just gave them each a ration of sweet feed. They really are pretty. What are their names?"

Walking back toward the gate, Lee and Abigail began a lengthy conversation about the horses. He told her their names and ages, personalities and quirks. The mares briefly looked up at Lee and Abigail but only Misty nickered a greeting. None of them would leave their feed until the last morsel was licked up and the final inspection of each other's spots was executed just in case one miniscule bit of grain had been overlooked.

Moving up to the trucks, Lee and Abigail negotiated a plan for the care of the horses as well as additional hay and sweet feed. They brought the four feed pans down to the area in front of the tack room for the evening feeding and then Lee transferred several bags of feed from his truck to the trailer. Chatting about mundane horse-related things, talking about Lee's adventures in locating a place to live, feeling as clumsy as teenagers, the two finally lapsed into an awkward silence that seemed to last for minutes.

Lee cleared his throat. "I just want to thank you again for putting up my horses. They seem to like it much better than Gary's back yard."

"No problem," Abigail said with a twinkle in her eyes, "I'm glad I can give them some 'horse-pitality'."

Lee let a deep-throated chuckle escape and shook his head. "I'll see you later," he said. "I have some follow-up calls to make and some property to look at. I want to get them settled for the winter as soon as possible."

"Well, you have fun with that," Abigail smiled, "I'll be praying that God gives you a speedy answer and lots of favor."

Lee left and Abigail went back into the house where she shed her coat. Carrie Sue had spent the night once again. She wanted to go home, but Abigail persuaded her to stay at least until Sunday after church since today was another demon revel. Walking through the kitchen and then down the short hallway to the guest room, Abigail knocked lightly on the door.

"Come in," Carrie Sue said softly.

"Hey," Abigail said as she poked her head through the doorway, "I just wanted to check on you. How's the foot? Do you want an ice pack?"

Carrie Sue's foot was elevated on pillows with an ace wrap holding the splint on her foot and ankle. "No, not now," Carrie Sue said, "maybe in a little while."

"What can I get you for breakfast?"

"I'm not really hungry, but I am thirsty and could use something to drink."

"Juice? Hot tea? You name it, I'll get it," Abigail offered.

"I'll get up. I don't want to be a bother; you've gone through so much trouble already."

"No problem. Besides, *you've* gone through so much trouble already!"

"Okay, thanks," Carrie Sue conceded, "how about one of your granola bars and some hot tea? And please don't make me have to make a decision about what flavor," she added with a hint of a twinkle in her eyes.

"Coming right up," Abigail replied with a smile. It was good to see Carrie Sue beginning to recover from her ordeal. Returning to the kitchen, she got the water heating on the stove and found a large mug before selecting a granola bar. Placing the items on a tray, she waited for the water to boil.

A few minutes later, Abigail brought the steaming mug of Constant Comment tea and a granola bar to Carrie Sue. "There you go," Abigail said as she set the tray on the night stand.

"Thanks," Carrie Sue said as she came to a seated position and tried to suppress a groan. "I'm sore all over. It feels like I've been run over by a Mack truck!"

"Well, I can understand that," Abigail said with a concerned nod and then broke into a grin. "Let's see, you spent the night dodging Satanists, tripping over rocks and roots and then falling into a ditch and crawling through the woods with a broken foot after you banged your face on Billy's car. Yep, I think you ought to be sore all over."

Carrie Sue attempted a quiet laugh and then turned serious. "I really need to talk with you about the last couple of days. God did some incredible things, but there are other things I'm a bit worried about."

"I really want to hear about it when you're up to it," Abigail responded. "Do you think you'd be up to it by tomorrow afternoon?"

"Sure."

"Would you mind if I invite Cindy over to be an intercessor? I think we need to go over that prayer of renunciations and affirmations again."

"Good idea, I'd love the extra support."

Gary and Cindy McCord were just finishing breakfast with their two children, Traci and Bryan. Traci had turned six in June and Bryan was going to be four in December. They were interrupted by the ringing of the phone. Gary leaned back and answered the phone.

"Hello," he said cheerily as he recognized Abigail's number, "how are things going?"

"Hey, Gary," Abigail replied, "I almost shot your cousin this morning, but other than that, everything is just fine."

"He probably deserved it." Gary joked but asked with a hint of concern in his voice, "What did that man do now?"

"Oh, nothing much," Abigail continued to banter with Gary. She considered him to be another brother that she loved to tease. "He just happened to have a truck that was dark enough and diesel enough to make some paranoid woman think he might have been Max coming after Carrie Sue or me again."

"Well, I guess you're not paranoid if they really are out to get you," he countered.

Abigail chuckled with him and then changed the subject. "Is Cindy handy?"

"She's right here." He handed the phone to his wife.

Abigail greeted her friend and asked her if there was any way she could come over some time on Saturday to pray with her and Carrie Sue. After a quick check with Gary, she told Abigail that she would be there as long as she was home in time to take the kids off of Gary's hands and make supper. They chatted for a little while before hanging up.

Lee Norris headed over to his real estate agent's office in Springfield. He was beginning to get a feel for the county again and was becoming more familiar with the secondary roads. Things had changed somewhat since he was a kid and when he visited as an adult he stuck to the main highways. Springfield was the county seat and had a population of about twenty thousand.

Unincorporated Kingston, where Gary and Cindy lived, had a population of nearly five thousand and Oakvale, where his grandparents lived, was even smaller. There were several unincorporated towns scattered throughout the mostly rural county. He liked the feel of the area and was hoping to find at least fifty acres that would suit his purposes.

Gayle Dillon looked up from her desk when she heard the gentle tinkle of the bells that hung from the handle of the heavy glass door. "Hello, Mr. Norris," she stood up and greeted him with her warmest professional smile, "how are you today?"

"Great; and please call me Lee. Mr. Norris is my dad," he replied with a smile. "I just got my horses settled with a friend temporarily but I'm eager to find them a place to call home."

"Excellent," Gayle said. "I've reserved the rest of the morning to show you several places that I think may work for you." She strolled over to the prominent topographical county map that was displayed on one wall of the office. "Let me show you the properties on the map and then we'll go check them out."

"Sounds like a plan," Lee agreed. He ambled over to the huge map and followed her practiced hand as she pointed out each property, gave a brief description of the land and any buildings, asking price, proximity to amenities, and other details that would give Lee a general idea of the property. He was impressed with her efficiency and was grateful to have a printout of each of the five listings.

They got into her full-sized, bright red, all-wheel drive SUV. Driving out of Springfield, using short cuts to get to Route 1950, talking like a tour guide about local points of interest, Gayle eventually turned east onto a narrow road a few miles just before Oakvale that wound past clusters of mobile homes, large estates, and scattered farmhouses.

Turning up a narrow lane, she pulled into the rutted driveway that led to a double-wide mobile home. The yard was spacious and well-manicured and there were several out buildings, including a modest barn. They got out and Lee referred to his print out: Thirty-seven acres more or less, 3 BR, 2 Bath ranch style home, newly remodeled kitchen, barn, shed, shop, mostly fenced, 2 ponds. Asking $199,000. There was more information about taxes, school districts, and utilities.

"Is there any way to drive the property?" Lee could see the crumbling remains of a very old farmhouse on the other side of the mobile home.

"Sure," Gayle replied. "I can take you down the lanes along the overgrown pastures. Apparently, the owner had some animals and raised some crops."

"Why are they selling?"

"It's an older couple and they just want to get a little place in town. It's getting to be too much to manage."

They finished the tour and Lee made some notes as they drove on to the next place on their list. It, too, had pros and cons that Lee would have to pray about. He was getting a bit frustrated that the places in his price range with suitable houses had too little land or else they had great land and fixer-uppers to live in. Lee was disheartened as they made their way back to Gayle's office in Springfield.

Gayle looked at the attractive man and suggested, "Why don't you come in for a minute and let me see if there have been any new listings that popped up while we were out."

"It wouldn't hurt," he replied. "I can review what we've seen today while you do that." He wandered over to the big topographical map with his papers and checked his notes.

She went to her computer and punched up the multi-listing files. Navigating the web site and finding the properties with acreage, she was disappointed to find only one new listing. "Well, there is one ... let me see what it says about the property...." She was half talking to herself, half talking to Lee, "receivership ... 80 acres more or less ... hmm."

Lee's curiosity was aroused. "Well?"

"Okay," Gayle said while looking at her screen, "we have a place that's in receivership and they want to settle this ASAP."

"What's a receivership?" Lee asked.

"Basically, it's a piece of property that gets taken over by a bank or a court appointed receiver because of unusual circumstances. Like the owner may have died and there's no family to deal with it, or maybe it's done to avoid foreclosure; I'm not exactly sure. It doesn't say here, but when a property goes on the market like this, it's usually a very good deal."

"It wouldn't hurt to check it out," Lee replied.

Gayle looked at her watch and made a decision. "I've got time now if you do."

"Let's go," Lee said hopefully. He really wanted to find a place soon. He was originally going to stay with his grandparents, but Gary and Cindy insisted that he stay with them. They were gracious hosts, and it was wonderful to get reacquainted. Lee had lived alone for so long, he missed the activity of a happy household, but he also wanted to get settled and get on with his life – whatever that would look like.

They got back into Gayle's SUV but this time they headed toward Kingston instead of Oakvale on what most people called the King-Spring Road. She moved efficiently through the small town and caught Kingston Road on the south side of town.

"I was just on this road this morning," Lee quietly commented. His thoughts wandered back to the wild adventure into which Gary had dragged him. *Was it just yesterday morning?*

"Oh?" Gayle responded, "What's out here?"

Lee did not want to get into a tricky conversation about Carrie Sue and Abigail since he was not quite sure of everything himself. "My cousin's friend has some property out this way. She's boarding my horses until I can find a place to put them."

"Well, let's hope that this place will give you some options. I'm sorry, but with the newness of the listing, there are very few details about buildings other than a barn and a mobile home. I have no idea about what shape they are in."

Turning onto York Creek Road, she followed the hills and curves rather slowly. Lee noted that this was also the same road he had been on earlier in the day, but he kept the thoughts to himself. Gayle slowed even more as they approached the top of a hill and was craning her neck as she looked for a driveway on the left side of the road.

"It probably won't be marked yet, but I'm sure we can find it. It says 1.25 miles from Kingston Road and that should be just over the hill," Gayle said as she checked her odometer.

To their relief, the listing agent's vehicle was in the rutted driveway and he could be seen pulling a sign out of the back of his truck.

Turning on her signal, Gayle slowed and made the turn, parking next to him. "Let's see if he can tell us anything," Gayle suggested.

Lee stepped out of the SUV and walked slowly behind Gayle, stopping to survey the property. He saw a stand of trees to the south and could barely make out the outline of a weathered barn further up the lane. He was starting to feel as if he was coming home but did not have any logical reason for such sensations. *Lord, is this the place You've prepared for me?*

Soon Gayle came over to Lee with the agent. "Lee Norris, this is Pete Cooper. He has this listing and we are all going to explore it together."

"Nice to meet you," Lee said as he extended a hand that engulfed Pete's.

"Nice to meet you, too," Pete responded. "I'm sorry to sound so uninformed about this property, but the bank wanted to get this off its books. Apparently, the owner died years ago under some kind of mysterious circumstances and his family squabbled about it so much that it was put into receivership until they could come to some agreement. Some wanted to sell, others wanted to keep it in the family, but no one could afford to pay for it. There are some back taxes that have to be caught up, but the price has been reduced drastically. This place won't be around much longer." He gave his best pitch.

Carrie Sue was still making her best arguments but finally agreed to stay with Abigail at least through Sunday after church. Abigail had made a compelling case by pointing out that Saturday night was another ritual night, but when she mentioned that Sunday night was a full moon and might pose a problem, Carrie Sue put a hand up and said firmly, "No, I need to go home. I've imposed on you for a week and I appreciate it more than you will ever know, but it's time for me to stand on my own two feet. No pun intended."

"Okay," Abigail agreed reluctantly. After all, she did not want to create co-dependency in her client-friends. "I think that after tomorrow's prayer session with Cindy, I'll feel better about your situation. I just want to make reasonably sure that they haven't put in some latent programming or something."

"Me too." Carrie Sue nodded her head just as the phone rang in the living room.

Abigail answered it on the second ring when she recognized the Taylor's phone number on the display. "Hello?"

"Abigail, I'm sorry to bother you, this is Twyla's mom," Nancy Taylor answered, "would it be all right if we cancel Twyla's appointment today? I'm really sorry that I'm calling so late."

"No problem," Abigail replied, "is there anything wrong?"

"No, actually, everything is all right. I mean, she's doing great. There's no more cutting or anorexia. I've got my little girl back," her voice broke with emotion. "I just want to thank you for everything you did. You're awesome."

"God is awesome, I'm just good," Abigail responded with a laugh. "I'll take her off the schedule. But don't hesitate to call if she needs a little more help later on."

They hung up and Abigail turned to Carrie Sue and said with a satisfied smile, "That's good news; I just love to work myself out of a job."

"Oh, is that what you're doing with me this week?" Carrie Sue teased.

"Funny." Abigail gave a close-lipped smile before moving on. "Well that leaves me with a two o'clock appointment today. I think you can stay out of trouble for a couple of hours while I'm gone."

They continued to banter back and forth for a few more minutes, ate a light lunch, and then Abigail made preparations to leave for her appointment with F. Amy Bolton. As she drove to her office in the First Baptist Church, she began to pray for their meeting. Amy was still on the bubble and Abigail was earnestly praying that she would whole-heartedly pursue God.

Pulling into the church parking lot, she walked to the side door, unlocked it, and went inside. *I think I'll lock it behind us today.* The events of the last week had Abigail feeling a bit more wary. Abigail went up to Pastor Spalding's study to see if he was still there. The lights were on, so she rapped lightly on the partially open door. "Hello?" she called out softly.

"Come in," Pastor Spalding responded, "Come in. I was just getting ready to head home. What's up?"

"Well, I just wanted to let you know that Carrie Sue is safely back at my house until Sunday afternoon. She went through quite an ordeal – three bones broken in her foot, a couple of scrapes, and a nasty bump on her head, complete with a lovely shiner."

"Oh, my!" Pastor Spalding was not accustomed to such drama in his congregation. His world consisted of an ordinary assortment of illnesses and accidents, births and deaths, weddings and baptisms. He did not know anyone involved in Satanism. "Thank you for letting me know; I have been praying."

"I'm so sorry I didn't think to call you sooner. It's been wild!" Abigail apologized.

"That's not a problem," Pastor Spalding responded graciously. "Oh, wait," another thought came to him, "when will you have time to sit down with me and talk? I haven't forgotten."

She mentally went through her calendar, "How about next Friday around one? I'll have about an hour between appointments."

Pastor Spalding scribbled a note in a square on his desk calendar. "Done. I'm looking forward to it."

"Well, I have a lady to see in a couple minutes, so I'd better head back down there." Abigail smiled as she left his office and headed back down to her office. She then set it up for the next appointment before returning to the door. Amy should be there at 2:06 as usual. *Amy and the number six!*

On cue, Amy roared into her parking place like she was late delivering a pizza. Actually, she had some teenaged personalities who drove like race car drivers. She popped out of the car and sauntered over to the door that Abigail held open for her. "Oh ho, I get a greeting committee today?" she asked with her typical sarcastic edge.

"It's the Friday afternoon special," Abigail joked back. "Actually, I'm going to lock us in because you're the only one I have this afternoon. The pastor and Ginny are gone already so I just don't want anyone wandering in."

Abigail locked the door and they went back to her office. Amy flopped into her chair in her customary way, folded her arms defensively, and waited for Abigail to open the session with prayer. Keeping her eyes on Amy during the prayer, Abigail noticed the physical shifts that marked personality shifts. By the time she finished praying, the host Amy had been displaced by someone else.

"Hi," Abigail ventured, "have we met?"

"I know you, but you don't know me," the personality replied.

"So, why are you here today; if you don't mind my asking?" Abigail hoped that he or she was friendly.

"I've been watching what's been going on. Amy's been on the bubble about her allegiances these days. She just wants to be left alone and not have to answer to anyone," the part continued. There was an analytical air about this part that left Abigail thinking that it was a male personality.

"I can't say that I blame her," Abigail replied, "unfortunately, she's caught between two warring factions. Her destiny, both in time and in eternity, will depend on the choices she makes here and now."

He looked a little puzzled by her reply and then continued, "Like I said, I've been watching. I think that she does need to make a choice and quit playing both ends against the middle. I think that she will continue to be used and abused by Levi, Darod, Prinz, and all the others in the cult. She may not survive another ritual. Monday, Tuesday, and Wednesday were brutal. What you did with her last week spared her from Saturday and Sunday's rituals, but they made up for it at the next ones. They're very angry at her for seeing you and they want to use her to destroy you."

"They've made that pretty clear. How can I help you?" Abigail was not sure where he was going with this line of thought.

"I want to see that she gets set free. I watch what's happening on the surface level with Head Warden, Caleb, and the others. I think that your strategy is working. I want to help you and Amy."

"And once you help them get free, then what?" Abigail asked. Did he want freedom for the sake of independence? Or did he want freedom in Christ?

"I know that it's a black and white issue. All in or all out. I don't know experientially about this Jesus you work for, but I do know about Satan. I haven't been personally involved in that because I am the intellectual one, the analytical one. There is a certain logic to what you say and do."

"Help me understand where you fit in the system," Abigail said, "and what do you want me to call you?"

"Hank," he said, "you can call me Hank. I'm not like most of the other personalities. I don't answer to anyone and I don't have anyone under me. I just think and analyze. I can influence by injecting thoughts into some of them, but I can't control them."

"Let me see if I understand you. You observe Amy's life and analyze the various factors and then try to influence key players to make logical decisions for the course of her life based on the facts that you discover."

"Yes. I think you have captured the essence of my role," he responded.

"How long have you been able to do your job?" Abigail asked.

"As long as she's been around," he answered with a quizzical look. He was not quite sure of where this line of questioning was leading.

"Logically, then, at some point you thought that Satanism was a beneficial option for all of you."

He was momentarily stymied. "Well, yes."

Abigail pressed, "At what point did you realize that it was not entirely beneficial?"

"The last couple of weeks have been very revealing. I did not have the quantity of information that I now have," he admitted.

"Why do you think you had limited information? Who or what kept you uninformed all those years?" Abigail pressed harder.

"Actually, I hate to admit this, but I am not really sure about that."

"I would like to suggest, as the Bible says, that the god of this world has blinded your eyes."

"I'm not accustomed to ambiguity. It makes logical sense, but I am not sure what to do about it."

"Let me give you some information that might help you," Abigail offered and then continued when he nodded affirmatively. "You've heard me speak about the programming and demonic control that the others have had to deal with. I want to suggest that you, too, have been programmed and demonized." She paused to let that sink in.

Hank sat with his hands together and the tips of his fingers pressed against his lips. He took a deep breath and then straightened as he looked Abigail in the eyes. "It would be consistent with the way Satanists work. I would like to be free of such things."

"I agree. Are you ready to pray with me right now to Jesus the Christ?"

"Yes, I want to align myself with Him and with His kingdom."

Abigail prayed for Hank and when she was finished, she could sense the change in him.

Hank opened his eyes at the conclusion of the prayer and smiled. It was as if he was able to tap into some emotions. "I feel different ... freer ... more peaceful. I can think clearer and understand so much more."

"Fantastic! What are you sensing that God wants to do with and through you now?" Abigail asked.

"I think ... no, I know that He wants me to do what I did before, but with His wisdom."

"I have peace about that," Abigail confirmed.

Hank retreated back into his place in Amy's system and was immediately replaced by Head Warden who was easily recognizable by his military posture and deeper voice as he greeted her.

"How are things going in there?" Abigail asked. "I have a hunch that this was a rough week."

"You can say that again!" he answered ruefully. "We have to make sure this doesn't happen again. My cells got loaded with new victims. We prayed for a bunch of them and got them integrated, but there are some that are a mess. They may be on to us. I think they diverted a lot more to Nicholai's hell hole. Pardon my language."

"No problem," Abigail replied and then moved on. "Unfortunately, we have a bunch of ground to recover and tomorrow is another demon revel. I think we can be encouraged that damage from at least two of the last five rituals was averted."

"So where do we start?" Head Warden asked.

"Let's pray and ask the Lord where He wants us to start." Knowing that he would agree, Abigail did not wait for his reply before launching into prayer and then asked Head Warden what he was sensing.

"I think that even though I'd like to see the newest ones healed up, it's more important to do a ... what do you call it? A preemptive strike on tomorrow's ritual."

"Let's do it," Abigail agreed. "Do you know any of the parts that are programmed for the demon revels?" After a discussion of the nature of this ritual, they assumed that there would be eleven of them since the ritual specified females aged seven through seventeen – one for each year.

"No, I think they're all down in Nicholai's area."

"Would Zuard know?" Abigail asked about the former spy that had gotten himself caught up with Head Warden's guards.

"I'll check." Head Warden ducked back inside and returned within seconds with his report. Zuard knew the general area where they were kept, but all of the subterranean areas were filled with murky mazes, hazards, and tortuous tunnels that were meant to confuse anyone who was unfortunate enough to try to find their way in or out without proper clearance.

In the three-way exchange, it was decided and confirmed through prayer that Zuard would go back down the secret passage and bring the demon revel parts back with him if possible. Zuard was willing to be recaptured if necessary. They prayed again and sent Zuard on his way.

Sliding down into the shadowy depths of Nicholai's labyrinth, Zuard shuddered. *Had it only been a week since I defected to God's kingdom?* He stayed behind a pillar and listened carefully to determine if he was alone or not. Convinced that he was, he crept to the right and followed the tunnel's curves. He could hear muffled moans coming from behind thick doors that were secured with chains. He knew that there would be guards posted at some of them and prayed that he could pull off the act of his life in convincing them that he was on a mission for Nicholai.

After taking many familiar twists and turns without incident, he came to the central area of this topmost subterranean level. He knew that this level had six "spokes" that fanned out from this central hub. He believed that there were a total of six levels, each with six hubs and six spokes. The deeper the level, the more intense the darkness – both physical and spiritual. The original core person was most likely kept imprisoned at the deepest level.

Since the November fourth demon revel was coming up soon, the participants would have been moved up to this level for their preparation. Zuard knew where they would be. He also knew that they would be very heavily guarded. "Jesus the Christ, I'm new at this; please help me pull this off and get these girls to safety." He moved quickly down the next corridor to the preparation room.

The two guards eyed Zuard suspiciously. "What are you doing here?" the first one demanded.

Zuard pulled himself up to his full height and snarled back at him, "I'm here to transfer them. Why don't you have them ready? Nicholai is waiting."

"We don't know what you are talking about," the second one retorted. "No one told us anything."

"*I'm* telling you," Zuard continued to bluff. "I need them now. I don't intend to take a beating because you're inept. Open that door, tie them together, and let me be on my way. I'll sign for them while you're doing that." He stepped toward the befuddled guards.

"I don't like this; we didn't hear anything about a move today."

"Suit yourselves," Zuard said, "but all I know is that Herrak got word from Prinz himself that these Revelers are vital to our future. Nicholai is going to prepare them himself."

The guards' bravado began to waver until one of them pulled out the keys to the bolted door. The other one crumbled and retrieved the shackles and ropes. After the docile revelers were secured, Zuard led them back out the way he came. Indeed, there were eleven females, a new one was added each year covering ages seven through seventeen. Disoriented and compliant, they followed Zuard to their inevitable fate. Since Amy was thirty years old, the oldest Reveler would have been created twenty-three years ago.

Zuard continued to pray, and miraculously they went unchallenged all the way to the secret passage that led to the boiler room. He assisted each one up to the surface level where they were nearly blinded by the unaccustomed light. They had existed in the dimness of the lower levels and were only out at night when they did surface. Head Warden had Caleb and several other guards assist them.

Head Warden reported to Abigail, "They're safely up here. Now what?"

Abigail noted that Zuard's internal mission took less than a minute. What a critical minute that was! "Well, since they are now under your jurisdiction, I suggest that you lead a prayer for their healing and deliverance. I'll pray in agreement."

Head Warden was taken aback. "You don't mess around, lady. Okay, it might not be as pretty a prayer as you do, but here goes." He launched into a prayer that covered the main points that Abigail covered for deeply wounded parts.

When he finished, Abigail prayed in agreement and then asked him how they were doing.

"They look great. They don't have that glazed look. They're not hurting. I think they're ready to go inside."

Abigail pressed him once again, "Would you do the honors? I'll pray in agreement."

They did so, noting that each of the eleven girls had "vanished" as they were integrated somewhere inside of Amy's system. Sometimes another personality could tell if there was integration into them, sometimes there was no idea of who integrated with whom. Abigail could only trust that God was reknitting them back into their rightful places. Often, they would go into the infant original person who would then begin to "age" as those parts merged with her. That was bewildering to the original person and it could endanger her as the persecutor parts and the demonic oppressors would note the subtle changes.

Next, they tackled the newly damaged parts that were resting in the various cells in Head Warden's prison. He and the other guards felt badly that they were unable to help all of them completely, but Abigail explained that when there was an unresolved issue or someone resisted healing, it was the signal to ask the Lord to reveal more about it. There would likely be some critical element that then helped them unravel the control of the cult, or perhaps an unexpected twist in the programming.

"One more thing," Abigail said. "I think we need to pray that no one else gets triggered, especially the one who drives you guys to meet cult people."

"That would be Issador," Head Warden said.

After praying for Issador and asking for a general covering for Amy et al over the weekend, Host Amy reappeared, and made her appointment for the following week. Reaching into her pocket, extracting a wad of crumpled dollars, she left them on the desk for Abigail.

"Thanks."

3

Saturday, November 4, Demon Revels

Cindy was cruising down the road in her minivan by two-thirty so she could to get to Abigail's home on time. She felt a sense of anticipation for this prayer session. That was not unusual, and in her experience, it meant that God was going to do something significant. She began to sing in the spirit to the tune of one of her favorite hymns as she drove.

Winding down the familiar roads, she reached the top of the final hill before Abigail's driveway and noticed a new For Sale sign on the left-hand side of the road. Turning her attention back to the road, Cindy continued the last mile to her friend's house where she was instantly reminded that Dude was not there to escort her to the farmhouse on the top of the hill. She breathed a prayer for her friend who acutely missed her canine companion.

Abigail appeared on the front porch with a genial smile on her face. They were like-minded, like-spirited friends who often marched shoulder to shoulder into spiritual battles together. Today was another one of those occasions that irked the members of the kingdom of darkness.

"Hey, lady," Abigail greeted her warmly. "Come on in, we've got the fire going." It wasn't extremely cold, but the overcast day and the breezes made the damp air feel quite chilly.

Cindy walked up the steps and embraced her friend before they went into the house. A warm puff of air that radiated from the wood stove greeted them as they came into the cozy room. Carrie Sue was seated in an overstuffed chair with her injured foot propped up on a pillow. They greeted one another as Cindy removed her coat and then got settled herself.

"Does anyone want anything to drink before we get started?" Abigail asked.

"No thank you," Cindy answered.

"I could use some water," Carrie Sue said. "I have a feeling my mouth might get dry."

Abigail got some water for Carrie Sue and then sat on the end of the couch that was closest to the wood stove. She had her Bible and notebook on the end table. "Well, if everyone's ready, let's open with prayer," she said. Leading the prayer for the Lord's direction, she then looked at Carrie Sue expectantly.

"I need to tell you things I remember that might be important," Carrie Sue began. She recounted the walk she took on Wednesday and the vague feeling that she had felt like something was wrong but she was unable to discern what it was at the time. She related that David had told her that one of the inside personalities noticed that they were being followed by demons once they left Abigail's property. She reported that they also saw some really big angels at the foot of Abigail's driveway, but they seemed stationed there.

"It was as if they wanted to go with me but couldn't desert their post."

Abigail was tempted to ask for a description, but she needed to let Carrie Sue continue with her narrative. She was taking notes that she could go back to later on when they prayed.

"I don't know why I decided to go up to Billy's car again. I'd intended to just walk the perimeter of your property." Carrie Sue continued her narrative and told Cindy and Abigail more about what David said. "Some big demon tripped us and that's how we smashed into the side of the car and got knocked out." She gently rubbed her forehead. "David said that it jumped on our back and dug its claws in. Our back is still sore." She went on to say that the child alter, triggered by their mother's presence, willingly got into her truck and was driven to the windowless lodge.

Cindy was taking some notes as well and trying not to act shocked by some of the strange things Carrie Sue was saying.

"I don't know how long we were out, but apparently they drugged us before they tied us up, gagged us, and brought us to the barn for the ritual. The funny thing is that I didn't feel drugged. Maybe one of the others held the drug for us so we could be clear-headed. And I have no idea how long I was gone."

Abigail made a note to follow up on the drugging issue and then said, "Well, if your mother picked you up around noon and the ritual started at midnight, then it was about twelve hours," Abigail calculated. "And you were back here by about nine a.m."

"It sure seemed longer than that!"

"It was a long night," Abigail concurred. "But, keep going; there's some important stuff you're telling us that we need to pray about."

"Okay, so they put a hood over my head and threw me in the back of a van and drove me to the barn down the road. Oh, wait! I forgot to tell you that we found a guy named Ichabod who was the leader of the group that was supposed to be at the ritual that night. It's a long story, but he and his group defected and got healed. And we all decided that we'd be like Daniel and his friends – no matter what, we weren't going to bow to Satanism."

"You go, girl!" Cindy said with a huge smile.

"I'm so proud of y'all," Abigail added with a wink and a smile.

"For some reason, they left me alone in the barn. I know it had to be God looking after me. I found a nail and used it to get free of the hood and the ropes. When Zorroz, er, Sheriff Bynum came in, he was shocked when I called him by name. I wish you could have seen his face! He grabbed me by the wrist and started walking me toward the fire. That's when I said, 'In the name of Jesus Christ of Nazareth, let me go!'"

Abigail and Cindy both grinned from ear to ear and laughed with delight.

Carrie Sue continued her narrative, "And then David switched in and punched him real hard in the throat. Zorroz let go and we took off.

"Way to go, David; I would have paid good money for a ticket to see that!" Abigail said gleefully and then hesitated. "Well, actually, on second thought; I think I prefer just hearing about it."

"So, the next six or seven hours were crazy. We went from feeling hopeful and like God was going to deliver us to being mad at God because we thought it should happen the way we thought it should."

"What do you mean?" Abigail asked.

"Like, why couldn't He have kept me from breaking my foot? What good does that do? It seemed like every time I asked for strength or help, something bad would happen. I said, 'help me, God' and promptly fell into the ditch because the moon disappeared behind a cloud and I didn't see it in front of me. But," Carrie Sue said as she hung her head momentarily and looked a little chagrined, "we found out that when we were weak, then we were strong."

"How's that?" Abigail was eagerly following the dramatic story.

"Well, after we crawled into the culvert, a huge dog came barking down the driveway. All of a sudden, a little girl named Leah switched in. I mean, we were so mad at God because our protector guys couldn't be out to fend off the dog," she paused and sighed, "but we had to apologize later because the dog would definitely have fought us. It protected Leah and lay down beside us and kept us warm. We got to rest for a little while until she took off after the men again. Oh, yeah! And before that we were trying to outrun the goons, but the more we prayed for strength, the weaker we felt. We just finally gave up and leaned against a huge tree. About five seconds later, the moon went behind a cloud and they walked right past us down the path. If we had been strong enough to keep going, they would have caught us for sure."

"Huh, I heard a dog barking a couple of times in the night," Abigail said thoughtfully. "I was up at 4:30 and remember asking God to put you in a safe place and keep you warm."

"Oh, so, you're responsible for the ditch and the culvert and the dog," Carrie Sue said with a tone of mock accusation.

"You're welcome." Abigail gave her a cheesy grin.

"You two!" Cindy joined them in the levity of the moment. She was getting an education.

Abigail looked at the time and got back to business. "Well, that's an amazing story. There's a lot to praise God for and I think we have a number of things to pray about – the demons that attacked you, the little girl that came out for your mother, whatever they drugged you with, any possible programming, uh," she looked back over her notes, "the physical traumas, and Leah, the little one that was triggered by the dog."

They prayed about the items one by one, ministering to the two girls who were triggered. Leah's healing was especially touching because she had been subjected to bestiality and other unsavory treatment. They were both completely healed and integrated.

"I think it would be prudent to pray that prayer of renunciations and affirmations that I adapted from Floyd McCallum's prayer," Abigail said while reaching for copies of the three-page prayer and then giving one each to Cindy and Carrie Sue. "Remember the last time we prayed through this?"

"Yep," Carrie Sue affirmed, "I skipped words and it changed the meaning of some of the sentences."

Abigail turned to Cindy to explain matter-of-factly, "Sometimes the enemy or maybe a demonized cult-loyal part interferes and words get missed or changed which changes the meaning. Sometimes the person has trouble seeing or hearing. Once in a while someone passes out."

"Oh, my," Cindy said. She was getting educated.

"It's no big deal," Abigail assured her. Turning to Carrie Sue she said, "Do you give me authority to complete this prayer on your behalf if you can't do it for any reason?"

"Absolutely!"

"Okay, then, let's begin."

Carrie Sue prayed the opening prayer affirming her belief in Jesus Christ as her Savior and then proceeded to alternate between the corresponding renunciations and affirmations. "I renounce, repudiate, and reject all occult involvement, hereby breaking all ties to the demonic realm of darkness. I claim every spiritual blessing that is mine in Christ ..."

She continued to pray through the first page without faltering, but when she got to the next page, she began to stammer and have difficulty with some of the words. "I claim ..."

"Reclaim," Abigail alerted her to the error.

"I reclaim rights given to, or taken by Lucifer/Satan. I choose to give all such rights to my Lord Jesus Christ since I have been bought with a price."

Abigail kept an eye on Carrie Sue and the words of the prayer. They were on the final page and Carrie Sue was now struggling noticeably. "I renounce the wrong belief/lie that I am unable to choose truth and be free of demonic and/or cult control and influence over me." Suddenly, she slumped over in her chair and the pages floated to the floor as she passed out.

"Cindy," Abigail said calmly, "would you go check her pulse and make sure she's still breathing?"

Cindy responded immediately with a worried look on her face that soon faded as she knelt beside Carrie Sue and found a strong pulse. *How does Abigail do this so nonchalantly?*

"In the name of Jesus the Christ on behalf of Carrie Sue," Abigail picked up the prayer where Carrie Sue left off. Within a couple of minutes, she concluded the prayer, "Father we fully trust that Your Holy Spirit is interceding according to Your will and that Jesus the Christ is also interceding for Carrie Sue, completing and correcting anything that we may have prayed inadequately. We ask that You would now declare that IT IS FINISHED! Thank You, Amen."

Immediately, Carrie Sue stirred and became fully conscious again. "Whoa, what happened?"

"You passed out so I finished it on your behalf," Abigail replied. "How about if we go back to the place where you stopped and you finish it? I just don't want some legalistic demon to say, 'Abigail prayed, but Carrie Sue didn't.'"

Cindy picked up Carrie Sue's copy of the prayer and handed the pages to her and was amazed that Carrie Sue finished it flawlessly, speaking fluently and with conviction that was not there previously.

"Whew!" Carrie Sue said, "That was hard work. I'm whipped. I need to use the bathroom." She moved her foot from the pillow and stood up. "Oh! Oh, my foot!" Carrie Sue exclaimed. Sitting back down on the chair, reaching down to the ace wrap, furiously unwrapping the splint, Carrie Sue exposed her foot.

Abigail and Cindy did not know what to think. Did she forget that it was broken and reinjure it when she stood up?

"My foot! My foot!" Carrie Sue stood and jumped up and down three times before she stopped and inspected the foot again.

Abigail and Cindy were astounded to see that there was no swelling, and only one tiny bruise remained above the little toe. It took them a second to realize that her foot had been miraculously healed and then they all began to jump up and down like schoolgirls.

Carrie Sue stopped and they all looked at her foot again. This time even the tiny bruise was gone and the skin looked pink and new like a baby's foot. Their happy dance began all over again while they joyfully laughed together until tears flowed.

"Um, Carrie Sue," Cindy said with a hushed tone, "you need to look in the mirror."

"Why? What?" She responded with some alarm as she put her hands to her face.

"Oh, my," Abigail said as she looked at Carrie Sue.

Carrie Sue was now as concerned as she was curious and walked quickly over to the mirror that was above the mantle of the woodstove. She looked in awe at the reflection of her fully restored face. The swelling and bruises were completely gone.

It was a few minutes after five o'clock and the sun was nearly set already. Streaks of orange, pink, and bronze slashed the western sky. Urdang, the territorial spirit of this county, shrieked his displeasure. He watched that property earlier as the multi-colored ribbons of incense were winging their way to the throne of grace where bowls were filled and the overflow dripped back to earth. Praise and thanksgiving to the Great Enemy on earth caused His angels to respond in worship and celebration in heaven. Urdang could not divert or stop or control any of it. His frustration heightened his fury. He would revel at the demon revel tonight.

Indeed, tonight was his night.

Abigail had said good-bye to Cindy shortly after their celebration and was heading down to feed the horses with Carrie Sue who had finally decided to venture back outside again. Carrie Sue waited at the gate since she was leery of moving among the large creatures.

Misty, Sassy, Lady, and Sparkles were warming up to Abigail and allowed her to pat their flanks or necks as she passed by. She did not want to push herself on them too quickly and then have to reestablish trust. Buster was enjoying their company immensely, but definitely showed signs of jealousy if Abigail gave one of the mares a little too much attention. He would cut between the mare and Abigail as if to say, "She's mine and I'm not sharing her with another horse."

"This is amazing!" Carrie Sue said for the umpteenth time since the Lord had healed her fractured foot and battered face.

"Isn't it interesting that God healed everything that the demons caused?" Abigail mused.

"It sure is," Carrie Sue agreed as she freely moved her shoulder. The palms of her hands were also healed.

"Do you remember asking why God couldn't have kept you from breaking your foot?" Abigail asked.

"Yeah," Carrie Sue sighed.

"Do you have an answer to that question now?"

"Hmm, well, I think He's trying to teach me to trust Him for one thing. I think He used the injury to slow me down enough that I was actually safer than if I was crashing through the woods at full speed," she paused and then added, "and I think maybe He wanted to use it to build my faith when He healed it."

"It's quite a testimony and I can't wait to see Gary and Lee's faces tomorrow when they see your face!"

Amy was returning to The Pizza Palace after delivering what she hoped was the last pizza for the night. Saturday nights were usually her best nights for tips, and tonight was no exception. She typically liked to work late and make as much as she could, but tonight she wanted to get home as early as possible. She was entertaining thoughts of going to Abigail's church the next morning when her cell phone rang. Automatically pulling it out of her pocket, she flipped it open with a practiced flick, assuming it was her supervisor. It was Levi, a lower level master Satanist that was very much involved in her programming. A series of tones and clicks was all she heard before the phone went dead.

Issador was being summoned. His mission was to drive them to the ritual that night. Levi did not know that Issador had been deprogrammed the previous day. "So that's what triggered me all these years," he said half aloud. Hank, the intellectual, was hovering nearby in case he needed to help Issador think. Caleb, now a protector, was also waiting in the event that he was needed. It was unnecessary today and the various personalities that were beginning to function as a team rejoiced in the small victory.

Issador switched back out and the pizza delivery girl resumed her job. Swooping into the back of The Pizza Palace's parking lot and skidding to a stop, she picked up the zippered money bag, the large insulated pizza box holders and headed inside through the back door. Her supervisor let her know that she could begin to help close up for the night so she logged in the receipts, turned in the money, and began to help tidy up the lobby and the kitchen. Finally, she said good night and headed home confident that she was truly going to go home and stay home.

Amy was still having trouble with "losing time", that is, she was not always conscious or even co-conscious when other personalities took executive control. As the host personality, she was in charge of most of the mundane activities of their day. Head Warden, Caleb, the guards and sentries, and Zuard all took turns that night to ensure that Amy was not accessed and brought to the demon revel ritual. Their prayers with Abigail to thwart the cult's plans seemed to be effective.

Nicholai was frustrated and furious that he could not find the Revelers. The guards that failed to deliver them were demoted and brought down to the lower levels where they were tormented by the internal persecutors. He was alarmed that he could not gain executive control of Amy and felt a deep sense of foreboding about his failure to perform his assignment.

4

Sunday, November 5

Carrie Sue had her bags packed before breakfast and was eager to go to church with Abigail and finally go home after that. It had been a harrowing week and she was grateful that she not only survived it, she was thriving. There had been so much healing internally as well as externally. *God is so good!* She was sensing a glimmer of hope that she was actually going to make it.

Abigail had just come in from tending the horses and they met in the kitchen for breakfast. "This has been one wild week," Abigail said. "I'm so glad that you were here."

"I am too," Carrie Sue replied, "I'd hate to think of what would have happened if I'd been home and if we hadn't gotten all those ritual parts healed. David never would have been able to punch out Bynum."

"Ooh," Abigail said with a little alarm, "he might be in church this morning, you know."

"Well, too bad for him," Carrie Sue said with more boldness than she was actually feeling.

"Well, he usually sits in the balcony and boogies out as soon as possible," Abigail said. "It's not likely that you'd meet him face-to-face. But if you do, I doubt that he'd try anything. I'll sit in back with you just in case."

"Actually, if you don't mind, I'd like to join you and Cindy and Gary."

"I'd like that."

They sat in silence for a while, each one absorbed in her own thoughts until they finished breakfast and then finished getting ready for church. Carrie Sue brought her belongings out to her car and when Abigail was ready, they each got into their own vehicles and drove to the church in Springfield. Parking next to each other, they walked into the church together and through the main entrance where Pastor Spalding was busy greeting as many people as he could.

When Pastor Spalding saw Carrie Sue walking next to Abigail, he furrowed his brows and cocked his head as he questioned what he was seeing. Disengaging as gracefully as he could from the couple he was greeting, he walked over to Abigail and Carrie Sue.

"You must be a fast healer!" he exclaimed.

Carrie Sue was somewhat rattled by the sudden attention and stammered, "Uh, yeah, I guess I am when God does a miracle."

Abigail was beaming, nodding her head up and down, and restraining herself from jumping into the conversation. It was important for Carrie Sue to testify.

"What happened?" the incredulous pastor pressed.

Carrie Sue took a deep breath and then launched into a brief description of what had happened the previous day when Cindy and Abigail had prayed with her. Pastor Spalding interrupted her several times to get additional details. He was so excited. "Would you feel comfortable with giving a brief testimony during the service today?" he asked.

Carrie Sue was taken aback and began to feel panic rising up from the pit of her stomach. She hastily gave Abigail a bail-me-out look.

"Cindy and I will both be glad to go up there with you," Abigail offered.

That was definitely not what Carrie Sue wanted to hear. She felt a little bit trapped but she also felt a boldness that she did not formerly feel. "Okay," she consented tentatively as the butterflies in her stomach began whipping up a tornado.

"Great!" Pastor Spalding boomed excitedly. "We'll do this just after the offering. And I'll ask for other testimonies so that you won't feel alone. We haven't had a testimony time in a long time."

"Yeah, great," Carrie Sue groaned under her breath and hoped that no one heard her. She and Abigail moved through the doorway and made their way about half way down the outside aisle and sat with Gary and Cindy McCord. Lee was sitting on the far side next to Gary carrying on a low conversation with him.

They looked up as Abigail sat down next to Cindy, gave her a brief hug and then leaned forward to whisper a good morning to the men. Gary's eyes looked past her and he glimpsed Carrie Sue's face. His jaw dropped slightly before he gave a big smile and stabbed a triumphant thumbs-up at her mouthing "Praise God!"

Lee joined the hushed celebration with a smile of his own. *I am so glad I moved here.*

Soon the worship team assembled on the platform and the parishioners rose to their feet ready to worship. About forty minutes later, Pastor Spalding came up to the platform while the worship team maintained soft instrumental music. He made some announcements and then concluded his remarks with, "Folks, I have been reminded that we have not had a testimony time for several months. Be thinking about something that will bless and encourage one another. I know God has been doing good things and we need to give Him glory. We'll make time for that just after the offering."

Too soon for Carrie Sue the offering time came and went. Pastor Spalding picked up an extra hand-held microphone and headed to the space in front of the platform. "Who wants to start the testimony time?" he invited expectantly, eyes roving across the crowd and up into the balcony.

"I do!" a chipper voice near the front called out.

"Maggie Carter!" Pastor Spalding identified the voice. "Come up here. And while she's coming, I want others of you to start to make your way forward. I want to get as many testimonies in as possible."

Inwardly, Carrie Sue groaned as Abigail and Cindy rose to their feet together. *I'm cooked.* She gathered enough strength in her trembling legs to stand and move into the outside aisle and let Abigail lead the way. She was barely paying attention to Maggie Carter's tearfully happy story of how her six-year-old granddaughter, Bethany, got saved.

"My daughter and son-in-law have raised her in the church and talk to her about Jesus all the time. So last week, little Bethany came up to her mom and said it so cute, 'Mommy, I prayed to myself and asked Jesus in my heart all by myself.'" Maggie was beaming with happiness as she returned to her seat warmed by the clapping and smiles of her church family.

Pastor Spalding turned his attention to Carrie Sue who was standing half a step behind Abigail and Cindy. He looked at the congregation and said, "Folks, this next one is going to make you want to dance! This young lady took a nasty fall this week." He thrust the microphone close to Carrie Sue's chin and said, "tell them what happened this week."

"Uh, well," Carrie Sue started off softly, "I was visiting Abigail Steele and I decided to take a walk. Somehow, I tripped and fell. I broke some bones in my foot and got a nasty shiner and a bump." She lightly touched her forehead.

"Well, you look fine today. Tell us what happened," Pastor Spalding prompted.

"Abigail and Cindy prayed with me yesterday and by the time we were finished, both the foot and my face were back to normal." She gave a close-mouthed smile as she shrugged her shoulders.

Pastor Spalding moved the microphone over to Cindy who spoke up, "It was the most amazing thing! Her foot and face were both swollen and bruised. When we were finished praying, she stood up and unwrapped it. There was one tiny bruise, but she danced up and down on it. When we looked again, it was completely healed. That was when I noticed that her face was healed, too." Abigail smiled broadly at Carrie Sue and Cindy.

"Praise the Lord!" Pastor Spalding rejoiced with them and the congregation erupted in more clapping and shouts of praise.

Suddenly, Abigail became aware of tingling on the back of her neck. She momentarily froze when she saw Roger Bynum striding down the center aisle toward the front. Maintaining the smile on her face, stepping in front of Carrie Sue, she grabbed her friend's elbow and nudged her toward the window aisle.

"Sheriff Bynum," Pastor Spalding quickly turned his attention to the burly man and said with mock concern,

"I hope you're coming up here to bring me a testimony and not a ticket." The congregation laughed at yet another one of his corny jokes.

Bynum's long legs quickly covered the remaining distance to the front. He turned and flashed his winning political smile before he cleared his throat and said, "I know I'm not usually very vocal around here, but I just can't help it today. I had an amazing healing this week, too." His eyes found and momentarily bored through Abigail and Carrie Sue.

"I was in a scuffle with someone I was trying to apprehend this week and got clobbered pretty good in my windpipe. I couldn't talk or breathe for a while because it was swelling inside. But, I was lucky enough to have someone with me who had the power of the man upstairs to heal me. He laid his hand on my throat and prayed."

And immediately an angel of the Lord struck him because he did not give glory to God.

Sheriff Bynum suddenly coughed sharply. "When he finished," he continued with a slight rasp, "I was healed. I could breathe and talk normally again." He maintained his smile as there was more clapping, but he could feel the familiar warm sensation of blood oozing into the folds of his vocal cords. He quickly waved and headed back up the aisle trying not to cough as he went.

Without returning to the balcony to rejoin his family, the stricken man headed for the foyer. Max Berryman, who had heard the change and sensed that his comrade was in trouble, met him in the foyer. Roger saw him and motioned for him to come with him. They hastily exited the building.

Roger Bynum rasped, "Get me to the doctor."

Max hustled Roger to his black truck and turned the key in the ignition. As the diesel warmed, he hit the speed dial that connected him with Dr. Bacchus, told him the problem, and arranged to meet him at the emergency room.

Meanwhile, Pastor Spalding had the praise team lead the congregation in a song to praise and worship God for the testimonies. He returned to the platform and opened his Bible, "I'm going to be preaching out of Matthew seven today. These are the concluding words of Jesus' Sermon on the Mount. I have got to believe that these are some very important words. Let's take a closer look at them."

The rustling pages soon quieted as the congregation found the passage and followed along while Pastor Spalding read the verses. He made several references to the contrasts that Jesus had made in the previous chapters. "Throughout this sermon Jesus made direct or implied contrasts of people who found themselves in different situations – whether it was the man who hid his lamp or displayed it, the one who reconciled with his brother before bringing his offering or the one who didn't, the one who made oaths or the one who let his yes be yes and his no be no, the one who practiced righteousness before God or the one who did it before men, the one who fasted or prayed so everyone knew it or the one who met secretly with God."

He continued to cite examples and then ended the sermon by reading the last few verses and making his concluding remarks. "We see one more contrast here: one man built his house upon the sand and another one built his house upon the rock. I can just imagine that the men built houses that looked identical. It's not the house that's the most important thing here, it's the foundation. The quality of the foundation will not be revealed until and unless there is a storm. Carrie Sue and Sheriff Bynum both encountered storms last week. We can see that their foundation, the Rock of Ages, has served to preserve their houses despite the winds and the floods that came their way."

Pastor Spalding closed his Bible and searched their faces before he said, "Folks, I can look at you and I know that most of you have weathered storms of life and revealed the Foundation that you are building upon. But I also think that there may be some of you who look just like the wise man, but your foundation is really built upon the sand. Won't you search your heart today? Won't you be like a child, like sweet little Bethany, and ask Jesus to come into your heart and be your Foundation, your Rock?"

He extended the invitation to come forward to pray about salvation, healing, or any other matter before dismissing them. Several people came forward and prayed with the prayer teams. Some others clustered around Carrie Sue, Cindy, and Abigail. Carrie Sue was more comfortable with one-on-one encounters these days, but she was eager to be on her way. It had been over a week since she had been home and seeing Sheriff Bynum, a.k.a. Zorroz, had nearly done her in.

The crowd finally dissipated and the McCords and Lee Norris went to the children's area to get Traci and Bryan. Abigail and Carrie Sue made their way back out to the parking lot.

"I'm going to miss you," Abigail said, "the house is going to feel very empty."

"I'll miss you, too," Carrie Sue responded while trying not to tear up. "You saved my life. I don't know how I can ever thank you enough."

"You can thank me by continuing to pursue healing so you can live the life that God has planned for you," Abigail said. "That would give me such joy. There just aren't that many SRA survivors that make it all the way out and stay out."

"Yeah," Carrie Sue nodded soberly, "I am going for it. I can do all things through Christ who strengthens me!" She flashed a bright smile.

With his Haitian heritage came a mixed bag of occult practices. Dr. Bacchus' family had been immersed in Macumba and Hoo Doo while he was living in Haiti. He quickly became occupied with Witchcraft, Satanism, and Wizardry when he moved to America.

Dr. Bacchus was annoyed that his day had been interrupted, but he had loyalties so he changed his plans in order to meet Sheriff Bynum and Max Berryman in the emergency room. Parking his Jaguar in a reserved space, he strode into the emergency department and inquired about Roger Bynum.

"We have him in six," the clerk informed him.

Without thanking her, he headed to the curtained off cubical and entered. He saw that Bynum had already been hooked up to an IV and was being given oxygen. He looked distressed and tried to speak but a husky croak was all that came out. His wife had been called and she was sitting nervously in a hard plastic chair in the corner of the room. Max left when she arrived.

"Don't try to talk," Dr. Bacchus instructed him. He noted that Roger's oxygen level was too low. Turning to the nurse that followed him into six, he barked out an order, "Get me a light and open the trach kit."

She slapped the light into Dr. Bacchus' outstretched hand. Having anticipated the need for a tracheotomy, she had assembled the instrument table and trach kit along with local anesthesia and surgical scrub. She placed the kit on the table and began to unfold the dark blue cloth exposing assorted instruments and devices that were necessary for the procedure.

"Roger," Dr. Bacchus addressed the distraught man professionally, "I'm going to do a tracheotomy right here to help you breathe and let me see what's causing the bleeding. We might have to go upstairs to clean it up better."

Roger Bynum visibly tensed up but Dr. Bacchus continued, "I'm going to have the nurse give you a mild sedative and I'll numb up the area. You'll feel some pressure and a little bit of pain, but that'll be the worst of it. You won't be able to talk until we remove the trach tube. It might be a few hours or a few days, depending on what we find."

After gowning up, Dr. Bacchus expertly used the scalpel to create the stoma and then slid the tube through the exposed cartilage and into the trachea. Immediately Roger was able to breathe better since the partially obstructed airway had been by-passed. Dr. Bacchus was then able to do a more extensive examination and determined that both the hyoid bone and the thyroid cartilage had been fractured. It was confirmed by the X-ray. One of the fragments had apparently damaged the blood vessel that was continuing to bleed.

"Roger," Dr. Bacchus said, "the good news is that you're breathing, the bad news is that we do have to take you upstairs to clean it up a bit and stop that little bleeder. We can't let you walk around with fragments in there waiting to cut something else."

Roger Bynum nodded and closed his eyes. He had questions that he could not voice. He was not only frustrated, he was scared. He knew that the Great Enemy had undone what Prinz had healed. Reflecting on his time in the church earlier that morning, he ruefully thought that he now had an inkling of what a Christian must feel like in the midst of a crowd of Satanists. He had been a Satanist standing in the midst of Christians. *At least we kill them. They didn't kill me – yet.*

The McCords and Lee Norris were finishing up their Sunday dinner of scrumptious pot roast and potatoes, applesauce and green beans. Their conversations were varied and only interrupted by Traci and Bryan when they wanted to go play.

"Isn't that something about Carrie Sue?" Cindy gushed. "I mean, I've seen God do some great things, but I never watched a foot just heal up instantly."

"I wish I could have been there," Gary said.

"Me, too," Lee agreed. "That woman was in a bad way. The last time I saw her, she looked like she had lost a boxing match with a heavy weight but today ... wow! It's a miracle for sure."

"Praise God!" Cindy exclaimed again. "That woman has endured so much. I'm tickled that she's getting healing from all the dissociation and the programming and whatever else the Satanists did to her."

"Just what *is* going on in this county?" Lee said with some concern. "Do I want to move here?"

"Lee," Gary said, "there are Satanists all over the world. We see a lot of graffiti and hear about someone sacrificing a cat on Halloween once in a while, but the real Satanists are more subtle. They don't want to be exposed. If you lived among them back in Montana you wouldn't even know it."

Lee's right eyebrow raised and he gave Gary a tell-me-more look.

"The only reason Cindy and I are aware of them in our community is because Abigail Steele regularly works with the survivors and Cindy's been her prayer partner. I had no idea until last month that Sheriff Bynum and Max Berryman are part of the cult. And they both go to our church."

"Why would a Satanist go to church?" Lee asked.

"I don't know for sure," Gary ventured, "Abigail can give you much a better answer, but I think it's a part of their cover and part of the way that they keep an eye on the good guys."

"What do you think of Sheriff Bynum's testimony this morning?" Lee asked. "Something didn't seem quite right." He was a very discerning, intuitive man.

"I think he was trying to save face or maybe trying to intimidate Carrie Sue and Abigail," Cindy said as she began to clear the table. "He sure gave me the creeps when he looked right at us."

"Aren't you worried that he'll try to do something to you, too?"

"No, not really," Gary said, "I mean, when I was face to face with him in Abigail's basement that day Carrie Sue's brother attacked her, he acted like he was afraid of me. It's like Abigail always says, 'no weapon formed against us will prevail.'"

"Carrie Sue's brother attacked her?"

"Yeah, that was about a month ago. He disappeared and we think he's been killed."

"What?" Lee was becoming more alarmed and more perplexed with each new revelation.

"It's a long story," Cindy said, "why don't you ask Abigail about it next time you see her? Hey, how are your mares getting along with Buster? And how's your search for a place?"

"They're fine, but I really want to get them to a place of their own. I hate to impose on Abigail much longer. I originally said it would be three mares, but I just couldn't leave Sassy behind."

"I happen to know that she doesn't mind. She likes the added company," Cindy spoke for Abigail.

"Gary, if you don't mind, can you take a ride out to a place I looked at Friday? I'd appreciate some feedback on the pros and cons. And I'd like to walk the property some. I only looked at it for a little while with the real estate agents."

"Sure," Gary said, "I'd love to." Then he looked at Cindy. "Do you mind?"

"No problem," she said, "the kids and I have plenty to do."

The men donned their boots and coats. Lee took along his spiral bound notebook that had his notes in it.

They settled into Lee's F350 and headed down the road talking about the property. Lee was becoming much more familiar with these roads and soon they were turning onto the rutted lane that led to the abandoned mobile home and old barn.

"Hey," Gary exclaimed, "this is within a mile of Abigail's place. When did it go up for sale?"

"Friday," Lee replied. "Gayle Dillon checked her computer when we got back from looking at some other places and this was just listed. There wasn't very much information, so I wanted to come back and take a closer look."

"I'll tell you one thing," Gary said as the old mobile home came into view, "you won't have to worry about air conditioning in that thing."

"Let me tell you what I'm thinking," Lee said, ignoring his cousin's humor, "this place is in some kind of receivership so they want to dump it quickly. I put some earnest money down on it and don't mind losing it if I decide against it."

"What are they asking?"

"$32,000 for eighty acres more or less," Lee replied.

"That's a steal!" Gary exclaimed. "Farmland around here usually goes for about a thousand per acre."

"That's what I figured. It's perfect for my horses and a few cows once I get some fences up. Anything else by way of buildings is just a bonus."

"So," Gary teased, "are you going to live in the trailer or the barn?"

"I don't know, they're both so cozy it'll be a tough decision." Lee shot him a grin. "Actually, I think it would be more comfortable to rent a small apartment close by until I can build something."

Lee parked his truck close to a dirty, abandoned car and they got out to explore the eighty acres. They did a quick inspection around the outside of the trailer and determined that it had once been hooked up to gas, electricity, and city water. Looking inside, they noted that it was a haven for every kind of rodent in the area. Old fast-food trash gave evidence that it had probably been used as a hangout by teenagers.

They wandered around the back and then walked completely around the weathered barn before entering it through a side door. Most of the boards were a dull gray and some of them were curled with age. A creaky but sturdy staircase led to the loft where half of it had been used as a hay mow and the other half was filled with old wooden barrels, a pile of boards, rusty pipes, pieces of sheet metal, and odd things that get tossed into attics over the years.

Shoving against the beams, they decided that other than some damage from a couple of leaks in the roof; the barn was generally quite sturdy and could be repaired with minimal expense. There was plenty of room for stalls and equipment storage. In his mind, Lee was moving in already.

They ambled down the hillside behind the barn and found what used to be a pond in the gully. It had been worn down on the lower end where erosion had done its steady work. It could be readily repaired as well. Working their way down through the fields behind the barn, walking toward York Creek and then back up the fields across from Abigail's place, they finally emerged from the wooded area on the same path that Billy and Zorroz, Carrie Sue and Abigail had previously taken.

"You know," Gary said frowning at the abandoned car, "I think this car might just be Carrie Sue's brother's car. This would be where she was knocked out and taken by her mother."

"Let's check it out," Lee said. He walked over to the passenger side of the car and opened the creaky door. Reaching into the glove box, he withdrew the rumpled scrap of paper that identified the car as being registered to William J. Wagner. This generated yet another set of questions that he had for Gary, Cindy, and Abigail.

"This could be a little fly in the ointment since the guy is unofficially missing," Gary observed.

"Well," Lee said with his dry humor, "other than this being a crime scene, what do you think?"

"I think that if you don't buy it, I will!"

Carrie Sue felt both exhilaration and trepidation as she drove home from church. It felt as if she'd been gone for a year. She had been through so much but she had also healed so much. She grew in her faith in God and was optimistic about her future even though there was a good deal of uncertainty about it.

Pulling into the empty parking space in front of her apartment, she heaved a sigh of relief. She was in the habit of looking around to see if anyone might be lurking nearby or if anything seemed to be out of order. Noticing nothing unusual, she gathered her belongings and unlocked her front door. Kicking the pile of mail that had been shoved through the slot, she scattered the heap of bills and junk mail. Taking a quick peek into her bedroom and the adjoining bathroom, she felt sure that her apartment was secure. She spent the rest of the day unpacking, sorting the mail, and checking her food supply. Tomorrow she would get some groceries but tonight she would relax.

Within an hour she heard the familiar sound of a truck that would soon need a muffler and looked out the window. *Oh, no; not Mom!* She quickly breathed a prayer for protection and made an announcement internally that was totally unnecessary. Her reliable protectors were already near the surface and ready to intervene if the mother switched into that aggressive personality like she did the last couple of times.

"Carrie Sue!" Susan Wagner called out loudly as she rapped on the door, "Carrie Sue, it's your mother."

Carrie Sue begrudgingly opened the door and then greeted her mother as warmly as she could, "Hi, Mom; come in."

Susan wasted little time in berating Carrie Sue. "Where have you been? Don't you know how worried I've been? How could you treat me this way? What kind of daughter are you? You're all I've got left, you know?" The personality that Carrie Sue identified as Martyr Mom was pouring it on.

"Sorry, Mom," Carrie Sue said, "I didn't mean to worry you." It was hard not to be blunt, but Carrie Sue realized that her mother's multiple personalities would be switching in and out so it would be useless to try to carry on a rational conversation.

"You should be sorry," Martyr Mom had switched out and Mean Mom had switched in, and then just as abruptly, Martyr Mom was back, "I've lost my sons and all I have is you and you just don't care...."

"Mom!" Carrie Sue said assertively, "Just stop. You do not get to put me down like this anymore. I'm not a little girl. I'm not programmed anymore. Just stop it! You need to get some help."

Susan Wagner's mouth dropped open as she stared and then glared at her daughter. "Why, you ungrat…"

"Mom!" Carrie Sue asserted herself again, "Just stop. Is there something you need help with today? Because if not, I'm afraid I'm going to have to ask you to leave."

"Well, you escaped this time, but we'll get you!" Susan bristled as Dorkas quickly switched in and out and then she stammered, "I, um, well … I'll just leave then. Good-bye!" With that, she turned and fled from Carrie Sue's apartment.

Good job! Carrie Sue heard a chorus of praises and encouragement coming from her internal protectors. *It looks like we're going to have to find a new job in here. Way to stand up to the bio-mom!*

Carrie Sue grinned a great big triumphant grin. "Lord, we plead Your blood over us and over this apartment and ask that You would cleanse it and keep any programming from getting triggered because she was here and we rebuke and renounce all oppressing spirits, amen."

Amy was becoming increasingly restless as the evening wore on. She was unable to focus on the sitcom that blared through her television. As the host personality that was usually in executive control, she often felt the emotions and thought the thoughts of the others inside. Until recently, she believed that everyone operated like this. Abigail had been trying to convey these principles to her, but she had not been ready, or perhaps, she was not healed enough to be able to recognize what was happening to her.

Amy, Head Warden here. Amy heard an internal voice that sounded much like hers, but a little deeper.

"Yes," Amy answered uncertainly out loud.

You know me, right?

"Yeah," Amy replied, "what do you want?"

It's a ritual night tonight and we need to do something about the Moonrakers.

"What can we do?"

Let's call Abigail

"I don't want to bother her," Amy protested.

Then let me, I think she'd much rather spend a little time preventing trouble than a lot of time cleaning up afterwards.

"Whatever," Amy feigned disinterest out of a long-standing habit. "Go ahead and call her." Amy faded into the background while Head Warden assumed executive control. He made the call.

"Hello," Abigail said. *This is unusual.* "Amy?"

"Actually, this is Head Warden."

"I was wondering how you were doing. You've been on my mind, so I've been praying."

"Thanks," Head Warden said gratefully. "Let me get right to the point," he said like the executive that he was, "the whole system is really restless and we've identified a sector that is supposed to be at tonight's ritual – the Moonrakers."

"That makes sense. Do you know where they are?"

"No, it's not as easy as the last group was. We think Nicholai has extra patrols running down there so we're going to need a different strategy for this operation."

They continued to discuss the logistics based on the limited knowledge Zuard was able to convey to the prison level leaders. They prayed together and Head Warden felt a strong impression. "You're not going to believe what I'm thinking," he stated.

"Oh, try me," Abigail said lightheartedly.

"I think God wants me to invite Nicholai up for a summit meeting."

"That will be interesting," Abigail said thoughtfully. They continued to debate various strategies and after praying again, they said good-bye. Head Warden and his loyal guards were going to implement the plan and Abigail would continue to pray.

The full moon was unimpeded by clouds. Silhouettes of the tall trees were showcased against the moon and their crisp shadows filled the countryside with shades of gray. Once again, the invisible world clashed as spirits contended in the age-old battle between the kingdom of darkness and the kingdom of light, the demons and the angels, the fallen and the redeemed.

Prinz was making his way to Zorroz' remote territory. He loathed having to go back to that paltry ritual site located just about one mile south of that damnable woman, but tonight he must. Amalek would fill in for him and lead the more prestigious big city festivities in his stead.

Daggett and his people would be joining him along with nearly fifty others from the surrounding counties. Darod and Herrak were heading to the local ritual site in their home county located about midway between the two diverse sites. Each county had its own local gathering places in wooded areas, churches, lodges, barns, or private homes. The public as a whole was unsuspecting and unaware of what occurred during the night in their communities.

By ten o'clock, most of the participants had arrived or were well on the way. By midnight they were all gathered around the fires. Instruments of torture were staged nearby. Victims were prepared with drugs that they were tricked into or forced into ingesting. Other participants also altered their mental states with drugs to enhance their experience. Drums began to beat their deadly rhythms and the festivities began in earnest.

At three o'clock in the morning, the darkest of the night hours, and the counterpart of Jesus' three o'clock in the afternoon cry, they cried out "it is finished" and sent out innumerable curses before disposing of evidence and making their way back to their homes.

5

Tuesday, November 7

Abigail was feeling very much alone after having had Carrie Sue as a guest, but she also appreciated the alone time and was grateful to be able to work around the little farm to finish the seasonal projects. It was chilly earlier in the morning when she fed the horses, and yet it was just mild enough to make her entertain thoughts of taking Buster out for a ride. *Maybe later this afternoon when it warms up a bit more.* She busied herself in her office until lunchtime. Weather forecasts were calling for clear skies this week and storms next week so she wanted to take advantage of the nice weather. *Who knows how many good riding days are left this year?*

Across the county, Lee was contemplating a ride of his own to explore the property that he had purchased the day before. The deal was still pending, but Gayle Dillon assured him that despite the complication of the receivership, he should expect to close on the deal in about ten days. He felt a little bit like a shy teenager as he contemplated calling Abigail Steele. *What's the big deal? I just need to call and let her know I'll be taking a ride.* He tried to settle his nerves.

Taking a deep breath, retrieving the phone number that was on a scrap of paper from his wallet, he began to tap the numbers into his phone.

He heard the answering machine engage, listened to Abigail's voice as she gave her humorous, slightly saucy message. "Calls are screened by this machine, but sometimes the lights are on and no one's home so please leave a message!" An annoying tone followed.

"Hello, this is Lee Norris. I'd like to come by early this afternoon so I can take one of the horses out for a ride. I come in peace," he added with his dry humor, "so don't shoot me." He was just about to hang up when Abigail picked up the phone.

"Hey, sorry, I didn't recognize your number so I was screening the call."

"Oh, no problem," Lee replied graciously, "I think maybe I'm beginning to understand your situation a little better."

"Sorry about that," Abigail said, "I guess Gary and Cindy didn't warn you about my crazy life."

"No, not much, but I don't think it's crazy; I think it's heroic. There aren't very many people who would help people like Carrie Sue."

"I'm just one beggar showing another beggar where to find bread." Abigail downplayed the compliment. "But back to your ride; what time were you planning on coming by today?"

"Oh." Lee remembered the original reason for his call. "I was thinking about right after lunch. I haven't had the girls out for a ride in quite a while and I also want to explore the property that's right across the road from you."

"Really?" Abigail was curious. "What for?"

"It went up for sale on Friday. I put some earnest money down and hope to buy it."

"That's exciting! But wait; there's no house up there, just some run-down trailer. Where will you live?"

"In the barn," Lee replied dryly before he broke into a light chuckle and then said, "I'll get a place in town while I build something."

"Well, come on over!" Abigail said enthusiastically. "I was going to take Buster out today. Do you mind if I tag along?"

"Not at all," Lee said heartily. "I'd like that. I'll see you around one then."

"Perfect!" Abigail did not hide her excitement. After they said good bye, she began to have second thoughts. *Oh, dear, was I too forward? I hardly know the man.* It did not matter. She was just going to enjoy the afternoon. No agenda. None.

Absolutely none.

Going to her bedroom, Abigail dropped to her knees. "Lord, I know that it's just been about a month since I mentioned that I'm getting lonely. If You are bringing this man into my life for more than just boarding his horses and maybe just being neighbors, please," she pleaded, "please don't let either one of us defraud the other in any way. Let us be authentic and real with each other." She paused for a minute. "Lord, I'm kind of excited and nervous, happy and sad, all at once. I miss my Darryl, but I know he's gone...." She continued to pour out her heart.

By the time she finished her lunch and cleaned up the kitchen, she heard the distinctive sound of a diesel coming up the driveway. Peeking through the front windows of the living room to be doubly sure that it was Lee and not Max, she breathed a sigh of relief. *Lord I need to stop being so much on edge.* Abigail quickly put her coat on and headed out the back door.

"Hey!" she greeted Lee as just he was getting out of his truck.

"Hello!" Lee said and then teased, "Nice to see you and not Walther."

"Oh, he's here," Abigail smiled as she patted the slight bulge on her waist.

"Good," Lee said approvingly.

"So, who are you riding today?"

"I think Lady will get the first workout."

Lee went to his horse trailer and selected the saddle and tack that he needed and then they strolled down to the gate and slipped into the pasture. Buster had heard the commotion and came thundering up the field. That got the attention of Lee's horses and they followed him to the tack room anticipating a treat. Abigail and Lee finished brushing and saddling their horses at about the same time and led them to the front gate.

"I want to make something that will allow me to open the gate without getting off of Buster every time I go in and out," Abigail said.

"I made several latches for all my gates. It saves time and sometimes it even keeps you from losing a few head of cattle. I'll fix one for both of your gates when things settle down," Lee offered.

"Really?" Abigail was impressed. "Thanks. Maybe we could build it together. I like to learn. My dad used to rig all kinds of things. He thought outside of the box a lot." *Points! Another man who can fix things.*

They continued to talk about horse and farm related things as they made their way down the driveway and across the road following the same path that Carrie Sue and Abigail had followed not many days before.

The sun was pleasantly warm and the aromas of the dried grasses and leaves added to the invigorating fresh air. They talked about the property and Abigail began to fill Lee in on the adventures of the last month or so. She had to be careful not to violate Carrie Sue's confidential counseling information, but since Lee had become involved in Carrie Sue's rescue and he now owned the property upon which Billy's car remained, Abigail could tell him a few more things.

They fell into comfortable silences as they rode along side by side through the fields and later with Abigail in the lead when the trail narrowed through the stand of woods. Arriving at the top of the rise near the derelict trailer and the weathered barn, they explored the land in widening circles, discovering discarded and rusty antique plows, tires, appliances, and other farm debris that had accumulated over the decades. Some of the out buildings would be useable with minor repairs and some would need to be burned. They also came across the remains of a foundation that had once supported the original farmhouse. A three-foot-tall cement block structure that was about four by six feet and covered with rotting boards was near it.

"What would that be?" Abigail asked. "It's too short to be a building and too tall to be an outhouse."

"I don't know; let's check it out." With one fluid movement he swung off of Lady. Lady was a striking bay horse, seventeen hands high with flowing black mane and tail.

Abigail followed suit and dismounted from Buster as Lee removed some of the cracked boards and peered inside. Abigail's curiosity drew her closer. "Pipes."

"I think this is an old well house," Lee said excitedly. "That's an answer to prayer." Abigail looked at him questioningly so he explained, "Whenever I pray about something, especially big things, I make a great big long detailed list of the desires of my heart. One of the things I asked for was both city and well water plus ponds and streams."

"Wow!" Abigail exclaimed, "That's really cool. And, by the way, I do the same thing – God gets a bunch of lists from me."

Points! A like-minded godly woman.

They remounted their horses and continued their exploration of Lee's new property. He told her of his plans to fence off certain fields for the horses and then for the cows that he would get later. He showed her the broken pond and some of the other things that he and Gary had discovered earlier.

They talked about disposing of Billy's car and the closing date and the buildings and fields and woods. They talked about the McCords and church and Pastor Spalding and the upcoming holidays.

They did not talk about loneliness.

"Hey," Abigail asked mischievously, "you want to go see where the five-sided ritual rock is? I mean, not actually go all the way to it, but I'll show you the trail that leads up to it."

Lee thought about it for a moment and then replied, "Actually, I think it would be a very good idea. I mean, if I'm going to live here, I'll need to learn all about the new neighborhood."

Abigail nudged Buster with a light kick and took off down the trail through the woods and back into one of a series of pastures. Lee kicked Lady and was right behind Abigail and Buster. It was exhilarating to let the horses gallop at top speed but too soon they were closing in on York Creek. They slowed their horses and picked their way across the creek at the same place that Abigail had crossed weeks before on the Saturday that she discovered the pentagram shaped rock and ritual site on the back side of one of the neighboring farms. She still could not pinpoint which property it belonged to but she was definitely not inclined to try every driveway along the road just to find out for sure.

After cantering through the fields, Abigail slowed Buster and pointed to her right up a fairly steep hill with a well-marked trail. "That's it," she said.

"Yeah," Lee said, "I can sense it from here. Let's turn around and head back."

"Good idea," Abigail agreed. *Hmm, he has the gift of discernment. Points.*

It wasn't long before Lee and Abigail were back at her farm. Neither one of them spoke much as they groomed their horses, sensing that their pleasant afternoon was drawing to a close. Too soon they were heading back up to the gate.

"I have a favor to ask you," Lee started awkwardly.

"I'll do what I can. What do you need?"

"Well, actually, I need two things. I won't close on this place until the week of the thirteenth. Can you keep the horses here until I can get some fences up for them? It might not get done until Thanksgiving."

"No problem, don't pressure yourself," Abigail said. "Besides, Buster likes the company. I hope he doesn't jump the fences wanting to visit all of his girlfriends once they move out." They smiled at the visual images that accompanied the thought.

"The second thing is that I'm hoping to go back to Montana this week. I have a neighbor back there who's been storing my other truck, a trailer, and some tools and equipment for me until I decided if I needed them or not. I need to fly out there and haul a bunch of stuff back. It'll be less expensive than buying replacements here. Can you take care of the horses until I get back?"

"Sure thing. They're easy to handle and it only takes a couple extra minutes to feed them," Abigail said.

"Thanks," Lee said visibly relieved, "I really don't want to impose on you."

"Like I said, it's no biggie," Abigail said graciously. "I love the horses and I'll miss them when they move out. So will Buster."

F. Amy Bolton looked through pained eyes into her bathroom mirror at the reflection of her swollen and split lower lip. She was moving slowly this morning, but she was feeling a modicum of satisfaction.

Somehow, Head Warden and his guards had kept Nicholai and his henchmen from getting them to the full moon ritual on Sunday night. She would have grinned with satisfaction if the puffy lip had not been so damaged. She had done some damage, too.

When she did not show up at the ritual, Herrak and Darod, the upper level masters for her area cult, had sent Levi and one of his buddies to beat her up and rape her. At four o'clock in the morning she was awakened by the creaking of the old wooden steps that led into her trailer. They had burst in on her before she could reach her knife so all she could do was kick and flail at her attackers until she was subdued; until they had vented their displeasure.

Amy was no longer fatalistic about her life and her future. She used to think that this was her destiny, her purpose, her lot in life; that she had no other recourse. Her parents and grandparents and great grandparents were caught up in Satanism. Why should she be the only exception? How could she possibly get away? They never did. Did they have a choice? Satanists had their world-wide network and Satan had his demons stationed everywhere, too.

But... what did Abigail say? Once the programming was dismantled and all the personalities were finally integrated they could not access her anymore. In fact, they might even be a mite intimidated by her because they would know that she possessed the *dunamis* power of the Holy Spirit of the Most High God. *Oh, God, how long will that take?*

Meanwhile, she would go to work and come up with yet another cover story about how clumsy she was. Amy had been through worse than this over the course of her life and she did not doubt that she would be ambushed a time or two before it was all over. Sighing a painful sigh, she began to ready herself for her shift at The Pizza Palace.

6

Friday, November 10

Caring for the horses, keeping the wood stove burning, checking indoor projects off her list, the week flew by for Abigail. Sometimes she would pause and look out her front windows. It was the same and yet it was all different now that Lee Norris would own that property. She had always appreciated the view as a picturesque country scene filled with fields and streams, woods and wildlife. What kind of changes would be coming to the landscape? What would it be like to be neighbors with Lee Norris? Other than Earl and Jan on the next hill to the north, she really did not know her other neighbors – an understatement in light of her discovery about the farm with the ritual site less than a mile south of her.

Abigail double-checked her schedule for the day and was reminded that she had that meeting with Pastor Spalding at one o'clock. *Oh, Lord, I need your wisdom! Put a guard over my mouth and keep a watch over the door of my lips. Let me say everything I need to and nothing that I do not need to say.* Abigail frequently prayed her Psalm-one-hundred-forty-one-verse-three prayer.

She prayed for her sessions with Carrie Sue and Amy as she packed a lunch and brewed some Constant Comment tea to put in her stainless-steel thermos cup. Making one final check of the woodstove, Abigail slipped on her insulated black jacket, adjusted her black and purple plaid woolen scarf, and headed to her truck. Starting the engine, blasting the defroster, she grabbed the scraper from behind her seat and cleared the windows. There was a hard frost the previous night.

Buster was at the near corner nibbling at the sparse grass. He looked up at her briefly as she cruised down the curved gravel driveway before returning to his grazing. The grass was usually meager at this time of year, but with the addition of Lee Norris' four mares, there was not much left to munch on. Abigail had been supplementing their grazing with hay from the barn. Soon she would have to wrestle another one of the round bales into the pasture.

The sky was blue and the sun was shining. Abigail was grateful for every sunny day. Soon, the weather would turn cold and dreary. In fact, it was supposed to rain on Sunday. Today, however, was a quintessential fall day – crisp and clear, invigorating and energizing.

Her thoughts drifted once again to the day ahead of her and she automatically began to pray for each appointment that she had. She almost chuckled out loud thinking that she was more comfortable talking with Satanic Ritual Abuse survivors than she was talking to her preacher. Of course, today was the day that he was going to ask her some pointed questions about the nature of her work and about SRA. Now that Carrie Sue had that abduction and escape, the trauma and miraculous healing, he would undoubtedly have even more questions.

Carrie Sue was waiting inside of her rusty old car when Abigail pulled into the church parking lot. They emerged from their respective vehicles at the same time and greeted one another with smiles. The ordeal that they recently shared had deepened their relationship. That's the way it should be between sisters in Christ. Sometimes it was tricky to have a dual relationship, that is, counselor and friend, but they were navigating it well enough that it did not interfere in either one of their lives.

After settling into the office with the music playing softly in the waiting area, they opened with prayer and began their session. "It sure seems like it's been forever since we've met here," Carrie Sue said.

"I know what you mean," Abigail agreed but got right down to business. "Where are we starting today? What are you sensing?"

"Well," Carrie Sue began, "I think there's someone in here that's really tormented but no one seems to be able to find him."

"Let's ask the Lord to illuminate and seek the 'lost sheep' for us." Abigail continued with a prayer to that effect after Carrie Sue nodded her agreement. Abigail had learned to watch and pray a long time ago. Body language and facial changes gave clues to switching personalities and other hints that aided her in sorting out the healing process. Today she noted a subtle shift after a few moments of silence.

"Hi," she said gently, "who are you?"

A suddenly alarmed personality quickly flinched and looked askance at Abigail and scanned the inside of the room.

"You're safe here," Abigail said reassuringly, "I'm Abigail and I've been trying to help Carrie Sue and the others inside." She continued after receiving a puzzled look by the personality, "Do you know Carrie Sue?"

Abigail was rewarded with a nervous shake of the head as the personality looked apprehensively around the room. Abigail sensed that this one had endured torment with some kind of a twist to it. But then, that would make sense because the so-called ordinary torment would have been absorbed by someone else. "Do you know anyone else in there?" Abigail pressed him or her quietly.

This time she got a slight nod with more nervous looks darting around the room.

"Is the person you know nice to you?" She probed. She had the sense that perhaps the personality was a young boy, maybe ten years old.

Again, the shake.

"Is the person you know mean to you?"

Another shake.

"Do you know where that person is right now?"

"He's dead," a tiny voice whispered sadly.

"I'm so sorry, it sounds like he was your friend," Abigail pursued the glimmer of a trail.

"He, he was..." his voice quavered and stopped as he pulled his knees up to his chin, folded his arms around his legs and dropped his forehead on top of them. It was amazing to Abigail how the adult Carrie Sue could get into such compact positions when the younger personalities switched in. Years of abuse had rendered the adult Carrie Sue incapable of some of those postures, especially full knee flexion.

Abigail waited silently until the little guy regained his composure. Heaving a great sigh, deciding to make this do-or-die decision, he raised his head and blurted, "He was my twin brother." He retreated back into his upright fetal position.

Again, Abigail was reminded of the myriad of ways that personalities might be programmed. They could be older or younger than the actual age of the person. They could be a different gender than the physical body with different assignments and different looks.

Why couldn't they be programmed to be twins or pre-borns or even dead?

"Can you talk about it a little bit?" Abigail invited.

She got the I-have-nothing-to-lose-and-she-seems-nice-so-why-not look. He began haltingly and then his story poured out. He began to describe a terrible ritual in which he and his twin brother were brought in front of everybody. "They put 'Azazel' and 'Lazarus' on two gold coins and put them in a fancy vase. Then the man with the scary eyes came up and took one of the coins and put it on my brother's head and he put the other one on mine." He looked confused as he continued the story. "He said those were our new names and we had to ... I forgot the word he said ... like we had to do what those names mean."

"You're doing just fine," Abigail encouraged, "keep going. I'm following you."

"The leader man said that my brother had to go to Jehovah because his name was Lazarus. I don't know where Jehovah is, but I want to know so I can find my brother. Then he looked right at me and said that I was chosen to be the scapegoat because my name was Azazel. I didn't know what that meant, but he said that everybody's sins had to go on me and I had to go far away where nobody was. Then they tied a purple scarf around my neck and said that if it didn't turn white they were all going to be in trouble and it would be my fault." He looked despairingly at Abigail hoping that she could make some sense of his life. "He said that I was evil and I could never come back."

"Well," Abigail said with a gentle smile, "I'm pretty sure that the mean man was wrong and we can get this all straightened out and you can see your brother again.

I know Jehovah and I know what He did for another guy named Lazarus who died."

"Really?" the boy asked. His saucer eyes brightened to reflect a shred of hope. "How?"

"I need to tell you about the real Jehovah," Abigail began. She continued to tell this personality many of the things she had told countless other parts of Carrie Sue about her history, her family, the real Jesus Christ of Nazareth, the Satanists, and other details that were pertinent to this boy. She told him about the Day of Atonement that was meant for Jehovah's chosen people and that what he experienced was the Satanists' way of mocking the real Jehovah God.

He drank it all in and eagerly consented to have Abigail pray for both he and his twin brother.

"Holy Father," Abigail began, "we come before Your throne of grace in the name of Jesus Christ who is the true, once-and-for-all atonement for all of our sins. We ask that You would now cover that ritual with Your cleansing blood and release these twins from every stronghold that has been created by any and all verbal assaults – the spiels, hexes, chants, judgments, curses, covenants, assignments, programming, and any other kind of verbal, written, engraved, tattooed, or other communication – render them null and void. We also pray against every direct and indirect unholy union, soul tie, and flesh link represented in sexual violations of these twins. We ask for Your healing balm to cover physical, mental, and emotional traumas as well as all body memories caused by whatever they heard, saw, smelled, tasted, touched or felt. We ask You to take the sting out of the memories and then heal and seal all their broken places. Fill them with Your Holy Spirit, truth, blessings, and above all, I speak life to the one they called Lazarus. Jesus, You are the resurrection and the life! We pray this in Jesus' name, amen."

"Oh, wow!" the boy exclaimed. "My brother is alive again! Thank you, thank you so much!"

"Is he okay now? Are you okay?" Abigail wanted to confirm that their healing was complete.

"Yep," he answered and then added with a smile, "Our real names are James and John."

"Well," Abigail laughed gently, "I think you two are like the brothers in the Bible that Jesus called the Sons of Thunder."

He giggled back in delight.

"I have one more question," Abigail said. "Do you think you'd like to be put back inside so that the mean guys can't get at you anymore?"

"Yes!"

"Okay, then, let me pray you in." Abigail beamed with delight as she asked the Lord to reknit them back into their rightful places with unity in a bond of peace.

Immediately Carrie Sue switched back in. "That was good! Thanks. I wonder why they showed up now. Wasn't Yom Kippur last month?"

"It is a little peculiar," Abigail agreed, "but, if you think about it, he said that he was sent away by himself and his brother was sacrificed. So, when we worked with the Yom Kippur group, they were probably inaccessible. For whatever reason, God brought them back today."

"I guess that makes as much sense as anything else in my life," Carrie Sue said thoughtfully. "It just makes me wonder how many other strays are running around in my system and," she paused and looked at Abigail,

"I know you can't answer this question, but how long will it be until I'm completely integrated?"

Abigail just smiled. They made their appointment for the following week and said their good-byes. Then Abigail went to the kitchen to eat her lunch and got ready for her meeting with Pastor Spalding.

A few minutes before one o'clock Abigail made her way to the main floor and entered the secretary's office. "Hi Ginny," Abigail greeted her.

"Hi yourself!" Ginny responded with her typical enthusiasm. She had a gift for making anyone who walked through the door feel as if they were the most special person on the planet. Ginny and her husband, Rod, were Sunday school teachers for the elementary aged children. They and their four children were active members of the church. "Pastor Spalding is expecting you, go right on in."

"Thanks," Abigail smiled back at her and walked to the open doorway of the pastor's book-lined study.

"Hello! Come in! Come in," Pastor Spalding hailed her. "Have a seat. I've really been looking forward to chatting with you."

Abigail settled in a comfortable chair across from his desk. Even though he was a fairly tall man, he did not make those who sat across the desk feel inferior or intimidated. She smiled and looked expectantly at him, waiting for him to begin what she thought might be a touchy conversation.

"Why don't we open with a word of prayer before we get started?" He didn't wait for her response and launched into a prayer asking for the Holy Spirit to give them both wisdom and understanding, insight and direction.

"Amen," Abigail echoed his amen.

"I know you only have about an hour, so let me get right to it," Pastor Spalding said. "And I know you've been having some personal challenges lately with your brake lines getting cut and your dog being poisoned. I'll just be blunt and ask you how much that has to do with some of the clients you see here." He stopped and looked expectantly at Abigail.

"Well," Abigail started slowly, while desperately hoping that she would not be asked to discontinue seeing them at the church, "I guess it has everything to do with them. The enemy is not pleased with the work that's being done."

"That's what I suspected. Let me ask you one more direct question," Pastor Spalding requested quietly. "Are you aware of any Satanists that attend here?" He then subconsciously held his breath as he waited for an answer that he did not want to hear.

"Unfortunately, yes," Abigail replied looking him in the eyes.

"That's what I was afraid of." He briefly pinched his eyes closed and then exhaled through clenched teeth making a slight hissing sound before pressing his lips together tightly.

Abigail remained silent as he attempted to process the confirmation of his worst fears.

Taking another deep breath and exhaling slowly, he dared to ask, "Just how many of these Satanists are around here?"

"I couldn't give you a number, I just know that they are a part of our community and blend in just like they were average citizens. I've got one living less than a mile from my house."

"You're kidding!"

"No," Abigail replied with a sad shake of her head, "I wish I were."

The grieved man gave a short huff and then began to tell Abigail about his recent visit to the hospital. "I don't know if you heard anything about it or not, but after Sunday's testimony time, Sheriff Bynum went to the hospital. He ended up having emergency surgery and had a tube put in his throat."

Abigail gasped, "Really?" It was her turn to sit and ponder the implications of his statements.

"It seems that whatever originally happened to his throat had to be surgically repaired. I don't understand how he could get up there and testify about being healed – and he seemed fine to me – and then the next minute, he's heading to the hospital. His wife called me and I went over there to see him after church. What do you think?"

"Well," Abigail said as she searched her memory of Sunday's testimony time, "I don't know if you heard him or not with all the clapping and stuff, but at the end of his testimony he coughed kind of hard."

"Are you saying that he undid the miracle?" Pastor Spalding was thoroughly puzzled.

"Maybe it was a counterfeit miracle."

"So, are you saying that he's one of them?" Pastor Spalding asked bluntly.

"I happen to know that he *is* one of them, but not just because of Sunday's testimony. He's always given me the creeps and I managed to see the tell-tale upside-down cross in the fold of his thumb a while back – I think he wanted me to see that. Plus, I asked Carrie Sue to look through our pictorial church directory a couple of weeks ago. She took one look at him and just started shaking. She said, 'that's Zorroz.' So that confirmed it for me."

"Zorroz?"

"That's his cult name."

"Cult name," he repeated flatly. That was another new concept for the beleaguered man. He had not been trained for any of this in his seminary. Pastor Spalding was quiet as he processed this information. Looking directly at Abigail once again, he asked yet another question that he really did not want to have answered, "Are there others?"

"Yes. There were others that Carrie Sue said looked familiar, and one of them is Max Berryman. I can also confirm that because he's the guy that was chasing me in his black pickup truck the day we found Carrie Sue."

"Is his whole family involved?" Blood drained from his face as he thought about his father, Ted Berryman, the upstanding elder in the church and the respected civic leader and businessman.

"I'm not sure about that, I mean, sometimes Mr. Berryman gives me the creeps, but that could be for other reasons. I am real sure about Max. I don't know if they're the generational variety of Satanists or if Max got rebellious as a teen and joined the cult or if he got suckered in."

"Why would Satanists be in a church? How can they hide it from everyone? I thought I was a fairly discerning man and now ..." He let his thoughts remain unvoiced. *Max? He was raised in this church.*

"Don't be so hard on yourself," Abigail encouraged him. "Satan's a liar, a deceiver, a murderer and a master manipulator; and these people are experts as well. If I didn't have all the experience that I do, I'd miss it, too. Anyway, it may well be God's way of shielding you from their attacks. They now know that I know, therefore, it's open warfare. You're safe."

She paused a moment and then added, "To answer your question – Anton LeVey's agenda was to create duplicitous people who serve God by day and Satan by night. He taught that the highest sacrifice to Satan is to pull off leadership in both kingdoms."

"So," he said slowly, trying to grasp the significance of the connection, "Ted Berryman could be trying to rise in this church while he's rising in Satanism? I work with the man, I can't believe that would be true about him. But let's set that aside for now. Is that why they are attacking you?"

"They don't like it that these ladies are getting deprogrammed which means that the cult is losing their control over them. And, more importantly, they are losing their powers."

Pastor Spalding furrowed his brows once again as he considered Abigail's last statement. "I'm not entirely sure that I follow."

"Let's take Carrie Sue as an example," Abigail started. "She gave me permission to talk about this since you are involved a bit. Anyway, when she and I go back to certain memories that involve rituals with their covenants, assignments, and so on, including all the programming; we basically put off Satan's stuff and put on God's stuff. We work with all the personalities that were created there. We get them deprogrammed, healed, and integrated. Most importantly, we demolish strongholds and renounce the demons assigned to her."

She paused and let him absorb this concept and then continued. "There's kind of a three-way deal that goes down: the Satanist gets demonized power of some kind and Carrie Sue gets tormenting demons. The Satanist is happy about increased powers. The demons are happy because they have a person to operate through. But Carrie Sue gets left holding the bag because of those tormenting demons."

"Makes sense."

"So, when we go after healing, then the demons – the ones assigned to Carrie Sue and the ones that empower the Satanists – get sent to wherever Jesus sends them. Reproaches get sent back to whoever sent them. Carrie Sue gets healed. She can no longer be accessed through those particular personalities because they're integrated and now inaccessible to the programmers."

"Okay."

"The Satanists lose demonic power. In fact, that's what happened to Carrie Sue's father. He just died a couple weeks ago. It happens a lot when I work with these people. And I also suspect that the higher-level Satanists are not very happy these days because I'm working with a couple of their people and the masters are weakening as well."

"I had no idea," Pastor Spalding said, "but that makes so much sense."

"That was how Carrie Sue was able to punch Sheriff Bynum in the throat that night and escape."

"Seriously!" he exclaimed incredulously. "*She's* the one that he said he was trying to apprehend? Oh, my!"

"Yes. She was able to stay in control, punch him, and run. They used to be able to call out a child or a very docile, programmed part."

"So, if he was damaged that night and then healed by... who did he say healed him?" Pastor Spalding asked thinking back to Sunday and then answered his own question. "Yeah, he said it kind of odd, like it was a man who had the power of the man upstairs or something like that."

"He said something about being lucky, too. It makes me think that there might have been some kind of counterfeit healing done at the ritual and when he didn't give God the glory Sunday morning, his so-called healing got reversed," Abigail mused.

"Counterfeit healing?" Pastor Spalding asked. He did not let much get past him.

"Satan has a counterfeit for everything that God has in His kingdom, including healing."

"Counterfeit everything," Pastor Spalding repeated the words while deep in thought.

"Everything gets counterfeited. God is the Creator; Satan is the imitator. Baptisms, weddings, communion, healings, spiritual gifts, books, trinity... You name it, Satan counterfeits it."

Pastor Spalding glanced down at his watch. "Dear lady," he said as he stood up, "it's almost two. My, how this time has flown by. We need to talk again. I want you to know that I fully support what you are doing and I would love to sit down again and talk more in-depth about these things. This little discussion has generated a lot more questions. And I will be praying much more diligently for you."

"And I will pray more for you," Abigail responded. "Thank you so much for your support. It means a lot to me. I always remind myself that no weapon formed against me will prosper. We *are* on the winning side."

"Amen to that!" Pastor Spalding responded heartily. "I'll see you later."

With that, Abigail made her way past Ginny's desk and said good-bye to her before heading to the stairs that led down to her office. Uncharacteristically, Amy was actually right on time. Abigail double-checked her watch. It was not six minutes past the hour. *Something has changed.*

"Hello," Abigail said, "come on in."

Amy quickly followed her into the office and closed the door behind her.

"It looks like you're ready to roll," Abigail noted.

"Yeah, we have a lot to tell you," Amy said. "I think Head Warden wants to talk."

"Then let's open with prayer and go for it," Abigail agreed. When she finished the prayer, she noted the shift into the ramrod military posture of Head Warden. "So, what did you guys do? I've been so curious about it ever since our phone call."

"We decided that we would send a message down to Nicholai. Zuard snuck down and left a message with one of the guards. He told him that it had to do with the Moonrakers and that it was important. We weren't sure Nicholai would come, but we hinted that we knew that he was getting some pressure because of the Moonrakers and Amy not showing for that last ritual. We offered to work with him because all of us would take the heat from Prinz, Darod, Herrak and the other masters."

"So, what went down?" Abigail could not disguise her inquisitiveness.

"He let us know that he was suspicious and wasn't going to come up without his honor guard. We told him that it would be fine and that we'd meet in one of the secure sound-proof rooms. He seemed okay with that so we set a time and they came up."

"Did they come up Zuard's secret passageway?"

"No. Apparently, they have other ways to invade our space and that really disturbs us. Zuard only knew of the one way, so there may still be some subterranean infiltrators walking around among us. We're keeping an eye out for that and doing a cell by cell and room by room search."

"Good idea," Abigail commended his thoroughness. "Amy is blessed to have you watching her back."

Head Warden ignored the compliment and resumed his story. "They came from outside of the guard house, so we think that they may have come up through one of the houses outside the prison complex. At least we hope so, but we still can't figure how we didn't detect them. We started the meeting and they wanted to have three guys inside with Nicholai and post two guys outside of the door. We told them that we would be comfortable with that and matched their guys. We also told them that they could sit at the far end of the table with their backs to the wall and we'd sit near the door."

"So, what happened?" Abigail could hardly contain herself now.

"We'd rigged a drop-down chain barrier. Once they were settled, we dropped it and they were trapped on the other side. Oh, that Nicholai is one hopping mad guy! They started yelling and cursing, but the sound-proof room kept the guards on the outside from knowing that there was something going on inside. We arranged for our guards to wait for thirty minutes and then take down the other two. Once that was done, they were brought inside the room and we began the real negotiations."

"Wow! That was bold!" Abigail said. "Then what?"

"Well, we told Nicholai that there was going to be no ritual that night for any of us. Amy is defecting to God's kingdom and that we already had. That really ticked him off! We told him that we'd be back later to talk, but before we left the room, we prayed and pled the blood of Jesus the Christ of Nazareth all over the room and bound all the demons associated with those six guys. It is, after all, under my jurisdiction." He gave her an uncharacteristic wink and continued, "We brought them food and stuff to keep them comfortable and said we'd be back."

"Excellent!" Abigail said enthusiastically. How long she had waited for Amy and the other personalities to take the initiative in her healing journey! "Now what?"

"Uh, well," Head Warden said, "that's what we were hoping you could tell us."

"Let's ask the Lord," Abigail replied. She prayed a simple prayer asking for the Lord's wisdom in dealing with the ruthless commandant of the demon-loyal, cult-loyal subterranean level.

"What are you sensing?" Abigail asked.

"I think Nicholai needs to talk to you."

"Let's do it if he's willing," Abigail agreed. Once again, she was faced with a lengthy, tricky negotiation with a hostile, programmed, and fiercely cult-loyal, demon-loyal personality.

"He's willing."

"But first I want to pray a hedge of protection around everyone and that he would be restricted from harming anyone." Abigail prayed a short prayer to that effect and was soon face to face with Nicholai.

"Hello," she said cordially as if she were greeting a good friend.

He was squinting a little bit and shielding his eyes from the brilliance of the lights. He remained mute, but soon was glaring at her as his eyes became accustomed to the brightness of the room. His usual domain was quite dim and he had never surfaced in daylight.

"Will you talk to me?" Abigail probed.

"You're a ..." he paused and did not curse as he spat out the rest of his thoughts, "a woman! Why should I deign to speak to you?"

"You don't have to," Abigail said agreeably, "you can go back." She deliberately looked down at her notebook and preoccupied herself as she wrote a few meaningless words.

"Hey! Hey lady!" Nicholai raised his voice, "You don't know who you're dealing with!"

"And you don't know who you're dealing with, but, like you said, I'm a woman and you don't want to talk to me, so I won't bother you. You have enough trouble as it is."

"What are you talking about?" he exploded. "What do you know about my trouble?"

Abigail deliberately put her pen down and calmly looked at Nicholai's reddening face. "Well, I might just know more than you think I do. And I might just be able to help you out."

"Ha!" he spat again. "What can you possibly know? Who says I need help?"

"Well," she replied gently, "all I know is that you're stuck, and Prinz and Darod are not very happy with your performance with the Moonrakers on top of the failure with the Revelers. You're losing it, man, and you need help. They'll send you to the deepest pit at the bottom of level six after they discipline you."

"Who told you about level six?" he exploded and began fuming and cursing a blue streak under his breath. He knew that she was right and he had very few options at his disposal right now. His pride kept him from asking for help even though he was more afraid than he had ever been in his life.

Abigail did not want to further humiliate him so she suggested, "You have nothing else to do except go back to that room. Maybe it would amuse you to hear what I have to say."

"Fine," he replied haughtily but with a little less venom. "Give it your best shot, lady. Amuse me. I could use a diversion."

"Story time," she announced. "Once upon a time a little girl was born into a line of Satanists. She was dedicated to Satan generations before she was knit together in her mother's womb. She was subjected to torture and split into a gazillion personalities. Each one was given an assignment for the benefit of Satan and the cult. You are one of those personalities. Your job is to do the bidding of the Satanists for a promise that they will never honor because they will make sure that you will always fall short. And now, you have fallen terribly short and cannot deliver the goods because you are a prisoner in your own prison."

She paused as he shifted uncomfortably and feebly protested, "I serve my king because I want to. I *will* be rewarded when I finish my job. I was well on the way until you interfered."

Abigail ignored his rebuff and continued, "The good news is that you can avoid all the punishment and truly make your own choices."

"I do make my own choices," he protested through clenched teeth. "I do what I want to do. I want to serve my king and all the masters he's placed over me. I'm loyal, not like those traitors, Amy and Head Warden and his guards."

"I beg to differ with you," Abigail said with a gentle smile, "you are programmed and every time you get triggered, you do their bidding."

"I am not!" he protested.

"What makes you think that everyone else in there has been programmed except for you? Think about it. Just because you happen to have a position of authority in there, you're no different than any other part that has a lesser role. You're all programmed and you're all controlled by demons."

"I am not controlled by demons! I use them to give me my powers."

"I'm not trying to inflame you, but your demons have been bound and gagged by a Power infinitely greater than any of them."

"Ooh! Lady! You don't know what you're talking about!" He stifled a string of curses.

"No sir! *You* don't know what I'm talking about," Abigail replied firmly. "Let me ask you something else. Are you able to think a little clearer since your demons were set aside?"

"No," he replied immediately, "I mean, maybe I'm thinking about some things I hadn't thought of before."

"Do you think that it's a coincidence? Or do you think it might have something to do with the absence of the demons?" Without giving him a chance to answer, she continued, "Think about the reasons that demons are assigned to other people during rituals. If you have demons, wouldn't they do the same thing to you?"

"I don't know," he said hastily. He was beginning to sweat as if he was in an interrogation. He was used to having the upper hand in any situation and this was making him nervous. He had not thought about these things. His life was his life. It had always been that way and he expected it to continue.

"Just for the sake of argument," Abigail continued, "let's say it's not a coincidence. Wouldn't it follow that you would also be programmed?"

"No," he said somewhat desperately, "well, maybe. I don't know. You're confusing me."

"Sorry," Abigail said gently, "that's certainly not my intention. Are you up for a little experiment to see if it's true or not?"

He eyed her with suspicion. "What kind of an experiment?"

"Let's just have any programming rendered null and void and you let me know if that makes any difference in the way you think or feel."

"No way! You're trying to trick me."

"How can I trick you if there's no programming? It would just prove that you're right and I'm wrong. You can go back to your life and I'll leave you alone."

Nicholai could not come up with a logical argument so he glared at her in silence.

"Look," Abigail said, "if you are programmed and the programming is removed, what effect would that have? I mean, how could that hurt you?"

"You're trying to trick me," he said, "I don't know how, but that's how you got to Head Warden and all the others."

"But the problem is that you don't know what you don't know."

"What do you mean?" he snarled back at her. "I know everything I need to know."

"Yeah," Abigail agreed with a hint of sarcasm and a light laugh, "everything you need to be a good little puppet for the cult and Satan." She knew that this would inflame him, but she wanted him to face the stark reality of his situation.

"Lady! I should kill you!" he spat.

"I'm not the enemy," Abigail said pleasantly and slowly, emphasizing each word, "but you really don't know what you don't know. You only know what they want you to know. Why do you think they're so intent on keeping Amy away from me?"

"What do you want?" Nicholai demanded.

"Just humor me," Abigail invited, "let me prove or disprove the programming and I'll leave you alone."

"Fine!" Nicholai snarled and glared at her. "Exactly what are you going to do?"

"I'm only going to pray for the programming to be neutralized and wait for you to tell me if it makes a difference or not," Abigail replied. "Are you ready?"

"Wait! Pray? To your God?"

"What's the harm? If you're right about Satan being equal to or superior to my God, then nothing happens. But if I'm right...."

"You're wrong! If you want to waste your breath, have at it," Nicholai said.

Abigail knew from experience and discernment that when a personality was in the presence of the Lord combined with the absence of demons, whether or not they recognized it, they began to soften and have an inkling that there was more to their life than what they had always thought. That was an important reason that she tried to engage them in lengthy conversations. It was as if they had to be "marinated" in the atmosphere of a Spirit-filled believer who was salt and light in order to be "tenderized".

She also knew that they had great difficulty with humbling themselves and admitting that they were wrong. If they were wrong, then they had to face the fact that they had dedicated all of their time and energy to a lie. And that would be hard for anyone to take. But if they were right, they were in deep trouble. Very deep trouble.

"Okay." Abigail had been praying silently during the entire encounter and now she prayed aloud. "God, I ask You to render all the programming pertaining to Nicholai null and void right now." Abigail purposely prayed as brief a prayer as possible and maintained eye contact with Nicholai.

Furrowing his brows and staring back at Abigail, Nicholai maintained his silence for several long minutes before he spoke. "They lied." He was seeing his entire history though unsullied lenses.

Abigail remained silent as he continued to process the implications of this discovery. She knew that this would rock his world, and she also knew that he would be furious. This time the objects of his wrath would be himself and the Satanists who had duped him.

She finally asked, "What would you like to do?"

"I don't know," he said sadly, "I want to be alone and think about it."

"How about if I ask God to provide you with a safe place where you can do that; and then, when you're ready, we can talk some more. Maybe next time?"

"Yeah, I don't want to be with the other guys right now. I need to be alone."

Abigail prayed for the Lord to put Nicholai in a safe place. He disappeared inside and Amy emerged.

"Ho-ly mo-ly!" she exclaimed emphasizing each syllable. She had been co-conscious during the entire exchange. "I can't believe it! You actually talked to Nicholai. This is bigger than big!"

They continued to celebrate for a few minutes before closing in prayer. Abigail took her time finishing her administrivia and closing the office. Walking out of the door into the chilly November afternoon, breathing a prayer of thanksgiving, she unlocked the truck and headed for the grocery store before going home after a very satisfying day.

7

Tuesday, November 21

Thanksgiving was two days away. It had always been Abigail's favorite holiday. She loved to cook and she loved to watch football. Yes, it was a great holiday and she would tell her guys, "We get to eat too much turkey and watch too much football." Of course, she made all of the traditional side dishes and desserts followed by a week of turkey sandwiches, turkey salad, turkey pot pie, and turkey soup.

But since her family had been killed, most holidays sometimes seemed hollow and far too lonely regardless of how much activity went on around her. Sometimes a holiday was just another day. *Hollowdays.* Sure, she had Gary and Cindy, her father and her siblings, but as gracious and hospitable as they might be, she felt out of place. Isolated. Solitary. Disenfranchised. They had spouses and children. They belonged to someone. She did not. "God, I'm lonely," Abigail cried out.

Despite her loneliness, or perhaps, because of it, Abigail decided that she would spend the day before Thanksgiving volunteering at her friend's restaurant again this year. Her friends, Ken and Paula Archer, owned The Iron Skillet Restaurant located about thirty miles north of Springfield on route 1950. Every year, they expressed their thankfulness to God by providing free food for anyone who wanted to come in; they especially wanted to serve the poor and the homeless. Volunteers served drinks in thick glass mugs and cleaned tables for the grateful patrons. Many of them also left generous tips which went into the fund for the following year.

The Iron Skillet Restaurant was famous for its fabulous buffet fare which was efficiently laid out in the log cabin style building. It was tastefully decorated with antiques. Dimly lit with lantern-type fixtures, long tables with a variety of benches and chairs, it was a relaxing place. Often families that did not know each other shared opposite ends of a long table. It was a popular gathering place and patrons were frequently seen interacting with each other as if they were enjoying a grand family reunion.

It had rained on Monday, but today was clear. This morning she decided to groom Buster and clean his hoofs or she would not have the opportunity until next week. She also used the grooming time to check for any cuts or health issues. Buster was still enjoying the company of the four mares and was a gracious host. His antics never ceased to amuse Abigail.

"Yes, you're so studly," she whispered as she brushed his thick coat. His winter coat was darker and duller than his glossy reddish-brown summer coat that was typical of a sorrel. When she was finished, Misty edged her way closer to Abigail. Lady, Sassy, and Sparkles remained more aloof.

"You want some attention, too?" Abigail crooned softly. She slowly stepped closer to Misty and lightly placed her left hand on Misty's left shoulder. Misty's sensitive skin reacted with a mighty quiver, as if a huge horsefly had landed on her. Misty eyed her nervously, but as Abigail began to brush her, she leaned into it and let her move from her left side, around her chest and over to her right side. Abigail spoke softly to her the whole time.

Buster finally walked back to Abigail and nosed her away from Misty as if to say, "Hey, this is my human."

"All right, you big jealous galoot," Abigail laughed. "Let me pick your feet and then you can go play while you still can. Pretty soon they'll be moving across the road." Pulling her tool from her back pocket, running her hands down Buster's front leg, she faced his rump and clamped his hoof between her knees.

After finishing his hoofs, she returned the tool to its place in the tack room and went up to the house. She was remembering the last ride she took with Lee and decided that after she ate too much turkey on Thanksgiving, she and Buster would take another ride. She was not interested in watching the battle between the Cowboys and Tampa Bay this year.

Lee Norris had closed on the property and then flown to Montana two weeks ago. He and his friend, Ernie, took a couple of days to sort through the remaining equipment. They thoughtfully chose anything that he could safely haul in his big white 5.7 liter Tundra while pulling the fourteen-foot tandem axle trailer. He could put up to seven thousand pounds of equipment on it. His tractor with loader and backhoe plus attachments was just under the weight limit. He could load the bed of the truck with various tools and hardware, fence posts and barbed wire.

The rest of it was given to Ernie, who kept asking, "Are you sure you won't need this?" Lee assured him that if he needed it, he could purchase one later, but he did not dare overload his vehicles. Lee was careful with his equipment and was rewarded with many good years of service.

"What are you going to do about Bullet?"

Lee heaved a sigh as he looked at his old dog. "You said he hasn't been eating lately?"

"Nope. Barely gets off the front porch to take care of his business. His hips are gone."

"I know. I've been dreading this day, but just in the short time that I've been gone, he looks like he's lost more weight. The vet said his kidneys are gone, too."

Bullet whined pitifully. He knew that they were talking about him. Lee walked over to the beloved dog that had once run with him all day and been his faithful watchdog all night. Kneeling down next to him, Lee scratched his ears. "I hate to have the circumstances dictate my decision, but he won't survive the trip and I won't make you have to put him down. I think I'd better take him to the vet. I've put this off too long."

"I'm sorry, Lee, but like you said, he's in pain."

Lee finished his difficult business. It was hard to say good-bye to his friend and neighbor. It was harder to let Bullet go. But he did. Soon the mountains were in his rear-view mirror.

Lee was glad to be back after the long trip. Today, he had the trailer hitched to his dark blue diesel. It handled heavy loads better than the Tundra. He pulled off of York Creek Road and onto his rutted lane. His intention was to unload his tractor and smooth the long-neglected lane that would be well travelled with all the work he planned to do. He loved this challenge. He loved working outdoors. He loved working with hand tools as well as machines. It was as if the modern man deep inside of him heard the ancient call of his Creator to work the land, to strive to find the eternally elusive Eden, to subdue the earth, to reclaim dominion.

He pulled onto a grassy area and turned off the engine. With a spring in his step, he walked to the trailer, unchained his tractor, let down the ramps, and climbed into the seat. It fired up instantly and Lee was soon driving it off the trailer. The backhoe was curled up behind him like a scorpion's tail and the swivel seat faced the loader. The tractor had three forward gears and three reverse gears, so he had both versatility and power for whatever job he faced. He had arranged for a local company to pour a load of gravel the entire quarter mile length of the lane on Wednesday so this preliminary work must be finished today.

Daylight waned and he looked with satisfaction at the work that he had gotten done. He had an analytical mind and could organize the tasks that were necessary to efficiently complete a project. With a great sense of accomplishment, he opened the double barn doors and parked the tractor inside.

"You're home." He then backed the pickup truck to the barn and unloaded fence posts and barbed wire. He wanted to begin to put up fences this week. *I've prevailed on Abigail's "horse-pitality" too long.* He smiled as he remembered her remark.

Lee gave two soft toots on his horn as he drove up Abigail's driveway. It was his signal that it was him and not Max Berryman since their diesel trucks looked and sounded identical. Although Max's truck was black and his was midnight blue, his looked black from certain angles. He did not want to give Abigail any unnecessary fright and he certainly did not want to be greeted by Walther.

Abigail was in the middle of the evening feeding so he called to her and walked down to the horses. They talked to each other about Lee's progress in his new place as he moved from Lady to Sassy, from Misty to Sparkles. They barely gave him their attention before greedily going back to their sweet feed.

"I found a little apartment in Kingston."

"Oh, yeah? Where is it?"

"Do you know where the chiropractor is across the street from the grocery?"

Abigail mentally pictured it. "Yes."

"There's a one-bedroom cottage behind his building facing the alley. Right price. Close by."

"Sounds perfect. How did you find it?"

"Gayle Dillon, my realtor, told me about it."

"That's nice," Abigail replied.

"Yes, she's a nice lady," Lee continued. "She invited me to Thanksgiving dinner with her family since she thinks I'm a newcomer."

Abigail felt a momentary pang of jealousy. "Oh. That's nice of her."

"I thanked her but told her that I'll be spending the day with my grandparents and some other relatives." Lee paused for a moment and then asked, "What are you doing for Thanksgiving?"

Abigail hoped that her relief did not show too much and she swallowed quickly before answering, "Oh, well, tomorrow I'm going to be a volunteer waitress at a friend's restaurant and then on Thanksgiving Day, I'm going to roast a turkey and take a ride on Buster to burn off the calories."

She went on to explain what Ken and Paula did and how much fun it was to volunteer there. They talked about the horses and the property, the weather and the church, the war in the Middle East and the minor feud between two of the McCord's neighbors. Finally, they wandered back up to the house. Abigail went inside and Lee went to his apartment where he was struck with an acute sense of loneliness for the first time in a long time.

Lee turned in early as was his custom and rose early on Wednesday morning in preparation for spreading gravel. At the same time, Abigail was going through her morning chores and preparing to be a waitress at Ken and Paula's restaurant. She wanted to get there early enough to help with as much of the prep work as she could.

Heading north on York Creek Road, she did not notice the black truck hidden in the brush by the creek when she looked to the right. Her mind was on the day ahead of her. It was hard work, but the adrenaline kept pumping and the cheerful atmosphere would not let her feel the fatigue until she was well on her way home tonight. Parking behind the building, Abigail walked into the back entrance and greeted Paula.

"Oh, I'm so glad to see you!" Paula exclaimed. She was one of those perky, upbeat people who seem to have a perpetual smile on their faces and a cup-half-full attitude no matter what the circumstances were any time of night or day.

"Where's my apron? I'm ready!" Abigail tried to match her enthusiasm. She breathed in the aromas of turkey and the tang of spices that intermingled in the busy kitchen. "Oh, my mouth is watering already. This smells great!"

Ken and Paula's chief cook and creator of many of their unique dishes and sauces, desserts and dips was Ken's Aunt. Everyone who knew her just called her Auntie Z. She, too, was a slightly plump and largely joyful woman with seemingly boundless energy who talked and laughed her way through the day.

Other volunteers began to arrive. They were each given tasks and responsibilities that were in their respective comfort zones. Two couples brought their children who were able to do age-appropriate tasks. By the time the doors opened an hour before noon, there was a line outside on the wooden porch. Hungry diners were engaged in small-talk and the sound of laughter was a musical backdrop for the scene.

Abigail spent the day clearing tables and setting up for the next family. She bantered with the patrons and served them with a smile. When the last group left and the front doors were locked, the volunteers assembled for their favorite part of the day – gathering around the tables to eat the leftovers from the buffet. They retold funny stories, confessed their blunders, and rejoiced when the meal obviously blessed a very needy family. Eventually, they cleared their tables, helped with the cleanup, and headed home to prepare for their own Thanksgiving Day celebrations.

Turning into her driveway, headlights illuminating first one side of the driveway and then the other as she followed the curves, Abigail was stunned by the sight of a horse in the front yard. "What in the world?" she exclaimed. She put the high beams on and was able to make out the dim images of horses. *Oh, brother! I must have left the gate open.* Abigail berated herself for this mistake. She knew that Buster would not roam away, but she was not sure about Lee's mares.

She slowed down and continued until she was in her usual parking place. The motion sensor lights flickered on. Exiting the truck, she heard Buster's soft nicker greeting her. "Buster, what are you doing out here? And where are all your girlfriends?" He walked up to her and she stroked his neck. "You just wait here while I get the lights on." She went up the front steps and turned the front porch light on before she went to the back door and turned that light on as well. She noticed that two of the mares were in the orchard. *Thank You, Lord! They're all here!*

Grabbing her powerful Maglite flashlight from the truck, she headed down to the tack room softly calling for Buster to come with her. Thinking he was going to get a treat, Buster followed her all the way down. The mares that were in the front yard followed him, but the other two were still in the orchard. She made sure that the sound of the sweet feed hitting Buster's metal bowl was as loud as possible. *Maybe that'll get their attention.*

Trudging up to the gate, she cautiously went to the orchard. Making a clucking sound, she approached Sparkles and Sassy. They looked up from their grazing with deer-in-the-headlights stares. "Come on Sassy, I have a treat for you." Abigail decided to skirt around behind them to try to herd them toward the gate. She was grateful for the yard light and was able, with a little coaxing, to get them through the gate and give them their evening ration of sweet feed.

Swinging the gate to the closed position, Abigail reached for the heavy chain that she normally looped over the post to secure the gate. It was not there. She flicked on the Maglite again and searched the ground near the post. Not there. *Okay, something's fishy.*

Suddenly Abigail was alarmed. Pulling Walther from her appendix holster, she chambered a round and returned it as she flashed the beam in widening circles. She did not see the chain so she walked back down to the barn where she had baling twine that she could use to secure it for the night. Finding what she needed, securing the gate, Abigail went into her house and warily moved from room to room. With Walther.

Max Berryman was still processing what had happened to Zorroz a couple of weeks ago in church and now he was disconcerted by his experience earlier that day. He had staked out that woman's house and waited for a lucky break. He got it when she left that morning. Max sauntered a couple hundred feet down the road and entered her property at about the same place that Billy Wagner had a couple of months ago. He, too, felt a strange loss of vigor. Rationalizing it away, continuing his assignment to intimidate her, carefully walking through the woods and slipping through the fence, he looked at the house just as the camera on the back deck recorded his image.

Max had not recovered his power and had gone to bed early that night. Although he was nearly twenty-five, he was still living with his parents. He worked at his father's dealership whenever it suited him. He was tolerated by employees and coddled by his parents.

Max made it his ambition to rise in rank in the dark world. He had gone to school with a young man, Levi, who introduced him to Satanism and lured him to a ritual with promises of sex and beer. He did not know that his beer was spiked and he was manipulated into killing a human sacrifice that night. They then owned his soul, celebrated his rite of passage, and gave him the highly esteemed cult name, Mot. He was named for the god of death and tonight he appealed to his namesake for renewed powers.

He was, after all, beyond redemption.

The death demon assigned to Max was eager to comply and came swooping down from the second heavens. Max grunted as he felt the impact when the messenger of death landed on his chest and delighted to dig his claws into the fragile flesh of this pitiful human. There was always a price to pay for such favors and Max would pay the ultimate price someday, but for now, he was a useful puppet in the hands of a power-greedy demon. Yes, one day the landlord of death would collect his rent.

George and Elsa McVeigh had all the leaves of their dining room table in place for the family gathering. It had been some time since the McCord, Norris, and Bradley families could all make it. Members of each branch of the family were coming today to celebrate Thanksgiving. Their three daughters each had one son. Those sons had married and produced their beloved great grandchildren.

Lisa Norris could not make it, but Scott and Jill Bradley's teenagers, Shane and Shannon, would be there as well as Traci and Bryan. The first cousins were fairly close in age, but their children ranged from four to twenty-one and the McVeigh's delighted in each one.

The dinner was scrumptious and festive; the family was animated and talkative. All too soon, the pumpkin pie and other desserts were consumed, coffee and hot chocolate flowed, and contented sighs were heard. The women chattered in the kitchen while the men retired to the spacious living room. The teenagers retreated to the family room followed by Traci and Bryan where they played games and listened to music.

Lee looked at his watch and sighed as he stood up. "Grandpa, I can't tell you how much I've enjoyed this gathering, but I really need to head out to the new place and get rolling on that fence line while I have a few hours of daylight."

Gary looked at him and said, "No football game?"

"No, I'll pass this year," Lee replied, "but if it turns out to be a good game, I'll watch your recording. You are recording it, aren't you?"

"Of course," Gary said. "Hey, wait! Let me check with Cindy and see if she'd mind if I tag along. I might be of some help."

"I'd appreciate that," Lee said. He was accustomed to being fairly independent but he was not too proud to accept help. He had neighbors in Montana who would help him and he would help them, too. There was an unwritten code among the ranchers that they honored.

Scott chimed in, "Hey, what about me? Just because I'm a city-slicker it doesn't mean I don't know a screw-wrench from a monkey-hammer."

"I'm sure you can be useful. Do you have some work clothes?" Lee asked.

Shane overheard their conversation and wanted to be in on the excitement. "Can I come, too?"

"Me too?" Bryan piped up hopefully.

"Sorry, little buddy," Gary said, "but you'll get to help another time. I promise." The young boy was not happy, but he took it like a little man and went back to play with Tracy and Shannon.

Grandpa McVeigh was listening to his grandsons and volunteered, "I have old coats and some coveralls that should fit you. Go out to the mud room and you'll find hats and gloves, too." He was excited and a bit envious. The boys probably inherited their enthusiasm for farming from him. They had his work ethic as well. Of course, they had visited the homestead often as youngsters and worked alongside their hard-working, indomitable mentor.

Abigail had finished her own meal and cleaned up the kitchen before dressing for her ride with Buster. She had spent the morning searching for the missing chain but could not find it. Her temporary repair would have to do until she got to the hardware store. This time she hoped to remember to get some hardware and work on a lift system that would allow her to more easily remain in the saddle when she opened the gate.

Abigail had looked at the pictures from her security cameras and saw the unmistakable image of Max. She felt the surge of adrenaline course through her body. *Ooh, Lord! I feel so violated. Please keep me and the horses safe.* She saddled Buster and they meandered down to the back gate and stopped at the camera where she retrieved the SD card and placed it in her shirt pocket.

"Oh, where shall we go today?" She wasn't entirely sure if she was asking Buster or herself. She answered her own question by letting Buster go west toward the river. She felt like she wanted to follow the trail to the north that led through the stand of pine trees and then maybe take a run through Lee's property and look for Max's tire tracks down by York Creek. It would not prove anything, but she wanted to know for sure where he had parked his truck.

She nudged Buster into a comfortable gallop and enjoyed the clear, crisp weather. The trail was mostly dry, but there were some puddles and mud that they either avoided or splashed through sometimes flinging clumps of mud in rooster-tails behind them. Buster was invigorated by the hint of winter in the air and appeared to be able to maintain the pace for miles. They only slowed to a walk when the trail got more tortuous. Breathing deeply, she caught the pungent scent of the pine stand and soon they were through that and heading down the abandoned road that intersected with York Creek Road just north of her neighbors, the Milners, and her new neighbor, Lee.

She and Buster carefully crossed York Creek Road. When they got to Lee's newly graded driveway, she decided to head up toward the barn and abandoned trailer to check on Lee's progress. Nearing the trailer, seeing the dark blue truck, Abigail saw the four men walking toward the barn. She immediately recognized Gary and Lee, but not the other two. She urged Buster forward and hailed them, "Hello!"

They turned around in unison. Gary broke into a grin and said, "Well, look what we have here. What are you up to?"

"Just taking a ride and being a nosy neighbor. What are you guys up to?"

"I'm going to teach these guys how to put up a nice, straight fence," Lee joined the bantering.

"Oh," Abigail said with a knowing smile. "But your MEN WORKING signs are missing."

"We'll be working so hard that it'll be obvious that there are men working here," Gary shot back with a grin. "Oh, by the way, this is our cousin, Scott, and his son, Shane."

"You have my condolences for being related to this one." Abigail jerked her thumb toward Gary. They all laughed light-heartedly together.

Her tone changed as she changed the subject. "Hey, guys, I'm glad I ran into you. Last night I came home and all the horses were out. Max cut the chain to the gate. Caught him on camera."

Gary's countenance instantly clouded. "Sounds like another warning."

Scott and Shane remained silent as they listened to the baffling conversation.

"Lee," Abigail said, "I'm getting worried that they're going to hurt your horses, too, simply because they're on my property."

"Don't you worry about that," Lee assured her. "I'm willing to take that risk for another day or so if that's all right with you. I'm almost finished with their pasture and if I can get this motley crew organized I can get the corner posts set while the rest of you drive T-posts." He looked at the men and got nods of approval.

"Meanwhile," Gary interjected, "how about if you and I go visit the sheriff's office tomorrow morning with the pictures?"

"What about Bynum?" Abigail asked with alarm in her voice. "He's one of them!"

"Well, as far as I know, he's still on leave of absence. I don't know who the acting sheriff is, but we have to let them know that we know and that we're not taking this lying down." Gary was indignant.

"He's right," Lee agreed, "I'll go with you since my livestock were compromised, too."

"Sounds like a plan," Abigail said. "Meanwhile, is there anything I can do to help with the project here today? And don't tell me that it's men's work because I've run my share of fence."

"Well," Lee said thoughtfully, "I only have one T-post driver. Do you happen to have another one?"

"I sure do," Abigail said. "Why don't I put Buster up and come back with my four-wheeler and the trailer. I can haul posts and wire." She nodded at the pile of eight-inch diameter wooden corner and gate posts and added, "while you take care of those babies."

"Works," Lee said with a nod and a smile before he turned and headed into the barn to get the tractor and the auger attachment. Abigail turned Buster and headed down the trail that was becoming more worn with all the recent traffic.

She did a quick grooming of Buster and rewarded him with a small measure of sweet feed. The mares knew better than to come between Buster and his feed, but they were curious about all the activity and soon gathered around. Abigail opened the barn door and prayed that the four-wheeler would start. Unsure of how much it would be used today, she added more fuel. It had been several weeks since she had used it last, but it responded to the turn of the key. Soon she eased out of the barn, hitched the trailer onto the back and dropped the thick clovis pin in place to secure it.

Running back inside, she pulled the heavy T-post driver from its hook and then placed the cylinder into the trailer with a loud clang that startled the mares. A handful of sweet feed scattered in the feeding area kept the mares from following her out of the gate.

The afternoon passed quickly and Lee's fence was one giant step closer to being finished. He had the augur attachment on one end of the tractor and had loaded the bucket with gravel which Shane used to fill the bottom of each hole. He would set the posts in concrete another day. Meanwhile, Gary and Scott used the T-post drivers and set a line of posts that ran roughly parallel to York Creek Road, went almost as far as Abigail's driveway, and then all the way back to the little creek that emptied into York Creek.

The sun was going down when they called a halt to the project close to five o'clock. The men had worked off their Thanksgiving dinners and they were ready for supper and more dessert. Abigail declined their kind invitation to join them citing the need to take care of Buster and the mares. After they arranged to meet at the sheriff's office at nine sharp the following morning, Abigail headed home with the trailer bouncing behind the four-wheeler.

Clouds had blown in from the west overnight and brought a drenching rain that was supposed to last all day. Abigail put her poncho on over her coat and tended to the horses. She made a mental note to stop at the hardware and pick up another section of chain for the gate when she was on her way home since she decided against trying to build a gate opener in this weather. *Maybe next spring.*

Gary and Lee were waiting for Abigail in their respective pickup trucks when she pulled up in hers. The sheriff's office was located in a former grade school just off the square and not very far from the county courthouses in Springfield. After greeting one another, they walked through the double doors into the foyer. Gary led the way to the sheriff's office and greeted the duty officer with a nod.

"Help you?" he said as he barely looked up from his computer screen.

"Yes," Gary said, "we need to talk to the sheriff about a little matter."

"Sheriff Bynum won't be back until next week," the deputy sheriff stated. He was obviously annoyed by the disruption.

"We just need to file a complaint," Gary persisted.

"What kind of complaint?"

"Someone trespassed on Mrs. Steele's property," he nodded toward Abigail, "cut the chain on her gate and let all the horses loose," Gary stated succinctly. "We want to make sure that it doesn't happen again."

The deputy sheriff sighed, "Do you have proof of who did this?"

"Yes," Abigail said and stepped forward, "I have the recording from my security camera." She produced the picture that she had printed from the SD card.

He heaved his ponderous body out of the protesting swivel chair and walked over to a file cabinet. After rifling through the files with his meaty hands, he produced a form and slapped it onto the counter in front of her. "Fill this out and we'll get to it when we have the extra time."

Lee stepped forward, stood on the other side of Abigail and said firmly, "Where I'm from, sir, messing with someone's livestock is very serious business. The horses are worth nearly ten thousand dollars. Stealing or jeopardizing them puts this in the category of a felony." It was a challenge without being a challenge.

The deputy sheriff considered his statement and his size and adjusted his attitude while trying to maintain his superiority. "Like I said, fill out the papers and we'll follow up on it as soon as we can. We're short a man until next week."

Abigail had already begun to fill out the complaint. She named Max Berryman and gave the date and time based on the image that her SD card produced. After handing it to the deputy sheriff, she thanked him. Lee made it a point to reach over the counter and shake the man's hand quite firmly. Looking him in the eye, he said, "We appreciate your help."

Abigail could hardly suppress a smile as they went back out to their trucks. "Thanks, guys; sometimes it just takes some testosterone to get things done."

Gary shook his head and grinned at her. Lee was not quite sure how to take it, but he waved as he got into his truck and they each headed to work. Abigail looked at her watch and decided that she had enough time to stop at the hardware store before going to the church. She paid for the length of chain and made a mental note to ask Lee about the kind of hardware that would be needed for the gate latch.

Carrie Sue was waiting for her at the church when she got there just before ten. They greeted each other and talked about Thanksgiving. Carrie Sue had made the effort to spend some time with her mother, but then made an excuse to leave as early as possible. "It was tolerable and it was amazing how much I noticed my mom switching and I was able to stay myself. I mean, I didn't switch to match her switches. And I think that frustrated her ... or some part of her."

"That's a real mark of healing. I'm proud of you. Too bad you weren't with me instead," Abigail teased, "I'll bet Lee would have let you ride Lady and we could have had a grand adventure."

"Oh, shucks!" Carrie Sue said sarcastically, snapping her fingers. "That's too bad. I hate that I missed it."

Abigail glanced at her watch and said, "Well, it's time to get serious, I guess. You look great. How are you doing? Really. Inside."

"I've been thinking about something you said a while ago about the host person and the original core person," Carrie Sue began. "I'm just wondering what you think. I always thought that I was the original one, but I keep getting the idea that you think I'm the host."

"What brought this up?" Abigail asked.

"Well, the other day, I was thinking about things and so I asked myself - feeling more nutty than usual - 'does anybody in here know about the original Carrie Sue Wagner?'"

"What did you get?"

"I heard a faint, kind of shy voice say, 'I do.' So, I asked her more, but I think I scared her away." Carrie Sue sounded somewhat distressed. "Did I mess up?"

"No!" Abigail said excitedly with a big smile, "That was great. How many times did I contact one of your parts and they would shut down? That's how it starts.

She has to start getting used to you, to figure out if she can trust you, to see if *she's* nuts or not, to see if she wants to risk change."

Carrie Sue looked relieved. "Oh, good. So, what do we do next?"

"Tell me a little bit about her. Were you able to visualize her?" Abigail was energized. This was one of the turning point issues for someone with multiple personalities. In her experience, the original person emerged after there was a significant amount of healing and integration.

Since the SRA survivor was fragmented at such an early stage of life, the original person was generally an infant. With more and more integrations, the original person received back that which she had parceled out to the various personalities. She would then begin to "age" and once again have the character qualities that had been developed in the various personalities. It is an amazing healing journey.

"Well," Carrie Sue began, "it seemed like she was a young adult, maybe early twenties, but," she paused and groped for the right words, "she seemed kind of hollow or maybe more like one dimensional. I mean, it was almost like I could see through her because she didn't have a lot of substance."

"That's interesting. What else did you notice?"

"I asked her what she knew about us and Satanism and stuff. She acted like she didn't know a thing. How could that be if so many parts integrated into her? I thought you said that when a part integrates into another part, they would get each other's information."

"I did. This does seem a bit unusual. Usually, the original doesn't show up as an adult. I'm not saying it couldn't happen. Everyone's system is different. Why don't we pray and see what the Lord shows us?"

Carrie Sue bowed her head while Abigail prayed for illumination, wisdom, and understanding.

When she finished, Carrie Sue said, "I'm getting a word – pseudo. What's that supposed to mean?"

"The Greek word pseudo means false or to deceive by lies." Abigail reached back into the New Testament Greek 101 department of her brain. "I would guess that this part is a pseudo-original, a pseudo-core; or maybe a part whose job it is to make us think that she's the real original, or she might be a part that is very close to the original and acts kind of like a buffer."

"What should we do?" Carrie Sue asked and then quickly added, "Never mind; let's ask the Lord."

Abigail couldn't stifle her delighted giggle. "Go for it." Carrie Sue was taking ownership of her healing journey in dramatic ways these days.

After praying an awkward, self-conscious prayer, she looked at Abigail when she finished and said, "I think she's hanging around listening to us."

"Okay," Abigail said, looked intently into Carrie Sue's eyes and addressed Pseudo. "It's safe to talk to us. Do you want to use Carrie Sue as a mediator? Or will you come out and talk to me directly?"

She got her answer when Carrie Sue faded into the background and Abigail watched the transformation of her countenance and a subtle shift in posture. Abigail also sensed the hollowness of this personality and greeted her gently, "Hi, I'm Abigail. Thank you for coming out to talk to me."

There was no audible answer, but a delicate nod indicated that she was willing to proceed.

"Carrie Sue said that you know something about the original Carrie Sue Wagner," Abigail started. "Can you tell me what you know?"

The hollow one swallowed deeply and began to talk in a voice that matched her lack of substance, "My name is Carrie Sue Wagner. There are two more just like me. We weren't supposed to be found. How did you find me?"

Abigail saw the fear and bewilderment in her eyes and reassured her, "You are not in trouble and you are safe. I think the reason you are here now is because of all the healing that has been going on. I have a feeling that the original Carrie Sue started out as a very little girl and has been growing up."

Pseudo Carrie Sue nodded her confirmation with short nods that reminded Abigail of a bobble head she once had on the dashboard of her first car.

"What can you tell me about her?" Abigail probed carefully. She did not want to overwhelm this one.

"She's hiding."

"Who is she hiding from?" Abigail asked.

"Nobody. She's afraid. She just doesn't want to be in charge."

"Is she listening to us right now?" Abigail asked.

"I don't know."

"Do you think you can give her a message?" Abigail tried another tack.

"I don't know."

"How about if I just talk a little bit and if she doesn't hear me you can let her know if you get a chance to get close to her?" Abigail asked. Abigail suspected that this one, like most of the others, knew more than she was letting let on.

"Okay," she consented.

"I just want to let you know that you, the original Carrie Sue Wagner, are one of my heroes. You have been through so much trauma and have found a way to survive it. You needed to dissociate, to split out those other parts in order to survive. Unfortunately, that also meant that you got depleted. You have some incredible parts that have gotten you to this point with the qualities that came from you. And now, you are in the process of getting all of that back and that's what's causing you to grow up and get stronger. You are not all the way there yet, but I promise you, based on what I know about your protectors and the host and all the others, you are going to be one amazingly strong and resilient woman once you are all reunited."

Abigail stopped to allow the message to sink in a little. "No one expects you to be able to come out today or even this month and take over all aspects of your life. I want to encourage you to just peek in and check it out as often as you can handle it. Ask questions. Talk to the host Carrie Sue or one of the others. And when you are all the way ready, you will know it and it won't be intimidating. I promise."

Carrie Sue's body visibly relaxed and Abigail was certain that the message had gotten through. That was confirmed when the host Carrie Sue resurfaced and said, "I think she heard you."

"Great," Abigail answered. "I'm really excited for you. This is a huge turning point for you, er, y'all."

"Funny," Carrie Sue replied and then frowned. "So, what's going to happen to me? To us? I mean, I know that we talked about this before, but I don't want to disappear. I just don't like the idea of me having to integrate into her, you know? I've been in charge of our life for so long. She should integrate into me. It's not fair."

Abigail smiled gently. "Carrie Sue, I promise you that however you guys integrate, the bottom line is that all of you together are Carrie Sue Wagner. Everyone is important. No one disappears. I can't wait to see the authentic Carrie Sue Wagner the way God designed you to be."

Carrie Sue's cheeks puffed out as she sighed. "If I were a dog, my tail would *not* be wagging." She tried to suppress a laugh but was unsuccessful when she heard Abigail's giggle.

They closed their session and Abigail walked Carrie Sue to the outside door. Frowning with displeasure at the heavy rain, saying their good-byes, Abigail turned to go to the kitchen to eat her lunch and prepare for Amy Bolton's visit. Time passed quickly enough and soon she heard Amy entering her office area.

"Anybody home?" a cheerful voice called out.

"Yes! Come in," Abigail answered. "I can't wait to hear how things are going."

"It's going," Amy replied with a grin. "It's been an interesting week."

"Let's open with prayer and then you can tell me all about it," Abigail responded. She opened with prayer and Amy, the host, was still in front of her. *There are definitely some good changes going on here.* "So, what happened after last week's session?" Abigail asked eagerly. She wanted to hear it all. Sometimes it felt like she was waiting for the next exciting episode much like the television drama series she watched years ago.

Amy told her that she would let Head Warden tell her the details. She faded back and Head Warden took over and recounted the week since their last session when Nicholai finally gave in and defected from the kingdom of darkness. He reported that Nicholai was instrumental in persuading the five guards to defect as well. Head Warden and Nicholai were now allies and were beginning to work on strategies to make changes on the first subterranean level.

"There are meaner and more entrenched leaders on levels two through six," Head Warden reported. "We have to assume that they all have infiltrators that spy on other levels, including my surface level. We think that the original Amy is hidden on the sixth level."

"That would make sense," Abigail agreed. "They think that they created a fail-safe system, but they still wouldn't want to take a chance that she might possibly run into someone that could get her free."

"It's pretty complicated. Nicholai was telling me about some of the structures and booby-traps that have been installed on his level. In fact, since his defection, there's been a lot of activity down there."

"Suicide bombs?" Abigail asked the question based on her experience with other survivors.

"Yes, you could say that," Head Warden replied. "There's a whole bunch of them putting a lot of suicidal thoughts into Amy's mind and others who are plotting to kill her. It's kind of scary when one of them takes over driving while she's trying to deliver pizzas."

"Well," Abigail said calmly, "we have a lot of work ahead of us. This coming week should be fairly calm, but the following week is loaded." She picked up the List of Satanic Holidays and looked at the first week of

December. "Of course, there's the first and the third which is also the first Sunday of Advent, St. Nicholas Day is on the sixth, and then there's the feast of the Immaculate Conception on the eighth." She looked at her calendar and added, "Oh, we have a full moon on the fourth, too."

"Great," Head Warden groaned with a when-will-it-ever-end tone.

They prayed and came up with a strategy which involved sending Nicholai and his five elite guards back to his level to access each of the personalities that would be programmed for the next series of rituals.

With the speed of thought, they descended to Level Two and were able to intimidate everyone, demanding the early preparation of each group using their recent failures as the rationale. Nicholai was able to bluster and threaten his Level One guards into complying unquestioningly. They feared him despite the subtle changes that they sensed.

There was very little resistance to defection into the Kingdom of Light once the newly liberated captives were deprogrammed and set free from their demonic tormentors. With amazing quickness, each of the six groups of personalities that would normally have been summoned to rituals were healed and integrated. Nicholai was changing by the minute as he not only experienced for himself but witnessed in others the transforming power of the Lord Jesus Christ.

"Lady," he said to Abigail, "I've got to say that that was the most fun I've had in my entire life." He then lowered his voice and hesitated a little, "I just want to thank you for not giving up on me."

Abigail broke into a big smile. "You're welcome. Now you know why I come to work. It *is* fun!" They laughed softly together and then he faded into the background while Amy resurfaced.

"Whew!" she said happily, "It feels like we just took a giant step forward."

"You did," Abigail agreed. "But, remember, there's still a lot of work to do on the other five levels. There could still be some we don't know about that could get accessed. Keep your guard up and let your protectors do their jobs. I'm proud of you taking back your life!"

8

Thursday, December 21, Winter Solstice

Prinz was in ill humor. That was not new. What was new was that he was literally ill; physically ill. Since ascending to his position as regional master just over one hundred years ago, he had never been sick. He had never been weak. He sold his soul to the devil and was rewarded with power, wealth, and any tangible or intangible item that fascinated or satisfied him. He looked at his reflection in the mirror and was not pleased that he was beginning to show signs of aging. His shoulders were more stooped. His formerly brisk pace was noticeably slower because of the unfamiliar pain in his joints.

He carefully made his way down to his private inner sanctum and positioned himself in the center of the Baphomet. Candles were lit and the flickering light added to the eerie atmosphere of the room that was dedicated to Satan and his minions. He called upon his highest-level demons for more power. He invoked the name of Satan as he chanted his appeals and promised deeper allegiance to his lord and king.

Dark streaks stabbed through the atmosphere and converged in the inner sanctum. Shadowy forms manifested and joined the prostrate man. "Yes, yes," he moaned, agreeing to the terms that would give him the power that he craved. He did not know that he was blinded by the god of this world and could not grasp that the heights he enjoyed in time would dictate the depths to which he would fall in eternity. He believed that Satan would fulfill his five great "I wills" and that Satan would recompense him for all the work that he had done during his time on earth.

Prinz arose refreshed and empowered. He donned his robe with a sense of satisfaction. He summoned his attendant and conveyed his desire for a choice young child to be delivered to his sleeping chambers. The gender of the child was not a concern. The attendant bobbed a quick bow and scuttled off to do his bidding. Prinz would test his competence in anticipation of the Winter Solstice ritual.

The Winter Solstice ritual was an important ritual. Astronomical signs and wonders have always been the focus of satanic rituals from the time mankind was evicted from Eden. Today was a new moon as well as the shortest day of the year. Daylight would last for ten hours leaving the darkness to reign for fourteen.

The participants were assembled for the regional festivities. On this long and dark December night, they would discretely assemble at the most liturgical church in the capital city and desecrate it in debased ways that its parishioners could never have imagined. Daggett and Darod, the area masters were present. Zorroz and Herrak, the local masters were present. Levi was there, but his counter-part, Mastiff, had died. Max was one of a throng of power-hungry young men with aspirations of rising in rank.

Carrie Sue and Amy were not there, but a host of other women were. Women! Those utterly despicable, inferior women! They were only good for one thing. If the Great Enemy would favor them, Satan would disfavor them.

To that end, scripture must be carefully taught using duplicity. Each verse and each principle was given double meaning or taken out of context by omitting or substituting words to alter the meaning. During the last series of rituals, several little girls were evangelized by their own parents. Quite a number of them were deemed to have believed in the true Jesus Christ. These were monitored and chosen for the festivities at the previous ceremony. They were prepared with mind-dulling substances that would render them incapable of resisting suggestions.

There was a risk that some of them would defect from Satanism, but it was a small one. It effectively mocked their Great Enemy. "Look, God! Look at what we're doing to Your child. Look, God! Look at what Your child is doing!"

Tonight, they were assembled in the middle of the menacing, but smiling crowd that included parents, grandparents, and siblings in most cases. They were questioned about their faith in Jesus. The atmosphere appeared to be benevolent as they recognized the church surroundings with stained glass and candles, pulpits and pews, banners and tapestry. Those who were deemed ready for the next phase of duplicity programming were exposed to a situation in which the Satanists tortured and raped another child. They were told to call on Jesus. They were goaded. "He said that He would hear when you call."

The children called on Him. "Jesus! Come and help her. Please stop that man!" Finally, after interminable minutes, someone dressed to look like Jesus wearing a white robe and sandals, entered the room and started to help the perpetrator torment their little friend. The children were horrified and sobbed. Finally, the Jesus and the perpetrator removed the inert body of the tormented child.

"Children," one of the women came to them and said, "God would never do that. The real Jesus isn't like that. That was a fake Jesus. You keep your faith in the real Jesus. They just tricked you." Her soft, sincere voice convinced some of the children that she was right, but it was nearly impossible to process what they had just witnessed. They were mere children.

They seemed comforted for the moment and were led away. The following night, at the Sabbat Festival ritual, that same woman would lead them through the ceremony and reinforce that they could trust the true God of the Bible. This time, the fake Jesus would abuse each one of them escalating the increasingly intense cycle of hope and despair.

The ultimate goal of the Satanist is to make sure that the child would never get to know the non-duplicitous God. They were programmed to believe that a non-duplicitous God does not exist and therefore anyone who is called a Christian would also be duplicitous. How often survivors would get only so far in the healing journey and then flee. Trust erodes as the survivor concludes that no one is trustworthy.

No one.

Not even God.

Especially not God.

Friday morning brought more cold rain into the region. It swept in from the northwest and Abigail was just grateful that it was rain and not snow. She loved the snow when she was snuggled in her cozy farmhouse, but even with high and low four-wheel drive options on the truck, she preferred not to have to drive in it. Lee had moved his mares to their new pasture about two weeks ago so her morning and evening chores took much less time.

"It's back to me and you again, Buster," Abigail muttered to her beloved horse. "I'll bet you miss all your girlfriends. One of these days, we'll go visit them, but not today." She finished the feeding and hurried back up to the house where she shed what she called her play clothes and got ready to go to work.

Carrie Sue was there and after setting up the waiting area, they settled into their chairs and began their session. Since meeting the pseudo-Carrie Sue for the first time, they had been able to access and negotiate with the two other pseudo-Carrie Sues. They were somewhat less "hollow" than the first one, but it was evident that they were not the true original Carrie Sue. They appeared to be a buffer or perhaps a diversion of some sort. They had no memories of their own; they just existed. They were a mystery, but even so, they were parts of Carrie Sue and needed to be integrated.

"I'm sensing that the original Carrie Sue is kind of on the fringes right now," the host Carrie Sue said. "I think that she, um, how shall I say it? She kind of uses these pseudo-Carrie Sues to peek out and see what life is like."

"So," Abigail said thoughtfully, "then it might not be a good idea to push for the integration of the pseudos so that she doesn't shut down or get overwhelmed."

"Yeah," Carrie Sue agreed. "She's pretty jumpy. Scared. I can feel it sometimes."

"Why don't you talk to her a little bit and let her know that we are going to help her, that we are glad that she's here and that you welcome her."

Carrie Sue was silent and looked down at her hands. After a few moments she looked up at Abigail and said, "I'm not so sure that I can say that."

"What do you mean?" Abigail asked.

Carrie Sue sighed, "It's that whole thing about me being the host and being in charge all these years and then having to integrate into her. It just doesn't seem right. It's not fair. I mean, I'm the one that held us all together. I'm the one that had to go through thick and thin. I'm the one that had to make the decisions about jobs and moving and, and well, just everything while she was hiding and letting everyone else hold the bag." She huffed again. "There! I said it. I'm mad."

"Okay," Abigail said slowly, "I guess that got her running again."

"Oh, I didn't mean to do that," Carrie Sue agonized; "it's just that it's so frustrating. Why can't she integrate into me? I don't want *our* relationship to change and if we integrate, it just won't be the same."

"Ah, ha," Abigail replied, "you're afraid that you'll disappear altogether or that you'll have to share me with everyone or that maybe I won't like the fully integrated Carrie Sue Wagner."

"Yeah, something like that," Carrie Sue admitted. She was nearly in tears because of the distress that the thoughts and fears brought to the surface.

"Will you trust the process?" Abigail asked. "Think about what you were like when we first met. Do you remember telling me that you wanted all of this to be done in a couple of months?"

"Boy, was I ever an idiot," Carrie Sue said with a rueful smile.

"No! Not an idiot," Abigail countered. "You were desperate to get healed as soon as possible, and yet, there were so many times, like today, when you said that it was going too fast. But God has guided us every step of the way just like it says in Psalm twenty-three, *'He restores my soul; He guides me in the paths of righteousness.'* He's done a great job so far. Trust Him. Trust the process."

Carrie Sue let out another sigh. "You're right. I'll see if I can contact the original Carrie Sue."

Host Carrie Sue did manage to briefly contact the original Carrie Sue and thought that she had patched up the damage she had done. Abigail also brought up the series of rituals that were coming up starting this evening – Sabbat, Hanukkah, Demon Revels, Christmas Day, and Kwanza. They systematically prayed for any programming that might get triggered and Abigail instructed Carrie Sue to call her if she felt stirred up at all. By then it was time to close the session and make an appointment for the following week.

Abigail ate her lunch and then prepared for the next counselee. It was a new young man from the church. Abigail asked that he bring his wife with him for the sake of appearances. She did not want to counsel a man unless someone else was either in the room with them or in the waiting area. Her office was like Pastor Spalding's and had a glass door and a window for propriety's sake.

Just before one o'clock the young couple poked their heads into the unfamiliar room.

"Hello," Abigail greeted them with a smile. "You must be the Johnsons," she said, looking at the tall young man with the middle linebacker build and then shifting her gaze to the petite lady next to him. "I'm sorry; I don't know your name."

Wes immediately answered for her, "This is my wife, Laura. We just started coming to church here a couple of months ago. We didn't know this was here."

"Lots of long-time members don't even know what all is down in the lower level. I'm glad you're coming here, this is a good church and it's nice to meet you," Abigail responded. "I'm glad that you were both able to come today. Let me get you to fill out these papers and then we can get started." Abigail handed him the clip board. "Come in whenever you're ready."

Wes busied himself with the paperwork and Laura sat next to him idly checking her phone. Soon, he joined Abigail in her office and sat in a chair opposite her. The window in the door and the other window opening allowed anyone in the waiting room to see Abigail, but not whoever was seated in the chair opposite her.

Abigail briefly looked at the papers and focused on the 'reason for counseling' line. "Can you tell me about your anger problem?" Abigail started.

"I guess I've always had an anger problem," Wes sighed. "It kind of came to a head last week when I was on the entrance ramp to the interstate. Some clown was tail-gating, honking his horn, flashing his lights; you know, just being obnoxious. I was okay until he passed me and gave me half a peace sign, if you know what I mean." He smiled ruefully.

"That's a tactful way to put it." Abigail smiled.

"I just lost it. I mean, I wanted to ... well, I'm not sure what I wanted to do exactly, but I hit the pedal and chased the guy for miles. Laura was begging me to stop and the kids started crying. It was like I just couldn't stop. I finally calmed down and that's when Laura said that I needed to get some help."

"Okay," Abigail said reassuringly, "this is all very fixable. Before we go too far, though, let's open with prayer and then I'd like to give you a general idea of how I work so that you're tracking with me."

"Sounds good," Wes said uncomfortably. He was still not quite sure what this counseling was all about.

She prayed and then went on to describe how she listened for "verbal assaults" such as the deceptions, misinterpretations, and faulty processing that may have been embraced; vows that may have been made, as well as curses and judgments. She explained what the Greek and Hebrew definitions of the words were and gave him some examples. Abigail also mentioned that sometimes there were generational curses and/or familial spirits that affect a person.

"You stated here that you have 'always had an anger problem'," Abigail stated. "Can you tell me about the circumstances of your womb experience? Have your parents ever talked about that time period?"

Wes was not expecting that question and cocked his head a little but did not ask why she would ask such a thing. "My father was a marine. I guess the story goes that he was home on leave one time and got my mother pregnant. They were planning on getting married but neither sets of parents wanted them to. They were too young. He was still in the service and she was still in college. Mom's folks were angry at dad's parents and vice versa. Mom's folks were mad at dad because they had 'a bastard grandchild,' uh, sorry. His parents were mad at Mom for 'seducing their son' and manipulating him into marriage."

"Ooh, that's ugly," Abigail commented.

"Yeah," Wes agreed, "but eventually, after the wedding and my birth, things simmered down, I guess. At least they all seem to get along now."

"But you were an angry kid," Abigail restated and then asked, "What kind of things made you mad?"

"Yes, I was," Wes affirmed and thought for a minute before answering. "I'd have to say that being made fun of, being called names, or being judged really ticked me off the most."

"Kind of like what happened while you were in the womb." Abigail stated it almost as a question.

His eyebrows came up in surprise as he connected the dots. "Exactly!" Wes was stunned as he mentally examined the parallels between his womb experience and his life experience.

"So, when some driver 'judges' your driving and calls you a name with his tall finger," Abigail brought it back to the present situation, "you get angry."

"Exactly!" Wes was stunned again. "That makes so much sense, but I don't understand how all that womb stuff can make a baby into an angry person."

Abigail took some time to explain that emotions are chemically based and can be transmitted from a mother to her developing baby. "Your mother and father, as well as both sets of grandparents, were angry so you were an easy target for Satan, the roaring lion, since you were so helpless. You inherited a familial spirit of anger on top of that womb experience."

"So, what can we do about that?"

"We can do like Ezra, Nehemiah, and Daniel did and confess the sins of the fathers. We can also ask the Lord to go back to your womb experience and bring healing there, too. How about if I pray and you pray in agreement?" Abigail invited.

"Let's do it," Wes said excitedly.

"Lord, You knit Wes together in his mother's womb. We ask that You go back to that moment when the seed and the egg united and cover that entire gestation period and beyond with the blood of Jesus Christ. We ask that You would render the judgments and curses of being a bastard null and void as well. We confess as sin and plead Your blood over any and all strongholds created by the anger, curses, and judgments that came from the previous generations. We ask that you would release Wes and his entire family from generational curses and familial spirits and then heal and seal this broken place. Fill him now with the fruit of the Holy Spirit and unity in a bond of peace that goes deep into these family relationships. And then as Wes prays in agreement, we ask You to declare that it is finished."

"I agree, Lord," Wes prayed quietly, "and I confess my own anger all these years. God, I'm so sorry for how I scare Laura and the kids with my anger. Please ..." Wes dabbed at his eyes and sniffed as he fought the tears, "please forgive me and the previous generations, amen." Wes reached for the box of tissues and looked a little embarrassed.

"Hey," Abigail joked, "I've heard from a reliable source that tears and snot are fruit of the Spirit, so be fruitful if you need to."

Smiling, Wes wadded up the tissue and threw it into the waste basket. "I feel better, lighter. Now what?"

"I think we need to talk about jurisdiction."

"Jurisdiction," Wes repeated flatly.

"Yes," Abigail said and continued, "Everyone has God-given and man-given jurisdiction. For example, I have been given jurisdiction over this office and the waiting area by the church leadership, but if I try to take over the rest of this level, there would be conflict and stress."

Wes nodded as he followed her explanation.

"But if someone else were to come barging in here and started to use my desk and diminished my rightful jurisdiction, there would be a different kind of conflict and stress."

"Right." Wes was attentive and trying to figure out how this applied to his anger issue.

"So," Abigail concluded, "when some clown – your judgment of him – invaded your rightful jurisdiction on the highway, you attempted to return the favor."

"Oh, you're right," Wes agreed dropping his chin to his chest momentarily before he looked her in the eyes again and said slowly with a sheepish grin and a slight wag of his head, "I am not the 'nice police'. I am not even a regular policeman."

"Not your job," Abigail agreed shaking her head slowly from side to side with a slight smile and a twinkle in her eyes.

Wes was a quick learner and immediately launched into a prayer, "God, forgive me for judging that man – calling him a clown and thinking some less than godly thoughts about him. God, I am not the nice police or a policeman of any kind. Please forgive me for trying to exercise jurisdiction that is not mine, amen." Wes looked up expectantly.

"What are you sensing? How are you feeling?"

"Actually," Wes confessed, "I'm exhausted, but I feel so much, uh, lighter. Yes, that would be a good word."

"Very good. Let's pray one more time then and ask the Lord if there's anything else that He might want to address today."

He nodded his assent and bowed his head as she prayed again.

"Are you sensing anything?" Abigail asked.

"Not really."

"I'm not getting anything either," Abigail confirmed. "We'll take it that this is enough for today. Let me pray a blessing over you and then we'll decide where we go from here."

Wes nodded, and when Abigail finished, he rose and thanked her. "What now?"

"Do you think that you need to schedule another appointment? Or would you like to play it by ear?" Abigail asked this when she sensed that the person needed to "life it out" a bit and test the healing.

"I think I'd like to see what happens, I mean, I know God did something here."

"I agree. And you can call me if anything comes up. Don't be disappointed if it does, though. This is a life-long issue and sometimes we just have to pray about several roots. It's more like whacking tentacles off of an octopus rather than plucking a carrot."

Abigail walked out to the waiting room behind him where they thanked her before heading out of the door. Checking her watch, Abigail was grateful for a short break before F. Amy Bolton's appointment which was due to start in less than thirty minutes.

It was not long before Amy came in with an I've-got-to-get-this-settled look on her face. She quickly sank into her chair, looked up expectantly and quipped with mock seriousness as she reversed their roles, "Are you ready to start?"

Abigail saw the twinkle in her serious eyes and shot back with, "Sure, why don't you open with prayer?" and was mildly surprised with the reply.

"Uh, okay," Amy said, "I'm not so good at this, but I'll give it a shot." She cleared her throat nervously and said, "Hey, God, it's me and Abigail and we really need for You to show up here today with Your Holy Spirit and tell us what we need to do. Thanks. Amen."

"Amen," Abigail echoed.

Head Warden came to the forefront immediately and changed Amy's posture and demeanor as he did so. Although Nicholai had been working closely with Head Warden, he preferred to have Head Warden interact with Abigail, indeed, with the entire outside world. His dimly lit subterranean world was still a comfort zone of sorts for him and he was not fully accustomed to daylight.

"Hello," Head Warden greeted Abigail and then got right to the point. "Nicholai has been a busy guy lately and we have a lot to report."

"Excellent. What's he been up to?" She was excited.

"You know how we've got all that 666 stuff going on in here. Nicholai told us that he's been in meetings in the past with the leaders of the other levels. It didn't happen very often, but he got to know who some of them are and knows kind of what their assignments are. We figure that we can use that intel to do what we need to do to get free."

"Go on," Abigail urged. This was intriguing.

"Let me just give you a rundown of the leaders and the general function of each level," Head Warden said as if he was debriefing another military operative. "You remember that there are six levels that are roughly in the shape of wheels with six hubs and six spokes. And there are wheels within the wheels, kind of like concentric circles, but there are also random tunnels and mazes attached to some of them."

"Uh, huh," Abigail was following him and was grateful for the overview.

"Level One, of course, is Nicholai. He has been in charge of holding and preparing ritual parts like the Moonrakers and Revelers. He's always had some of them on his level, but some have been passed up from the lower levels depending on the importance of the particular ritual."

"Okay," Abigail said, "that makes sense."

"Level Two is headed by Achan. His people keep stealing from Amy."

"What do you mean?"

"His job is to keep Amy impoverished. When she gets a paycheck, someone finds a way to spend it on stupid stuff, lose it, give it away, hide it, or whatever. They just generally make her finances chaotic."

"No wonder she's struggling so much."

Level Three is led by a guy named Beor. His job is to get Amy involved in sexual relationships. She's been quite promiscuous over the years, but she doesn't really know all about it because she loses time when those tramps are out."

Abigail sighed but said nothing right away. She ached for the day that Amy Bolton would no longer be under the control of the cult and their programming. Besides the dangers to her, there were risky behaviors that constantly threatened her life. "Who's next?"

"Level Four is Jonah. His job is to make sure that Amy stays as far away from God as possible. That's why she won't go to church and whenever there's a God encounter, like after sessions with you, someone starts talking trash to her and pointing out all the flaws and inconsistencies, the hypocrites and jerks. They really trash talk you."

"Unfortunately, that wouldn't be too hard with most of us Christians. Our behavior does not always line up with our identity in Christ. I'd be the first to admit that I haven't arrived yet."

"Level Five is Judas. He would be what you call a persecutor. His job is to punish traitors who defect into God's kingdom. He's been really frustrated by all the integrations because he knows that they are somewhere but he can't find them." Head Warden gave Abigail something as close to a smile as she had ever seen on his usually serious face.

"Level Six is the bad one. It's led by Apollyon. It's got a bottomless pit and that's where we think that they keep Original Amy. Their job is to destroy and corrupt. We think that's probably where most of the suicide bombers are."

"Well," Abigail said, "that's a lot of info, but it gives us some idea of what we're up against. She paused momentarily as she reflected on the thought that most of her survivors had an Apollyon or Abaddon in their system. They usually had a David as well.

"Let me ask another question." She didn't wait for his answer before posing her query. "Who is the head honcho over all of the level leaders?"

Head Warden jerked back involuntarily as if he had been slapped. "I don't know anything about that but I'll check with Nicholai if you want."

"Was that you reacting, or someone else?" Abigail asked as she looked intently into his eyes.

"It wasn't me," he replied. "I'll be right back." He conferred with Nicholai and was back with Abigail in a blink. He reported, "Apparently, the head honcho, as you called him, has been listening in and he's the one that reacted to your question."

Abigail was not surprised. She frequently found that references to a particular personality would bring that part forward and sometimes that part would even switch into executive control. However, she did not expect it with whoever was the top dog of the entire cult-loyal, Satan-loyal side. That would usually come much later in the healing process. "Yeah, they don't think I know what I know and it surprises them."

"So, where do we go from here?" Head Warden asked and then immediately answered the question. "Wait, I know. Let's ask God."

Abigail smiled broadly and led them in a prayer. She looked expectantly at Head Warden, but he was displaced by someone else. "Hi. Who are you?"

"Just a messenger, lady," he snarled. "You need to back off."

"I'm only doing what Amy has asked me to do," Abigail answered pleasantly.

"*She's* not in charge! *We* make the decisions and *you* need to stop," he growled.

"Sorry," Abigail replied calmly, "I've been asked by Amy to do this. We have an agreement."

The enraged messenger clenched his teeth and disappeared. Amy resurfaced once again and seemed a little shaken despite her attempt at bravado. "I don't know who that was but I've made up my mind that I don't want to be a Satanist anymore." She grimaced and exhaled suddenly.

"What's wrong?" Abigail asked with concern.

"It feels like someone's kicking the crap out of me," Amy grunted in obvious pain.

"It must be Judas or one from his level punishing you for being a traitor," Abigail observed.

"Oof!" Amy felt another internal blow. "How can we make him stop?" she gasped desperately as she hunched over with her arms wrapped around her belly.

"I believe that this is a demon-driven personality. Remember the principle that if a demon is manifesting or acting out in any way, it's not in its so-called legal place. Let's ask the Holy Spirit to fill that void so he has no place to retreat to. Then we can go from there."

Amy was in pain and vigorously nodded her head in agreement. Abigail prayed and the internal torment abated somewhat. She was still feeling pain, but not with the same intensity. "It's let up," she reported with a sigh of relief.

"Good." Abigail was pleased with the report. "I'd guess that what you are feeling now is non-demon driven torment. Whatever you are feeling is coming from the part without its demonic strength."

"No doubt," Amy concurred. "But I want this to stop, too."

"Why don't you pray and ask God to deal with this guy? Like maybe put him in protective custody or something," Abigail suggested. She could have prayed on behalf of Amy but it was always more effective when the client prayed with authority.

"God," Amy started her prayer uncertainly, "would You do something with this guy? He's hurting me and I'm asking You to stop him however You want." She looked questioningly at Abigail as if she needed approval or further instructions.

"What are you feeling?" Abigail asked.

"Oh!" Amy was surprised. "It worked. I mean, God did it. Cool!"

"Very cool," Abigail agreed. "You're learning about the authority that you have in Christ."

Too soon, it was time for them to end the session so they closed with a lengthy prayer about the upcoming rituals and then made their next appointment.

Oh, Lord, please protect her, we can't lose another one! Abigail often thought of those who were entrusted to her by God as her own; her brothers and sisters, her sons and daughters. And she loved them fiercely.

Driving out of the church parking lot, reflecting on her day, Abigail was not aware of the black truck with the tinted windows that shadowed her all the way to the grocery store. Arriving at the store, looking briefly around her, seeing nothing alarming, Abigail went on to do her shopping. Despite the heavy rain, the store was crowded as people shopped for their last-minute Christmas groceries. She ran into several people that she knew and they exchanged Christmas greetings as the festive atmosphere infected the shoppers.

After checking out, Abigail quickly made her way to her truck in the unusually full parking lot. Once again, she scanned the area but did not notice anything, did not sense anything. Unlocking the passenger door of her truck, placing the bags on the floorboard, Abigail was abruptly shoved forward as the door was jammed forcefully into her. Grasping for a logical explanation, ignoring the sharp pain in her right knee cap, Abigail twisted around and saw the man that was trapping her in the door of her truck.

Max Berryman! Adrenaline surged through Abigail's body, her mind analyzing and processing the situation with the speed of light. She momentarily thought about introducing him to Walther but did not want to risk starting her jail ministry – from the inside. With the corrupt legal system, she would surely have been prosecuted. Or worse.

"Lady," he growled with a low voice, "you don't know who you're messing with, and I'm not just talking about me. Back off, or else!"

"Max Berryman," Abigail retorted, "do you want an assault charge on top of your criminal trespassing charges?" She lunged over to the steering wheel and sounded the horn.

"Back off!" he snarled, emphasizing his message with a final shove on the door.

Abigail winced with the sharp pain which served to intensify her outrage. "In the name of Jesus Christ, get out of here!" Abigail shouted. Already drawing the attention of several customers who were scurrying through the parking lot, he backed off. Whether it was the horn or the shouting or the invocation of the name of Jesus Christ, Abigail was not quite sure, but just as suddenly as he appeared, he disappeared. She pushed the door open and bent down to rub her knee. *That's going to leave a nasty bruise.* Moments later, she could hear him roaring out of the parking lot.

Abigail was visibly trembling when an older couple who had witnessed the incident approached her. "Are you all right, dear?" the woman asked. "We saw what that man did."

"Yes, I'm okay, just a couple of bruises and a little shaken up." Abigail paused a moment and then asked, "Would you be willing to make a statement to the sheriff? I'm going to report this."

"Uh, no," the man immediately injected, "sorry, we don't want to get involved. We just wanted to make sure you were okay." With that he tugged on his wife's sleeve and guided her toward the store, looking back once just before stepping out of sight.

Abigail finished securing the grocery bags, limped around the back of the truck, and drove home. Having put the groceries away and taken care of Buster, she called her friend, Cindy.

"Hey girl," Cindy chirped. "Merry Christmas! How are you doing?"

"I'm fine," Abigail said and then confessed, "well, actually, I'm kind of shaken up and pretty mad. I know you're probably busy fixing supper, but I could use some prayer support." She gave Cindy a narrative of the encounter with Max Berryman and then they prayed together.

"Hey," Cindy said brightly, "why don't you come over for dinner after church on Sunday?"

"But that's Christmas Eve," Abigail protested, "that should be for your family; I'd be an imposition."

"Nonsense!" Cindy countered, "You're family. The kids are crazy about you. Besides, Lee Norris is going to be here, too."

Abigail was silent for a moment as she absorbed this information. "Are you and Gary trying to...?" She let the question dangle.

"Oh, no, nothing like that," Cindy insisted and then giggled in her mischievous way, "but if something were to develop ..." She let her answer dangle.

"Well, it would be good to be with your family again," Abigail conceded. "All right, I'll come. What can I bring?"

9

Sunday, December 24, Demon Revels

The storms had passed but they had left the ground a soggy mess. Abigail slogged through the mire at the entrance to the tack room. The area would never grow grass because it was constantly being trampled. Buster raced up the pasture kicking clods of mud up behind him. He stopped as suddenly as he normally did but slid leaving parallel gashes in the muddy surface. He was tossing his head in an unusual manner when Abigail noticed the rope.

"Come here, boy," she said soothingly. He walked over to her so Abigail was able to clearly see that someone had tied a noose high, and just tight enough, under his jaws to allow him to breathe uncomfortably. *Oh, Lord, don't let them take it out on Buster, too!*

Unable to untie the knot, Abigail frantically went into the tack room and found a wire cutter on the bench. Holding the rope firmly, she edged the blade under it and snipped it, freeing Buster. He responded with throat-clearing snorts. Abigail gave him a scoop of sweet feed and made sure that he was able to eat. "You're just too trusting, buddy. We have to be a lot more careful!"

Abigail turned to go to the end of the pasture to retrieve the SD card from the lower camera. Carefully scanning the area before retrieving the two-step ladder that she had hidden in the brush, she berated herself.

I should have known. Lord, how are we going to keep Buster safe? You know, I'd really be upset if they killed him, too. Abigail prayed fervently as she returned to the house, scrolled through the images from the SD card and found several that showed a man about the size of Max Berryman coaxing Buster to the gate with a carrot.

Glancing at the time, Abigail realized that she had to put it into high gear if she did not want to be late for church so she expertly downloaded the images onto her computer and then uploaded them onto a thumb drive. She would take these to the McCord's. *Maybe we can figure out something.*

She continued to pray for the Lord's presence on the property and was pleased that this time, at least, Max did not step onto the property. *Lord, would You place Your warring and guardian angels outside of the perimeter of this property so they can't get close enough to reach Buster?*

The church was tastefully decorated for Christmas. Boughs of fresh evergreen and poinsettias with bright red bows, candles and holly adorned anything in the path of the zealous decorating committee. Abigail enjoyed the festive atmosphere and looked forward to the rest of the day in spite of the rough start.

Pastor Spalding bounced up to the podium after a selection of traditional Christmas hymns and carols. "Merry Christmas!" he boomed cheerfully into the microphone. He presented a traditional sermon based on Luke two and was careful to keep it short and sweet. He knew that his parishioners would have Christmas celebrations to attend.

The McCord family was no exception. Bryan burst out of children's church, his red and green Grinch tie askew, clutching a candy cane. "Mommy, can I eat it now? Teacher said I have to ask you."

"Do you think it will spoil your appetite for lunch?" Cindy asked.

"No, Mommy, I have a great big tummy," he said with all the seriousness a four-year-old could muster.

"Oka-ay," Cindy said, "you can eat it in the car on the way home." Bryan was delighted and did a skip-hop-gallop next to her as they collected Traci from her class and headed for the parking lot. Gary was already warming up the van and got out to help buckle the kids in the back seat. It was a joyful ride home with the children competing with each other to tell about the fun they had in church and asking when they could open Christmas presents.

Abigail had pulled into their spacious driveway right behind Lee and just before the McCords arrived. The sound of doors opening and closing was followed by Christmas greetings and chatter as they hustled out of the cold and into the warmth of the cozy house. Appetizing aromas greeted them and started their mouths watering in anticipation of a ham dinner with all the trimmings. Abigail's marzipan bars were added to the pies and cookies that filled the desert trays.

After dinner was over, the adults lingered over tea and coffee as they talked about Gary's work, Lee's farm projects, and the kids' Christmas vacation plans. Cindy gave Abigail a quick look, and knowing that her friend would not bring up the subject, asked, "Abigail, how is your knee doing after Friday?"

Lee's questioning look went from Cindy to Abigail and back again but he did not say anything. Gary knew what had happened and intended to have a discussion about it today. He did not wait for Abigail to answer but looked at Lee and explained, "It seems that Max followed Abigail to the grocery store and accosted her in the parking lot."

Lee did not say anything, but the thunderclouds that formed in his eyes rumbled volumes of thoughts.

"I'm okay," she downplayed her feelings, "I'm just a little bruised. And a little stiff."

"Let me see," Cindy demanded like only a close friend could and scooted her chair back so she could look at the injuries.

Abigail complied, turning sideways in her chair, rolling up her pant leg, and exposing the extensive bruising high on the front of her right shin. The right leg took the brunt of the trauma and had bled a little bit. A large adhesive bandage covered the abrasion but bruising was evident under the fringes of the bandage as well as on the back of her leg. No one said anything for a long awkward minute as the various emotions bubbled up in each of them.

"So, what are we going to do about this?" Cindy demanded. "They're escalating their attacks on you. They're getting bolder."

Abigail bent over and rolled her pant leg down and smoothed it carefully. When she sat up, she looked up with moisture in her eyes. "When I fed Buster this morning, he had a noose around his neck."

"What?!" Gary exploded.

"I cut it off. It wasn't tight enough to choke him, but he wasn't very happy. It was Max Berryman again. I have the images on my thumb drive if you want to look at them." She pulled the lanyard with the thumb drive attached to it from around her neck and held it out.

"Yes!" came from both Gary and Lee. It was evident that it would not have taken much provocation for either one of them to confront Max. Gary snatched the thumb drive and headed into his study with Lee on his heels. Cindy and Abigail could hear the men muttering in the study. When they returned, Gary's face was red. He was angry that Max was harassing and threatening his friend.

"At least he didn't come onto the property again. I asked God to move His angels a little bit further out so they can't get close to Buster."

"This needs to be reported to the sheriff," Lee said.

"I thought about that, but the law is so stinking corrupt in this county that they won't do anything to him and *I* might be the one that ends up in jail," Abigail said with a hint of despair. "I think we need to pray and brainstorm with God. We're in the middle of six days of rituals and things are escalating because my clients are getting set free. They're getting desperate."

They huddled up and began to pray for discernment and direction, for wisdom and understanding. They prayed for safety and protection for Abigail and her clients, and for all their property and animals. They prayed for justice and mercy. They appealed to God as the Judge and God of all to bring swift justice regarding the "defendants" on behalf of Abigail. She was, after all, the plaintiff with Jesus as her Advocate.

When they were finished, Gary decided that the mood needed to be lightened up, so he leaned over to Cindy and whispered a question. After she nodded her approval, he bellowed out loudly enough for Traci and Bryan to hear him, "I think we have some Christmas presents to open."

Squeals of delight resounded from the family room and the sound of hurried footsteps drummed closer to the kitchen.

"Really, Daddy? Right now?" Traci asked through her toothless smile. She had recently lost her top front teeth in yet another rite of passage for the first grader. Bryan was right behind her jumping up and down, pumping his clasped hands vigorously.

"Let's go to the living room," Gary said exuberantly. He loved his family and loved being a dad. He looked from Abigail to Lee and said, "I hope you don't mind helping us celebrate a little."

"My pleasure," Lee replied with a faint and mildly bitter-sweet smile. He was thinking of other happier Christmas festivities when he and his wife celebrated with their daughter, Lisa.

"Oh, I'd love to," Abigail said, also smiling. "I have some stuff in the truck, let me go get it." With that she stood up a little gingerly and went to get her coat.

Lee noticed her try to cover up the slight wince and offered to help. "Let me come help you." His parents had raised him to be a gentleman.

"Thank you," Abigail responded.

Gary nodded toward the retreating couple and winked at Cindy behind their backs. Cindy responded with a satisfied and slightly mischievous smile.

The children were delighted with their presents. Abigail had bought Bryan a little matchbox tow truck and a red car that he could tow with it. Traci loved her set of watercolor paints and a couple of coloring books filled with princess pictures. She wrapped up a basket and filled it with various pint jars of fruit jams from her orchard and vineyard as well as some of her traditional holiday baked goods.

Lee looked pleasantly surprised when she handed him a similar basket. Receiving it with a smile, he thanked her profusely and apologized for not having something for her.

The adults enjoyed another round of coffee and chatted about more pleasant topics while the children busied themselves with their new toys. Soon Abigail announced that she needed to get going. "I want to get home way before dark and make sure that Buster is okay. Thank you so much for including me in your festivities." She went to each member of the McCord family and gave them a hug.

Lee stood up and stretched, "Thank you, Cindy, for another fabulous dinner. I've got some livestock to check up on, too, so I'll see you tomorrow at Grandpa and Grandma's." He turned to Abigail and said, "I'll try to keep an eye out for Max when I'm out that way."

They walked out together and Lee impulsively stopped Abigail. "I don't want to be presumptuous, but would you like to meet me at my farm and see what I've been up to? We still have plenty of daylight."

"I'd love to!" Abigail hoped she didn't sound too enthusiastic, but it was certainly more appealing to spend time with someone on Christmas Eve than being alone with her memories. Besides, she was beginning to like this man. "Let me go home and get changed. I'll put on some play clothes and shin guards and meet you there in, what? An hour?"

"I need to change, too." Lee smiled at her humor. "An hour would be about right." He hesitated just a moment and then added, "How about if I pick you up? I'd like to walk the perimeter of your property with you. We might find something."

She agreed and they got into their respective trucks, Abigail backing out first and Lee following her at a distance. Abigail arrived at her home without incident and excitedly changed into her play clothes. Actually, they were work clothes and boots, but she really did enjoy attending to the activities of her little farm and considered it play.

Abigail was ready when Lee came up her driveway in his dark blue pickup. Heading down the stairs and angling toward the pasture gate, she joined him as he headed there from the driveway.

"Hello!" Abigail greeted him.

"Hi," Lee answered with a smile. "Got your shin guards on?"

"I'm ready. Where do you want to start?" Abigail saw that Buster had already started to move to the top of the pasture.

"Can I see the noose?" Lee asked. "Sometimes you can tell something about someone by the knots they tie. It might mean something and it might not."

"I tossed it into the tack room. Come on, I'll show you." With that, Abigail removed the newly rigged chain that replaced the one Max had taken.

Lee frowned and said, "I'll see what I can come up with to fix your gate."

"Thanks," Abigail was touched by his willingness to fix it. But then, that was kind of a guy thing. They fix problems. But there seemed to be more to Lee's offer. His protectiveness was much like his cousin Gary's and it was very touching to Abigail. With her own brothers and father living so far away, she was accustomed to fending for herself. It felt good and reminded her of Darryl's protectiveness that he modeled for their sons.

Lee looked at the noose and did not make any comment. When he was finished, they walked down to the bottom gate and looked for footprints. Once again, the hoof prints of a very large horse were evident.

"Well, that solves that mystery," Abigail said. "The guy with the big horse is Max."

"But didn't that guy have a long braid or a ponytail or something?" Lee asked.

"Oh! You're right!" Abigail gasped. "Humph. Well I guess it means that they both have access to the same horse or the braid-guy came around after Max did."

They continued to ponder the possibilities as they walked the perimeter of the property. Abigail was praying as she did. *Lord, every place I put the soles of my feet belong to me. Keep the trespassers away.* She led the way though the familiar trails that crisscrossed the pasture and woods. Finally, after completing the circuit, they were back up at the house.

Lee walked to the passenger side of his truck and opened the door, "Ready?" he gestured toward the passenger seat with an exaggerated sweep of his arm and a slight bow.

"Thank you," Abigail responded and climbed up into his full-sized truck. It was noticeably bigger than her mid-sized model.

He started the engine and expertly turned the truck around. Within minutes they were bouncing to a stop in front of the barn. Abigail did a controlled slide from the high seat and stood firmly on the ground. "Wow! You really have gotten some work done here," she exclaimed as she looked around. "Whatever happened to Billy's old car?"

"I had the real estate people take care of getting it towed to impound or whatever they do around here." They walked side by side toward the barn.

"You are so smart. That keeps you under the radar," Abigail said. It was a genuine compliment. She had wondered how that car situation would play out. "I hope you prayed for cleansing on the property."

Lee gave her a quizzical look. "What do you mean?"

"Oh," Abigail said, "I guess maybe I should tell you a couple of things about Billy."

"Like what?"

"Well, you know that he was Carrie Sue's brother and that he was a Satanist like his parents, right?" She waited for his nod and then continued, "Carrie Sue and I came up here back in October to look at the car and we found some things under the back seat."

Lee's eyebrows rose up. "Like what?"

"There were three bags. One had a stash of whacky tobaccy, one had some occult rings and jewelry that he probably used in the rituals, and the third one had a bundle of money."

"Really!"

"Yeah," Abigail replied, "we dropped the first two bags like hot potatoes. We wore gloves and were very careful not to leave fingerprints." She tilted her head and looked him in the eye as she said, "You're not paranoid if they're really out to get ya. Anyway, Carrie Sue took the money and is trying to sneak it back to her mother a little bit at a time. She thinks that either Billy stole it from her or, if he got it some other way, she should have it."

"So, explain why I need to pray over the property. I think I have an idea, but I'd like to hear your take on it," Lee said with growing interest. He had wanted to pick Abigail's brain about spiritual warfare ever since he met her and this seemed like a good opportunity. This was all new to him.

"Well, here's my philosophy: There's not a demon under every bush, but if there is, I want it out of there. Demons are legalists and squatters. They were, in a sense, invited into that car because of the drugs – spirits of pharmakia – and because of the occult jewelry and whatever demons were associated with Billy. Basically, whenever there is sin, strongholds are established and that's where the demons have a so-called legal right to be. Any one of them could decide to hang out here simply because they're looking for a new home now that he's dead."

"That makes sense," Lee said. "I wasn't raised in a church that talked about demons and Satanism so this is kind of new to me. Don't be offended if I look at you sideways sometimes."

"No problem. I wasn't raised with this stuff either, but I've become kind of an expert in it over the years."

"So, how do you pray over your property?"

What followed was a fairly extensive discussion prompted by insightful questions. They continued the conversation as they walked down to the pasture to check on the horses. Their water supply was steady with the stream and the round bales of hay that Lee had secured kept them happy. He had cleaned and moved the old abandoned chest freezer down to the gate. It was perfect for storing the sweet feed since it was weather proof and would keep the raccoons and rodents from stealing or contaminating it.

"I plead the blood of Jesus Christ over everything that is legally mine. I ask Him to station warring and guardian angels all over the property and I ask Him to evict any trespassers. I pray over the history of the property in case there were crimes, traumas, or other sins committed by or against former owners. Then I rededicate it to the Lord." She continued to talk and quote some Scriptures that were pertinent.

"Could we do that?" Lee asked, "I mean, would you walk the perimeter and pray with me over this land?"

Abigail beamed. "Absolutely!" She loved to teach and apply biblical principles. "Right now?"

"As good a time as any," Lee agreed but then he furrowed his brow a little, "but how's your leg? Are you okay with a long walk?"

"I'm good," she said convincingly.

"Where do we start?" Lee asked.

"I guess this would be a good place. We can head to the entrance of the driveway and go all the way around and then come back up the driveway so we can pray over all the buildings. Are you comfortable with what I call tag-team prayers? I mean, I'll pray something and then you pray in agreement and maybe add a little something to it or pray it from a different angle that I might not know about."

They walked and prayed over the property and by the time they got back to the barn and the old building sites, it was starting to get quite cool with the sun going down.ABC Lee drove Abigail home and after an awkward farewell, reminiscent of teenaged years, Lee headed back to his apartment; his empty apartment. And Abigail went into her house; her empty house.

Demon Revels were being celebrated all over the world in communities that had no tangible reason to suspect that various diabolical activities were regularly spilling blood onto their land. Prinz and his underlings were also prepared to gather for their rituals. Zorroz had finally recovered from his tracheotomy and was able to rejoin the festivities. He had not yet returned to church. He was determined to regain his powers and continue his climb to upper level master. Max had not been seen in church either, but his father continued to rise in the church and in the community as a respected leader and businessman.

The frenetic activity in the second heavens was filled with dark bands like spears which stabbed the earth's atmosphere after having been summoned by their hosts. Most of the demons came and went as they needed to. Some took up permanent residence in some of their hosts rendering them demon-possessed like the man of the Gadarenes.

Demons did not like any talk about what the People of the Cross called "the demoniac of the Gadarenes." A legion of demons had been entrenched in the naked tomb-dweller who terrorized the citizens of that region with his howling and screaming, chain-breaking and rock-gashing behavior. That Great Enemy decided to visit the region one day. Demons stirred up a fierce gale and tried to sink His boat before He even got there. Oh, how they tried to keep Him away! But He merely stood up and rebuked the wind and the waves.

Those inept spirits were further tormented for the humiliating powerlessness that kept them from killing Him and His followers. How infuriating! They vowed vengeance but were further disgraced when the free will of that captive superseded the will of the legion of demons and brought him to the feet of the Great

Power. The best they could do was kill off a herd of swine and try to alienate the now free man. No, it would not do to be reminded of this failure for it did not comfort them regarding Satan's final plan to be like the Most High.

Fires were ignited, sharp implements were readied, and goblets were produced. Sacrifices were prepared and tormented. Frenzied demon-driven, power-hungry men and women partook and indoctrinated the next generation. Communities slept in the cold and dark December night.

Most children anticipated waking up to gifts and goodies. Not these. They just wanted to endure, to survive, or perhaps it would be better to die tonight. Did they really want to wake up one more time? Those that survived the night had been further fragmented, programmed, and demonized.

Carrie Sue Wagner felt some minor tugs but was able to pray and maintain control. She did not go to the ritual that she would have been lured to just one year ago. She was able to sleep a restless, nightmare-ridden sleep. She awoke at three o'clock in the morning and put a praise and worship CD into her player and then drifted back to sleep while her cautious protectors kept a vigilant watch on her behalf.

It was not so simple for F. Amy Bolton who had not travelled as far along the healing journey. She felt the mighty inner turmoil as Nicholai and Head Warden and those who had defected from Satanism strategized and warred against those who would have schemed to maneuver her into a vulnerable position and thus, to a ritual. No one slept that night and by morning Amy was exhausted but feeling triumphant that they had successfully resisted. This was the first year of her life that she did not go to a ritual for this demon revel.

The following night was a repeat of the same for both of them. Carrie Sue had a slightly more difficult time because she felt obligated to visit her mother and share Christmas dinner. Her mother, Susan, switched personalities as various topics were discussed. Carrie Sue chuckled inwardly as she could now understand why Abigail kidded her about the need to wear a rolodex instead of a name tag.

10

Friday, January 5

Abigail did not pay much attention to holidays since she lost her family. She spent New Year's Day, which fell on Monday this year, much like she did any other day. She kept up with the insatiable appetite of the wood stove by periodically bringing more wood up to the holder on the front porch. She attended to Buster, cleaned house, wrote out the bills, and spent some time writing. Some favorite desserts were baked and some projects that had been put on hold for a while were finished. Someday she hoped to publish a devotional. So far, she had a collection of notes in her Bible and a few pages in a document on her computer. She added several pages to the growing file and was satisfied with the new chapter.

Finally, it was Friday and Carrie Sue had agreed to meet at noon today instead of their usual ten o'clock time slot since Abigail had no one scheduled between her and Amy. Abigail did not like to have idle time. It was another stormy day which was so fitting for a week laden with ritual days – the first and third of the month, which also happened to be a full moon. The third also happened to be Carrie Sue's birthday.

The SRA survivor's birthday was purported to be the absolute worst ritual the survivor could endure. It was always couched in the duplicitous double-binds that lent to the already deep confusion. "Oh, we're just honoring you." That so-called honor usually meant the most degrading, horrific torture that *honored* them because it gauged their ability to withstand the so-called momentary and light afflictions for their king. They were being groomed and trained, prepared and mentored. The survivors reported pre-birthday rituals which meant enduring six weeks of additional torment.

Carrie Sue looked a little bit stressed but she tried to hide it. They talked about her holiday visits with her mother. "I was finally able to get some of the money Billy stole back to her," Carrie Sue said and smiled triumphantly. "I bought a bunch of stuff she needed. Of course, the nice mom came out and thanked me profusely before the nasty mom came out and cussed me." Carrie Sue laughed a genuine laugh. "I can't believe that I lived with that kind of insanity for so long. It's a wonder that I haven't gone screaming into the sunset!"

"It is remarkable," Abigail said, "but, that's the gift that dissociation is. I know it doesn't always work *for* you, but you really would have been in a rubber room if you couldn't cope by dissociating."

"Yeah," Carrie Sue agreed. "It's amazing how much more clearly I see things now. I'm not losing time as much and I'm really sure I haven't been suckered into going to any more rituals. Uh, well, except for the 'Great Escape' night." She shuddered involuntarily.

Abigail abruptly changed the subject. "Well, we have a lot of work to do today. What do you say we open with prayer and get started?"

"Good idea."

After seeking God for direction, the host Carrie Sue sensed that they needed to do something about the original Carrie Sue. "I've been talking to the pseudo-originals. They mostly just listen, but I think that's progress. They won't say anything about the original core person – or whatever we're supposed to call her. I get the impression that they're afraid that they'll be punished or something."

"No doubt there were plenty of threats," Abigail agreed. "Let's pray and ask the Lord to illuminate this issue." Abigail led the prayer and looked expectantly at Carrie Sue.

"Birthday," Carrie Sue said flatly, "I heard the word 'birthday' and I feel a lot of terror."

"Your birthday is this month, right?" Abigail asked. She remembered a lot of facts about her clients, but did not have everything committed to memory.

"It was Wednesday, the third," Carrie Sue answered.

"Well, isn't it interesting that we have your birthday and your original person's issues coming up today?" Abigail said half to Carrie Sue and half to herself. "It's also interesting that your birthday is one, three; January three – a couple of their favorite numbers."

"Yeah. Interesting. I'm just feeling terror," Carrie Sue repeated.

"Let's ask the Lord to show us the root of this kind of terror," Abigail suggested. They prayed and it was not long before Carrie Sue reported the results.

"We were supposed to have died on Wednesday," Carrie Sue said. "I don't know how I know this but that's what I'm getting. It has something to do with the year 2007 and something about my life finally being completed. What's that supposed to mean?" she asked with a puzzled frown.

"The first thing I thought of was that the number seven means completion or maturity or perfection. I wonder if they were thinking that you completed your job, your purpose, so you get to die – they'd probably figure that it would happen at your birthday ritual."

The mention of the birthday ritual caused Carrie Sue to jolt upright in her chair. It was obvious to Abigail that there had been another switch in personalities and the next words out of her mouth confirmed it. "So, the brilliant counselor finally figured it out," a snotty voice taunted Abigail.

"Oh, I think it's fairly predictable," Abigail quietly countered. "So, who are you, if you don't mind my asking?" Abigail continued as if she were having a pleasant conversation with a friend.

"You can't stop us," she, or maybe he, continued. "She's going to die and even *her* Jesus can't stop it. Ha! He didn't make it to thirty-four; why should she?"

Abigail quickly did the math. She knew that Carrie Sue was born in 1973 and this was 2007. Interesting. "Correct me if I'm wrong," Abigail continued amiably, "but she's thirty-four now. She survived her birthday."

"You don't know what her real birthday is," the irate one sneered. "*She* doesn't even know."

Abigail considered that. Many cult families were known to falsify the birth certificate information. They had plenty of physicians within their circles who gladly abetted them. "Okay, then, if Wednesday wasn't her birthday, then we still have time to thwart your plans."

"We'll kill her! You just wait and see. And it won't be very pretty."

"What do you mean, *her*?" Abigail countered. "If she dies, you're toast, too."

"So what? As long as I do my job, it's all good," the personality retorted.

"What'll happen to you when you die?" Abigail asked. She wanted to gauge how deeply this part of Carrie Sue had been indoctrinated.

"I'll live on in someone else. I'll be rewarded for a job well done," the personality said smugly. "I'll get a better assignment." Abigail was beginning to sense that this was a male personality.

"What if you're wrong?"

"I'm not," he gave his cocky answer.

"Oh, okay, you're probably right," Abigail replied with a slightly sarcastic edge to her pleasant tone, "Satanists never lie and they've treated you just great so far. Thanks for the warning, but do you mind if I talk to the Birthday Girls?" She had another Holy Spirit hunch.

Frustrated by not being able to fluster Abigail, infuriated at the dismissal, shocked by Abigail's sudden change of subject, the personality blurted out his threat. "You'll see! She'll be dead by midnight of her birthday and you can't stop us!" With that, he was gone and a cowering and visibly trembling personality appeared before Abigail.

Abigail sensed that this was one of the Birthday Girls that carried the terror. As soothingly as possible she said, "You're okay. You're in a safe place. I'm Abigail. I won't hurt you."

The trembling continued, but the little girl ventured to look briefly at Abigail as if to assess how soon this lady would lie to her and eventually betray her tenuous trust. Desperate for relief, she thought she would try one more time. What was there to lose? Maybe, just maybe, there really were nice people out there.

"I know what that guy said and I have a pretty good idea of what you have gone through and I know that Carrie Sue's birthday is a problem, whenever it is," Abigail said gently. "I also know that you've never met anyone who could actually help you out of this mess and you don't have any reason to believe that I won't turn on you, too."

The little girl did not change her downcast look but nodded in agreement and looked as if she were bracing herself for the worst.

"I don't have any way to prove what I said," Abigail continued, "but I do know that you know what the Satanists' eyes look like – evil and sometimes red or orange, right?"

She was rewarded with a slight nod of assent so she continued, "Would you be brave enough to look at my eyes while I look to the side of you a little bit? I know it makes you nervous to make direct eye contact. Then you can maybe decide if you can let me help you. Can you do that?"

Before the little one could answer an older, more assertive personality switched in and demanded, "Who do you think you are working on a little kid like that?"

"I'll assume that you are another Birthday Girl or maybe a protector," Abigail responded evenly. "So maybe I should ask you why you would let a little kid show up to test the waters."

"That's not what happened!"

"You have the control now," Abigail observed, "why not earlier?"

The flustered personality was casting about for a retort but found none.

"Listen," Abigail said gently, "I'm not the enemy. And to answer my own question, demons do the same thing – they send out the lower ranking ones. So, back to the main issue, what do you want to do about your thirty-fourth birthday, whenever it is?"

"There's nothing that we can do about it. We just have to get through it like we always managed to do without your help. Thank you very much," she ended with a sarcastic note.

"Ah," Abigail disagreed quietly, "but I believe that there is something that can be done. How about if I run it past you and then you and all the other Birthday Girls can think about it and decide what you want to do? You've got nothing to lose but a little bit of time."

The personality did not want to sound desperate or grateful. She did not want to lose face, so she gruffly gave her grudging consent. Abigail talked to her about programming and demonic oppressors, cult agendas and internal persecutors, complete physical, emotional, and spiritual healing and integration for all of them. "So, what do you think?" Abigail asked, "Does any of this make sense?"

"Maybe," came the grudging answer. Was she ready to have her hopes dashed once again? Could she trust this woman with the kind eyes? Yes, she had been listening in on the previous conversation and had stolen a look into Abigail's warm brown eyes. She could not detect any evil, but she had been tricked before. Duplicity. Double-binds.

Abigail noticed the quick movements of her eyes. It was interesting how the movements of the natural eyes traced internal conflict. "Would you like for me to make them stop threatening you?"

She was startled by Abigail's question and began to respect her uncanny insights. "Uh, sure," she said with more humility in her tone.

Abigail launched into a brief prayer, "Lord Jesus the Christ, I plead Your cleansing blood over these parts of Carrie Sue and ask that You would bind all demonic oppressors that are associated with them. Do not allow them to speak or threaten in any way and set them aside. I also ask that You would put the persecutors in protective custody for now." She waited a moment and then followed up with, "How are you doing now?"

"Fine. I mean, it's a lot quieter in here," she replied with wonder.

"Well, now that you can think for yourself a little bit better, what do you want to do?"

"I think that I, I mean, we don't want to go to the Birthday Ritual. We like the idea of integrating so they can't access us," she replied thoughtfully. Then she added with a hint of mischief and a wry smile, "We also like the idea of messing with them for a change."

"I like the way you're thinking!" Abigail smiled and received a genuine smile in return. "Are you ready?"

She looked as if she was taking an internal poll for a few seconds and then announced that they were ready to get healed and integrated. Abigail prayed a "sozo" prayer, customized it for this group, and followed it up with prayer for integration when it was confirmed that there was nothing upsetting or uncomfortable left for any of them. She then addressed the persecutor whose job it was to kill Carrie Sue by midnight of their birthday. She found a more contrite personality and was able to also pray effectively for him and his group.

Abigail and Carrie Sue continued to pray until they were confident that Carrie Sue was safe from imminent danger associated with the Birthday Ritual – whenever it happened to be. They scheduled the next session and Carrie Sue left.

F. Amy Bolton arrived a few minutes later, once again, right on time rather than her former six minutes late. She was ready to do battle. This was a tricky time in the recovery of an SRA survivor. Too many times cult-loyal, demon-driven personalities would literally move them out of state to stop the healing process. One of Abigail's former survivors even moved to Europe! After a short time of catching up on ordinary events in Amy's life, they opened with prayer.

Reviewing the information about the other level leaders, she got an update from Nicholai about the continued progress he was making on his level. That was the good news. The bad news was that the key personalities from the other five levels now knew that there had been a major defection on the top level so they were fortifying their positions and increasing pressure in various retaliatory ways.

Suicidal thoughts increased. Time losses were more frequent and coming at critical times in Amy's day-to-day activities. But she was determined to get free.

Head Warden was becoming a familiar face lately. "Hello," he began as if he were once again chairing a debriefing. He brought Abigail up to speed on the internal workings and informed her that there was considerable turbulence coming from the lower levels.

Nicholai's people recently caught several of Achan's people who had come up to steal things from some of his people like they had in the past. They did not know that they were walking into a trap despite their careful disguises. Nicholai had them locked up, dismissed their demons, and deprogrammed them. He was also a quick learner and loved the principles of jurisdiction that complimented the newly found authority he had through Jesus Christ. "We're getting things done, but it seems like it's one step forward and ten steps back."

"I know it seems like it, but you really are making serious progress. As distressing as the backlash is, it lets us know that they're rattled. Hang in there and the balance will tip even further in your favor."

"You know best," he acknowledged. "Where do we go from here? These are some pretty nasty parts."

"Let's take a step back and look at the big picture," Abigail said thoughtfully. "We have to remember that there are no bad parts, just parts that have bad jobs." She paused to let this sink in and then continued, "We can continue to battle through each level down to the pit on Apollyon's level to get to the original Amy and that will take a lot of time and energy. I mean, why do we have to follow their rules?"

"What do you mean?" Head Warden asked. His curiosity was roused.

"God said that He can lower the mountains, raise the valleys, and make crooked paths straight. Just because the Satanists have used all these complicated strategies, tunnels, pits, hiding places, programming, pseudo-personalities, and whatever other scheme they have; it doesn't mean that we have to undo everything the same way it was done." She used her index finger to draw squiggly patterns in front of her.

"God can just put His finger on whatever it is that we need to do and take us straight there." She made a straight line with her finger from eye level to waist level. "We don't have to follow their so-called rules."

"Okay, so how do we do that?" Head Warden asked ready to implement the strategy.

"Let me talk a little bit about the system. Think of the system as a tree. Ground level is birth, the roots are the pre-borns, and the main trunk is the original Amy. Out of that trunk come three main splits. One is the pain side with the painful memories. One is the denial side. They typically deny the pain *and* the dissociation. The third main split is a buffer zone that's confused by the arguments of the pain side and the denial side."

Head Warden was following her analogy but failed to see the relevance. "That makes sense but how do we use that to our advantage?"

"We've been working with the branches and leaves most of the time until now. And that's all necessary preliminary work, but I think we might be able to contact the primary splits, or Head Honchos, as I call them, and see if they would be willing to step aside and let Jesus minister to the original Amy."

"How do we do that?"

"Let's ask if there's anyone who knows what we're talking about," Abigail replied. Getting the nod from Head Warden, she prayed and then asked, "Is there someone who knows what we're talking about? Can we talk?"

They waited a few moments and then were soon rewarded with a voice that said, "I do." Head Warden relayed that information to Abigail.

"Do you want to come out and talk to me, or are you more comfortable with Head Warden as the middle man?" Abigail asked.

She answered by switching in and adjusting the rigid posture that Head Warden had held to something more relaxed. "I'm Abnego," she introduced herself, "I guess I'm the one you call the denial head honcho."

"Thanks for coming out," Abigail said, "I hope you won't mind my getting directly to the point. Do you deny just the pain or all the dissociation and multiple personalities, too?"

"Well," Abnego said sadly, "I used to deny it all, but it's kind of hard to deny something that's so obvious, I mean, there were a lot of different characters coming and going just today. And I've been watching what has been going on for quite some time. No, I don't deny the dissociation or the multiple personalities anymore."

"What about the memories, the pain, the emotions, and all the stuff that the pain side personalities are talking about?" Abigail asked mildly.

"*That* I'm just not so sure about," Abnego said. "I don't have any memories like that. I've never been to a ritual. Our parents took good care of us."

Abigail noted Abnego's reference to herself using plural pronouns but did not comment about it. It would indicate that there was a group of denial side personalities. "Would you be okay with talking about dissociation and pain and see if maybe we can connect the dots for you?" Abigail asked.

Getting a nod, she talked about dissociation as an effective coping skill that was needed to deal with overwhelming unprocessed trauma and concluded, "No one wakes up one morning and decides to dissociate, to make up wild and crazy stories about rituals. Your parents wouldn't have let you read books or watch movies with that kind of content even if it existed. The pain parts didn't make it up. So, these stories, these memories had to come from somewhere. How do you explain it? Were you co-conscious one hundred per cent of the time with every personality that ever took executive control since the beginning?" Abigail put the burden back on Abnego.

"Well, of course not, I mean, um, uh," Abnego began to stammer with frustration. She was stumped and knew where Abigail was heading. She was feeling like a failure for not maintaining the denial and for not protecting the system from the overwhelming pain.

"Abnego," Abigail said tenderly, "you have one of the toughest jobs in the system. And, you are a huge key to healing. You have done a great job and have helped Amy function. How else can a kid hold onto two equal and opposite truths? 'My parents love me and take care of me – my parents are evil and have harmed me.' There had to be dissociation and denial to go with the pain."

"I know you're right," Abnego conceded, "I just don't know…" She softly let the thought evaporate.

"Let me ask you this," Abigail took a different tack. "What would it mean if all of the pain side memories are true?"

Abnego wrestled with her thoughts for several minutes before replying with tears welling up in her eyes, "It would mean that we were never loved." She choked back a sob. "We were never wanted; that our parents didn't care about us; that they just used us." This time she could not hold back her emotions or the tears that coursed down her cheeks.

This is the deepest pain a human being can face. Rejected. Despised. Abandoned. Neglected. Abigail's eyes welled up with tears, too. She had to resist her mother-heart that wanted to give this distressed part of Amy the most motherly hug she had. But she had learned early in her practice that it was too risky. There was no way of knowing who might switch in and, having limited understanding, might misinterpret the hug. Instead, she prayed silently for the Comforter to minister to this profound agony. Even though the session ended on a somber note, Abigail was encouraged about the progress that the denial side had made. F. Amy Bolton had turned another significant corner in her healing journey.

Abigail switched up her routine and shopped at the Oakvale grocery. She did not want to risk another Max encounter. She had a taste for eggplant lasagna and efficiently gathered all the special ingredients that she did not normally keep at home. Fresh mushrooms and special cheeses, tomato paste and eggplant all found their way into her cart along with her usual staples.

Looking very carefully around the parking lot, she made her way without incident to the truck and soon was on her way home. She was thinking about today's sessions and was intrigued by the name Abnego which sounded a little like a Greek or Latin word. She made a mental note to research it in her old textbooks when she got home.

Lee was happily working on his new farm. He had made good progress repairing the barn, reinforcing some of the smaller out-buildings, running electricity to the barn, locating the well and attaching a new pump. He built a well house using the existing foundation and soon was able to pump water. He was not sure if it was potable or not, so he would take a sample to be tested at some point. It was a beginning.

It was getting dark and Lee had put in a long day but first he wanted to check on his mares. Actually, he just missed messing with them and determined that he would take a ride one of these days soon. When he got to the gate, he heard a diesel revving its engine close by. Curious, he walked through the horse pasture and positioned himself to be able to see through the thin tree line that separated his field from the adjacent one that bordered York Creek. *A black pickup. Could Max be stupid enough to try something again?* It looked like he was settled into his hiding place again.

Lee quickly reached into his pocket and retrieved his cell phone.

"Yo!" Gary barked. "What's up?"

"How long would it take for you to get down here to my farm?"

"About ten minutes. What do you need?"

"I think that Max character is parked at the end of that field by the creek again. What do you say we pay the man a visit?"

"I'll be right there. I'll get Rusty to close up." Gary continued to talk to Lee as he headed for his truck and together they came up with a strategy.

Max was idly smoking a cigarette and listening to his radio. It was almost dark and he was unconcerned that anyone might see him from the road. He felt smug because he knew that the judicial system would do little more than slap him on the wrist if he got caught. Slouched down in his seat with his cap pulled down, he waited until it was just dark enough to complete his mission. If he could not get onto the property, his tranquillizer dart surely could. He had already loaded the 1.5 cc dart and locked it into the chamber. Having pumped it three times, he was just biding his time.

Gary and Lee easily slipped through the rough edges of the field and approached the quietly idling truck. "That's definitely Max," Gary said. "I recognize his truck."

"Good," Lee responded. "Ready?"

"Let's give the man a taste of his own medicine," Gary said grimly. Neither man was given to violence, but there came a time when a man needed to talk man-to-man to get a point across. If governing authorities would not protect its citizens, then the citizens must protect each other.

Gary crouched and crept unnoticed to a position just behind the door. Lee was right behind him. Suddenly, he yanked the door open and before Max could react in any way, Gary punched him hard in his left temple. The stunned man slumped and before he could regain full control of his mind and body, Lee stepped past Gary and covered Max's head with a feed sack.

"Wha..." Max was trying to make sense of this situation in his somewhat disoriented condition. He began to thrash around and fight back but another fist to his face got his attention. "Okay, okay," he whined desperately, "what do you want? I ain't got no money. Don't hurt me!"

"Don't hurt you?" Gary asked. "Did you give that little lady an option in the parking lot last week?"

"Did you give her dog that option before you poisoned him?" Lee asked, not knowing if Max was the actual offender or not.

"It wasn't me! That wasn't me," Max protested. "I know who you are. You better watch out. You don't know who you're messing with." He began to grope the seat next to him for the tranquilizer gun.

Seeing it in time, lunging over him, wresting it from his grip, Lee elbowed Max's nose as he withdrew from the cab with the gun in his hand. "Well, well, what have we here?" he asked as he turned the gun over in his hand. "I think someone was about to tranquilize someone's horse."

"I wonder what's really in the dart," Gary said. "I think we need to have this analyzed. Or maybe we should just use Max as a guinea pig."

"No! No!" Max screamed in alarm.

That confirmed the malicious intent to the men. Lee checked to see if the safety was on and then tossed the gun onto the ground near the back of the truck. He was infuriated. Gary was simmering.

They exchanged a look with each other, nodded in unison, and dragged the man out of his truck. What followed was not pretty. Max's cries were muffled by the feed sack. Lee and Gary gave Max a blow by blow description of how a gentleman should treat a lady. When they thought that they had sufficiently made their point, they threw Max back into his truck and ordered him to leave and never come back.

Snatching the bloodied feed sack from Max's reeling head, slamming the door, picking up the gun, the pair retraced their steps back to their own trucks. Adding the feed sack to the burn pile and lighting it, Lee and Gary stared intently at the small fire. Each man silently reviewed their recent adventure.

"Brings back some old memories," Gary broke their silence, rubbing his knuckles.

"Yeah, I was just thinking that," Lee agreed. "We still got it!"

"Of course, those were legal hits on the football field," Gary added.

They broke into a tension-breaking chuckle and then soberly discussed the possible ramifications of their encounter with Max. They might have to deal with the legal system. They may have to deal with the local cult.

"Hang on a second," Gary said. "I have an idea." He reached for his cell phone and speed-dialed their grandfather.

"Hello," George McVeigh answered.

"Hey, Grandpa, it's Gary. I have a question."

"What is it, son?"

"Do you still have those old arsenic testers you used to have?" Gary asked.

"Oh, let me think," the older gentleman paused and scratched his forehead, "I haven't used one since we got off the well water, but I'm pretty sure I still have some in the shop."

"Can I stop by and use one?" Gary asked eagerly.

"Sure, boy, come on over."

"I'll be by in about twenty minutes. Lee will be coming, too." Gary glanced at Lee and got the nod.

"I'll be watching for you. Meet you at the shop."

Quickly raking through the last of the ashes and crushing the last ember, Lee and Gary headed for their respective trucks and drove over to their grandparents' home in Oakvale. George McVeigh wanted to be sure that he could locate the testers and was already in the shop when the two cousins arrived.

"What have you boys been up to?" Grandpa asked with friendly suspicion. He had an intuition that had proved to be quite accurate over the years. "Come on! Out with it!"

Lee produced the tranquilizer gun and said, "We found this on a guy who was up to no good by that creek near my place and across from Abigail Steele's place." He was unloading the dart as he spoke, being careful to keep his gloves on.

"We think he was going to do something to Abigail's horse, or maybe even to Abigail," Gary took up the narrative. "That's the guy that roughed her up in the parking lot last week."

"Oh?" Grandpa McVeigh pressed.

"Long story," Gary said, "I just want to see if he put arsenic in this dart. I have a hunch."

"I want to know what you did before we go any further," Grandpa insisted.

Gary and Lee took turns filling their grandfather in on the rest of the story. When they finished, he asked them, "How do you reconcile stepping outside of the law with the Scriptures that call us to submit to the authorities that God placed over us?"

"Grandpa," Gary said, "the law in this county is part of the problem. They look the other way."

Lee looked his grandfather in the eye and added, "Grandpa, the way I figure it, the authority in this country is 'We the People'. We elect officials, including the sheriff, judges, and other politicians. Therefore, *they* are mandated to submit to 'We the People' who are the God-ordained authority in this country. If they do not abide by the constitution or the law, we need to enforce it. I'm not talking about vigilantism; I'm talking about obeying God rather than men."

"Hadn't quite thought about it like that before," Grandpa replied thoughtfully. "All right then, let's see what we got."

They opened a kit and reviewed the instructions before carefully putting the recommended number of drops on the test surface. Within a few minutes, the test surface darkened and showed positive for a strong concentration of arsenic.

"That's enough to kill a horse!" George McVeigh exclaimed. "If we got a faint gray in the well water, we had to add filters to the system. That must be straight up arsenic!"

Abigail was unaware of all the drama that had taken place across from her property on her behalf. Buster was taken care of, she checked his water and made a mental note to fill the trough tomorrow. Going to her study, pulling down her Vine's Expository Dictionary, she found what she was looking for: "Abnego – to deny utterly" from the Latin. It was a perfect name for a denial personality. *How do those Satanists know so much more than the average Christian about the Bible and the ancient languages?*

11

Sunday, January 21

Max Berryman finally dared to show his face at church on Sunday morning. He slithered up the stairs to the balcony and slouched down in his usual seat behind the Bynum family's usual pew. His father, Ted, was an elder in the church and he made it clear that his son must attend church every Sunday. "An elder must rule his family well!"

Max despised the hypocrisy of the placid man that showed up in church but acted like a dictator in his own home. Even though his father was nearing sixty, Max knew that he dare not challenge the old man. He might have an edge on him physically, but that was all. Max nursed his wounds and his grudges while making his plans. *I'll show him! I'll show everybody!*

Carrie Sue joined Abigail in Abigail's usual row near the front of the church – a bold move for her. Deciding to take back her life, she was not going to let the fact that several Satanists were in the balcony, and perhaps scattered throughout the congregation, dissuade her anymore. It was a great mark of healing as she realized her identity in Christ and how intimidating that was to those Satanists.

The last chords faded and the worship team secured their instruments and then joined their families in the audience. Pastor Spalding shook hands and patted the shoulders of several of them as he passed them on their way off of the platform. Always smiling, he took his place behind the podium and boomed, "Isn't it great to be in the house of the Lord today?" A chorus of amens echoed throughout the sanctuary.

"Today I want to talk about success and what it will take to be successful in life; but we'll need to talk about something that might get some of you squirming," he began. "Now, I don't want you to think that I'm just pointing fingers and preaching hell fire and damnation because I've had to squirm a bit myself. You know, that old practice-what-you-preach thing." He was able to disarm his audience by couching his messages in humor and genuine humility.

"The title of my sermon is called, 'If You Want Success, Get the Sin out of the Camp'. If you would turn to chapter one in the book of Joshua, we'll look at what happens when you don't get sin out of the camp." He paused long enough for them to find the passage before he opened with prayer.

After giving a summary of the first few chapters to put his teaching into context, he said, "I was struck by how many times God told Joshua, *'I will be with you. I will not fail or forsake you. I'm with you wherever you go.'* He also said that as He was with Moses, He'd be with Joshua. Joshua must have had a tremendous amount of confidence when they went up against Jericho in their first battle since he had it in the bag because of God's promises. Right?"

He saw that the people were following him so he continued, "But, there was a condition that God gave Joshua. Let's look back at Joshua one verse eight. *'This book of the law shall not depart from your mouth, but you shall meditate on it day and night, so that you may be careful to do according to all that is written in it; for then you will make your way prosperous, and then you will have success.'*

God made it clear that obedience and success were linked. Now let's fast-forward to chapter six."

Pages rustled and he continued, "The seventeenth verse gives the instructions for the battle of Jericho. It was their first battle and the first fruits belonged to God. The soldiers were to take nothing. All the gold and silver, bronze and iron articles were to go to God's treasury. They obediently marched for seven days and successfully crushed their enemy, preserving the spoils for God."

Pastor Spalding continued to take them through the next battle scene with the tiny town of Ai where the now confident Israelites were defeated. Most of them were ready to head back across the Jordan River and all the way to Egypt. "What was the problem?" Pastor Spalding demanded as he leaned over the podium.

Answering his own question, he said, "The problem was that there was sin in the camp. God said to Joshua in chapter seven verse eleven, *'Israel has sinned... and have taken some of the things under the ban and have both stolen and deceived.'* Someone had disobeyed the orders and took some of the spoils for himself. Disobedience of the one man led to failure for the whole nation."

He continued with the account of how they purged sin from the camp by finding the man and stoning him and his entire family and all of his possessions. "Wow! Was that an overreaction? I mean, Achan did it, not his family or his sheep; yet they all had to go. The guy even confessed. Why couldn't he have given the stuff up and been restored? What is God trying to teach us here?" Again, he paused to let the congregation ponder these questions.

"Folks," he said as he came down the steps and walked back and forth in front of the stage, "God wants you to be successful. God really, really, really wants to bless you, but He can't if there is sin in the camp. So, take a few moments and ask God to reveal any area of disobedience. Is there something that might have been stolen from God? Is there something in your life that belongs to God? Your finances, your energy, your job, your relationships, your leisure time... Is there an area of deception or compromise? Is there sin in the camp? Don't let another day go by without confessing it, taking it out of your camp, and utterly destroying it."

He let the sobering questions sink in before he extended an invitation. "Our prayer teams are ready to pray with you about this issue. Come down if you need prayer for health issues or anything else." With that, he unclipped his microphone and began to pray with some who had come up for prayer.

Carrie Sue and Abigail made their way back up the aisle and headed for the main exit through the foyer. They were nearly to the door when Max Berryman slunk down the balcony stairs. He had intentionally timed his exit to be able to intercept them. Following closely behind the two women who were walking side by side down the sidewalk, Max waited until they got to the parking lot and then breathed his sneering threat in a barely audible voice, "Ladies, I am going to visit you, tear your precious Bibles to shreds, and screw you on the pages."

Abigail abruptly stopped, faced him, and said loudly enough for the entire town to hear, "Max Berryman! I am tired of your threats. Leave us alone in the name of Jesus the Christ!"

Not expecting that bold response, Max quickly retreated, waving at them with a big smile for the benefit of the people who turned to look their way. Moments later, he roared out of the church parking lot.

"Are you okay?" Abigail asked Carrie Sue.

"Yeah," Carrie Sue answered, "are you?"

"Yeah," Abigail sighed. "Let's pray a minute."

"Good idea."

"Lord, You said that no weapon formed against us will prosper. God, as far as we know, we do not have sin in our camps, so we pray for You to protect us wherever we go and thwart any plans of the enemy. Lord, Max is not the enemy, but the enemy is using him; please transform him. Save him and keep us safe from his threats, amen."

"Amen," Carrie Sue agreed. "Thanks, I'll probably see you Wednesday for church."

Max Berryman was vying for Mastiff's position in the local cult. Mastiff was the cult name for Ron Wagner, Carrie Sue's father. His sudden demise was a shock to the entire region and they knew that Carrie Sue and Abigail Steele were somehow responsible. Taking those women out or at least down a peg, would elevate Max. His cult name was Mot and it meant death. He would live up to his name and rise in the kingdom. He would make them respect him.

Calling on two other young men who were being recruited, Max laid out his plan in the local diner in Kingston, one of the few establishments in the area that did not close on Sunday.

"Hey, guys," Max began after they had ordered, "You want to have a little fun tonight?"

Unsure of what Max had in mind and not altogether sure that he wanted to follow Max, Nathan asked for more details. Jason just quietly waited for the answer. They were younger than Max and so far, hanging out with him had been heady stuff. But lately, the changes that they were seeing in Max were beginning to disturb these normally adventurous fellows. Max talked about power and drugs and women – all appealing to guys who did not always bother to figure out the possible consequences to involvement in any given venture. Immediate gratification was the norm.

"There's a little business that I have to take care of tonight," Max sneered conspiratorially, eyes shifting back and forth between Jason and Nathan.

"What kind of business?" Nathan asked.

"There are two ladies who need to learn a lesson. They need to know when to back off." Max hissed venomously. "When's the last time you got some?"

"Uh," Jason gulped incredulously, "are you talking about rape?"

"No!" Max barked, looked around the diner to see if he had attracted anyone's attention, and then lowered his voice. "Look! If you guys want your share of sex, money, and power, this is the way to go. I'm telling you that if you stick with me, you'll get that and more. We're calling the shots in this county! Whose side are you on?"

Max set the challenge before the two young men who recently graduated from high school. They were not college bound and were still drifting through life looking for easy jobs and good times. They were perfect recruits. Draw them in, give them drugs and alcohol, parties and girls, and then sucker-punch them with a crime that would be used to blackmail them and ensure their continued participation into deeper and darker cult activities until they would despair of ever getting out. Any residual bent toward conscience or morals, God or religion, would wither.

Max should know.

Max had met them though their church and he made sure that his dad hired both of them at the dealership to prove his influence. It was especially gratifying to be able to turn someone away from the Great Power. The young men had parents and grandparents who had attended the Baptist church for decades. Max had an instinct for finding malcontents. Nathan and Jason did not take much convincing.

"What would we have to do?" Nathan asked.

"As much as you want," Max said with a leering smirk. "You can watch or you can have some fun, too."

Jason and Nathan looked tentatively at each other. Neither one of them wanted to be the first to say yes or no. Finally, Nathan wilted under Max's scrutiny and said, "Okay, count me in." They both looked at Jason whose backbone sagged and then stiffened.

Saying nothing, pressing his lips together tightly, Jason stood up. "Not tonight. I gotta get home; maybe another time." Jason did not wait to hear the taunting that he was sure Max would dish out, but turned and left the diner. Moments later, tail lights confirmed that Jason was heading out of the parking lot.

Max reached over and gave Nathan an approving slug on the shoulder and said, "I know you have what it takes. Come on, let's go! We have some scores to settle." With that he opened his wallet and thumbed through the bills until he found just enough to cover the tab. He was not a very generous tipper.

Nathan followed Max in his own little red pickup truck. It was dwarfed by Max's full-sized truck and Nathan hoped that he could keep up with Max. Max drove like he owned the county, like he was immune to traffic tickets, like he could replace any vehicle that he smashed because he had gotten away with it so many times. Indeed, his father bailed him out of every bit of trouble he ever had with the law. Yes, and dad fixed or replaced every damaged vehicle.

Soon Max slowed down by an apartment building and parked in a shadowy area on the street. Nathan parked right behind him. They walked down the sidewalk side by side until they came to Carrie Sue's apartment. Looking up and down the quiet street, not noticing anyone around, Max boldly walked up to the front door and kicked it in.

Nathan was too shocked to do anything more than follow Max into the apartment and hastily close the door behind them. He wanted to run, but he dared not bail on Max right now. He sensed nothing but evil and he wished with all his might that he had the courage to walk out like Jason did.

Carrie Sue had been sitting on her couch half dozing in front of her television. Bolting upright, slightly disoriented, she was too slow to block Max's hard slap. Max let a string of expletives loose, "I told you that I was going to tear up your precious Bible and screw you on it!" He continued his intimidation as he looked around the room.

Seeing the Bible on the end table, stepping over to it, grasping the open book with both hands with the intent of tearing it apart page by page, Max suddenly screamed in agonizing pain. "Get it off of me! Get it off of me! It's burning my hands!" Max turned to Nathan with a look of anguish mingled with fury.

Nathan was shaken from his shock as he watched Max drop to his knees. It was as if his hands were stuck to the Book with hot glue and he could not drop it. Backing toward the door, tripping over the corner of a chair, he half fell, but managed to right himself and regain his footing. Jerking the door open and running to his truck, Nathan fled.

Cursing and swearing through agonized screams, Max gasped, "Okay, okay, I give!" Looking at Carrie Sue, he implored, "Make it stop. I won't touch you."

"Okay," Carrie Sue said uncertainly. "God, please let him loose so he can leave."

Instantly, his hands were loosed from the pages of the Bible. He staggered to his feet, totally humiliated and glared at Carrie Sue with as much curiosity as malice. The defeated man turned and bolted out of the door. Jumping into his truck, turning the ignition, his blistering fingers left bloody skin on the key. Roaring down the side streets until he connected with the route that wound toward his father's house in Springfield, he groaned after he finally dared to look at his bloodied, blistered, throbbing hands.

About midway between Kingston and Springfield, Max was forced to slow down because of an accident. Blue lights from county sheriff units, red lights from an ambulance, and amber lights from a tow truck pulsed through the darkness. Joining the line of vehicles,

gaping at the accident scene as he slowly drove by, Max was startled to see the mangled wreckage of a small red pickup truck.
Could that be Nathan's? Now he was thoroughly alarmed. *What power did those women possess?*
Meanwhile, Carrie Sue had gathered her wits about her. She tried to shut the front door, but the hardware was broken so she shoved a chair under the knob and secured it well enough to keep the cold drafts out. Picking up the phone with a shaky hand, she speed-dialed Abigail's number.
"Hello," Abigail's welcome voice answered on the first ring.
"Abigail," Carrie Sue immediately poured out her story, "Max was here with another guy. They broke the door in and Max was going to rape me on my Bible like he said at church."
"Oh, Jesus!" Abigail responded with alarm, "Are you all right? What happened?"
"You are not going to believe this," Carrie Sue said a little more calmly, "but when he picked up my Bible, his hands started burning and he couldn't shake free of it. It was the weirdest thing I ever saw!" Carrie Sue continued to relate every detail she could remember and concluded with, "and the other weird thing is that my Bible is perfect. Nothing happened to it."
"Wow!" Abigail marveled, "I think God has His angels watching over you."
"He sure does," Carrie Sue agreed.
"Out of curiosity," Abigail changed the subject a little bit, "what chapter was your Bible open to?"

"Oh, just a sec, let me look." Carrie Sue took the time to walk over to her open Bible and then exclaimed, "Psalm 91! Oh wow!"

"How appropriate," Abigail said with equal wonder at God's confirmation. She picked up her own Bible and scanned the chapter. "Ooh! Look at verse eight - *you will see the recompense of the wicked.* I guess Max got his recompense tonight and you got to see it."

They continued to praise the Lord and then the ever-practical Abigail asked about the condition of the door. If they called the landlord, questions would be asked and the sheriff might be called. That seemed too risky so they made plans for Abigail to come over with some tools and see if they could repair it themselves. She also asked if it was okay to call Cindy and ask for more prayer support.

Sheriff Bynum was called out to the accident on the King-Spring Road. The coroner had been called, the body was positively identified, and he was transported to the morgue. Sheriff Bynum then had the unsavory duty of notifying the next of kin of the death. It was ironic that a Satanist who relished the torture and sacrifice of the rituals found it distasteful to encounter death in his other life.

As expected, the Powell family was devastated. Nathan was the oldest of their three children. Deborah crumbled the moment she saw the sheriff. She sensed that something dreadful had happened. Her husband, Rob, caught her as she sagged to her knees wailing inconsolably. The unfamiliar noise brought Marie and Joel scrambling down the stairs to the living room.

"Is there anyone I can call?" Sheriff Bynum asked with a modicum of sympathy. "We'll need someone to come to the morgue to officially identify the body and sign some papers."

Composing himself, Rob answered shakily, "Pastor Spalding; I think we need Pastor Spalding." He turned back to the impossible job of consoling his broken-hearted, shock-ridden family while the sheriff made the call to their pastor.

Fortunately, the Spaldings lived close by and he quickly arrived with his wife, Natalie. Natalie stayed with the family and Rob went to the morgue with Pastor Spalding. Sheriff Bynum excused himself after expressing his condolences. He had a single-vehicle accident to finish investigating. When he got to the scene, his deputies gave him their preliminary findings: Apparently, a coyote had run across the road causing the young man to swerve, run off the road, over-correct his steering, and finally hit a large oak tree located just off the shoulder.

"Bum luck. If he had been just three feet one way or the other, he'd be sitting in the corn field and we'd be at home watching Sunday night football," one of the officers remarked.

"Yeah," the other agreed. "Bad luck."

The third agreed and nodded at a mangled carcass that was thrown by the impact. "It was a bad night for that coyote, too."

Roadside flares sputtered out and the deputies left to fill out their reports and catch the last of the game.

Jeering spirits mocked the humans. Luck! What did they know about luck? Everything was orchestrated. Ha! A curse without a cause shall not alight? Well this was a curse with a cause and it did alight. This one was about to bail and they had to stop him before he returned to the Great Power and did damage to their king. Frustrated that the messengers of the Great Enemy came and escorted Nathan's spirit through the second heavens, these wicked spirits vented their frustration into the frigid night air.

Absent from his body, Nathan was safely present with the Lord.

Zorroz met with Daggett after he was finished with his official duties. It would not have looked suspicious for the county sheriff to be talking to a county judge.

"There's something going on here." He cleared his throat and continued, "that kid was one of the newer recruits. He was with Mot tonight and they were supposed to make a point to Mastiff's kid and then go after that Steele woman."

"Tell me what you make of it." Daggett was also unusually subdued. He was as mystified by the new development as Zorroz was. Every time they tried to take those women down a notch, their plans were thwarted. He, too, was constantly fighting to maintain his powers.

"It has something to do with those two women, and especially that counselor," Zorroz replied. He did not want to admit his concerns. Neither of the men wanted to admit any fear or weakness.

"I have heard of people like that counselor. I am beginning to believe Prinz was right when he said that there would be more and more people like that as we approach the time of the final battle." Daggett assessed Zorroz for a minute before he continued. "Tell me," he said, "you have been close to her and on her property several times. What do you feel when you're around her?" He cocked his head and eyed Zorroz much like he did when he was on the bench using his authority to draw the truth out of a witness.

Zorroz hesitated. He was reluctant to tell the truth, but he had little to lose. Absentmindedly, he rubbed the tender tracheotomy scar. "I seem to lose power. I feel like I've instantly come down with the flu, but I know it's not physical; it's spiritual."

Daggett uncharacteristically allowed himself to be transparent as well. "I have sensed the same thing. We shall have to redouble our efforts to appease our king and regain the upper hand in this region. We have nearly two weeks of rituals to regain our status."

He was referring to January twenty through twenty-seven being abduction and preparation week for the February second Candlemas Sabbat Festival. St Agnes Eve was January twenty-ninth and was devoted to casting of spells. There was also the first and the third of the month as well as the thirty-first – all plays on the number thirteen.

They already had the appropriate females between the ages of seven and seventeen for the other nights. The breeders had been very fruitful and their offspring would be used for the purpose for which they were created. Society would never miss them because those children were non-existent as far as the rest of the world knew.

It was important for another victim to be abducted for Candlemas. Zorroz was commissioned to abduct the appropriate child; preferably blonde-haired and blue-eyed; preferably the offspring of the clergy or one of the People of the Cross.

12

Thursday, January 25

News went out through the prayer chain. Friends called friends. Neighbors called neighbors. One of their young people had been struck down. It was on the local radio stations and the newspaper carried pictures of the little red truck wrapped around the oak tree. Only a handful of people knew the inside story. This was not just a random unfortunate accident; Nathan was a casualty of war.

When Jason heard about it, he instinctively knew that it had something to do with whatever Max had planned on that fateful Sunday night. While he felt tremendously relieved on one hand, he felt guilty, tremendously guilty, on the other. Survivor's guilt is what they called it. He knew nothing about that; he just knew that he should not have walked out on his friend. *Nathan might be alive today if only...* And he was angry! *Why did Max have to put them in that position? Why did he and Nathan even hang out with Max?*

Jason spent a great deal of time in his room thinking morose thoughts ever since the accident. His parents checked in on him because they were worried about their son. He had been such a fun-loving, outgoing child but he had changed in the last couple of years. He dropped out of the church youth group. He complained about having to go to church all the time. One of the bright spots was that he and his best friend, Nathan, both had jobs at the Berryman car dealership. They had hoped that having a Christian employer would help keep him pursuing God.

The Wednesday night service on the previous night was almost as full as a Sunday morning service. There were many people from the community who came as well as the regulars. Pastor Spalding took his text from First Thessalonians four verse thirteen, *"that you may not grieve, as the rest who have no hope."* They believed that Nathan was with the Lord and so there was hope. Many people went from the memorial service at the church to the visitation at the funeral home which was located two blocks away.

Thursday dawned clear and cold. Pastor Spalding was grieved. He and his wife, Natalie, barely tasted their breakfast and then got ready to go to the church. "We have a great opportunity to preach the Gospel today," Pastor Spalding remarked.

"I expect that there will be a lot of young people at the funeral," Natalie agreed. They took the time to pray together for the strength and grace to make it through an arduous day.

They arrived early for a meeting with the immediate family and for the private viewing. Although Pastor Spalding had officiated at many funerals over the years, he never got used to it. The smell of flowers met him at the door and reminded him of so many other funerals. *Oh, death where is your sting? I'm feeling it.* He covered his private thoughts and emotions for the sake of the grieving family. There was unhindered weeping during the eulogies and the brief sermon which included a salvation message. The graveside service ended with an invitation to come back to the church for a dinner.

The all too familiar smell of the post-funeral fare diminished his appetite. Graciously thanking the ladies who volunteered to serve the bereaved in this practical way, visiting tables filled with relatives and friends, he remained until the last of the guests had left. Making his way up to his office, he closed the door and sank to his knees. The deeply grieved man groaned as much as he prayed.

Ginny, the administrative assistant, lightly rapped on his door around two o'clock. "Pastor?" she called softly. She heard him grunt as he came to his feet and then settled back into his creaky chair.

"Come in," he said wearily, "come in."

"Jason Miller is here and wonders if he can talk to you a minute."

"Sure, sure," he said graciously, "please have him come in."

She turned and beckoned for Jason to come into the pastor's office and patted him on the shoulder in a motherly gesture of comfort. It was obvious that the young man was distraught.

Jason came in and closed the door before turning to face Pastor Spalding. Standing and gesturing to one of the chairs that was off to the side of his large desk, sensing that this needed to be a close face-to-face, man-to-man talk, Pastor Spalding shook Jason's hand before sitting down. "What can I do for you?"

"Well, uh, sir," Jason stammered uncomfortably, "I guess I need to talk to someone about Nathan and me."

"Sure, I'll be glad to listen," Pastor Spalding replied tenderly, "take as much time as you need."

"Um, I have one question first," Jason said looking directly at the pastor. "Is this confidential? I mean, if I tell you something do you have to tell my parents or the authorities or anything?"

"I generally say that whatever is discussed here stays between you and me and God, but if there's something illegal or dangerous to you or others, then I might have to notify the appropriate authorities. Can you live with that?"

"Yeah," Jason said, still edgy but somewhat relieved. "Okay then, I guess that I'll just plunge in." He started talking rapidly. "I was with Nathan the night he was killed. I was supposed to go with him and Mot, uh," he hesitated and tried to cover his slip, "Max Berryman and pay back some ladies for something. I don't even know who they were but it just didn't seem right. I didn't want to do it. Max just looked so evil, like, I thought he was a Christian even with all his drinking and all, but man! It just felt really creepy so I took off. Nathan didn't and I don't know if he was on his way to do whatever Max wanted to do or if they had done it and he was heading home."

"I see," Pastor Spalding said slowly. "Did I hear you refer to him as Mot?"

"Yeah," Jason said, not quite sure of how much he could confide in this man, "that's what he wants us to call him when we're doing stuff like that with him. He said that it's his power name."

"All right." Pastor Spalding filed that information away for the moment. "What can I help you with?"

"I guess I'm mostly just mad at myself for getting suckered in by Max. I should have said something to Nathan, I mean, he was hesitating. Maybe if I had just said something." He stopped and picked up with his previous train of thought. "Max got us our jobs at his dad's place and he flashes a lot of money around. He promises a lot of … well, girls and even drugs if we want it." He hung his head and confessed, "I smoked some weed with them."

Pastor Spalding kept his face from showing shock or condemnation and continued to listen to Jason, a boy that had been raised in his church, a boy that he had baptized only a few years earlier, a boy who was even now confessing some of the petty crimes that Max had encouraged – including ripping off tools and tires, oil and filters from his own father's business.

"What do you want to do about all of this?" Pastor Spalding asked.

"I feel like I just can't face another day. I feel like I should be dead, too. I feel like I've crossed a line and lost my salvation," Jason blurted out in frustration and despair as he leaned forward, elbows on knees and face buried in his hands. He slowly raised his head, eyes pleading for relief. "And I'm afraid of Max. He said he'd kill us if we ever crossed him; if we ever told."

Pastor Spalding was beginning to understand the depths of Jason's dilemma. He, too, was now stuck in a double-bind as surely as Jason was stuck in a double-bind. Pastor Spalding now knew that Sheriff Bynum was a Satanist. Already suspecting that Max Berryman was as well because of his close tie with the sheriff, it now looked more certain, especially after his recent talk with Abigail.

"Jason," Pastor Spalding said gently, "I can help you somewhat today to get started, but I know a counselor who can really help you with all this mess and I'd like you to meet with her. She's the expert in these things."

Jason was just desperate enough to agree to Pastor Spalding's plan. They spent some time praying and Jason felt relief after confessing his sins – the thefts, the marijuana, the abandonment of his faith. However, he still needed to get extricated from Max and whatever Max represented.

Pastor Spalding made a quick call to Abigail before he left and they were able to arrange for Jason to meet with her the following morning at ten o'clock.

Max was nursing his wounds and what was left of his ego. Second and third degree burns on the palms and fingers of his hands reminded him of the humiliation. Most of the skin had sloughed off and tender pink skin was beginning to appear except for a couple areas of infection. He avoided his parents and kept his fists balled up under his sleeves when he was out.

He was miserable. He was irate. He was scheming about how to get even. Carrie Sue and Abigail Steele were on the top of his list. Jason would have to be dealt with for walking out on him. And then there was that farmer and his buddy that ambushed him three weeks ago. The list went on and on and on. The growing root of bitterness that defiles many was expanding rapidly and driving itself deeper into his empty heart.

Dr. Bacchus was a busy man lately – Zorroz with the throat injury, Mastiff before him with the sudden cancer, and now Mot with the mysterious burns on his hands. What was going on in this territory?

Prinz found himself drawn to his inner sanctum, his worship chamber in the bowels of his abode. He was alarmed once again at the physical changes that he was seeing in the mirror. He vowed to redouble his efforts. January twenty-nine was his current focus beyond all the other rituals that were on the calendar – Casting of

Spells on St. Agnes Eve. Yes, he was prostrate before his lord continually seeking inspiration for the spells and incantations, spiels and hexes, curses and oaths that would help him regain his prowess. There were too many just waiting in the shadows and watching for any indication of weakness.

Abigail hustled through her Friday morning routine of breakfast for herself and Buster so that she could get to the church on time to meet with a new client. Arriving at the church, she noticed the nervous young man looking through the window of the locked door. *Good, he's ready for healing.* She got out of her truck and greeted him, "Hello, I'm Abigail Steele."

"Hi," the young man replied, "I'm Jason Miller. I guess I'm here to meet with you and Pastor Spalding."

"That's the rumor I heard. Are you ready?" Abigail flashed him a friendly smile and busied herself with unlocking the door to the church as well as the one to her office. "You look familiar ... do you attend here?"

"Yes, my whole family goes here. I just haven't been around much lately. I used to sit in the balcony."

She handed him the clipboard with the new client forms on it and instructed him to come into the office when he was finished. Meanwhile, she set up the music and waited for Pastor Spalding. Even though Jason was only nineteen and young enough to be her son, she still wanted to maintain good appearances. She was pleased to have Pastor Spalding sit in on the session so that he could be mentored in the matters that would likely come up today.

Once they were all settled, they opened with prayer and then got into Jason's concerns about Max. Jason told Abigail about Sunday night and his suspicion that Max wanted him and Nathan to come with him and rape a couple of women. "He said that they needed to be taught a lesson."

"Did he tell you why?" Abigail probed. She could not violate Carrie Sue's confidentiality nor did she want to reveal the fact that she, herself, was one of the women. She had to navigate through this potentially sticky conversation carefully.

"Something about them messing with his powers." Jason looked confused. "I don't really know what he's talking about. How could a couple of women mess with his powers? He's always bragging that he can get away with murder."

"Has he ever taken you to meet anyone else? Have you witnessed him killing anyone?" Abigail asked.

"Well, one night." Jason stopped, checked himself, and looked at Pastor Spalding before answering. "No one will find out about this, will they?"

"It depends on what you're about to tell us. You have clergy and counselor privilege here, but if there's something dangerous or illegal or if it affects someone else, we have certain legal obligations. Do you want to take a chance?"

"Yeah, I gotta get it off my chest," Jason sighed and picked up his story. "One night a couple months ago Max got me and Nathan a bunch of weed and a bunch of beer. We smoked most of it and I was pretty high, but I remember what he said. He started talking about taking us to the most amazing all-night party ever. He said that anything goes – alcohol, drugs, sex anyway we wanted it – and then he said something that made me sober up real quick." Jason hesitated and looked uncertainly from Abigail to Pastor Spalding and then back again.

"He said that if we wanted the biggest rush ever, we could kill someone. He said that if we did that, the sky was the limit and we would be in. He said that was what he did for his initiation."

"Do you know who these people are that he parties with?" Abigail asked.

"No, not really," Jason answered. "I thought he was just blowing smoke because we were all drunk and high, but the next week he took us on a horseback ride through the Blue River bottoms. We rode for a long time and ended up at some kind of a camp. There was a small building that was locked up. He found a key, went in, and took out a shovel. He searched around a little bit and then started digging. He turned up a human skull and laughed and said that we were now accessories after the fact or something like that." Jason was really distressed now.

Abigail watched the troubled young man rake his fingers through his hair and then began to talk in a soothing voice, "Jason, you are *not* an accessory after the fact. What you have just described is the way that people like Max get recruits for the cult. They promise them money and sex, drugs and power and then they involve their recruit in some crime, telling them that if they tell or try to leave, either they'll end up in jail or they'll end up dead." She stopped and looked for Jason's reaction.

He nodded and confirmed, "That's pretty much what Max said."

"That was probably what Sunday night was all about. If he could have involved you and Nathan in rape or murder, then he would have had you."

"Yes." Jason was amazed at how much this woman seemed to know. "That's what I was worried about. That's why I left the diner. That's why I'm afraid that Max is going to go after me, or even worse, go after my family." Jason paused and lowered his head as he raked his fingers through his brown hair again. "He said something about my little sister being just perfect. Perfect for what? She's just seven."

"Let me guess," Abigail said, "she's blonde-haired and blue-eyed."

"Yes! How do you know?" The startled Jason was even more anxious but very much intrigued.

"Okay," Abigail paused as she made a decision, "can you handle some scary facts?"

"I think so."

Abigail told Jason that there was a satanic cult in the area. There were Satanists, in fact, who attended their church. Max was one of them. Sheriff Bynum was also one of them. She talked about the authority of the believer and the armor of God. She talked about being at a crossroad in his life and that she believed that this week's circumstances were God's way of getting his attention so that he did not end up like Max, or even worse, like Nathan.

Jason absorbed this information soberly and it was obvious that he was weighing the facts and their implications. He looked incredulously from Abigail to Pastor Spalding. "Is this true?"

"I'm afraid so," the pastor confirmed grimly.

"Why don't you kick them out of the church? Why didn't you warn us?" Jason asked respectfully. He sincerely wanted an answer.

"Son," Pastor Spalding said, "I recently found out all of this myself. We shouldn't be very surprised, though. Doesn't the Bible warn us that there will be wolves in sheep's clothing and tares growing up in the wheat and Satan disguised as an angel of light?"

"Yes sir," Jason answered thoughtfully, "but what can be done about it? I mean, we can't be having these people in the church and endangering my little sister or suckering guys like me..." His voice drifted off but his thoughts continued to percolate. He did not want to voice his fears about Sheriff Bynum's involvement in Satanism, but it made sense as he reflected on things that he observed and heard from Max.

Mot.

"The bottom line question is," Abigail intruded on his thoughts, "what will *you* decide to do?"

His cheeks puffed out as he exhaled through barely parted lips. "I've always known that my rebellion was wrong. I know I've grieved my parents. I destroyed any Christian witness I might have had," he came clean and looked at his feet before abruptly looking up at Abigail and Pastor Spalding. "I want to start over. I want to fight this evil but I don't know how."

"Son," Pastor Spalding said with triumphant smile, "you've already started over. And as for how, let's just trust God to let you know where you go from here."

"Well," he said with resolve, "I know where I'm *not* going. I'm not going to work at Berryman's anymore. I'm going to quit tomorrow and I'll apologize to my folks today."

They talked and prayed about the decisions that he would need to make in the near future. They prayed about the conversation that he was going to have with his parents. Finally, they prayed for his protection and protection for his family – especially his little sister.

After Jason left, Abigail and Pastor Spalding spent some time debriefing and praying about Jason and the church in general. She ate lunch and was back in her office by the time Carrie Sue came breezing through the door. She was ready to work.

They talked about Sunday night's break in and once again Carrie Sue thanked Abigail for helping her repair the door. "I sure don't know how to fix things like that."

"No problem," Abigail said and then quipped, "I always say 'cut it close, slam it in, caulk the gaps, and paint it.'" They chuckled and then moved on to the more serious matter of her birthday.

"I think I know when it really is," Carrie Sue said, "January thirty-one. I don't know why, but it just came to me."

"Maybe one of the pseudos or the original leaked it to you. It would make a crazy kind of sense," Abigail affirmed. "They're using the same two numbers only they're backward – one, three – three, one." Stopping abruptly, she suddenly had a startled look on her face.

"What?"

"Your brother, Danny, died on October thirty-one," Abigail said pensively.

"And Billy's birthday was on July thirty-one," Carrie Sue was following her train of thought.

"Which means," Abigail finished her thought, "he was probably conceived on October 31."

"Oh, wow!" Carrie Sue said, "That makes so much sense. I really think my birthday is next Wednesday – another ritual day, right?"

"Yep, it sure is," Abigail agreed. "Okay, we have some work to do because there are all those other rituals coming practically non-stop all week." They prayed. Since Carrie Sue had been working with Abigail for several years, many of the personalities who had originally been programmed for those rituals had already been healed. They still found and ministered to small pockets of hidden ones. That cocky male alter who threatened Carrie Sue's demise by midnight of her birthday was a little more difficult. He was one of several with the same assignment.

"Okay," Abigail said after a lengthy but fruitless negotiation with the resistant personality, "I need to talk to Carrie Sue again."

"You're just dismissing me?" He was incredulous.

"You've already dismissed me. You don't leave me any choice. I don't want to waste your time." Abigail did not add *or mine*.

"Fine! Be that way! You'll see; we win! We always win." He faded back into his internal place and Carrie Sue resurfaced.

"What are we going to do?" She was distraught.

"He doesn't leave us with much choice. We tried negotiating with him and we need to give him the dignity of believing that what he's saying is true. He made his choice which leaves you with the option of taking authority in this situation."

"What do you mean?"

"I wonder if all his bravado is his way of saying, I-don't-really-want-to-die-and-you-might-be-right-so-get-me-out-of-this-without-getting-punished." Abigail let that sink in and then continued, "As much as we don't want to resemble the cult in any way by coercing anyone, he left you with no other option that I can think of."

Carrie Sue nodded in agreement, "We've done this before and I think you're right." She launched into a prayer asking God to strip all the programming and demons from those who were assigned to kill her, she prayed for their healing and then looked to Abigail to pray in agreement.

When they were finished, Carrie Sue reported that she felt relief.

"Let's see if he's willing to come back and talk again," Abigail suggested.

In a blink, the formerly cocky personality appeared. "I'm glad you finally figured it out; thanks."

"No problem," Abigail smiled, "sorry it took so long. Are the others good?"

"Yeah, we all are. We're tired!"

"Ready for integration?" Abigail asked.

"Yes!"

Abigail handed the privilege of "praying them in" to Carrie Sue who was getting less and less awkward and intimidated by praying out loud. Reporting that she sensed that they were all in, they closed in prayer and made arrangements for their next session.

It was not long before Amy bounced in and flopped into her usual chair in Abigail's office.

"Well," Abigail reacted with amusement, "you look happy today."

"I am," Amy said and then added, "mostly."

"I was a little concerned after the last session with the denial part being so down."

"Well, after the last time, I guess we all just kind of looked at each other, shrugged our shoulders, and said, 'this is what is' and pretty much accepted our reality." Amy said it glibly but had to be masking the deep pain that facing their reality brought to them. Utter rejection is never easy to accept.

"I'm really proud of you; all of you," Abigail said sincerely. "Let's open with prayer and see where the Lord wants to go today."

Head Warden showed up and greeted Abigail in his usual officious manner and then got to business. "Last time you said we needed to look at the big picture and then we got the denial person. Now what?"

"Can you brief me on whatever is going on in the lower levels?" Abigail used Head Warden's vernacular.

"It seems that last week had a positive effect in some ways. It's as if there are a lot of them that don't have to act out any more to prove their point that something bad happened. But there are still those demon-loyal ones who are hell-bent on doing their jobs."

"Let's pray and see who shows up."

Head Warden was displaced by what appeared to be a thumb-sucking child alter who immediately slid to the floor, assumed a fetal position, and began moaning and rocking with her eyes tightly closed.

Abigail prayed that this was not a pre-verbal child alter and silently observed her for a few minutes before saying, "Hey, sweetie, I'm Abigail and I would really like to talk with you. Can you talk?"

"Nuh uh."

"Okay, then, you don't have to talk, but I'm glad that you are smart enough to understand me." Abigail hoped to coax the child into communicating somehow. She had an idea that she was dealing with a deeply wounded six or seven-year-old.

No response.

"Do you know Amy?" Abigail probed gently.

"Nuh, uh."

"Can I tell you about her?"

The little girl's shoulders shrugged.

Abigail took it as I-don't-care or do-what-you-want so she proceeded slowly. "You're a part of Amy. She's the adult. There are a bunch of you in there who are all different ages. Some are grown up and some are still kids like you. If you open your eyes maybe you can see how big your hands are now."

After a few moments the child looked through squinted eyes at her hands which were close to her face. Unable to check her natural curiosity, the child unclenched the fist of her free hand and turned it from the palm to the back of her hand several times but she continued to suck her thumb.

"It's bigger than it used to be, isn't it?" Continuing when she got no further response, Abigail explained, "That's because you stayed stuck at six and Amy kept growing into an adult."

"I'm seven!" the little one asserted as she withdrew her thumb and quickly returned it to her mouth.

"Oh, sorry, I was just guessing. It's hard to tell how big you are because you're all curled up like that. Would you like to sit on the chair? It's nice and soft."

The little one shook her head, but she did sit up keeping her knees under her chin and crossing her ankles. The thumb was removed from her mouth as she looped her arms around her legs. She also dared to venture a quick glance toward Abigail before focusing on the carpet in front of her toes.

"Do you know why you're here today?" Abigail began to probe again. She suspected that the girl was supposed to be involved in the rituals that occurred at the end of January or the beginning of February.

"Nuh, uh."

"I think that some bad people did some bad things to you and they want to do it again."

This brought involuntary full-body shudders and a tighter grip on her legs.

"I want to stop them from doing that, but I need your help," Abigail said. "Can you be brave and tell me what happened the last time?"

Like a turtle peeking out of its protective shell, the little one ventured to look at Abigail as if to decide whether or not she would hazard taking yet another chance on another stranger. After a lengthy silence she finally sighed and began her story pausing frequently. "The bad people had a little baby and they said that I was s'posed to ... supposed to ... take the knife and ... and stab her ... stab her in the heart."

She faltered frequently in the grisly story of how she was supposed to kill the baby who was the featured sacrifice at the ritual that night. Somehow this amazing little girl had the grit to refuse. She described the large metal trash can into which they forced her, sealing the top so that she could not escape. They drummed on the can all throughout the ritual and at the end of the evening, they opened the lid and callously dumped the eviscerated infant on top of her and resealed it, leaving her to nearly die of hypothermia. She sat in the can in virtually the same position that she presently displayed in front of Abigail.

"The next night, the bad people took me out and... and they had another baby. They told me that I had to kill... to kill this baby... and they said... they said that if I kill this baby no more babies would have to die. But if I didn't... if I didn't kill her... they would do it really mean and make the baby hurt more. They said that... they said that they would kill another baby every night until I did it... and then it would be all my fault."

Abigail listened as the little one haltingly continued to relate her gruesome story. She had refused once again because she knew it was wrong. Once again, she was thrown back into the trash can and the second baby was thrown in when the cult finished ravishing her tiny body. Night after night this one had to endure being in the trash can with the stench of dead babies and the bloody slime oozing over her. She said that she did not remember what happened after the sixth night.

In Abigail's experience with these survivors, the cessation of memories meant that this one would have shut down completely and another personality would have split off of her and taken over the ghastly duties. Often there were "chains" of personalities who each split off of the previous one.

Generally speaking, each personality's first and last memories were the most horrific as they continued where the previous one shut down and then shut down themselves and handed the baton to the newly created personality. This scenario might be repeated hundreds and hundreds of times resulting in thousands of new personalities from just one horrific ritual.

Abigail was able to find the protector of this one and was not surprised to discover that there were sixty-six more little girls and teens between the ages of seven and seventeen. After some negotiation, Abigail was able to pray the comprehensive "sozo" prayer with all of them and they were healed and integrated.

Amy resurfaced feeling much relieved about the healings and integrations. They closed with prayer and made arrangements for the following week. Amy was feeling like she made the right decision about getting out of Satanism.

Closing the office and approaching the outside door, Abigail heard footsteps echoing through the hallway and coming toward her. Whirling around quickly, she was relieved to see Pastor Spalding coming around the corner. *I'm getting jumpy these days.*

"Hello," she greeted him with a smile, "or maybe I should say good-bye, I was just heading out the door."

"I'm glad I caught you. Do you have a couple of extra minutes?"

"Sure," Abigail said with a twinkle in her eye, "I don't actually have much of a life."

"Well, you sure seem to be in the middle of a lot of activity from what I can tell," he countered with a hint of humor coming back into his tone. "And that's what I wanted to talk to you about."

"Okay."

"Let me get to the point and let you get on your way," Pastor Spalding continued. "I'm a part of a small ministerial alliance in this county. Once a month three or four of us get together and discuss our churches and our outreaches into the community. During our last meeting, I told them the story behind the story about

Nathan Powell. I told them about Jason's narrow escape from the cult and then I told them that I have Satanists in my congregation."

"Oh, I'll bet that got a reaction."

"Yes, but not what I expected. Dennis Walsh, the pastor of that little charismatic community church, told me that he's suspected something for quite a while. Paul Overton, the Methodist pastor, didn't dispute it, but seemed open about the whole matter. I mean, he wasn't going to call me a liar or a storyteller. And Mike Griffin, from the Presbyterian church across town, said that he's found some very peculiar things in his church over the years – things moved around a little bit, stains in the carpet, and just a sense that something was not quite right."

"Interesting."

"I told them that I had a counselor in my church who worked with SRA survivors and they seemed very anxious to learn more," Pastor Spalding continued. "I told them that I would ask you if you would come to our next meeting and answer questions and maybe explain some things."

"Yes." Abigail jumped at the opportunity. "I'd love to. When is your next meeting?"

"The first Monday of the month," he answered, "I know it's short notice, but can you make it February fifth? We rotate churches and this month it'll be right here at noon. Ginny will make us a light lunch and we can talk and pray between bites."

"Like I said," Abigail said, "I don't have a life, so count me in."

13

Monday, February 5

February brought forecasts of cold and snow, clouds and bitter winds. Abigail put Buster into his stall in the barn when the temperatures dipped into the single digits or below. He did not like to be confined and preferred the old lean-to where he could come and go as he pleased. Abigail preferred not to have to haul water down to the barn, but she fired up the four-wheeler to haul water and did what was necessary to keep her horse comfortable until the temperatures rose.

Although she had not met any of the other pastors and was not sure of what to expect, Abigail was excited about the meeting with the Ministerial Alliance. Breathing a brief prayer as she made her way to the church just before noon, Abigail was at peace. "Lord, allow me to say exactly what needs to be said and nothing more. Increase my discernment and bless me with favor, amen."

She brought some handouts with her just in case they would be needed – "Abuse Symptoms in Ritual Abuse Children" and "Abuse Symptoms in non-Ritual Abuse Children." She thought that would be a good introduction. She did not want to overwhelm them or sound like someone with a vivid imagination, but she brought along copies of the "List of Satanic Holidays" just in case it got that far.

By the time Abigail made her way to the fellowship hall just off of the kitchen, Ginny had already set a table and had the tempting aromas filling the kitchen and spilling into the hall. "Abigail!" Ginny exclaimed in her usual effervescent manner, "How are you? Are you keeping warm?"

"I'm great," Abigail replied, "and whatever you've got cooking in there smells wonderful."

"Thanks. It's just an old family recipe for a thick 'venistrone' soup."

"Venistrone?" Abigail asked.

"Yeah," Ginny said with a twinkle and a laugh, "it's minestrone soup made with venison."

"Yum!"

They both looked up as Pastor Spalding entered the far end of the fellowship hall with the other three men. Ginny retreated and began to put out the pot of soup and a basket filled with crackers and breads, a plate with sliced cheeses and one of raw vegetables, a pitcher of iced tea and a pot of coffee. One last trip back into the kitchen produced a plate piled high with homemade oatmeal raison cookies.

"Enjoy!" Ginny chirped. "Call me if you need anything and don't worry about clean up," she did a mock scolding as she shook her index finger in their direction and bustled back to her office.

Pastor Spalding thanked her and the others voiced their thanks as well. They found places around the table and bowed their heads as Pastor Spalding prayed a blessing over the meal. After looking up, he said, "Gentlemen, this is Abigail Steele. She's a counselor here and she's an expert when it comes to the things that we discussed last time. I asked her to join us to answer your questions and help us come up with a strategy to deal with this problem in our area."

They each nodded and smiled at Abigail as they began to pass platters of food in the family-style meal.

Pastor Spalding went right to the heart of the matter after he opened with prayer and began to tell the other ministers about the conversation that he and Abigail had with the other young man that was connected to the death of Nathan.

"Now, I don't want to violate confidentiality, so I won't mention any identifying details, but suffice it to say, that after that session with the young man and Abigail here," he nodded toward Abigail, "I know that we definitely have a problem with Satanism right here in our own county."

The three men looked expectantly at Pastor Spalding and then at Abigail. Finally, Reverend Mike Griffin, the Presbyterian minister, spoke up, "Well, I'm not sure where to start," he said looking at Abigail, "but I've seen some suspicious things in my church and now I'm really beginning to wonder. I mean, I had no idea that Satanists would show up in church let alone do rituals there. How does that happen?"

"What leads you to think that there have been rituals in your church?" Abigail asked pointedly.

"Well," he hedged a little, "it's just a bunch of little things that I didn't think were even related until I spoke to Daniel here." He nodded at Pastor Spalding and continued, "I found what looked like small blood stains and wax on the carpet around the communion table. Stuff gets moved around a bit once in a while, but I know our janitor; he's a stickler for putting everything back exactly where it was after he vacuums and cleans. In fact, he's the one who alerted me to some of these things."

"I wonder if there's any way you and your janitor could come up with dates, or at least the weeks when you noticed that these things happened. Do you happen to remember the last time something seemed amiss?" Abigail asked.

He thought for a moment and then said, "Yes, yes I do. It was about a month ago." He paused and stared up at the ceiling for a moment with his eyes casting back and forth as he searched for the information. "It was," he paused and reached into his pocket for his phone and thumbed the surface until he found what he was looking for, "it was the first Sunday of January; the seventh." He looked expectantly at Abigail.

Abigail prayed silently and then reached into her office-in-a-bag and pulled out a folder. Extracting a stapled document, she glanced over it, put her index finger on the date and then looked up at the minister.

"January seventh was Orthodox Christmas. January sixth was Epiphany. They're both satanic holidays as well. It was cold and it would make sense that they'd go indoors and desecrate a church on those holy days."

She paused as eyebrows rose in surprise and then continued, "Actually, that entire week was pretty active. There was the first, which was New Year's Day and the third, which was also a full moon. Those are both ritual days."

"What is that you have there, if I may ask?"

"It's a list of satanic holidays," Abigail replied. "I brought extra copies for each of you."

"Where do you get something like this?" Pastor Walsh asked incredulously.

"I don't remember exactly where I got this one. There are several variations, but basically you can count on a satanic ritual to counter any Christian, Judaic, Catholic, or other religious holy day. Then there are the full moons and often new moons, eclipses, solstices, and other astrological signs. And they love the number thirteen, so they celebrate the first and the third of each month; they love it when the thirteenth lands on a Friday, and then there's the thirty-first of the month because it's the reverse of those numbers." Abigail heard their involuntary gasps as they began to mentally calculate the sheer number of satanic rituals that would occur every year.

"I'm just blown away," Reverend Paul Overton said. "And you think this is happening in our county?"

"Unfortunately, I *know* it's happening in this county. I work with survivors who live here."

"Okay," he pursued, "so some kids paint graffiti on trains and overpasses. Some cat gets hung or burned or whatever they do. Isn't that just normal stuff that they grow out of?"

"Perhaps that kind of stuff is," Abigail conceded, "but I'm talking about Satanists who were raised by Satanists generation after generation. These people infiltrate our communities and, yes, our churches, and do not want anyone to know about their cult activities. These Satanists try to keep a low profile while they raise families and run businesses and attend church."

The ministers continued to pepper Abigail with question after question. She was able to field them well and give concise answers. She went into more depth only when they pursued it. Finally, Pastor Spalding looked at his watch and said, "Why don't we table the discussion here? I have a feeling that we could talk for hours more but I think we all want to spend some time praying about a solution. How can we eradicate this evil from our county? How do we begin to transform this community?"

"Abigail," Pastor Walsh turned and asked, "what do you recommend?"

"First of all, we have to remember that the enemy is the enemy, not these people. I think that on a practical level, we need to pray for God to expose the darkness and increase our discernment so that we recognize a person or a site or an activity." Abigail paused and was grateful that all their heads were nodding. "We must remember our authority in Christ but we also must operate within our own jurisdiction."

"What exactly do you mean by that?" Reverend Overton asked for clarification.

"We can cast demons out all we want, but if they've been given a legal right to be in our community, we're not only wasting our breath, we're risking attack. But you each have God-given and man-given jurisdiction over the property and souls of your churches. Let's pray for spiritual house cleansing, safety, discernment, wisdom, and more warriors."

"Okay, that makes good sense," Paul Overton said. "If it's all right with everyone, would you lead us in a prayer today?"

"I'd be glad to," Abigail agreed, "but when I'm finished, it would be good for each of you to pray out loud and in agreement with what I pray and then add anything else that the Holy Spirit might quicken to your mind."

They did just that. This small group of five believers launched a missile through the heavens that screamed past hordes of infuriated demons who were powerless to stop it. The incense-laden prayers of the saints added to the bowls being filled before the throne of their God. Soon the bowls would overflow and pour out answers to the earnest prayers.

On Wednesday, Abigail met Carrie Sue in the foyer and they chatted for a few minutes before the service. They talked about mundane things for a minute and then Abigail asked, "So, how was your birthday?"

"It was interesting," Carrie Sue responded. "I really believe that the thirty-first is my true birthday. It just fits and my mother came by. She's been mostly staying away, but she showed up last Wednesday."

"What did she do?" Abigail was curious.

"It was odd," Carrie Sue said and then laughed. "But then, what isn't odd when it comes to my life? Mom started talking about wanting me to help with sprucing up the flower beds. Hello? It's winter!"

"What did she want you to do?"

"She said something about how dad just loved tending to the flower beds, the roses, especially. And when she said that, I just got chills all up and down my spine. What's up with that?" Carrie Sue wondered.

"Well, I guess someone got triggered. Remind me when we meet on Friday and we'll pray about it," Abigail responded.

Just then the door opened and a gust of cold air infiltrated the foyer. Eyes ablaze with hatred, face contorted in a sneer, Max approached the two women and snarled through gritted teeth in a barely audible voice, "You're responsible! You'll pay and pay dearly!" Looking Carrie Sue in the eyes, he hissed, "You got away once, but that ain't happening again, you'll see."

"I renounce that in the name of Jesus the Christ, Max Berryman," Abigail responded fiercely pointing an index finger at his heart. "No weapon formed against us will prosper. Give it up, Max! Get right with God."

"Enjoy that horse while you still got him!" Max hissed his venomous retort before he turned and fled from the church.

Carrie Sue and Abigail looked at each other in stunned silence and said nothing. Looking around, Abigail noticed very puzzled looks on the faces of a handful of people who happened to see the exchange between Max and the two women.

"Come on, let's get a seat," Abigail said.

"Good idea," Carrie Sue agreed. "Let's sit by Cindy and Gary.

"Good idea."

They settled into the pew and Abigail quietly told Cindy and Gary about the most recent threat. Lee was sitting on the other side of Gary so he got the message from Gary. He was not pleased. Gary was not pleased. God-given protectiveness flared up in both of the men. The group decided that they would stop at the local diner for a discussion and prayer session after church.

Their conversation was interrupted when Pastor Spalding took the microphone and began the service. The musicians quietly left the stage as he opened with a prayer and then began to teach.

"Turn with me to the ninth chapter of Mark." Pastor Spalding waited for the rustle of pages to quiet and then read verses fourteen through twenty-nine. When he finished, he began to go through the various points of the story of the demon that the disciples could not cast out.

"Picture this scene," he said, "Jesus just got back from the transfiguration with His A-team – Peter, James, and John. The other nine guys were asked by a father to cast a demon out of his son. They could not do it so the father came to Jesus and told Him that his B-team failed. Here the father is – describing how the demon dashes the kid to the ground, makes him foam at the mouth, grinding his teeth, and so on. It sounds kind of like an epileptic seizure."

He paused and let his gaze drift over the small crowd before he continued. "How does Jesus respond? He said, '*O unbelieving generation, how long shall I be with you? How long shall I put up with you? Bring him to Me!*' It sounds like Jesus is a bit frustrated; exasperated with these people. If we go back to the original Greek, we see that 'unbelieving' means 'twisted thinking.'"

Noticing the nods as the congregation followed him, he continued. "I would love to have been there to watch this. I mean, they brought the boy to Jesus and the demon throws him into a fit. Right in front of Jesus! That takes a lot of nerve! But then, I think that when a demon is about to lose its assignment, it gets a bit desperate. Did you ever notice that in people? When they are cornered, when they are sensing defeat or doom, they get angry and vindictive and do irrational things and threaten people."

Several people nodded in agreement. Carrie Sue nudged Abigail lightly. They looked at each other with knowing smiles and slight nods.

"Okay, picture this scene." Pastor Spalding was warming up. "The kid is writhing and foaming at the feet of Jesus and Jesus casually asks his father, '*so, just how long has this been happening to him?*' The father answers Him and gives a fairly lengthy description of how the kid had been thrown into water and fires and was nearly killed ever since he was a little guy. Hello? Just heal the poor kid!" Several chuckles were heard throughout the auditorium.

"The father finally gets to the point and implores Jesus to have pity on them and heal his son if He could. It sounds like Jesus was irate and responds, *'If you can! All things are possible to him who believes.'* To which the father answered, *'I do believe, help my unbelief.'* He's saying, 'I believe, but my thinking is twisted which makes it hard to think that my son would ever be healed. My twisted thinking leads me to believe the compelling lies of the enemy because of what I see happening in my son.'"

Pastor Spalding leaned over the podium putting his hand on his heart and looked around the room, "How many of us fall into that trap? I know that I have from time to time." He always made sure that he was not pointing fingers but honestly including himself.

"Well, Jesus noticed the crowd gathering so He quickly rebuked the demon. Would you believe that insolent demon had the nerve to throw the kid into one last terrible convulsion? It was so bad that the people thought the boy was dead. But Jesus took him by the hand and he stood up."

Pastor Spalding made a few more observations about the incident and then moved to his conclusion. "Okay, folks, this is where the rubber meets the road. The disciples later asked Jesus why they couldn't cast out the demon. Listen to Jesus' answer, *'This kind cannot come out by anything but prayer.'* And some versions add *'and fasting.'* Most of us have been taught that the 'this kind' that Jesus was talking about was the kind of demon." There were many nods of affirmation.

"Yes, the demon was powerful and insolent. He was bold and desperate enough to do what he did right in front of Jesus. But that is not what Jesus is talking about. Look back at this passage. In these few verses, the focus of Jesus is on belief and unbelief, right thinking and twisted thinking, not on the demon. The demon was just there because of their unbelief, their twisted, faulty thinking. The only power a demon has is the power to deceive. Jesus did not pray or fast before He cast out the demon. He didn't have twisted thinking. He was thinking like His Father thought. He knew His authority. The disciples did not. The father did not. The crowd did not."

Pastor Spalding paused again and said, "Folks, how many of you are like that father bringing your concerns, your family, your job, your health, your friends, anything and everything to Jesus and all it does is convulse and roll and foam and grind at your feet? And you start thinking, 'this has been happening for such a long time, it'll never be healed or fixed.' How many of you are fighting the battle on the wrong front, perhaps? You're focused on the demon when you should be focusing on your doubt and your twisted thinking. How many of you have whispered in despair, 'I do believe; please help my unbelief?'" The congregation was pensive in the brief silence before Pastor Spalding gave his invitation and the musicians filed back up to the stage to play quietly.

Several people came up front to do business with God. The McCords and Lee, Abigail and Carrie Sue made their way to the back making plans to meet at the little Greek restaurant nearby. Abigail, Carrie Sue, and Lee Norris got there about the same time since Gary and Cindy had to pick up Bryan and Traci from children's church. They grabbed a large round table in the corner and waited for the McCord family.

Carrie Sue felt awkward and kept quiet, but Abigail engaged Lee in a conversation about the progress he was making on his new property. "Every once in a while, I hear you fire up that back hoe-tractor thing you have and I wonder how the place is shaping up."

"You ought to come down some time and see," Lee said cordially and nodding at Carrie Sue, he added, "you're welcome anytime, too. I'll give you the nickel tour." He proceeded to describe how he had built a lean-to for Misty, Sassy, Lady, and Sparkles so they could get out of the weather. He told them about the progress he was making on weatherizing the barn and the other out buildings. The new pump for the well was in place and working. He was just about to tell them about clearing the site for the house that would be built as soon as the weather broke when Gary and his family came in the door.

The waitress efficiently brought their drinks and took their orders in spite of Bryan and Lee's animated conversation. "When can I ride your horsey?" Bryan asked and then peppered Lee with more questions about riding the 'whacter' – his pronunciation of 'tractor' – and building his barn.

"Pretty soon," Lee answered patiently.

"Hey, little buddy," Gary addressed his son, "the adults need to talk about some important stuff right now. How about if you and Traci work on coloring those papers while we do that? You'll have time to talk to Cousin Lee pretty soon."

The little guy was clearly disappointed, but he nodded his head and reached for the three crayons that came with his place setting. Traci was already busy diligently filling in the pictures without going out of the lines. The adults began to talk about Max, using general terms and tried to speak in code so that the big ears of the little people would not pick up something that they should not misinterpret.

"I think God was reminding us through Pastor Spalding tonight that our friend is feeling desperate, like he's going to lose his assignment and therefore, he's getting angry and nasty," Abigail said.

"I agree," Gary said, "I think God's going to give him just enough rope to hang himself."

"But," Lee injected, "what kind of damage can and will he do before he's finished?"

"I'm concerned about the safety of his targets, too," Cindy added. "I know that no weapon formed against us will prosper but look how far he got the other night. And," she looked at Abigail, "look at what happened to another pet."

"I think," Lee said looking at Abigail and Carrie Sue, "that both of you need to go to the sheriff's office in the morning when it opens and file a complaint about the threats. Get a copy of it and if something happens, you will have it on record."

"I really don't like the thought of facing the top guy and I'm not sure who else is like him, but I think you're right," Abigail agreed reluctantly.

"I'll be glad to go with you, if you like," Lee offered.

"I think that's a good idea," Gary concurred. "I remember what it was like the last time we visited there. It'll be good to have someone with you. I'd go, too, but someone has to work." He winked at Cindy.

"I'll go!" Bryan looked up from his coloring and volunteered enthusiastically. He had no idea where they were going, but any place with two of his favorite people was all right with him.

They chuckled at Bryan and the conversation turned to the food as the waitress brought their selections. Gary prayed over the meal and asked for continued favor, blessings, and safety for everyone. He also blessed Max Berryman and asked God to bring him transformation. They enjoyed their time of fellowship and before they parted ways, the men each told Carrie Sue to be careful and extra watchful. She gratefully accepted their phone numbers and promised to call if there was anything suspicious.

Max Berryman was cruising through town ever on the prowl for trouble. He was a magnet for disgruntled teens. Tonight, he swung by the park and was pleased to see a small group of about six or seven hanging out under the street lights, leaning against their vehicles despite the cold. He was also pleased to see several of them smoking cigarettes because it usually indicated rebellious or defiant kids. They were much easier to prey upon. He needed to redeem himself and bring in more recruits. Nathan was dead and Jason quit his job and said that he was done. He meant more than just being done with the job. *I'll deal with him the next time I see him.*

The thought of Jason made his blood boil and he decided that this would not be such a good night to try to recruit anyone, after all. It was time to soothe his wounded ego. Hitting the accelerator and jamming the stick into gear, he roared out of the park and headed for home. His parents either did not know that he used drugs or they did not want to know. Crushing a roxy, adrenaline rising, introducing the powerful pain killer into his system, Max was soon drifting into that peaceful place that never lasted long enough, that never satisfied well enough.

Unknown to him, however, illicitly using that potent drug was an open invitation to the spirit of pharmakia. The demon lured and lulled Max into a passive state while deceiving Max into believing that he was still in control. Not tonight, oh no, not tonight; but eventually at a more opportune time, this spirit, the drug landlord would require a payment for penalties and back taxes. If Max could only hear in the spiritual realm, his blood would have run cold at the sound of the diabolical shriek that came out of the fang-lined, drool-spattered lips of this triumphant principality who was patiently waiting to collect.

Jason attended church with his parents that Wednesday night for the first time in a long time. He even sat next to them in the pew with his sister. He was surprised at how interested he was in the sermon; he was surprised at the hunger he felt to know more. When he got home he rummaged through his book shelves until he found his old Bible. It was one that he received many years ago when he was baptized. His name was embossed in gold on the cover. Opening it reverently, Jason began to read where the book opened naturally to Psalm thirty-six. He read about the contrast between the ungodly man and the children of men. *Wow! Was I ever on the wrong path!* Jason began to pray one of the first genuine, heart-felt prayers of his young life. He asked for forgiveness and for direction. When he rose off of his knees, he felt like a different man and he was determined to live for Christ.

"Mom! Dad!" Jason called as he bounded down the stairs and into the living room where his parents were watching the news. "Can we talk?"

"Sure, son," Paul Miller replied as he muted the television. "Sit down, what's up?" His mother, Cassie, remained quiet but was just as curious about the recent changes in their son's life.

"I dug out my old Bible and started reading one of the Psalms. I understand it like I never could before. I mean, I was reading about how the ungodly were so deceived and defiant against God." He hung his head momentarily before he continued, "that was me and now I just want to be one of God's children. Do you know that it says we drink from the river of His delights? I don't exactly know what that means, but I want it. I want everyone I know to have it." He rattled on in excitement while his parents sat listening happily astounded at the transformation in their son.

When he stopped, Cassie looked at him in mock seriousness and said, "Just who are you and what have you done with my son?"

"I think I am the real Jason. I mean, the Jason that God wants me to be is what I want now. I want to go into the ministry somehow and be like Pastor Spalding or Mrs. Steele. I want to reach teenagers, especially, so they don't have to get suckered down a dark path like me and Nathan did."

"Are you talking about going to Bible College?" his father asked.

"Yeah," Jason replied thoughtfully, "yeah, I think that's what I need to do. I mean, I've just been drifting since high school. It's about time I do something right for a change." He looked expectantly from his mother to his father and back again.

"Well," Paul answered, "I think that sounds great. Do you want help researching Bible Colleges? We'll certainly help you with scholarship and grant apps."

"Yeah," Jason said gratefully, "you've both been to college, you kind of know the ropes. But I'll get on the internet tonight and start looking."

Cassie was suddenly confronted with the thought of her son leaving home for the first time. It was what every parent worked toward, but when the nest began to empty, there was a tug especially on a mother's heart. "Well," she said, "you have a lot of decisions to make – campus size, denominational affiliation, cost, location, and so much more. How exciting!" She tried to make her voice sound enthusiastic even as her heart was simultaneously breaking and bursting with joy.

Carrie Sue met Abigail at the sheriff's office. Lee pulled up two minutes later. They greeted one another and then Abigail suggested that they pray a minute before going inside.

Once inside, Lee led the way to the desk and asked, "Where do we go to report a threat?"

The deputy sheriff looked up from his computer and said flatly, "Right here. What kind of threat?"

Lee stepped back and Abigail stepped forward. "Last night a man threatened to kill my horse and to attack me. He also threatened this lady." She nodded toward Carrie Sue.

"We can't do anything unless there's been an actual attack." The deputy sounded bored as he recited the official protocol.

"He already broke into my house once but I was afraid to report it then," Carrie Sue added.

The deputy huffed as he stood up and walked over to a bank of file cabinets behind him. Looking at the labels, he opened a drawer and withdrew two sheets of paper. "Fill out these forms and bring them back to me," he said dryly.

Carrie Sue and Abigail took the forms and went over to a clear part of the counter and began to fill in the date, time, name of the alleged offender, and other details pertaining to the threat. Once they finished, they brought them back to the deputy who took them and laid them aside on his desk.

"Excuse me," Lee interjected, "would it be possible for these ladies to get copies of these complaints?"

"We don't normally do that." The deputy tried to come up with a reason for denying the request.

"I've been here before with complaints," Abigail said, "it would help me keep this documented. I know you'll follow up, I'm just one of those people who need a little help remembering details." She gave him her friendliest smile.

"Well," he conceded, "I suppose it wouldn't hurt." He turned to the copy machine, made the copies and handed them back to the ladies.

"Thank you so much," Abigail said, "we really do appreciate it and we'll feel better knowing that you're going to keep this man from hurting us again." She said it but did not believe it. "Since I'm here, could you tell me the status of my last complaint?"

Looking at her last name on the current complaint, sighing loudly as he took his seat by the computer, the deputy looked at the keys, pecked at six of them, and waited for the screen to give him the information. "Sorry, nothing's in here under your name," he said. "You spell it s-t-e-e-l-e, right?"

"Yes, sir," Abigail replied. "It was filed just a few weeks ago."

The deputy did not reply but grunted and went back to his computer. "I don't see nothing." He was clearly annoyed. "Look, I have things to do here; I'll check later and contact you if I find anything."

Abigail was not surprised, but there was nothing further that they could do. The three friends went out the door and to their vehicles. The ladies each thanked Lee for being there. "Well, at least that's done," Carrie Sue said. "But I don't have very much confidence in their protection."

"Me either," Abigail echoed, "but I *am* confident in the Lord's protection."

Carrie Sue opened her car door and smiled at Abigail as she said, "See ya tomorrow!"

"See ya," Abigail said.

"So," Lee ventured as they watched Carrie Sue back out of her parking space and head down the road, "do you want to come up to the farm and see what I've been up to?"

"I'd love to," Abigail replied, once again hoping that she had not sounded too eager. "I'll follow you."

Abigail followed Lee up his driveway and they awkwardly approached each other. "Come on into the barn, I'll show you what I've been working on." They went into the side door and were greeted with earthy, musty, oily combination of aromas that are unique to old barns. Lee flipped on the lights.

"That's new. When did the electric get hooked up?"

"It's been a couple of months. Now I can see and I can hook up a heater in my shop." They wandered down the middle of the spacious old barn and Lee pointed out the repaired stalls and windows, the feed bins and his shop.

Abigail was impressed with his organization and complimented him, "This is quite a change from the last time I saw it. You really have been working hard." Her eyes roamed over the shelves and the items that were hanging along the walls. "Nice tools! Carpenter, machinist, and mechanic. And you're a welder, too?"

Lee was pleased that she was not only impressed, she was knowledgeable. They continued to meander around the property and ended up down by the horses. After some time, Abigail thanked Lee for the tour and his presence at the sheriff's office earlier and then left for home.

If they could have read each other's mind, they would have known that they were having similar thoughts and feelings. Hopeful, yet tentative; excited, yet cautious; lonely, yet unsure about giving up solitude. They each replayed every word spoken by themselves and by the other.

14

Friday, February 9

In the clear and crisp morning Abigail could see her breath as she walked down to take care of Buster. She felt a momentary lurch in her stomach when she did not see him immediately. *Lord, please don't let Max or anyone else hurt him.* Finally, she heard him pounding up the trail, nostrils flared, and head tossing in exaggerated nods as he circled around her. Settling down with muffled throat-clearing sounds, Buster quickly nibbled his sweet feed.

Abigail made out her grocery list, started a load of laundry, and ate an early lunch. Getting into her truck, she drove slowly down the winding driveway on her way to the church where she hustled into the church and efficiently got things set up in the office. Carrie Sue was not far behind and soon they began their prayer session.

"You told me to remind you about the bio-mom's flower garden thing," Carrie Sue started.

"I'm glad you remembered. Let's open with prayer and see what the Lord shows us," Abigail responded. She led the prayer and then waited to hear what Carrie Sue sensed.

"Rosebud; I just hear the word rosebud."

"Okay, let's keep praying." Abigail prayed for the Lord's illumination and watched as Carrie Sue shifted in her seat. It was obvious that someone else had switched in. "Hello," Abigail said softly, sensing that it was a child, "I'm Abigail, who are you?"

The personality slowly took in the room and when her eyes finally settled on Abigail, she said, "My name is Rosebud."

"Oh, you must know something about your father's rose garden," Abigail said.

The little girl shuddered. It was very apparent that whatever she saw or remembered was frightening or repulsive. She nodded her head and shrank back into the chair.

"You're safe here," Abigail assured her. "Are you scared or do you have yukky memories? Or both?"

"Both," Rosebud replied softly. Her eyes were as big as saucers and it made Carrie Sue look so young.

"Do you know that your father died recently?"

Surprise registered on her face as she slowly shook her head. Her eyes opened even wider. She did not ask, but it was apparent that she wanted to know more.

"He got real sick, I think it was pancreatic cancer and he died a couple of months ago. Does that make you feel a little bit safer?"

"Yes," Rosebud replied with obvious relief.

"Do you think you can tell me about your father's flower gardens? Why is that so scary?" Abigail had a hunch but she did not want to ask leading questions.

"Daddy always said that our roses needed special fertilizer. He called it bone meal or something like that." She paused and looked deeply into Abigail's eyes as if to reassure herself that it was safe to proceed with her story. Taking a deep breath, she launched into her account of being her father's gardening assistant. He would take her with him into the workshop and take blackened bones out of a bag and grind them up. Together they would go to the rose garden and rake it into the dirt. "Sometimes he just buried the bones in the dirt because he said he didn't have time to grind them up."

Abigail had a pretty good idea about the source of those bones. Satanists were careful to dispose of any remains after their rituals. *Could he really be that bold or careless as to bury the bones in his own back yard?* Abigail sensed that there was more to the story. "Why are you so scared? You made Carrie Sue shake when we talked about the rose garden," Abigail intentionally probed.

"Daddy said that if I told, he would put me in the ground, too, and I really would be a rosebud," the little one said bravely.

"Well, he can't do anything to you now. What else besides bones did your daddy bury there?" Abigail asked, hoping to solve the mystery of Rosebud's fears.

"One time a man came to our house and he and daddy had a big fight in the kitchen. They were yelling at each other and then they started hitting. Daddy hit the man with Mommy's big pan right over his head. He was bleeding a lot and then it looked like he was sleeping on our floor."

"What happened then?" Abigail asked.

"Daddy looked at us kids and told us that we had more fertilizer for the pretty flowers. He went outside and when he came back inside he made Danny and Billy help him. He told us that it was our family secret and that we should never, never tell."

"How old were you when that happened?"

"Nine."

Abigail was doing the math in her head. Carrie Sue was now thirty-four so this would have happened about 1981 or 1982. She made a mental note to search for missing persons on her computer.

Engaging the child in further conversation, Abigail was able to ascertain that there were several other murders that she had witnessed in her parents' home. While Rosebud herself was not traumatized more than witnessing the murders, there were several other little ones who had been subjected to worse torment. One of them was put into a make-shift coffin with a dead body overnight in their basement. Abigail accessed each one in this group as well as their protectors and prayed with them for healing and integration.

"Whew!" Carrie Sue exclaimed when she resurfaced. "That explains a lot. I always wondered why I had such creepy feelings around the flower beds and why I have an aversion to roses. Do you really think there are bodies buried in their back yard?"

"I wouldn't be surprised," Abigail said. "I'll tell you what you might want to do now that you have their memories and a rough idea of the date. Try checking the internet for archives of the local newspapers to see if there was anyone missing."

"You know, I might just do that."

They closed with prayer and made their next appointment. Shortly after Carrie Sue left, Amy Bolton arrived for her appointment. On time. They fell into their routine banter for a couple of minutes and then opened with prayer. As expected, Amy receded and Head Warden appeared.

"How's it going?" Abigail knew that she would get a no-nonsense report on the internal situations.

"Mostly good," he replied, "but there is one concern. It is getting dark in here, at least that's the best way I can describe it. Kind of like an eclipse, light but dark. And it feels heavy. You have used the word oppressive in the past and I think that might best describe it."

Abigail almost smiled at this very analytical part of Amy who was using words that bordered on feelings. "Let's pray and ask the Lord to take us to the root of this oppression."

He nodded his assent and they prayed together. Immediately, a very hostile personality switched in and glared at Abigail. "Just who do you think you are summoning me?" he demanded.

"I didn't summon anyone," Abigail replied mildly.

"Then what am I doing here?" he asked insolently.

"You tell me," Abigail countered. "We're just trying to figure out why the darkness is more apparent lately and why the extra oppression."

"Ha!" he spat. "You think you're so smart and you can't figure that out. Why should I tell you anything?"

He's stalling for time and wondering what I really know. "I know that you're controlled by programming and a demon and that he's the reason for the darkness. It's probably there because some moon phase is about to happen and that means that you and your buddies have an assignment to carry out." Abigail paused and almost enjoyed his consternation which confirmed that what she was sensing from the Holy Spirit was on target. "And, you're probably from Apollyon's level."

Trying to hide his shock, the caustic part countered with the usual vitriolic denial of being controlled. He let loose a venomous tirade filled with threats against both Amy and Abigail.

Abigail made it a policy to intercept abusive tirades, especially when they were filled with spicy language. "In the name of Jesus the Christ, shut up."

Immediately, the personality stopped and looked incredulously at Abigail. He was not accustomed to being ordered by anyone but his superiors. "Woman, who do you think you are telling me to shut up?"

"I have jurisdiction over this room and authority from Jesus the Christ. Who do you think you are?" Abigail countered. She was cautious about answering questions because the one who asked the questions was the one in charge.

Puffing up his chest, throwing his shoulders back, he said, "Craven."

"Huh! Appropriate," Abigail replied.

"What do you mean?" Craven asked suspiciously, eyebrows furrowing.

"You'll just go into another tirade if I tell you," Abigail sighed lightly as she responded with an almost bored tone. She was intentionally stringing him along so that she could gauge how much she wanted to continue the dialogue.

"I can control that," he conceded. "But I still think that you're a cocky, know-it-all b..." he cut himself off before he finished his thought.

"Okay," Abigail said, "I'll take a chance that you're a man of your word. The definition of the word craven is 'cowardly, gutless, spineless, weak,' and other fear-driven descriptions like that. Why would they name you Craven?"

Face flushing, veins popping out on his forehead, he spoke with a staccato, "I am not a coward. You have no idea what I am capable of." He stopped out of sheer frustration and grunted.

"I believe that you have done some pretty tough stuff, but I also believe that you did it because of programming and demons," Abigail was attempting to calm him down again. "And, I also believe that you are probably the low man on the totem pole and that the ones above you sent you out here to test the waters."

With that, Abigail noticed another change in Amy's body as a different personality switched in and took Craven's place. She was greeted with an icy glare, but it was from more than just a demonized personality. Abigail was staring at the demon behind Craven and the others as Amy's eyes took on a dark, flat, shark-like appearance. *Shark eyes! Demon!*

A low, raspy, growl was emitted through Amy's bared and clenched teeth. Although the demon was manifesting through Amy's body and would have had the power to kill Abigail or Amy if God permitted it, the demon sat there glowering at Abigail. Finally, it disappeared and another personality emerged.

It reminded Abigail of Craven so she assumed it was one that was over him. "Hi," Abigail greeted him in a pleasant voice. "You must be the guy over Craven."

"Brilliant," he dripped with sarcasm.

"Thank you," Abigail quipped and smiled as if she had received a genuine compliment.

The misdirection momentarily threw the personality off but he quickly regained his hostile composure. "I am Draven," he announced as if he expected some kind of deference to his position or person.

"So," Abigail ignored his attitude and pursued her interview, "who's the demon ruling over you guys?"

Draven was not expecting that query. "He doesn't rule us. We have a mutually beneficial arrangement."

"Ah, kind of like two ticks and no dog?" Abigail bordered on antagonism.

"No," Draven answered with a huff, "like two allies in a battle who use each other's strengths to get our assignments done."

"So why are you here today, if you don't mind my asking?" Abigail took another tack.

"You tell me," he countered. Abigail could see the barely concealed hostility in his eyes and wondered if the demon would show up again.

"Okay," Abigail agreed, "you're here because Head Warden and I prayed and asked Jesus the Christ to show us where the darkness is coming from inside. I would assume that you and especially that demon had no intention of showing up today."

Draven did not want to admit that he emerged involuntarily. Pride. Control. Appearances. "You do not know who you are messing with, lady," Draven said. "You will pay and pay dearly. So be careful or you'll get hurt. Not that I care."

"No weapon formed against me will prosper," Abigail countered. "I think it's time that I talk with Head Warden again."

"Have it your way," he smirked and retreated to his internal place.

Head Warden reappeared and described what he observed from his internal vantage point. "He's a big mean one," he said, "and I think I'd heed his warning. I don't know what they have planned, but I agree with you that it has something to do with the moon."

Abigail looked up at the calendar above her desk. "Hmm," she mused, "it looks like we have a quarter moon coming up in a couple of days." For some reason she added, "A crescent moon."

Head Warden jolted when Abigail said crescent. "Whoa," he said somewhat bewildered, "what is that?"

"Maybe the name of the demon is Crescent," Abigail ventured an educated Holy Spirit-inspired guess.

He jerked again at the second mention of the word crescent. "I think you're onto something. What do we need to do?"

"Let's pray," Abigail began her prayer after Head Warden nodded in agreement. "Oh, Lord, we pray for Your wisdom and discernment for a strategy that will keep all of Amy safe on Sunday. Please illuminate things that are hidden in darkness, amen."

"Amen," Head Warden echoed. "I'm sensing that this is a really big demon. It's kind of like he's there to protect deep secrets."

"That would make sense since he's at Apollyon's level," Abigail mulled over the information. "I wonder if he has anything to do with the original Amy."

"I just sense that he's really agitated. I get the idea that he never expected to be exposed."

"That's pretty standard for the way the Satanists set up systems. They never really expect anyone to get very deep, but they still put in a ton of booby-traps and blockades and fail-safe structures just in case."

"So, what do we do?" Head Warden asked. "We can't just let that demon have his way on Sunday. Who knows what they have planned?"

"Let's see if we can have another conversation with Draven or Craven," Abigail suggested. They prayed together and asked for the Lord to bring out the one that needed to come out.

They were rewarded with the smirking personality.

"Draven, I presume," Abigail greeted him cordially.

"Brilliant," Draven responded sourly. "What do you want with me now?"

"Oh," Abigail responded pleasantly, "I just thought you might want to get free of Crescent."

Draven jerked as if he had been kicked in the head at the mention of the name. "Like we said," he countered defensively, "it's a mutually beneficial arrangement."

If Head Warden felt the jolt indirectly, Abigail could only imagine what Draven was feeling. As obnoxious as he was, Abigail knew that he was a part of Amy – and she loved even the unlovely parts of Amy.

"So, I see," Abigail's words were slightly mocking, but spoken with a congenial tone, "Crescent gets to beat on you and you get to do whatever he wants you to do."

"It's not like that!" Draven spat after yet another kick. "Look, lady, you need to back off. You don't know who you're messing with. He will get you and don't say that you haven't been warned."

"Okay," Abigail conceded, "I'll back off and not mention that name for your sake. I'm not out to get you more punishment or discipline or whatever you call it."

Amy's countenance took on a sinister change and Abigail assumed that Crescent had once again manifested. Shark eyes appearing, head lowered with teeth clenched and bared, a thunderous snarl erupted as the demon tried to leap out of the chair to pounce on Abigail. Abigail was struck by its inability to rise up more than a couple of inches off of the cushion. This further infuriated the creature who roared again, saliva dripping from the corners of the down-turned lips. It was as if he were held down by a seatbelt.

A God-sized seatbelt.

Abigail calmly prayed, "Holy Spirit, this demon is not in its assigned place right now. Would You fill its vacated place so it can't return and then remove it?"

The demon was now panicked. It could not retreat. It had lost its assignment and was doomed to reprisal from its superior.

"You can cut your losses and go to the feet of the true Lord Jesus Christ," Abigail informed him.

The demon knew exactly what she was talking about. He did not want to face the wrath of Satan or one of his cruel henchmen. Abigail could visualize him leaping heavenward to become a POW in this war. Once he was gone, Amy resurfaced and sagged into the chair with relief.

"Wow!" she said when she regained her composure, "That was one tough demon. Thanks."

"Was that Crescent?" Abigail wanted confirmation.

Amy was jarred. "I don't know but I sure got a kick out of that name." She tried to make light of it but it was obvious that she was concerned that Crescent or some other demon was still present.

"Is there anyone who can tell us what's going on down there?" Abigail addressed the system.

Head Warden appeared in Amy's place. "Nicholai says that there was another demon that got sent out to take you-know-who's place and he got ousted instead. He also said that what's-his-face has disappeared deep into the abyss on Apollyon's level with Draven and Craven and another one called Raven."

"Interesting." Abigail was quiet as she prayed and thought. "It would make sense that each of those three would each have a ruling spirit and it's consistent with how they work – send out the lower ranking one to test the waters."

"What are we going to do?" Head Warden showed concern about this latest development. "We can't let them run around inside the system wreaking havoc."

"Why don't we ask the Lord?" Abigail suggested. "I don't like the idea that there will be a quarter moon on Sunday with him still running loose in there either."

They prayed for wisdom and specific strategies. Head Warden said that he sensed that the Lord was directing them to seal off the abyss and so they prayed to that effect expecting that Amy would be safe until the next session.

After confirming their appointment for the following week, Amy left and Abigail closed up her office. Hearing footsteps coming down the hallway from the direction of the kitchen, Abigail waited to see who was coming. It was Pastor Spalding.

"Hello," Abigail said with a smile.

Pastor Spalding returned the smile and said, "I just happened to be down here a little while ago and I heard some pretty loud noises coming from your office. Are you all right?"

"Yes," Abigail answered, "it was just a growler."

"A growler?"

"A demon manifested in that last lady."

"A demon."

"It happens sometimes," Abigail responded calmly.

"I'm glad you know what you're doing," Pastor Spalding smiled a half smile as he shook his head and turned back up the hallway. "I'll see you Sunday."

His mood was as black as his truck while he sped through the streets of Springfield that Friday night on his way to a meeting with his friend and mentor, Levi Blevins. They had originally met during high school. Max was much like the small marble that bounced and sprang inside a pin ball machine until it inevitably fell past the lowest flippers and was gobbled up by the black hole at the base. He bounded and rebounded through life thinking that he was in full control. His attitude was unchanged despite recent setbacks.

Levi, a more analytical man, took his cult name from the middle of his last name. Levi was a scrambled spelling of evil. It was prophetic. Levi had been raised by Satanists and was being groomed for a future as a master. He belonged to the region ruled by Prinz, but he fell under Darod and Herrak's jurisdictions a couple counties east of Daggett's area. It was east of the area in which Max lived and the area in which Amy resided.

Although they were about the same age they had different motivations. Max was always an immediate gratification type of person. He was vying for Mastiff's vacated position. If he could recapture Mastiff's daughter, then he might be able to regain points with his superiors. If he could torment or eliminate that Steele woman, it would bode even better for him.

Levi, on the other hand, was a delayed gratification kind of man who shrewdly calculated his moves. He was patiently ambitious, biding his time to move into leadership. That was his goal from the time his father and grandfather began to groom him for such a role. Levi was currently just below Herrak who was just below Darod who was just below Prinz.

It was ironic that those in the cult wanted to promote advancement. Masters encouraged and enticed their protégés with grand promises. At the same time, those masters were constantly looking over their shoulders lest they become overtaken by their charges.

Max pulled into their usual meeting place by the lake. Levi was already there and pacing as usual. He was a foxlike young man who moved gracefully and, like a fox, could quickly pounce upon and devour his prey. They greeted one another with a hand signal and then set off down one of the trails, plans fermenting in the darkened cauldrons of their souls.

They had one common problem: Abigail Steele. She was responsible for the changes in F. Amy Bolton and Carrie Sue Wagner. Karkass and Carrion. They were dead meat, both of them, if they did not return to the cult and conform. Levi and Max were commissioned by their upper level masters to deal with the errant ones. They knew that their own well-being rested on their success. They would collaborate for that success.

Max did not want to admit the weakness he felt in the presence of Abigail Steele. He did not want to divulge the reason for the burn scars on the palms of his hands. He did not want to own up to his recent recruiting failures – one of them dead and the other one pursuing the Great Enemy even harder. Max did not want to confess how the recent events had shaken him up and he certainly did not want to acknowledge his own ambivalence. But he thought about every wicked thing he had ever done since Levi recruited him in high school and believed that he had surely committed the unpardonable sin. Many unpardonable sins. He was irredeemable so he might as well go for whatever reward he could obtain in Satan's realm.

Saturday's dawn brought another clear, cold day. Abigail tended to Buster, filling his water trough and making sure that he had enough hay. His nicker was music to Abigail's ears. She was lonely. *Huh, this must be a little bit like what Adam thought – the animals all had mates and he looked around and saw no one suitable for him. God, I'm sorry to complain again, but I'm lonely and all the friends and relatives and clients and critters in the world don't fill that vacuum. Please take this away or ...* She did not finish the prayer.

Pouring sweet feed into Buster's bowl, Abigail was startled as she clearly heard the voice of the Lord with her spiritual ears, *"Abigail, sell your horse."*

"Oh, Lord," she pleaded, "not Buster, please."

She sensed His clear words coming to her again. This time she was startled by the message. *"You will find him dead in the pasture with his throat cut if you don't sell him."*

"Okay, Lord," Abigail was sure, but not sure. So, she laid out a fleece as Gideon did. "Lord, if this is truly of You, then bring me the buyer today and I'll sell him. I don't want him killed. Thank You for the warning."

Abigail found the curry brush and tenderly brushed Buster's thick coat. He did not mind her presence when he ate his sweet feed. He could not know that their time together was short. He stood there sensing her sorrow as Abigail groomed him. As she stood at his shoulder, he bent his long, muscular neck around Abigail, trapping her between his head and shoulder in a hug. Abigail broke and sobbed. Buster nosed her back and soon released her. Then in a majestic display of his power and speed, he broke away in a canter, bucking like a rodeo horse, and then disappeared into the woods.

Abigail went to her office and pulled out her Bible. She had been reading in the book of Hebrews and it lay open to chapter twelve. Her eyes fell on the words at the end of the chapter. She read and re-read them out loud, *"See to it that you do not refuse Him who is speaking. For if those did not escape when they refused Him who warned them on earth, much less shall we escape who turn away from Him who warns from heaven. And His voice shook the earth then, but now He has promised, saying, 'YET ONCE MORE I WILL SHAKE NOT ONLY THE EARTH, BUT ALSO THE HEAVEN.' And this expression, 'Yet once more,' denotes the removing of those things which can be shaken, as of created things, in order that those things which cannot be shaken may remain. Therefore, since we receive a kingdom which cannot be shaken, let us show gratitude, by which we may offer to God an acceptable service with reverence and awe; for our God is a consuming fire."*

Abigail was stunned by the Word of God. It was *rhema*, the living Word; not just *logos*, the written Word. "Okay, Abba Father, I get it." *This is a scary prayer but here goes...* "Abba," Abigail cringed as she formed her prayer, "I will not refuse you and so whatever is created, whatever is shakable that stands between You and me... remove it. I want nothing to come between us. Not Buster, not the house, not the truck, not all the land or buildings... nothing, amen."

Abigail half expected the house to fall down around her, but she felt peaceful. "Lord, can I have one last ride on Buster?" She did not sense anything one way or the other so she decided that she would take Buster for a final ride after she finished her Saturday morning housework.

She and Buster headed out the front gate and across the front lawn, crossing the road near the mailbox. Turning to the right, they followed the road to the trail that was just before York Creek where Max typically parked. They headed down the trail that bordered the creek. Buster lifted his nose to the wind and got excited when he caught the scent of Lee's horses one field over. Soon they came into view and it was clear that Buster wanted to go visit them.

"Not today, boy," Abigail said and gave him a light kick. He obeyed and picked up his pace down the trail. After going back through several fields, Abigail turned Buster uphill toward the woods. She wanted to explore the trail and wooded area that belonged to the neighbor whose land was adjacent to the back side of Lee's. She had no idea who he was or even how he had access to that parcel of land. She supposed that there was a back road somewhere.

They wound through the woods on the trail that was regularly used by horses, four-wheelers, and deer. When they came to a bend in the trail, Buster balked. With ears flattened and nostrils flared, he began to snort and toss his head. Abigail stopped him and looked around carefully. Nothing was apparent, but then, she did not have the keen senses that Buster did.

When she tried to urge him forward, he stopped as if he were up against a fence. "All right, buddy, let's go back," Abigail said disappointedly. She turned him and he moved about ten feet down the trail before he stopped again and acted as if he were blocked.

"Buster!" Abigail was getting annoyed. This was not like her well-trained horse. *Lord, what is going on here?* She nudged him a little harder with her heel. Putting his head down, Buster bucked, trying to dislodge Abigail. Now Abigail was not just annoyed, she was afraid. She doubled her fist and gave him a smack between his ears. "Buster, you get going now!"

Again, Buster tried to buck her off.

Thoroughly alarmed by this unusual behavior, Abigail dismounted and checked under his saddle blanket thinking that he might have gotten some burrs under it when they went through the rough areas of the fields. Nothing. Abigail remounted and Buster still would not take a step. Dismounting again, Abigail grabbed the reins close to his muzzle and led him down the trail in utter frustration. He followed and seemed to calm down.

When they got to the open field, Abigail remounted and prayed that he would behave. He did for a short lope and then he began bucking again. Abigail held on to the back of the saddle and the pommel until he settled down, panic clawing at her heart. She fought him all the rest of the way home, dismounting and leading him, remounting and rodeo riding. Abigail was upset and weeping as she led him up the front lawn and back into his pasture.

Removing the saddle and grooming him, Abigail did not know if she wanted to clobber him or hug him. She was hoping that their last ride would have been sweet; something she would look back on fondly. *Lord, I think this is Your way of confirming that I really need to sell him. Send the buyer.*

Urdang congratulated his cohorts for their excellent work that day. They spooked the horse when they boxed him in and caused the thorn in their side some consternation. Yes, it was a good day, indeed.

Lee Norris was frustrated. He wanted to set some more posts, but he could not find his post driver. It should have been with the rest of his fence posts, wires, and attachments, but it just was not there. He finally decided that if he were to take advantage of the ground conditions, he would visit Abigail Steele and ask to borrow hers.

Getting into his truck, he made the short ride down his driveway, down the road less than a mile and then up her driveway, tooting his signature toot as he neared the upper curve. By the time he had parked and gotten out of his truck, Abigail had donned her coat and walked out to meet him.

"Howdy, neighbor," Lee greeted her.

"Hello, yourself," Abigail responded. "What brings you up here?"

"Well, I'm embarrassed to say that I have looked all over for my fence post driver and can't find it," Lee said sheepishly. "I would have sworn that it was with all my other fencing stuff."

"So, you're hoping that I can find mine and lend it to you?" Abigail guessed.

"Yes; if that wouldn't be too much trouble."

"No trouble at all. Come on down to the barn with me and I'll get it."

Buster had galloped up to the top gate when he heard the sound of Lee's truck coming up the driveway. He stood there alert and curious as the couple made their way to the gate.

"I'd love to have a horse like Buster," Lee said as he stroked Buster's muzzle and looked at him carefully while subconsciously appraising him. Looking back at Abigail with a mischievous grin, he asked, "Is he for sale?"

"Actually, yes. I have to sell Buster," Abigail said with a slight tremble in her voice.

"Wait. What?" Lee was flabbergasted. "I was just kidding." He knew how much Abigail loved Buster.

"Um," Abigail sighed and blew out a lung full of air, "God told me to."

"Serious?"

"Yeah," Abigail said sadly. "He said that if I didn't, I'd find him dead in the pasture."

Lee removed his hat and ran his hand through his hair. "What are you asking for him?"

Abigail paused and answered, "I'm not even sure what he's worth. I paid around six hundred for him when I got him. He was just green broke back then. He's a quarter horse from a good line, but I never bothered to get the official papers on him because he's a gelding so there was really no point."

"I'll give you eighteen hundred for him," Lee said decisively. "Having him in with my mares would be a good thing. And you can ride him any time you want."

"You don't have to," Abigail thought he was taking pity on her by making the offer. And then she stopped in her tracks as if she had just been smacked.

"What?" Lee asked with furrowed brows as he also stopped and looked at her carefully.

Abigail huffed, "I just remembered that after the Lord told me to sell Buster I said something like, 'okay, then, will You please bring the buyer here today' and here you are. But I can't take that much for him."

"Why not?"

"Because I consider you a friend and I just don't think he's worth that much. Besides, it just doesn't seem right that you would have to feed him and pay vet bills and I get visiting privileges *and* money." Abigail was trying to talk him out of it and all the while thinking that it would be the perfect solution for her. For Buster. "Besides, I don't think he'll let me ride him anymore."

Lee shook his head in a quick double-take not understanding her last statement. "What's going on?"

"I took a ride on him earlier today and it was like a rodeo event. We were okay going out, but when we got into the woods behind your place a ways, he went nuts. He wouldn't go forward or turn around. He tried to buck me off, too, so I led him down to the fields and he bucked me some more. I ended up walking him most of the way back home."

"That's peculiar," Lee mused as he looked from Abigail to Buster and back again.

"I took it as a 'drop-kick' from the Lord confirming that He wanted me to sell him. So, I am. To you. For six hundred and not a penny more. I don't need the money, okay? I just want him in a safe place with a horse-lover."

"Okay," Lee conceded. He instinctively knew that he would not win this negotiation.

"Thanks," Abigail said sadly as they resumed walking down to the barn to get the post driver. "Can you take him now?" It was hard not to burst into tears.

"Now?" Lee asked.

"Yeah," Abigail quavered. "I just have a feeling that the Lord wants him safely away today."

"Okay," Lee's mind was churning trying to work out the logistics of the transfer. "How about if I ride Buster over to my place and you follow in your truck so you can bring me back to my truck?"

"That will work," Abigail agreed. "You can keep his bridle and bit if you want, it fits him well."

Lee soon had Buster bridled and leapt onto his bare back. Buster was not accustomed to Lee's weight but he did not balk. He sensed that he was being ridden by a very experienced rider. Lee walked him all the way to his pasture where he let him mingle with his mares. There was much head tossing and whinnying, prancing and running as they got reacquainted.

Walking back up to his driveway, he found that Abigail had turned her truck around and was waiting for him, tears glistening as she could not hold back the emotions. Lee did not know what to do. He did not want to be forward, but he could not stand to see this beautiful woman's sorrow. He settled for awkwardly patting her shoulder. "You come visit him any time."

Levi and Max each drove to the ritual site at the farm located a mile south of Abigail. Leaving their trucks there, waiting for the cover of darkness, Levi and Max ambled down the path that Carrie Sue had traveled not so very long ago. They were able to avoid being seen by anyone travelling on the road as they covertly crossed York Creek Road at about the same place Carrie Sue did. The Rottweiler was silent today. They slipped into the woods and crossed the creek at the shallows. Max had come this way before.

Without stepping onto the Steele property, Max and Levi walked parallel to the fence line on the York's property in the cover of the brush and trees until they were nearly back to the road again. The wind was in their favor – blowing gently toward Abigail's property.

Approaching the barbed wire fence, they got as close as they dared as they sensed the enemy's presence. Finally, Max lit his package, nestled it in dry tinder and watched with satisfaction as the flames grew and began to spread. Levi had done the same thing nearby. Sure that the fire was going to take, they hastily retreated and took the same paths back to their trucks.

Abigail realized that she had not eaten lunch and was ravenous. She was making a late supper and was just about to sit down when the phone rang.

"Hello," Abigail said cheerfully as she recognized her neighbor's number. It was Earl.

"What are you burning, girl?" he asked. "It looks like your woods are on fire!"

"Just a minute," Abigail said in alarm. She took the phone with her and stepped out onto the front porch. She was shocked to see that the woods were on fire. It looked like the front quarter of her woods was being consumed by the fire. "Oh, Lord, Jesus," she cried, "it *is* on fire! I'm going to call 911."

Earl said that he would be right over, but she did not hear him because she had already hung up and was punching in 911. The dispatcher wanted her to stay on the phone, but she said that she was going to try to fight the fire. With that, Abigail pulled on her coat and rushed out to the water hose praying as she ran. "God! Should I just let it burn? Are you taking everything?" Abigail wanted to know how futile her fire-fighting efforts might be if this was God's response to her recent scary prayer. *God is a consuming fire.*

She heard Earl coming up the driveway and handed him the hose when he got out of his car. Running to the shed, grabbing a shovel, she slipped through the fence and made her way to the leading edge of the fire. The wind was blowing smoke into her face but she started to pat the glowing line of leaves and forest debris that fueled the fire. Off in the distance she heard the welcome sound of sirens from the volunteer fire department. Soon volunteers with their dome lights were visible as they parked along the road and entered the woods with their equipment.

Arms aching, back protesting, Abigail continued to pat embers with her head down intent on not letting it get past her. She did not notice that a fast-moving finger of fire had zipped around her and she was now caught in the middle of the charred section that the fire raced through. Suddenly, she heard a sound not unlike a miniature tornado and felt the air being sucked out of her lungs. Running as hard as she could, Abigail made it back up through the fence and into the driveway. Throwing down her shovel, coughing, gasping for clean air, Abigail sagged against her truck.

Earl had relinquished the water hose to a volunteer fire fighter and came over to her side. "Are you, all right?" he asked with great concern.

"Fine," Abigail coughed out her answer and looked up at what was left of the fire. At what was left of her woods. Fortunately, it was mostly a brush fire with only noticeable damage to the smaller trees and trunks of the larger trees. Volunteers had made short work of putting the fire out. Now they were combing the edge of the fire line looking for the cause of the fire.

"Where's Buster?"

"At Lee's," she coughed out another answer. Her throat was raw and her eyes were watering. She would have been appalled if she could have seen her soot-blackened face in a mirror. And she was unaware of how badly she reeked of smoke.

The captain approached Abigail and Earl, supposing that one of them was the property owner. "Who's the owner?" he asked, looking from Abigail to Earl.

"I am," Abigail answered without a cough this time.

"We believe that this fire looks a bit suspicious," he said gravely. "You're lucky that your house and out-buildings are safe. It was close. Are your neighbors mad at you? Do you know anyone who would want to burn your woods?"

Abigail did not know who she could trust in this county anymore. She opted to shake her head and take the matter to God's higher court for justice. If they found any solid evidence, nothing would be done anyway. She was sure the paperwork would get lost.

"Can I get you to sign this report? We'll make sure that there will be an investigation by the state arson unit from the capital." He took the clipboard back from Abigail after she signed it and left with his team.

"Abigail," Earl scolded her, "you know who did this, don't you?"

"I don't know for sure, but I am sure it's someone from the cult - probably Max Berryman. He's been making a lot of threats lately and I'm getting pretty sick of it. I file reports at the sheriff's office and they have no record. They're all in on it," Abigail said angrily.

"I'll keep a sharp eye out whenever I can," Earl assured her. "I guess we can see how much damage was done when there's daylight."

"Thanks, Earl," Abigail said gratefully.

"Go take a shower!" he responded trying to lighten up her mood. "You're a mess!"

"Thanks, Earl." Abigail managed a weak smile and another cough.

15

Sunday, February 11, Last Quarter Moon

Abigail had gotten out of bed for the last time to stoke the fire at six-thirty, just before sunrise. She did not sleep well, thinking that an ember might have been overlooked and she would see a renewed blaze coming at her. She kept the curtain covering her south window open, and watched vigilantly. As the fog of sleep lifted, Abigail had two gray thoughts: Buster was gone and her woods were burned. She stood by the window of her bedroom that faced the charred woods and looked at the blackened surface in the early daylight. It was ugly. The weapon did not completely prosper.

Finding her Bible, Abigail returned to the end of Hebrews twelve. *For our God is a consuming fire.* "God, I don't understand. Was that of You? Should I have let every created thing that I own just burn up?"

Abigail knew the answer. She knew that this was of the enemy who was not getting away with anything. In fact, the enemy's choice of fire only confirmed God's word to Abigail. She spent time thanking Him for mitigating the damage, for Earl's phone call, for the effective work of the volunteers, for the timely transfer of Buster to Lee's safe pasture. And she found herself remarkably at peace. "It's just stuff."

Without Buster to tend to, she had extra time that morning. She prepared a leisurely breakfast and, thinking ahead, took some ground beef out of the freezer for lunch. Frowning at the dishes that she did not wash last night, she began to run hot water into the sink. Adding a squirt of dish soap, putting the dish drainer on the clean counter, Abigail heard the pile of silverware shift under the water just as she dipped her hands under the surface.

"Ouch!" Abigail felt like she had just been bitten by a snake. Withdrawing her right hand, looking at the dripping blood, Abigail noted the two crescent shaped gashes on the tips of her index and middle fingers.

"God? Can they do that?" Abigail was indignant. She was not angry at God, she was angry that weapons seemed to be prospering against her. What was giving them the so-called right to do this? Dude, Buster, the break-in, the noose, Max, the fire, and now this?

Abigail went to the bathroom and pulled out her first aid kit. Awkwardly using her left hand to open bandages and apply ointment, Abigail managed to staunch the flow of blood. *Well, so much for washing the dishes.* She went back to the sink and used a tablespoon to pull the stopper out to drain the water. She looked at the pile of silverware and saw her dull, old paring knife. It was the only thing that was remotely sharp enough to do that kind of damage.

As curious as she was about the condition of her woods, she was determined not to go there before church. The cameras could be checked later, but she was not optimistic about finding anything useful on them. In fact, she assumed that by bringing pictures into the sheriff's office the last time, Max or whoever it was, knew about where they were placed.

Driving down the road to church, Abigail craned her neck to the right to see if she might get a glimpse of Buster and Lee's mares. It suddenly struck her that Max might have set the fire to get Buster. He did make that threat. "Oh, Lord, thank you that Buster was gone already. He would have been terrified. You *did* protect him. You *are* protecting me."

It had become a habit over the last couple of months to sit by Cindy, Gary, and Lee and today was no different. Abigail slid into the pew next to Cindy and they briefly hugged. Abigail had expected Carrie Sue to come any minute, but she did not come to church that morning.

"Got a lot to tell you," Abigail whispered just as the music began.

Noticing her fingers, she asked, "What happened?"

"Later," Abigail promised.

At the end of the service, Cindy pumped Abigail, "What's going on? What happened to your fingers?"

"One of my SRAs has a demon named Crescent. When I went to wash my dishes this morning, I filled it like usual, had my silverware in a pile at the edge and when I put my hands in, I heard the pile shift and I got cut by my dull paring knife or the razor-sharp claws of the demon."

"Serious!"

"And I'm mad. I'm totally outraged that that thing attacked me. I don't know what we missed. I thought it was contained."

"Well, we'll be praying." Cindy did not always understand the wild things that her friend told her, but how could she deny the physical evidence here?

"And then there's Max. Max, or someone, tried to burn my woods down last night," Abigail said quietly, but not quietly enough that Gary did not overhear.

"Max?" Gary asked, "What's he been up to now?" Lee was just over his shoulder listening, too.

"I'm pretty sure it was him, or at least the cult," Abigail replied. "The fireman said it looked suspicious to him and that the state arson team would investigate. I'm going to go down there after lunch and take a look around myself."

"We'll join you," Gary answered for Lee who was nodding his agreement.

Abigail could see their anger rise from them like steam from a boiling pot. "Lee, I'm so glad Buster was safe with you. Thanks."

That exchange brought bewildered looks from both Cindy and Gary. They were unaware of the recent transfer of ownership.

They made plans to meet at Abigail's at two o'clock.

Sunday afternoons should have been peaceful and quiet. Abigail was beginning to see a pattern here. Just how many Wednesdays and Sundays had been ruined by chaos? Today was another one to add to the list.

The men arrived promptly at two o'clock wearing their boots and work clothes. Abigail was dressed in her outdoor gear as well. She got a strong whiff of her smoke saturated coat and recoiled as she put it on.

"Hey, guys," Abigail greeted them.

They were looking at the woods with mouths agape. "That's nasty." Gary wrinkled his nose. "Give it a little time and it'll all come back."

"I brought my camera. It wouldn't hurt to take a couple of pictures."

"Good idea," Lee concurred. "Do you have any idea where it started?"

"Somewhere down by the south fence line," Abigail said. "I think they were trying to get Buster and I also think that they now know that there's a camera on the back gate since our county's finest probably let them know about our photos."

"Ooh. I hadn't thought about that," Gary replied thoughtfully. "Maybe we need to relocate the cameras for a while or get some more."

They started their inspection by going down to the bottom of the pasture to retrieve the camera. After deciding on a strategic angle near the corner of the property, they installed and camouflaged it in its new position. Next, they walked along the path that Abigail kept clear along the inside of the fence line until they came to the charred areas. Some of the fire burned into the York's land, but because of the prevailing winds, it was driven toward Abigail's house and out-buildings. They found two similar patterns within twenty feet of each other.

Lee crossed the fence to the neighbor's property and began to cast enlarging circles around the area. He was looking for a boot print or some kind of evidence. He found a distinct heel print and took a picture of it with his cell phone camera. Now he had a direction and he followed it like a hound tailing a raccoon. He followed it along the back of the York's property and all the way to the creek. There he found two sets of prints in the soft mud that had been made very recently. Snapping pictures of them, he returned to Gary and Abigail who had taken pictures of the damaged area.

They went up to the house and retrieved all the SD cards on the way, hoping that something might show up. They eagerly looked at the pictures, but all they saw was the activity of the fire and the fire fighters, along with Earl and Abigail. They were able to get a close approximation of the start of the fire because of the time stamp on each frame.

"I'm going to start a detailed log and keep records and pictures of all this stuff. Maybe someday there will be an honest sheriff in this county and something will be done," Abigail said.

"Good idea," Gary said. "I'll download the pictures of Billy from my cell phone and get them to you, too."

Raven, Craven, and Draven might have been contained deep inside of Amy's system, but Crescent managed to escape the notice of the very astute Abigail Steele and the wary Head Warden by shoving an underling out to take his place. His sinister laugh was the closest the creature could get to mirth since his plummet from the throne room eons or ages or epochs ago. Or perhaps it was merely days before time was created and it was merely six thousand years. The timelessness of eternity was impossible to gauge. Forever is forever.

This time capsule began to tick with the daily cadence of sunrise and sunset when the Great Power spoke it into existence. Time, meaningless in heaven, was now measurable on earth. Time was getting short for these fallen ones, the formerly glorious ones who once worshipped tirelessly and joyfully in the throne room of the Great Power. But since their fall, their demise, their dismissal from heaven, these furious beings were becoming more and more aware of the incessant, irreversible swing of the solar pendulum. The earth spun perpetually like a gear in a clock.

That Great Power was unpredictable, and yet there were things that were consistent. He loved the number seven. Completion. Divine perfection. Maturity. Rest. There were nearly six thousand years of human history already past according to the Jewish calendar; and then there was the predicted one thousand years of the millennial kingdom. That would make seven thousand years. That would be so much like that Great Enemy to have planned for seven thousand years of time.

Oh, yes, Crescent was also there when the prophets wrote their prophecies. He and his kind peered over the shoulders of the prophets: of Ezekiel and Daniel, Isaiah and Jeremiah. They knew what John saw from the isle of Patmos because they watched him pen the words. Just as the Dusty Mortals of the Empty Tomb were beginning to understand and see the fulfillment of the prophecies, to watch for the Great Enemy's second coming, his fellow-creatures were also sensing that they were in the eleventh hour. Time was short and getting shorter. If Satan did not defeat the Great Enemy, they were all doomed.

Prinz ordered his masters and several key members within his region to gather at their inclement weather ritual site. There was a time when nothing bothered Prinz. Not heat or cold, rain or snow, wind or storm. But these days, he was feeling an ache in his bones and a decreasing tolerance for climate conditions.

The last chords of the huge pipe organ quieted. The church had emptied fairly rapidly as coats were pulled tightly and hats and gloves were put on in anticipation of the nippy night air. Greg Hinton, the janitor of the Springfield Presbyterian Church had carefully gone through his closing routine to be sure that every door was locked and every window was secure. Tomorrow morning, he would come in to clean and straighten. As he took one final look around the sanctuary, he noticed that someone had knocked over a potted plant, righted it and put most of the dirt back into the pot. Crumbs of dirt remained on the carpet between the baptismal font and the communion table. It had not been ground into the carpet so it was a simple matter of vacuuming the area. Making a mental note, turning out the lights, he left the building, and locked the door behind him.

By ten o'clock, the ones who had been summoned began to move toward the Presbyterian church. They were experts at not attracting undue attention to their presence. Their inside man had a key and unlocked the back door. The inside ground level landing offered two choices. Steps to the right led to the sanctuary. Steps to the basement were straight ahead. The group initially gathered in the basement and prepared for the night's festivities. There would be an infant baptism followed by a communion service.

Levi had ambushed Amy Bolton as she left The Pizza Palace. He flashed a signal with his hand to summon Craven. Much to Levi's consternation, Craven did not appear. He flashed another sign and was able to cause a child personality to switch in. He then approached her and guided her to his vehicle. Plunging a needle through her uniform pants, he emptied the contents of a sedative into her system. Within a minute, Amy sagged in the seat next to him, head rolling from side to side. He strapped her in with the seatbelt and headed to Springfield with his prize.

Born on New Year's Day, the infant had come from one of the breeders. The little boy did not officially exist since he was delivered by Dr. Bacchus at the New Year's ritual. There was no birth certificate, no social security number, not even a name. He had only one purpose and he would fulfill it tonight when he turned six weeks, six hours, and six minutes old as the crescent moon moved across the heavens.

Zorroz was wary of Amy. He sub-consciously rubbed the scar on his throat as he remembered the last time he tangled with one of Abigail Steele's people. Remaining on high alert, he helped Levi half walk-half drag the drugged woman into the church. Leading her to one of the side rooms in the basement, a pair of women prepared her for the upcoming ritual. She must be cleansed from defilement and adorned with the proper robe.

Head Warden, Nicholai, and the guards were also weakened by the sedative, but they kept fighting to regain executive control of Amy's body. So far, their efforts were futile. Their prayers went unanswered. By midnight, Amy was strapped down tightly to the communion table. She would be impregnated tonight. The seeds of the thirteen men would vie to fertilize the egg. The physical and sexual torture caused Amy to split off still more personalities.

The sacrificial infant was baptized, sprinkled with the blood of Prinz, Darod, Daggett, Zorroz, and Herrak. Slowly stepping from the baptismal font to the communion table, Prinz lifted the infant above his head in a dedication to Satan.

"Unless you eat my body and drink my blood," Prinz intoned in a mock communion service, twisting the words of the Great Enemy, "you have no part with me." He passed the tiny body and the warm blood to the participants using the very chalice and serving plate that Reverend Griffin used just last Sunday.

All evidence of their presence was removed and the group dispersed stealthily, silently. Amy was driven back to The Pizza Palace and roughly thrown back into her car. They had calculated the precise amount of sedative that would keep her under their control for as long as they needed for her to be physically compliant. She groggily put herself back together and was able to make the short drive back to her trailer. Stumbling and weeping, Amy collapsed into her bed and slept deeply, jerking and twisting as nightmares plagued her mind.

Greg Hinton was an early riser and Monday was no exception. Kissing his wife good-bye, he left the house and drove to the Presbyterian church to clean up after the Sunday services as usual. Entering the back door that led to the basement, descending into the fellowship hall, he turned lights on as he made his way past the kitchen and into the maintenance room that was filled with all the janitorial supplies. He straightened chairs in Sunday school rooms, vacuumed the floors, emptied trash, dry mopped the fellowship hall, and sanitized the restrooms efficiently.

Vacuuming the entire sanctuary took a long time. He methodically worked his way from the back to the front. Frowning at the remains of the spilled dirt, Greg took a closer look. He was startled to see the distinct impression of a heel print in the dirt. *I know that was not there last night!*

Stopping the vacuum, he retrieved his cell phone from its case on his belt and snapped pictures. *Lord, what is going on here?* Without knowing exactly why, he decided to look more closely at the furniture that was dedicated to sacred rites. Removing the lid from the baptismal font, he saw nothing remarkable. He felt a prompting to remove the white basin from its wooden frame. His heart froze as he saw fresh blood coagulated on the underside of the basin and on the wooden rim.

Amy stirred in her bed and groaned as pain began to register in her conscious mind. Still groggy, she fought the urge to shut down. She vaguely remembered last night. It had a surrealistic quality to it. Was that real? Was that a flashback? Was it a nightmare?

Head Warden had a busy night. He and his guards along with Nicholai and his men spent the night searching for and retrieving most of the newly split off personalities. They prayed effectively for them and got them reintegrated. Noticing that Amy was coming around, Head Warden apprised her of the internal status and let her know that she was not dreaming. They had been abducted and taken to a ritual. He did not need to fill her in on the details.

They were all outraged that it happened. They were all wondering how it could have happened. What had they missed? Didn't they pray effectively enough with Abigail? They decided that the best thing would be to call Abigail. Amy thanked her internal protectors and made the call.

"Hello," Abigail greeted Amy as she recognized the number. *It must be important, she rarely calls.*

"Hey, Abigail," Amy said and then hesitated, "I hate to bother you, but I really need to talk. Do you have a couple of minutes?"

"Sure do, what's up?"

"We got taken to a ritual last night," Amy blurted. "I'm a mess."

"Can you meet me at my office at ten?"

"Uh, sure. Are you sure? I mean, this is your day off and all."

"Don't worry about me. I'll see you soon, okay?"

"Thanks; I'll be there."

Abigail put some nicer clothes on and headed to her truck. *Oh, Lord, bless Amy. She must be so discouraged by this setback.* She continued to pray in the spirit all the way to the church and arrived there before Amy did so she decided to stop in at the office to let Ginny know that she would be down in her office for a while.

Amy was distraught and outraged, discouraged and yet wanting to fight. "I'm not used to feeling all these feelings," the bewildered woman said. "I don't know how to handle them."

Abigail gave her a gentle smile with a hint of a twinkle in her eyes. "Congratulations. You're normal. I know it's tough for you right now, but it's a good indication that there has been significant healing."

"Well, I'm not so sure I want to be so normal if this is what it feels like," Amy said ruefully. "It was a lot easier to let the others take care of stuff."

"It was definitely easier on you, but not so easy on the ones who had to carry all the tough stuff. This is how God intended for all of us to live," Abigail said sympathetically. "We get to feel the good, the bad, and the ugly. Sometimes it's not so much fun, but it gives us a fuller, richer life."

Amy sighed and then said, "Well, I'm not giving up. I'm so mad at those..." Amy held her tongue and then finished, "...those jerk-faces!"

"So am I. Let's war."

They opened with prayer and then Abigail was given an update on the internal situation by Head Warden. Apparently, Crescent escaped containment and was able to keep the God-loyal parts like Head Warden and Nicholai subdued while keeping those programmed to be cult and demon-loyal parts active.

"I need to show you something," Head Warden said.

"Okay," Abigail replied cautiously.

"This is embarrassing," he said slowly, "but I think it's important." With that said, he carefully tugged at the neckline of Amy's sweatshirt stretching it so that Abigail could see a fresh crescent-shaped cut directly over Amy's heart.

"Crescent!" Abigail said, holding up the recently cut fingers. "We need to do something about that demon. I think we'll have to deal with Draven, Craven, and Raven again."

"That's what we figured," Head Warden agreed.

They continued to discuss possibilities and strategies before praying. They sensed that the Lord would have the trio brought back to the surface again for another round of negotiations. Craven was the lowest of the three with Raven and Draven above him.

"You again!" Draven spat his disdain for Abigail.

"Sorry about that. I'm really not trying to aggravate you, but Amy needs to get this, uh, quarter moon shaped thing settled." She wanted to avoid using Crescent's name.

"You'll never get rid of him," Draven asserted. "Head Warden showed you that cut, but that's not the only place he's marked us. We belong to him and he belongs to us. You can't separate us."

"Sometimes," Abigail ventured, "I run across parts that feel helpless and hopeless..."

"I am not helpless or hopeless!"

"Let me finish," Abigail said evenly, thinking that he protested a little too much.

"Fine!"

"Some feel that way because of their experiences, or because of the presence of powerful demons and strong programming, or because of introjected objects, cuts, and maybe blood tattoos," Abigail instructed patiently.

"What's that got to do with me?" Draven demanded. He was getting agitated because Abigail was striking close to home. He tried not to look surprised when she mentioned those specific items, but Abigail noticed.

"Let me continue. Maybe it'll be relevant and maybe not. I'm just asking for a couple minutes of your time." Getting no response, Abigail continued, "Some parts really do hope and pray that there really is a way out, but are afraid to tip their hands for fear of receiving greater punishment."

"I'm not one of those," Draven insisted.

"There are some," Abigail spoke as if she had not been interrupted, "who are fully cult-loyal and demon-loyal, but, because they're a part of the original person, they may have to have their will violated for their own good and for the good of the whole."

"You better not pull some kind of stunt here, lady!" Draven threatened.

Abigail stopped and looked Draven intently in the eye and said, "I have prayed that the true Lord Jesus Christ would prevent any demon from hearing or interfering with this conversation. If you would like a way out, just nod and we'll get on with it."

Abigail was met with an explosion of insults and a hail of four-letter words.

"Okay, have it your way," Abigail said as Draven dropped out of executive control and was replaced by Head Warden.

"What now?" he asked.

"I guess he made it clear that he was not going to cooperate. It may be that he really hopes to be freed and hopes that we'll intervene on his behalf. But either way, we can pray about the cuts, tattoos, introjects, and whatever else happened in any of the rituals involving that demon."

"Sounds good," Head Warden agreed.

"I think it would be good for you to have a quick meeting with as many inside who might know specifics about the locations and numbers of C-shaped scars," Abigail consciously avoided using Crescent's name so that there would be no more physical reprisals on any part of Amy.

She waited less than a minute before he came back with his report. There were crescent shaped scars from every ritual that Amy attended that occurred on a first or last quarter of the moon. They were between her toes and fingers, they followed her hair line and natural skin contours. Thirty-some years of rituals would add up to a lot of cuts.

Blood tattoos would not be as obvious since they were made with needles. A tiny syringe of demonized human or animal blood leaves virtually no physical evidence. However, each injection was accompanied by curses and demons leaving ample spiritual evidence of their existence.

They prayed over her history, assuming that every crescent moon ritual produced fresh scars and/or tattoos. They pled the blood of Jesus the Christ over curses, chants, covenants, and programming associated with them as well as the strongholds, demons, body memories, and more. Believing that they had prayed thoroughly, they concluded their prayers by asking Jesus to complete or correct anything they may have prayed incompletely or inadequately.

"What are you sensing?" Abigail asked.

"It's much lighter in here," Head Warden reported. "It feels a lot cleaner, too. I think that demon is gone."

Abigail gave a quick smile. "But you're not sure enough to mention it by name?"

"Uh, yeah." Head Warden hung his head briefly. "Busted."

"You want to try it?" Abigail asked.

"Why not?" he replied and took a deep breath as he braced himself just in case. "I think Crescent is gone." After a slight pause he gave a tight-lipped smile and reported, "No kick that time."

"Excellent. Do you have any sense of where Draven, Raven, and Craven are?"

"They're nearby."

"Draven," Abigail asked gently, "will you talk with me some more?"

"I'm here." Draven appeared quickly and answered curtly, "what do you want now?"

"Just want to check in on you, that's all," Abigail answered sincerely. "I wanted to see if you see things a little differently now."

"Hello! You took away my power and protection."

"Would you be interested in some genuine power?"

"I can arrange for a replacement. Thank you very much! I don't need your God."

"Okay. I tried."

"What's that supposed to mean?" he demanded with narrowed eyes and furrowed brow.

"Nothing that concerns you directly; I need to get back with Head Warden." Abigail dismissed him.

Head Warden showed up at the mention of his name as Draven disappeared simultaneously. He reported that Draven, Raven, and Craven had gone back down into the abyss on Apollyon's level. They asked the Lord to seal the area off so they could call it a day. Amy was exhausted and they sensed that she would be safe until Friday after they prayed about the rituals coming on the thirteenth and on St. Valentine's Day. Amy went home to rest before her next shift at The Pizza Palace and Abigail headed home.

"Hello, Mike," Pastor Spalding responded to Reverend Griffin's call. "How are you?"

"I'm fine, Daniel, but I think I have a big problem at my church."

"Oh?"

"I'll get right to the point," Rev. Griffin continued. "Greg Hinton, my custodian, called me earlier and told me that there were some suspicious things at the church again."

"What kinds of things?" Pastor Spalding had an inkling of what was coming.

"He found a footprint in the dirt from a knocked over plant. He said he's positive that it was not there last night when he looked at it before closing up." He paused and added, "He also found fresh blood in the baptismal font."

"Oh, my." Pastor Spalding's heart sank.

"Can you and your counselor meet me at the church today? I told Greg not to touch anything until I got there."

"I'll call her right now and get back to you," Pastor Spalding offered.

They hung up and Pastor Spalding made his call to Abigail. She had just walked in the door as the phone rang. Recognizing the number, she picked it up right away and they made arrangements to meet with Rev. Griffin and his custodian at one o'clock. Abigail had a quick bite to eat and then headed back to Springfield to the Presbyterian church.

After listening to Greg's account of the previous night and the evidence that he found in the morning, they carefully examined the baptismal font again. By now, the blood was darker and some of it was dried.

"What should we do?" Rev. Griffin asked Abigail.

"Well, we sure can't go to the authorities, because we know that they are Satanists. We must assume that one of your parishioners is a Satanist and he probably has a key and let them in." Abigail was processing the situation aloud. "This is a spiritual battle. Our enemies are not flesh and blood."

"What do you recommend?"

"It's likely that there was a ritual done here last night because of the crescent moon. They would have done a counterfeit baptism using the blood of the victim. I would guess that it was an infant since your tradition baptizes infants and they would enjoy the mockery." Abigail continued to process out loud in a matter-of-fact tone, "and they would likely have had a counterfeit communion service using the flesh and blood of the child."

That brought sickened looks and collective horrified groans from the men much like air being released from a punctured tire.

"Have you checked the chalice and serving plates?" Abigail asked looking at Greg. "They would likely have desecrated them as well, but sometimes they bring their own."

"No, I didn't," he said, "they didn't seem to be out of place."

Shifting over to the communion table, carefully examining each goblet and plate, removing the covers from the servers that held the individual cups, using a flashlight to carefully inspect them, they found nothing obviously awry. This time there were audible sighs of relief.

The sound of a door opening and closing made the edgy men jump. Looking at one another, they waited tensely until they heard a man's voice call out, "Hello? Anybody here?"

Rev. Griffin recognized the voice of one of his elders and relaxed. "We're in here," he called back. "Is that you, Russ?"

The large man made his way into the sanctuary and approached the group. "I saw all the cars in the lot as I was coming through town and was wondering if everything was all right."

Hair standing up on the back of her neck, Abigail was instantly on alert and wanted to run. She did not know who he was, but her discernment caused her to be wary. There was something familiar about him. She quietly backed up a few steps.

"Yes," Rev. Griffin said, "everything is all right." He was not sure what more he should say. At this point he was not sure who the inside person was.

Russ squinted through his thick lenses, eyes shifting from man to man, from the baptismal font to the communion table, from the rug to the potted plant like an archeologist sifting through dirt before his eyes settled on Abigail. "Well, who's this pretty lady?" His words were congenial, but his eyes, minimized by the thick lenses, bored into her eyes as he stepped purposefully toward her holding out his hand in an attempt to shake Abigail's hand before introductions were made.

Abigail felt his intimidation, but she stood firm as she saw the small cross that was tattooed in the now exposed flesh between his thumb and forefinger. She also noticed a flashy gold ring on his right hand. Holding her right hand up, she said, "Sorry, I don't shake hands, and I have a couple of bum fingers." She was grateful for the two bandages.

Thrown off a little by her counter move, retreating a step, trying to retain a façade of charm, Russ Ranson smiled and looked to Rev. Griffin.

"Russ, this is Abigail Steele, a counselor at Pastor Spalding's church." He made the introduction nodding at Pastor Spalding and then he looked back at Abigail. "Abigail, this is Russ Ranson, one of our elders here."

Abigail gave a polite smile and simply said, "Hi."

Russ appeared to have no intention of leaving. There was an awkward silence until Mike Griffin finally said, "Well, Russ, thanks for stopping. We're getting ready to leave in a minute."

"I'll just wait and head out with you," Russ said. "I'm not in a hurry to go anywhere."

Abigail spoke up. "I have an appointment that I need to get to." With that, she headed toward the doorway that was just behind the massive organ. She was not concerned about what anyone thought at that moment; she just wanted to get away from that man. *Lord, where have I met him before?*

Descending the steps to the landing, she opened the outside door and headed to her truck. She saw a large, new SUV with a Berryman Auto Dealer decal on the back parked behind hers. She was blocked in. And mad. *He had the whole stinking parking lot and he had to park behind me?*

It was not long before Pastor Spalding, Rev. Griffin, and Russ Ranson emerged from the church. Abigail was standing on the driver's side of her truck leaning on her forearms, keys dangling from her gloved hand.

"Oh, I'm so sorry," Russ called out, "I'll move right away."

Abigail did not reply. She merely nodded, got into her truck, and started the engine. She looked into her rear-view mirror as he completed his three-point turn and headed out. She saw his profile dimly though his tinted windows and then it struck her – that was the man who followed her and Carrie Sue that day in the large sedan! He had the same profile. *I never did follow up on those plates.* Pastor Spalding came around to her door and indicated that he wanted to say something to her so she rolled the window down.

"Are you all right?" he asked with concern.

"I don't know how I know, but he's the inside man," Abigail said evenly. "He had one of those crosses tattooed in the fold of his thumb. I saw it when he tried to shake hands with me. I couldn't make out the ring, but I wouldn't be surprised if he belonged to the lodge as well."

"Let me get Mike. Do you have time to talk a little bit more?"

"Yeah," Abigail said and added with mock penitence, "forgive me, Pastor, for I have lied. I don't have an appointment; I just needed to get out of there."

Mike Griffin came over to the truck and Pastor Spalding filled him in on what Abigail had just said.

"I'm pretty sure he was one of the guys who has been following me lately, but the guy was driving a BFOMC."

"A what?" Rev. Griffin asked.

"Sorry. I call those full-sized sedans BFOMCs – Big-Fat-Old-Man-Cars because ya usually see old men like my dad driving those big, fat cars."

"Well, I can tell you that he just traded in his Marquis for that SUV not too long ago," Rev. Griffin replied. The wheels were turning in his head as he was trying to process the probability that one of his elders, a man who attended the church, who prayed with him, and worshipped with him was actually a part of the local cult. Too many pieces were falling into place. Things were making sense and he was uneasy.

Russ Ranson was trying his best to rise to the highest standards of Satanism: serving God by day and Satan by night, achieving leadership by attaining position in both worlds, and being a Christian by day and a Satanist by night. However, being blinded by the god of this world, he did not fully appreciate that he would have thoroughly negated serving God at all by serving Satan in any capacity. He had been suckered by duplicity training to his eternal damnation. Billy Sunday once remarked, "Hell is the highest reward that the devil can offer you for being a servant of his." Satanists did not believe it.

Russ contacted Herrak who contacted Darod who contacted Prinz. Prinz then summoned Daggett and Zorroz as well as other key area and regional leaders who fell under his jurisdiction. Their covert meeting took place in Darod's office. The weasel-faced man was the county commissioner and he was known to have meetings in his office after hours. It would not have looked suspicious. Besides, he was a powerful man in the county and none dared question him.

"You were careless!" Prinz spoke vehemently to all of the men gathered in the office. "You left evidence that a child could have detected." He was furious and the men were not sure if it was wiser to meet his glare or to avoid his eyes. He looked from man to man and then settled on Russ Ranson.

"You were there today," he spoke as if he were accusing the man. "What did they say?"

Russ groveled, apologized, and ended his answer with an insipid, "I don't know, your preeminence, they just clammed up and said that they were about to leave. That woman was there and she said she had an appointment and had to leave." He tried not to boast, but pride among these men was difficult to keep in check. "I think I made her nervous. She wouldn't shake my hand and backed away from me."

"She's no airhead," Prinz growled. "All you did was give her something else to piece together."

Russ Ranson quieted instantly. Although they each had aspirations of someday replacing Prinz, none dared challenge him, especially the lower level masters like Russ. They all noticed that Prinz was diminishing in some of the same ways that they were but, even so, Prinz was allied with demons who were more powerful than theirs. They would wait. They would bide their time. One of them would eventually ascend to his position and inherit his powers.

Tuesday was the thirteenth and Wednesday was St. Valentine's Day so they had rituals to plan. They had demons to summon. They had victims to procure and prepare.

A tiny orb-shaped cell detached from its origin and was guided by the finger-like cilia to the entrance of a long tube. Once safely on its journey, the cell tumbled down the passage just as others had done month after month. The vast majority of them had been unimpeded and therefore passed out of Amy Bolton's body. This egg, however, encountered a menacing stream of much smaller cells. Each of the tadpole-like seed with shark-like character vied with one another to be the first to penetrate the outer covering of the ovum, thus precluding the entrance of any other seed. The mix of seed from the various masters imitated the masters themselves. It was do or die.

Millennia ago Urdang's fellow reprobates had tried to sabotage the Genesis prophecy by co-mingling with the beautiful daughters of men, creating the miscreant Nephilim. Even Satan did not know from whom the Anointed One would arise or when the Holy Spirit would come upon the virgin and generate the head-bruising Seed. The best Satan could do was to spawn the heel-bruising seed that he could only hope to empower enough to overcome the Great Power. However, the great wickedness was too great. Satan had over-played his hand once again. The Great Power found one line, the line of Noah, which had not become tainted. Noah found favor.

Urdang and his ilk witnessed the fate of the dark angels who did not keep their own domain, but abandoned their proper abode and are being kept in eternal bonds under darkness for the judgment on the Great Day. They could not afford to have all their hard work wiped out again with flood or fire. The best they dared to do was infest, oppress, plague, torment, and yes, possess certain willingly demonized men and thus create a fouled seed.

Barrenness for the Jewish women was more than mere maternal longing for a baby. Those women knew that the Messiah would come, but no one could know through whom, or exactly when, this would happen.

Satan, sharing the same uncertainty, tried to ensure that there were always potential antichrists available. Ha! Eve, herself, thought that Cain was the immediate fulfillment of the prophecy. He had to be disqualified with his murderous rage. How many times had Satan come within one man of snuffing out the Messianic line, of destroying the entire nation? Oh, the rage fueled by his frustrations! Kill. Steal. Destroy.

16

Friday, February 16

The blustery winter day did not keep Abigail's spirit down. She enjoyed the dusting of snow that fell during the night – it disguised the blemishes in her woods and brightened the winter-drab landscape. The roads were a little slick, but she had nothing to worry about with her truck. Even though it had been months since Dude was killed, she still caught herself going to the cabinet to get his food once in a while. The intense sadness had passed, but she missed him.

And it had only been a week since she sold Buster to Lee. Grateful that he was safe, Abigail still missed him, still questioned God. *If no weapon formed against us will prosper, how come Dude is dead, the woods are burned, brake lines were cut...* Abigail stopped her curiosity from going too close to the edge of bitterness or resentment. *Someday this will all make sense and meanwhile, God, I trust that You know the end from the beginning and know what is best for all.*

She and Carrie Sue met at the church office for their usual noon appointment. After opening with prayer, Carrie Sue mentioned that she had received an unusual delivery on Valentine's Day – a dozen roses.

"Who did they come from?"

"I have no idea. There was no card and when I called the shop, the lady said that the order was placed by phone and it was paid for with cash."

"It sounds like someone is trying to rattle you."

"Yeah. Who'd know that we were talking about the flower gardens and that Rosebud had shown up?"

Carrie Sue was clearly upset and someone inside briefly appeared and looked at Abigail with suspicion. Abigail caught the look but did not comment on it. She knew that she would be tested over and over again until the last personality was integrated. It was part of the duplicity training and programming that was deeply instilled into every SRA survivor.

"Demons are messengers. We always pray and ask for protection here and I hope that the Lord doesn't permit those tattletales to eavesdrop."

"Hmm," Carrie Sue mused, "I wonder if it might have anything to do with my missing persons search."

"Oh, I didn't think of that, but that's a possibility. Did you find anything?" Abigail was quite curious. Satanists seldom left any evidence that was traceable back to them; or if it was, they would have a plausible explanation.

"Yes. There was a man reported missing in 1982. I saw his picture and he looked familiar. I'm really sure he was the guy that got in that fight with the dad. He might have been a neighbor."

"Interesting."

"Yeah. I made copies of the article, but I didn't bring them with me."

"That's okay. Hmm. I was just thinking that there aren't very many survivors who have any kind of corroboration for their stories."

"You're right. It gives me kind of mixed feelings, though. I'm glad that I'm not crazy but I hate it for that man. What about his family? I mean, after all these years they still have no answers."

"Let's keep this quiet for a little while longer. It's not like we can report this to Sheriff Bynum. Besides, we don't have proof positive yet."

"Yeah, I don't think I'm going to exhume bones from Mom's flower gardens."

"You don't suppose that she's onto something and is trying to get rid of evidence?"

"She did ask me to come help her."

"Let's pray and ask God to keep all evidence intact and then let's see where else we need to go today."

They prayed together and Carrie Sue sensed that they needed to deal with the pseudo-core personalities once again. She faded into the background and the boldest of the three pseudo-core alters surfaced.

"How have you been doing?" Abigail noticed that she seemed to be fuller, bolder.

"Fine. I think I'm catching on to some things and so are the other two."

"How is the original Carrie Sue doing?"

"She's growing. It's kind of weird to watch her grow up. I mean, she was an infant most of the time, but with so many of the integrations going into her, she's getting older."

"How old do you think she is by now?" Abigail tried to restrain her excitement.

"I'd guess she's about eleven or twelve."

"That's fantastic. Do you think she would be willing to talk with me for a little while?"

Abigail was able to have a brief conversation with the original Carrie Sue and was able to encourage the youngster and answer some of her questions. The girl reminded Abigail of a typical middle school child who was caught between yearning for her toys and dolls one minute and wanting to try make-up and high heels the next. She was not entirely sure about growing up and yet remaining the same or retreating back to infancy was an intolerable, if not impossible, option.

"A lot of them don't like me," she stated flatly.

"A lot of them think that you split them off on purpose and made them feel the pain. I think they don't realize that they kind of did the same thing when they were pushed too far and 'quit' so that another personality had to split out and pick up where they left off." Abigail said this knowing that many of the critics of this original Carrie Sue were probably listening. "I hope that each one will be able to extend grace to all the others because all of you were just trying to survive."

"Thanks."

They talked for a short while and then host Carrie Sue resurfaced. They spent their remaining time praying about the next week's rituals. Monday was the beginning of the Eastern Orthodox season of Lent. Tuesday was Shrove Tuesday and Wednesday was not only Ash Wednesday, but it was also a new moon. There was plenty of potential for Carrie Sue's system to be disrupted. It was no wonder that her mother was trying to intrude into her life again. No doubt it was her assignment and she was paying a price for having been ineffective.

Abigail took a break for a quick snack and when she returned to the office, Amy Bolton was already there just a few minutes early this time. That was a good sign and probably an indication that she had some serious business that she wanted to resolve.

After opening with prayer, Head Warden surfaced to give Abigail the week's debriefing. He was pleased to report that they had made it through the rest of the week without being accessed again largely due to increased internal security and the absence of Crescent as well as the inability of Draven, Raven, and Craven to interfere with things. He also reported that Amy was healing up physically from the things they did to her at the ritual. Abnego, the primary denial part, was deeply shaken but was on board as well.

"I've been wondering how Abnego has been doing. Would she be okay with talking for a little while?"

"I'll check." Head Warden disappeared and then quickly emerged with his report. "Not today, but she said to tell you that she appreciates your concern."

"Okay." Abigail continued to pray silently and then sensing an impression from the Holy Spirit, she related it to Head Warden. "Here's what I'm getting. You know how the system is organized in levels and areas – the outside ground level buildings, your surface level prison, and then the subterranean levels – and how each of those areas has a head honcho. You are the one for the prison, we know the leaders of the six subterranean levels, but we haven't met the head honcho there yet. We've pretty much left the outside area untapped, but we can be sure that there is a leader there, too."

Head Warden was nodding his head. "What are you thinking?"

"Well, with all the SRA's I've worked with, there seem to be three divisions, each with a leader, and a top guy over each of them. And, even though the leaders and divisions seem to be at odds with each other, they all have a common problem. That common problem is distracting enough that they are usually willing to work together to resolve it."

"What are you talking about?"

"The pre-borns, newborns, infants, and toddlers."

"They are a problem. At least they were on my level. It's a lot quieter and the protectors and others can do their jobs better without the distraction, like you said. But, if it makes the others more effective, isn't that going to work against Amy? I mean, then guys like Draven or Apollyon would be more effective on the dark side."

"That is one of the down sides at this stage of the game, but in the long haul, anything that benefits them will ultimately benefit everyone, especially Amy."

"Well, how do we do this?"

"As I recall... what was it? About a month ago when you were giving me info on the subterranean level leaders I mentioned a Head Honcho over each of them and some messenger showed up and told me to back off."

"Oh, yeah, I remember. He was not very happy and Amy got kicked a lot by that persecutor – Judas or at least someone from his level."

"Thanks for reminding me. We'll need to ask God to have everyone play nice for this meeting."

"Good idea. I'm ready if you are."

"Lord, we ask for Your presence during this meeting and that everyone would be cooperative and protected. We ask that no demon would have influence in this meeting and that each personality would be able to make decisions independent of demons. And now, according to Your will, would You bring out the other two head honchos as well as the leader over all of them if he's needed here today. Amen."

"Lady, you've got a lot of nerve calling us out like that!"

"Yeah, I know. Sorry about that, but I think you understand submitting to authority and even though you don't like my Authority, you know what it's like not to obey."

"Humph!"

"So, which leader are you?"

Pulling himself up into an even more erect posture than Head Warden's military-like bearing, he replied, "You may call me Joktan. I am the highest authority in the subterranean levels."

"Thank you for coming up." Abigail noted the squinting eyes in this personality that did not spend much time in natural daylight or in the presence of the Light of the world for that matter. "Is the leader of the outside community around?"

Abigail was rewarded with the tell-tale change in posture and eyes that did not squint. That would make sense since he was from the above-ground group of personalities. She had no idea of the population that inhabited that area. It had not been the focus of any of the sessions so far.

"I'm Mayor," the part said. He was decidedly uneasy for being in the spotlight as well as being in the presence of Joktan. He had witnessed many of Joktan's people as they used the tunnels that connected their respective areas. They were not hesitant to hurt anyone who happened to be nearby when they came through.

"Thank you for coming. Are we going to be able to talk to your leader today, too? Or is she going to leave the negotiations up to the three of you?" Abigail saw eyebrows rise in surprise.

"How did you know our leader is a female?"

"My Leader tells me things when I need to know them."

"I think she's just going to listen in and if we go too far, she'll let us know."

"Fair enough. Are you ready to hear the proposal?"

Amy's head nodded.

Abigail could not know if it was a collective nod or a nod by Mayor on behalf of Joktan and Head Warden. It did not really matter, she had their permission to proceed.

"Let me lay out the proposal and then I'd appreciate your feedback. Once we have a consensus, we can take care of business and you guys can go back to your areas. Here's the bottom line: In each one of your areas, there are lots of pre-borns, newborns, infants, toddlers, and little kids. They are miserable, hurting, and take up a lot of time and attention by their protectors. Each of them has been assigned demons. We all know that demons are messengers. Their job is to access you and narc on you to both the higher up demons and the cult members, thus, keeping one step ahead of you guys. For those of you who are against demonic and cult control, taking care of the little ones is one very effective way to eliminate it. For those of you who are demon and cult-loyal, this is one way for you to be more effective in your climb to the top. The demons and cult might not be pleased with this move, but sometimes you have to look out for yourselves."

"So just exactly what are you proposing, lady?" Joktan asked with slightly less hostility than he previously exhibited.

"I'm proposing that you allow the little ones – up to whatever age you are comfortable – to be healed and integrated into their respective protectors. That way, they're not going into the original F. Amy and remain under your jurisdiction until you're ready to release them." Abigail knew that Head Warden would be okay with it since all of the little ones that he was aware of were already healed and integrated, but she was unsure of the reactions of Joktan and Mayor. She was equally unsure of what the top leader would allow. The brief minute of silence while she awaited an answer seemed like an hour.

"All right," Joktan answered. "We consulted with our leader. She said she's comfortable with anyone who is preverbal. But you better not pull anything!"

"No problem. I'll start praying and if any of you are uncomfortable with anything I pray, just step in and stop it. Okay?"

"Trust me, we will."

Not wasting any time, Abigail launched into this very crucial prayer, knowing that two of the three of the leaders would be very uncomfortable with dealing with God. "Holy Father, we come before Your throne of grace in the name of Jesus the Christ on behalf of these leaders who desire to have the pre-borns, newborns, infants, and pre-verbal toddlers healed and integrated into their respective protectors. We ask that You would heal them of all verbal assaults, including programming; all direct and indirect unholy unions, soul ties, and flesh links from sexual traumas; and from all other kinds of traumas. We ask that You would cover them with healing balm so that their body memories and emotional pain would be soothed and healed. We plead the blood of Jesus the Christ over all strongholds created by sins against these little ones and ask that you would send their assigned demons to a place where they would never afflict anyone ever again. Please heal and seal all the broken places and fill with the fruit of the Holy Spirit. Father, please complete and correct anything prayed inadequately so that there will be no problems for the protectors who receive these little ones. Please integrate them now according to Your will and their willingness. Amen."

Head Warden took the lead and reported, "There were a bunch of little ones that I didn't know about. They looked really happy before they went into their protectors. Their protectors looked a little bit better, too."

Joktan begrudgingly reported the same results. Mayor looked relieved and stated that he felt a little bit better himself.

"I don't suppose you guys are up for including the next age level."

"Don't push it, lady."

"Uh, no, this is enough for me."

"Hey, I gotta try. Thanks for coming today and maybe when you process the changes you'll be up for some more."

Joktan and the Mayor disappeared and Abigail assumed that the top leader had retreated as well.

"Wow! That was a brazen move!" Amy was back in executive control.

"That was a God thing."

They prayed for protection from next week's rituals – the beginning of the Lenten season, Shrove Tuesday, Ash Wednesday with the new moon. The session went by quickly and it marked another major turning point in Amy's healing journey. Abigail closed with a prayer of blessing and protection from reprisals. After making an appointment for the following Friday, they went their separate ways.

Abigail looked at the skies and took a deep breath. *Lord, it smells like snow.* She made up her mind to stock up on a few extra items for the weekend. There was nothing like the smell of a turkey roasting in the middle of a snow storm. Sometimes snow was a nuisance, but sometimes a heavy snow gave her a good excuse to stay home and read a good book or work on the manuscript for her devotional. *Someday… someday.*

It seemed that others had the same idea and the grocery store was more crowded than usual for a Friday afternoon. Selecting a twelve-pound turkey and fresh cranberries, celery and sweet potatoes, Abigail added some of her staples to the cart and stood in the checkout line behind two more customers. Lost in thoughts, she suddenly felt a sharp pain in the back of both of her calves and found herself pushed forward by another cart.

"Oh, pardon me, ma'am!" a man with thick lenses apologized. "I'm so sorry, I wasn't paying attention. Are you all right miss?" He came to the front of his cart and got close to Abigail who was trapped between the two carts and the candy display. The only escape was blocked by the man who leaned over and whispered, "We're watching you, missy. Back off, or else!"

Abigail recoiled at the sound of a very familiar voice. Russ Ranson! "Or else what? Are you going to beat me up, too?" Abigail's strident retort had everyone within earshot turning around to look at the scene.

"Lady, you don't have to get so upset, I apologized and just wanted to make sure you were okay. You don't have to be so unchristian about it."

Wow, he's good... making himself look so good and me so bad. Lord, please deal with this oaf.

"Hey! Abigail!" A familiar voice hailed her.

Sagging with relief and a prayer of thanks to God, Abigail turned toward the voice as Russ abruptly walked away from his abandoned cart and headed toward the exit. Pastor Spalding and his wife, Natalie, were coming toward her. "Hello. Great timing!"

"Was that the guy from Mike Griffin's church?"

"Sure was. He rammed his cart into the back of my legs and made like it was an accident. When he came over to me, he whispered 'back off, we're watching you' or something like that and when I reacted, he acted all offended and tried to make me look bad."

"Are you okay, dear?" Natalie asked.

"I'm fine. Just a few more bruises to add to my hematoma collection."

The line moved up and Abigail placed her purchases on the conveyor. Soon she was checked out and on her way home. Snow was beginning to fall and so were the temperatures.

A heavy wet snow blanketed everything by Saturday morning. It further masked blemishes in the landscape and emphasized the graceful curves of the branches and wires. As pretty as it was, there was danger of the wet snow causing branches to snap off and sever power lines. Abigail was invigorated. After a late breakfast she set about baking her cornbread from scratch so she could make corn bread stuffing. Listening to her Christian radio station and cooking up a storm in the kitchen was both a joy and a sorrow. The baking and cooking were calming for her, but it reminded her in yet another way that she was alone.

"Lord, would I be out of line to ask Lee to come over for a turkey dinner? Is that too bold? Would You make it clear one way or the other and, well, maybe kind of make it happen?" She threw the prayer heavenward and went about making the dressing and preparing the cranberry sauce. Her grandmother taught her how to make it years ago. Scrubbing the sweet potatoes, she wrapped them in aluminum foil and readied them for the oven along with the turkey. Noting the time, she figured that she would be feasting by mid-afternoon if she started the oven now.

She planned to eat in her dining room using her grandmother's wedding china that she inherited. The pattern was quaint. There were hand-painted gold numbers on the bottom of each plate and serving piece of the Royal Bavarian Hutschenreuther china. Being the only girl had its privileges. Abigail broke into a faint smile wondering how many elegant and proper dinners had been served by her grandmother over the decades.

The ring of the phone jarred her out of her reveries. Walking over to the phone, she recognized Lee's number and picked it up. "Hello."

"Hello, how are you today?"

"Great! I love it when I don't have to be anywhere when it snows. It looks like we might get a pretty good accumulation. How are you?"

"I'm doing just fine. I'm still in town and I need to head out to the farm to move the horses up to the barn. How do the roads look by you? It's getting a bit treacherous here already."

"Well, I'm not sure. Come to think of it, I haven't noticed much traffic, but then, I was busy in the kitchen most of the morning. I'm looking out the window and it looks like someone has been driving on it. No snow plows or anything though."

"I'm not too worried with my four-wheel drive truck, I, um, well… would you like to check on Buster and the girls with me? I was thinking that it would be a beautiful day for a ride. I'd kind of like to explore some of the trails and I could use a guide."

"I'd like that. Wow, yes, that would be fun."

"I can be at your place in about thirty minutes. You still have your saddle, right?"

"Yep."

"Okay, then, I'll pick you and the saddle up and then we'll head over to my place."

"Great, I'll bundle up and be ready."

They said their good byes and hung up. Abigail could hardly contain her excitement. "Thank You Lord for a clear and quick answer to my prayer! I love You!" She put the turkey into the oven and set the temperature. It would be ready in about three or four hours. Perfect for an early supper!

By the time Abigail had gotten her boots on, found her oh-so-flattering stocking cap and a scarf, she had about five minutes to get the saddle from the barn.

That is, if Lee was punctual. She dressed in layers and could put things in the saddle bags if necessary. *Water. It's cold, but we'll get thirsty.* She grabbed some bottles of water and headed out the door to get the saddle. "Lord, will Buster behave today? I couldn't bear it if he acted up again."

Lee tooted his horn as he rounded the final bend in the driveway and turned the truck around as Abigail trudged through the accumulating snow. It was coming down hard and visibility was limited at times. Lee lowered his tail gate and took the bulky saddle from her. Escorting her to the passenger side, Lee opened the door, waited for her to get settled and closed the door behind her.

"This is going to be fun," Abigail gushed when Lee got in his seat. "Who are you going to ride today?"

"Maybe I'll take Sassy out. She's white and maybe people will think I'm just out there floating on a saddle behind a pair of eyes."

"It could happen."

"Actually, I think I'll go with Lady today. She's tall and strong and I might need that combination."

"Thanks for inviting me along. I miss riding and I do enjoy your company."

"I was afraid of being too forward, but I'm kind of tired of being alone and I enjoy your company, too."

"Actually, I was praying, or maybe whining, to God about being alone and lonely so I asked Him if I would be out of line if I were to ask you over for a turkey dinner today and could He please arrange it if it was okay with Him."

Lee's deep laugh interrupted her explanation.

"So, when you called, I took it as God's okay on the deal."

"I was kind of praying the same kind of prayer and was looking for an excuse to get together with you." He paused briefly and then looked her in the eyes. "Did you say turkey dinner?"

"Yep. It'll be ready in about three hours."

They continued to talk and chatted about the horses and Lee's progress on the farm, his plans for the new house and buying some beef cattle. They talked about Abigail's garden and orchard, plans to raise chickens and maybe get another dog. Someday. Lee told her about the loss of Bullet and plans to maybe get another dog. Someday.

Parking close to the barn, Lee grabbed the saddle, opened the door and headed to the tack room that he had built into one of the corners. Abigail was right behind him.

Pulling out leads for the horses, he handed them to Abigail. "Well, I think the best thing would be to walk down there, grab the horses and then saddle Lady and Buster up here."

"Sounds like a plan. I guess your mares are used to snow."

"We'd ride in a foot or more of snow, sometimes. This is nothing for them. Will Buster be all right?"

"I don't see why not. I've taken him out only a couple of times in the snow and he can get frisky in it. I just hope that he doesn't decide to do like he did on our last ride."

"If he does, I'll ride him. He'll be all right."

They fell into a silence as they walked side by side down the trail. About six inches of good packing snow had already accumulated and it was still coming down hard. Soon they were at the gate of the lower pasture. The horses were not in sight.

"Lady! Sassy! Where are you? Misty! Sparkles!"

"Buster!"

"This is strange." Lee looked worried. Opening the gate, he let Abigail in and secured it behind her. Looking for signs on the ground, Lee walked toward the lean-to that he had built. There were no fresh hoof prints in the immediate vicinity.

"What do you want to do? I mean, after we pray."

"Good idea. Let's pray and then walk the fence line. They must have gotten out somehow."

"Oh, Lord God, we pray for your protection over all the horses. We pray for clear signs that we can follow and we ask that You would cause that to happen very quickly, amen."

"Amen," Lee echoed. "I'll tell you what. Why don't you start at the gate and work your way around toward the road and then down to the creek. I'll go back up to the barn and get the four-wheeler and come pick you up and we'll go from there. It might take me a while because I need to fill the gas tank."

"No problem."

They quickly walked back up to the gate together. Abigail angled toward the road while Lee briskly hiked up to the barn. Abigail shuffled through the snow out to the corner of the fence and then turned south and was walking parallel to the road. It was slightly down hill and she made it to the far corner without slipping too much. Taking another turn, she started to follow the fence line that ran roughly parallel to York Creek when she saw the cut wires that curled back and left a gap large enough to allow a small herd of horses to escape.

Lee was going to follow the fence line the opposite way that Abigail had gone, but first he stopped to scan the area to see how much of the fence line Abigail had covered. He saw her at the opposite end of the field giving him come-down-here motions with her arms. *She must have found something.* Accelerating, Lee sped across the field without worrying about destroying any possible tracks or clues.

He saw the gap in the fence line where someone had clipped all five lines. Stopping just short of the fence line, Lee left the machine idling and walked closer to look for signs. Despite the deep snow, it was relatively easy to see that five horses had trampled through the muddy area and headed into the next field in the general direction of York Creek.

"It looks like they headed out toward the creek," Lee observed. "But the question is whether or not they were following their own noses or if somebody else led them or drove them."

Abigail was thinking similar thoughts and asked, "What's next?"

"Let's follow their trail for a little bit and see if there are five sets of tracks or if it looks like more. Why don't you walk on that side and I'll walk on this side and we'll just pray that we catch a break and see something definitive."

"What are you thinking?"

"That whoever cut the fence would have led them or herded them."

"That's rustling."

"Yep. Horse thieves." Lee was angry and worried but was self-controlled enough to hold his tongue and wait for a final verdict before verbalizing his thoughts. Actually, he learned a long time ago that he did not like to eat his own words. They did not taste very good.

Abigail set out slowly, not knowing exactly what she was searching for, and prayed fervently that whenever she did see it, or not see it, she would recognize the significance. Lee was doing the same thing about ten feet away from her. Nothing was obvious to either one of them after walking about fifty feet. "Let's get on the four-wheeler and follow their trail. Maybe we'll see something further on."

They retraced their steps back to the four-wheeler. Lee got on first and Abigail hopped on the back. She suddenly became self-conscious and uncertain as she realized how close they would have to sit. *Wow, this is close contact.* It brought back memories of Darryl and how she missed his touch. Forcing herself to focus on the task at hand, Abigail grabbed the brackets behind her and leaned to the right to watch the trail better.

It was fairly easy to see the snow-filled depressions left by their hoofs. Lee suddenly stiffened as he pointed to the ground, "Look! See those prints there? Look at how much bigger they are and how much further apart they are."

"The big horse!" Abigail felt a chill go down her back as she imagined that the cult people had captured all of Lee's horses. "I'll betcha these tracks will lead to that ritual site! Remember we rode up there one time?"

"We'll see. He probably clipped the fence and took off. Maybe he didn't realize that they followed him."

"I hope so."

"Hang on!"

Lee torqued the throttle and they sped through the snow following the predicted trail all the way through the field that bordered the creek, turning away from the road and deeper into the checker-board of fields that graced the countryside along the creek. Finally, they reached the shallow crossing and splashed through the elevated creek, fish-tailing in the mud as they came out on the other side. Neither one of them cared that they were wet and muddy. It was actually exhilarating. It had become obvious that their guess was right and the tracks led through the fields to the south of the creek and up the incline.

"Buster!" The truant sorrel gelding was pawing at the snow and nipping at whatever grasses he could find. Abigail leaped from the four-wheeler as Lee came to a halt about one hundred feet away from the base of the trail. He did not want to spook Buster or alert anyone who might possibly be lurking on top of the hill. Reaching under his coat, making sure that he had a bullet chambered, he scanned the trail and the hill top. Turning off the machine, he joined Abigail who was happily leading Buster over to him.

Lee opened the storage compartment on the front of the four-wheeler and pulled out a halter and let Abigail slip it over his head. "Where are all your girlfriends?" Turning to Lee she said, "I'll bet he wouldn't go up there because he remembers that ritual rock."

"They probably followed the big stud up there. You stay down here with Buster and I'll go up there and look. Do you have Walther with you?"

"Sure do." Abigail patted her belt line twice.

"Okay then, I'll take these halters with me and be back as soon as I can. If you hear shots, you get on Buster and head for a phone. Call Gary."

Abigail nodded and began praying immediately. *Lord, this kind of drama is supposed to happen to my clients, not me!* She watched the man that she was growing very fond of begin his trek up the slick, steep, snow-covered trail.

Lee's ground covering stride got him to the top of the trail in just a few minutes. He scanned the area and saw what he had hoped to see – four mares. Making a clucking noise, he got Misty's attention first. Her ears pricked up and she nickered a greeting as she started to amble over to Lee. The others looked up from their grazing and followed her lead. Within a couple of minutes, Lee had halters and lead ropes on all four of them and was walking back down the hill with a triumphant smile.

"Yes! Thank You, Lord!"

"Well, now we have to get these delinquents up to the barn. Are you comfortable driving this thing?" he asked with a nod toward the four-wheeler.

"Sure. It's a lot bigger than mine, but I think I can handle it."

"All right, then. I'll ride Lady and tie the others together. We'll probably walk so it might be a while."

"No problem. Anything I can do to help on the other end?"

"Yeah, why don't you open the stalls and put out some sweet feed and hay for them. I'll take care of the water when I get up there."

Their plans went as smoothly as herding the five horses could be and within the hour all the horses were safe and secure, groomed, fed and watered. They were sheltered in the barn from the snow storm which seemed to be increasing in intensity. The winds blew small drifts through some of the larger gaps in the barn's planking.

"Well, so much for a beautiful, leisurely ride," Abigail said with a twinkle in her eye.

"Sorry about that," Lee said.

"Actually, it's not your fault at all. It's probably mine. I'm just glad that they're all right. The thing that concerns me is that now you're a target of their pranks that could turn deadly."

"Yeah, I was thinking about that. We'll just have to be extra vigilant and keep praying. And don't you dare blame yourself for any of this. I sort of knew what I was getting into here."

Changing the subject, Abigail asked, "Hey, are you as hungry as I am? There's a turkey waiting for us."

"I'm starving!"

17

Sunday, February 18

The church was not very full Sunday morning. The snow kept many of the elderly parishioners and those without four-wheel drive vehicles safely home. The snow had stopped falling sometime in the middle of the night, but not before it dropped about ten inches of glistening snow. The gusts of wind left bare patches in some places and made up for it with drifts as high as two feet in others.

On the way to church, Abigail smiled wistfully as she saw the evidence in many yards of children who had played in the snow. Forts and snowmen dotted the county. Hills were striped with the smooth runs of the saucer sleds or toboggan-like plastic sleds that were all the rage these days. Abigail was adept at squelching thoughts about her sons but today she let her memories roll for a little while as she fondly remembered her sons' enthusiasm for playing in the snow.

The partially filled church did not diminish Pastor Spalding's enthusiasm. He bounded up to the platform in his characteristic style, beaming at the congregation. "Good morning! I'm so glad you made it here safely this morning. I am thankful for the guys who were out most of the night clearing the main roads." Continuing with some more opening remarks, he prefaced his opening prayer with information about two of their congregation who had been hospitalized that week.

"Folks, I don't know if you're aware of it or not, but this week marks the beginning of the Lenten season. I believe that our Catholic brothers and sisters are more diligent about revering this season than we Protestants typically are. I want to challenge each of you to search your heart and seek the Lord about how you should observe the time that leads up to Easter. We will have Shrove Tuesday which comes before Ash Wednesday. Palm Sunday, Maundy Thursday, and Good Friday occur toward the end of the Lenten season."

Seeing puzzled looks in some of the congregants, he went on to explain, "Shrove Tuesday started out in the Middle Ages as a day of confession and it marked a period of cleansing from lusts and appetites. People would fast during that time, but because they did not want to waste their food, they feasted. Unfortunately, it devolved into a day of indulgence and became known as 'Fat Tuesday' or in France, it was called 'Mardi Gras.'"

The "aha moment" flickered in peoples' faces as they heard the explanation.

"So, all that to say, I don't think it would be a bad idea to look at some Scriptures today that reference prayer and fasting. Sorry, but I'll be preaching from the Book of Concordance again."

He started in the Old Testament and pointed out some of the passages where the Israelites had annual fasting times. He had them look in the book of Esther where she called for a three day no eating or drinking fast. They looked at Ezekiel's extraordinary fast with a certain amount of specialty bread and a certain amount of water per day. Daniel fasted and waited for an answer to his prayers. In the New Testament, he covered many references to fasting and the purposes of the fasts.

"Folks, I intend to do some fasting during this season. I'm not sure why they call it a fast because it sure seems to go slow!" They chuckled at his wit.

He paused for a moment before returning to the solemnity of the subject. "Seriously though, I want to challenge each of you to inquire of God for your own situation. You may want to take three days like Esther, three weeks like Daniel, or an extended time. You may want to eliminate certain foods. You may need to fast from media. No television, radio, or internet might give us more time with the Lord and His Word."

He closed in prayer, as was his custom, and invited them to come up to the front to pray about sickness or infirmities, mental or emotional anguish.

Carrie Sue did not come to church that morning, so her spot in the pew was empty. After the service concluded, Gary and Cindy chatted with Lee and Abigail before heading downstairs to pick up Traci and Bryan. Lee and Abigail shuffled with the rest of the people up the aisle, shaking hands or hugging as they exchanged greetings.

"I enjoyed hanging out with you and the horses yesterday."

"I enjoyed it, too. I'm not sure I could have gotten the job done without you. Thanks. And thanks for the turkey dinner."

"My pleasure. I love to cook and it's nice to have someone around who enjoys it."

"The leftovers are great, too. I really appreciate it. I can cook, but mostly I pick up something at a fast food place or just make a peanut butter sandwich. Not so healthy, I suppose."

They continued to chat as they made their way to the back of the church, bundling up as they neared the doors and the felt the blast of cold air that invaded the foyer as people left the building.

"I need to go check on the horses today. I'd love to pick your brains about Max and his kind. Would I be too forward if I came up to visit with you for a while?"

"That saves me from being too forward and asking you if you'd like to share some leftovers. I made a turkey pot pie."

Rev. Paul Overton had prepared his United Methodist congregation for the up-coming Lenten season. The denomination traditionally had prescribed topics that each minister presented in sermon form nearly every Sunday. Many of them also had distinctive drapes for the communion table and the pulpit that corresponded to the season or the celebration. It was meaningful for some; it was a religious ritual for others.

Pastor Dennis Walsh's church was not affiliated with any denomination. As such, it was more informal and definitely was not liturgical. However, he mentioned the fact that Easter was not very far away, encouraged his congregation to ponder its meaning, and then completed his series on the Beatitudes.

Rev. Mike Griffin was keenly aware this year of all the forces that were competing for power – both human and demonic. He felt as if he had to tread a very fine line in his sermons because he did not know if Russ Ranson was the only Satanist in his congregation or if there were others. And if there were others, who were they? How many of them were there? What would happen if they knew that he knew? Who could he really trust? He found himself searching the faces of his congregation more intently than perhaps was polite. He was looking forward to the next Ministerial Alliance meeting and hoped that Abigail Steele would be with them. He had more questions.

Prinz and his cohorts were having their own services. They reverently partook of communion, they fervently prayed, and they thoughtfully prepared for the Lenten season. They planned for the crescendo of wickedness that would culminate on Easter.

They were much like people who despised having been raised by an alcoholic but then married an alcoholic as if by fixing the present they could mend the past. If the Satanists could rewrite Easter this year, they could fix the outcome of that first Easter. It was not logical, but desperation and corrupted wisdom kept all of them on their respective hamster wheels.

They discussed the various acts of vandalism. Prinz berated them for their sophomoric harassment attempts against Abigail, Carrie Sue, and Amy in particular. He knew that their fear was not of the women themselves, but of the presence of the Great Enemy within each of those women.

"They keep filing complaints," Zorroz said. "We won't be able to keep losing paperwork and delaying investigations forever."

"Why not?" Prinz snarled. "Have we had a problem before? We have the top county commissioner and the judge on our team." He nodded at his top henchmen, Daggett and Darod. "Do you see any problems?"

"No sir," they chimed in unison.

"Then I suggest that we get down to the business of winning this region for our father and king."

Lines were drawn in the spiritual sand. Both teams were vying for the same tangible and intangible territory. One was out of malevolence, desperation, and greed; the other was out of love, compassion and benevolent anguish for perishing souls.

Their respective cheerleaders were battling it out in the heavens as the Lord of hosts commissioned His messengers, His warriors, His worshipers to come to the aid of His people. It was much like long ago when Jehovah's shining warriors surrounded the hostile army that sought to kill Elisha.

Satan's hosts, mimicking yet another aspect of the Kingdom of God, came to the aid of those pathetic dust-puppets – but only insofar as it served Satan's purposes. He had no intention of sparing anyone pain. There was never any intention of sharing his glory with another. He would be like the Most High.

Max Berryman had dutifully attended church that morning as well. Sitting in the balcony behind the empty seat that Sheriff Bynum normally occupied, he fulfilled his obligation to his father by looking like the son of an elder. He had hoped to have contact with Zorroz this morning just for some contact with a like-minded, like-spirited comrade. Even with the tension of trying to rise in the ranks, Max found it invigorating to be near powerful men that he wanted to emulate.

Today, Max was eyeing that traitor, Jason. He had come with his family and was sitting down in the front of the main auditorium. Max timed his descent to the foyer so that he would encounter Jason. Falling into step beside Jason, Max whispered, "Look at the goody-two-shoes coming to church with Mommy and Daddy."

Jason was startled and drew back from Max. "That's not what's going on, Max. I've made a commitment to Jesus and I don't want to be a part of your gang."

Max was not expecting an assertive answer from Jason. "This isn't just some gang. You just made a big mistake and you'd better watch your back."

"I didn't make a mistake, you did. Max, you need to get out of that cult."

Again, Max was not expecting that kind of response from his former trainee. He quickened his pace to put a little distance between them on the sidewalk. Looking over his shoulder he said with as much sincerity as he could muster for the sake of appearances, "You take care of that cute little sister of yours."

Jason was pierced by the words. He knew exactly what Max meant. Stopping in his tracks, immediately turning around, he scanned the thinning crowd in the foyer looking for Pastor Spalding. Spotting him at the doorway, Jason edged closer to the man and waited until he could catch his eye.

Seeing the concerned look on Jason's face, Pastor Spalding turned his attention to the young man. "How are you doing, son?"

"Well, I'm a little upset right now. Could we talk in private for a couple of minutes?"

"Sure, let me just say good-bye to a few more folks and we can go over to my study."

"Thanks."

Jason was trying not to be impatient with the little old ladies who had to tell Pastor Spalding about their grandchildren or the long-winded man who had much to say about nothing. But finally, after interminable minutes, Jason and Pastor Spalding made their way to the study and sat down on the same chairs that they had in their last chat.

"You look upset. What's going on?"

"Well, you know Max... he ran into me in the foyer a little bit ago and told me that I'd better watch my back and he made an indirect threat about my little sister."

"Oh?"

"Yeah, he told me that I'd better keep an eye on her. I remember what Mrs. Steele said about little blonde-haired, blue-eyed kids. I mean, I just got cold chills all over me when he said that. Do you think he'd really do something to her?"

"I'd like to think that he was just blowing smoke, but unfortunately with all the mess that's been going on around this county, I think we would be prudent to take heed and pray accordingly."

"What can we do? There must be something we can do. What should I tell my parents? Maybe you can say something to them. I'm not sure what to say."

"Whoa, hold on there. Let's not panic. We should say something to your parents and I'm very willing to talk with them. Maybe we could even have a meeting with Mrs. Steele, too. But meanwhile, we certainly can pray together right now for protection over your sister and you, too, for that matter."

Heaving a sigh of relief, Jason felt some of the tension draining from him. "I'd like that."

"You know, I've been reading in the Book of Esther lately and I see some interesting parallels between the threats against the Jews because of a guy named Haman who wanted to destroy them and the threats that the cult and a guy named Max is making against you and your family. I hope you don't mind if I go into this briefly because I think we can pray more effectively about this situation."

"No problem, I kind of remember that story from Sunday school."

"Okay, so Haman plotted against Mordecai the Jew because Mordecai wouldn't bow or honor him. Haman bribed the king so that he could have a law made that would allow everyone to kill and plunder the Jews. Once that came to light, the king allowed Mordecai and Queen Esther, his cousin, to write a counter-edict that allowed the Jews to fight back. They did it and won. And, unfortunately for Haman, everything he wanted to have happen to the Jews happened to him and his whole family was wiped out."

"Vicious!"

"Well, I don't think I want to pray such a vicious prayer against Max, I mean, as malicious as he is, God is not willing that anyone should perish. He was a pretty decent kid at one time. I wish I knew what went wrong." Pastor Spalding was momentarily thinking of the young Max who appeared to have been just as normal a kid as any of the others. "Anyway, what if we pray that God would do whatever it takes to get his attention and transform him?"

"Yeah, I really don't want him burning in hell or anything, I just want him to not be able to hurt my little sister or anyone else for that matter."

"We can definitely pray for protection. Ready?"

"Yes sir."

"I'll start, then, and you can pray as the Spirit leads." With that said, Pastor Spalding launched into a prayer appealing to God as the King over this situation and asked Him to issue an "edict" that would counter the decrees of the enemy's kingdom. He prayed for Max's salvation and for safety for the entire Miller family.

After he finished, Jason self-consciously prayed, "Yeah, God, I'm really worried about what Max keeps saying about hurting little Ariel, please stop anything that he or the rest of the cult might try to do and change him, in Jesus' name, amen."

"Amen," Pastor Spalding echoed. "Do you feel any better now?"

"Much better, thanks. I think I'd better head home, I didn't tell my folks that I was going to be a bit late. I don't want them to worry."

Pastor Spalding marveled at the changes in the young man and praised the Lord as he walked him out of the office.

The roads were still slick in some areas despite the best efforts of the overworked snowplow crews. Black ice posed a threat, especially over some of the bridges that crossed the many creeks that flowed into the Blue River all across the area. Most of the roads in the low-lying areas were built up almost like levees so that they would not flood. Shoulders were narrow and sloped sharply downward in the lowlands. Those who had ventured out for church services that morning were carefully making their way home, grateful that the conditions were somewhat improved over their early morning drive. One miscalculation could put them into a precarious, if not fatal, situation.

Max felt invincible as he roared down the streets in his big four-wheel drive diesel and he was definitely too cool to use a seat belt. He was impatient with the slow drivers, he tail-gated and flashed his headlights, sounding his horn and cursing as he went. He did not care if everyone in the county knew who he was. He did not care if his father lost some business because of his antics. Max was only concerned about Max.

Always having a sense of urgency, he wanted to get to his destination as quickly as possible even when he had no particular plans. He liked the sense of power as his vehicle surged whenever he pressed the accelerator.

Adrenaline!

Today was no different and as he came upon a cautiously moving mid-sized sedan not very far out of town, he began his impatience routine. Approaching a longer bridge that crossed one of the wider creeks, Max decided to pass them since there was no on-coming traffic in sight. Nearly clipping the back bumper of the sedan, he passed closely alongside of them, frightening the elderly gentleman and causing him to ease off of his accelerator. The man did not see the finger that Max extended toward him as he passed; Max did not see the patch of black ice at the end of the bridge as he moved back into his lane.

Max's momentum caused his truck to turn to about a forty-five-degree angle as he slid down the highway at nearly fifty miles per hour totally unchecked. Too late, he realized his foolishness and there was no correcting his error despite frantically spinning the wheels into the skid. There was no traction until he hit a patch of dry pavement. Then the wheels bit. The truck lurched and spun uncontrolled onto the shoulder until the downward slope and his momentum started the truck to roll and then somersault into the semi-frozen marshy terrain that bordered this section of the road.

The abrasion-inflicting airbag punched Max hard in the face and chest and then collapsed allowing Max's body-turned-projectile to hurtle head-first through the windshield on the passenger's side of the cab. He heard the crack of the impact like the sound of thunder and felt the reverberation echo down his spine just before everything went black. The truck finally lost its propulsion and settled to a stop just before Max's inert, twisted body also came to a halt half in and half out of the cab. The only reason that he was not completely crushed was because the front of the mangled hood rested on a large rock.

The horrified couple cautiously slowed to a stop and peered over the edge of the road to the overturned truck which had come to a rest on its roof. "Honey, call 911!" Herb tried to sound calm, but the high pitch of his voice betrayed him.

His wife, Henrietta, nervously sorted through the collection of items that women carry in their purses just in case they ever needed them. Finally grasping the seldom used cell phone, she pulled it out, flipped it open and pressed the power button. It took thirty interminably long seconds until the musical tones let her know that she could make her call. Pressing the three digits, she responded to the dispatcher, "Yes, I need to report an accident. A truck just went off the

King-Spring Road just south of that long bridge outside of Springfield."

Herbert put his hazard lights on and stepped out of the car. "Tell her I'm going to see if he's all right."

"You be careful Herb! Don't you go down there!" She was clearly alarmed and tried to focus on the questions coming from the dispatcher while nervously watching her husband make his way to the edge of the road where he had a better view.

He turned back to her and shook his head. She related the urgency to the dispatcher. Another vehicle had stopped and the driver rolled down his window and leaned out. "I don't see him moving and I hope that water doesn't drown him if he's still alive," Herb called out to the other driver. "My wife is calling 911 so maybe they can get here fast enough to save him." Noticing that more vehicles were lining up behind him, Herb decided that the best thing he could do was to get out of the way.

"Do you think he's alive?" Henrietta quavered as they drove away.

Sirens sounded and lights flashed as the various agencies were notified about the accident. They had had a busy night already but the dedicated firemen donned their uniforms and leapt into their trucks. Even with no reported fire, they responded whenever the ambulance was called out. A deputy sheriff arrived and began to direct traffic flow while the tow truck maneuvered so that he could hook a line to the overturned pickup truck to stabilize it while rescuers used the jaws-of-life to free the lifeless figure who had been tossed around like a rag doll.

Much later, just as the Spaldings were settling down for the dark winter evening, the telephone rang.

"Hello?"

"Pastor Spalding, this is Ted Berryman. I'm so sorry to bother you this late, but my son, Max, has been in a terrible accident. We've been here all afternoon. They finally got him stabilized and have just taken him to surgery and I don't know if he's going to make it."

"Are you in the Springfield Hospital?"

"Yes."

"I'll be right over."

"I'm sorry, I hate to call you out on a terrible night like this, but I sure would appreciate it. We're in the surgical waiting room on the second floor."

"I'll be there as soon as I can."

Pastor Spalding told Natalie that he would be going to the hospital to be with Ted Berryman and his wife. Then he began to pray earnestly, "Oh, Lord, is this the result of Jason's and my prayer today? Is this Your way of getting Max's attention? Oh, God, have mercy on Max and his family. Save his life and save his spirit." He continued to pray as he bundled up, grabbed his Bible, and headed back out into the cold winter night for the short trip to the local hospital.

Pastor Spalding knew the hospital about as well as he knew his sprawling church building because he had been there so many times on so many occasions. And it really was not necessary for him to wear his clergy ID because most of the employees knew who he was. He found Ted and Barbara Berryman huddled together in the corner of the waiting room talking in low tones to a small group of friends and relatives.

"They had to use the jaws-of-life to get him out," Ted rambled in a monotone as if repeating the facts would help him make sense of the senseless situation. "They said that it was a miracle that he was even alive. He has a lot of internal injuries and his spine is broken. They won't know if he'll ever be able to walk again." At that point, the executive who always had solutions, crumbled. His shoulders shook as he sat back down on his chair.

Barbara had never stopped crying and she continued to dab at her eyes with a mascara-blackened tissue. Leaning onto her husband's shoulder, she broke into another loud sob. They were each preoccupied with their own thoughts and fears.

Pastor Spalding had too much experience over the years with these kinds of scenes. Pulling a chair directly in front of the distressed couple, he asked if they would like to pray. Getting their affirmative nods, he prayed, "Heavenly Father, we come before Your throne of grace in the name of Jesus on behalf of Max. Father, we implore You to have mercy on his spirit, soul, and body and bring him healing. Father, we know that Max has been drifting. We ask You to use this accident to get his attention and cause him to turn to You. We ask that You would redeem his life from destruction in the name of Jesus, amen."

Pastor Spalding scooted his chair back a few feet. An informal circle of supporters sat huddled together. Sometimes they sat in complete silence; sometimes engaging in small talk; sometimes venturing into best and worst-case scenarios for Max, but mostly praying with groanings too deep for words.

Finally, after hours of waiting, a volunteer answered the phone at her desk, uttered a few syllables and returned it to its cradle. "Berryman?" she asked as she looked their way. "The surgeon will meet with you in the consultation room." She pointed to the door just in front of her desk.

Ted stood first and helped Barbara to her feet. "Pastor Spalding, would you join us, please?"

The three of them made their way into the small consultation room. Soon a weary surgeon entered through the surgeons' door and sat down opposite the three expectant people.

"I have some good news and some challenging news. Your son is alive. He's had extensive internal damage. We removed part of his ruptured spleen, but he'll be able to function just fine without it. His left kidney had a tear that we could repair and it seems to be functioning just fine. We'll have the urologist keep an eye on that. His sternum was broken and so were some of the ribs at that level. We wired the sternum to stabilize it until it starts to mend on its own. The hematomas and other contusions will heal nicely. We sutured some lacerations on his face. His left arm is also broken just below the elbow and is in a cast."

"Oh, my God!" Barbara gasped.

"Is that all the challenging news?" Ted was not sure he wanted to know the answer.

"Actually, that was the good news."

"Oh, my!" Barbara gasped and clung tightly to Ted as she sagged momentarily.

"The most challenging thing, actually, there are two potentially very challenging things: his head injury and his spinal injury. He has had a severe concussion. He was unconscious when they brought him in. He came around before we had to put him under for surgery, but he's going to have a severe headache and we won't know if there has been any damage to his brain. He may have temporary or permanent problems with his memory, but that remains to be seen."

"Oh, my poor baby." Barbara was openly weeping.

"The other challenge is the spinal injury. He'll need surgery to stabilize the fractured vertebrae that are at about the same level as the rib and sternum fractures. We think that the spinal cord is still intact because he was moving his legs a little, but it may be impinged by bone fragments. We will have to let him heal from the surgery he had today and allow the spinal swelling to go down before we can assess that more accurately. Meanwhile, we'll keep him sedated in the ICU and he will get excellent care."

Word quickly spread around the community. Relatives were called. The church's prayer chain was notified.

Cassie Miller was on the prayer chain. She related the news to her husband and son after she hung up and called the next person that she was responsible to call. Fortunately, Ariel was already in bed for the night so she was not there to ask innumerable questions. Jason thought she would make a great interrogator.

"What happened to him?" Jason asked with alarm. The prayers that he and Pastor Spalding had prayed after church that day were running through his mind. He had the same questions that Pastor Spalding did: *Did we cause this? Did our prayers set this in motion?*

Jason's weighty thoughts and heavy emotions churned like a cement mixer's load.

"They say he hit a patch of black ice at the end of the long bridge. His truck rolled several times and he was ejected and then nearly crushed under it. It's a miracle that he's alive at all!"

Jason's brow was deeply furrowed as he processed his thoughts.

"Penny for your thoughts," Paul interrupted him.

"Dad. Mom. I need to tell you something. I'm sorry I didn't tell you this stuff before. I don't know why except that I didn't want to worry you."

"What are you talking about, son?"

"Okay, you know how Max is involved in some kind of cult. Well, it's more serious than any of us knows except for maybe that counselor, Mrs. Steele."

"Just say it, Jason," Cassie urged.

"Max bumped into me at the end of church today. He told me that I ought to watch my back and then he said something like, 'take care of that pretty little sister of yours.' He's been really mad at me for not following him anymore and he keeps hinting that he's going to do something to Ariel."

"Oh, my!" Cassie's hands instinctively covered her mother's heart.

"When I met with Mrs. Steele and Pastor Spalding last month after Nathan was killed, she mentioned that the cult prefers blonde-haired, blue-eyed children to sacrifice because they're considered to be purer."

"Oh, dear!"

"Mom, we prayed about it then and this morning – that's why I was late coming home after church – I told Pastor Spalding about Max's threat after church. We prayed again and… well, we asked God to do whatever He had to do to get his attention and transform him."

"And so, you think that this accident is no accident," Paul said.

"Yeah, and I don't know if I'm feeling relieved because he can't hurt Ariel now, or if I'm afraid of more pay backs, or if I just feel kinda guilty."

"Son, all those feelings and more are normal. You didn't do anything wrong. In fact, you did right. But next time, maybe you can talk with us about these things so that we can all be vigilant on Ariel's behalf and pray more intentionally about it as a family."

"Yes, sir, I just didn't want you to be upset."

"I appreciate that, but I am still the head of this household. It's my responsibility. You are growing up, and I'm proud of you, son. Why don't we spend some time praying for our family's protection right now?"

"And for Max's transformation."

18

Wednesday, February 21, Ash Wednesday

Amy Bolton's internal life had gotten quieter with the latest healings and integrations of the very young ones within the system. It seemed lighter inside, somehow, despite some of the very dark characters that inhabited her nether world. Amy was enjoying a respite from some of the intensity that had always surrounded her life; however, there was a bit of discomfort of sorts that came with it because peace was not her normal comfort zone. She did not know how to live with anything but crises and chaos. But she would learn.

The demonic oppressors who were assigned to Amy were not pleased with the decisions of Head Warden and now Mayor and Joktan were starting to get on board. They knew that it was just a matter of time before Joktan, leader of the subterranean levels, would be duped by more and more of that woman's schemes. They decided that this would be a good time to stir up their lackey, Levi, and have him bring some retribution.

Levi Blevins was only too eager to do the bidding of his masters. The more he did for them, the more they had promised to do for him. Levi was not particularly pleased with the sophomoric stunt that he and Max had collaborated on last time. The Great Enemy's woman warrior suffered very little ill effect from the dismal fire. Max was sloppy and despite having cult members in high places, Levi did not want to risk getting caught. He wanted to stay under the radar as much as possible.

Levi was raised by Satanists. His mother had been selected for his father by his grandfather. Actually, his grandfather might well be his biological father. There were no rules, no honor, no loyalty; only gratification and domination.

Levi felt a stirring deep in his spirit and focused his attention on the thoughts that flowed to him. He was practiced with this kind of spiritual communication and it was as clear to him as any conversation that he might have with any human being. He was being directed to have another encounter with F. Amy Bolton.

The so-called legal right that Levi had to rape Amy was the authorized opening that was made when her father named her. While Levi was not privy to the details, he understood enough about these kinds of transactions. Indeed, he had experienced a number of positive and negative effects of the name that he had been given. Levi. Leviathan.

Driving to her trailer, stepping out of his sleek sports car, looking casually up and down the deserted street, Levi moved with his usual quiet grace to the front door. Just like the previous times, he could not prevent the boards from creaking. It was irrelevant. He quickly shoved his shoulder into the flimsy trailer door and broke in without much fanfare. Closing the door behind him, he quickly surveyed the disheveled living room and then the kitchen to his right. *She must be in the back bedroom.*

Amy had heard the commotion of the break in and assembled her protectors. Head Warden directed his strongest man to handle the situation. They breathed a quick prayer to keep any programming that might be triggered which would cause a small child to be put in charge instead of an adult. They prayed that Levi's demons would be stripped off of him so that they could not empower him.

Levi confidently walked down the hallway peering into the utility room, the first closet-sized bedroom, and the tiny bathroom as he passed down to the bedroom at the very end of the trailer. Just as he suspected, Amy was there.

He flashed a quick sign that looked like he was making the well-known "okay" sign. It was also a sign that is used by the deaf community for the letter F. The letter F. The sixth letter of the alphabet. His goal was to bring a certain young part of F. Amy Bolton to the forefront – one that he could easily dominate because of programming that had been installed decades ago.

"You know what you're good for," Levi muttered. "I'm here to teach you a lesson and let you live up to your name."

Michael, Head Warden's strongman, feigned the part of a submissive little girl, at least until Levi came within striking range.

The unexpected uppercut to his chin caused Levi's head to jolt backward and he staggered back into the hallway. Metallic taste of spurting blood let him know that his tongue had been caught between his molars. Adrenaline kicked in and he was ready to fight.

"You worthless whore!" Levi regained his balance and came after Michael.

"In the name of Jesus the Christ, get out of here!" This command was accompanied by a step forward followed by another punch to Levi's face.

Blood trickling out of his nose, Levi was stunned once again. He began to retreat, totally bewildered by his loss of power. Turning quickly, stumbling down the hallway, Levi fled to his car. Only when he was off of the property did he once again feel the presence of his empowering spirits. They were unhappy with the whole situation because they were accountable to their superiors as well. They took it out on Levi. Barely able to drive because of the internal torment, Levi limped to the nearby truck stop and parked in a remote spot to lick his wounds and try to comprehend what had just happened to him.

Meanwhile, Amy and the internal protectors were triumphantly whooping it up. They had a victory – a smashing victory. They were beginning to sense more hope. She had felt so helpless and hopeless all of her life. They could not wait to tell Abigail.

Mayor and Joktan were in the background as usual, but they were near enough to the surface that they were fully aware of the fight between Michael and Levi. They were dissociated enough that they were as unconcerned about the outcome of the conflict as if they were observing the event on a television show. There was no affinity or loyalty between them and anyone else in the system of personalities that made up F. Amy Bolton. Such was the life of a person with multiple personalities. They each had their own jobs to do. What did they have to do with anyone else inside or out? Everything and nothing.

The temperatures steadily fell. Clouds formed a perfect canopy over the region. Snow began to fall once again. Because of the risk of leaving the evidence of too many tracks in the snow, the ritual tonight was being held in the windowless lodge. Weather never really deterred faithful followers. So, was it programming? Threats? Greed? Pride? Coercion? Or perhaps, like a gambler on the last hand of the night, the desperation of staking their very souls on winning the whole pot drove them to pursue ascendancy.

Levi tried to keep a low profile. He knew that it was just a matter of time before he would be called into account for the absence of F. Amy Bolton, better known as Karkass in their circles. Things seemed to have come easy to Levi most of his life, but tonight plans that were fermenting in his mind were just turning sour. It was as if his IQ had dropped fifty points. *Was it just from the beating? Do I have a concussion?* He kept his head down and stayed in the shadows as much as possible. He was humiliated and that disgrace fueled rage that simmered under the surface. He was angry at Karkass. He was angry at his demons – after all, they had an agreement and they deserted him at a critical time. They were supposed to help him.

Levi embarked upon a plan to attract stronger spirits that would be loyal to him and empower him to do whatever he needed to do to continue to rise in the ranks. *I'll be more powerful than Prinz, himself!* With that vow in place, Levi locked himself into a quest for power that would consume his life. Starting tonight. The new moon and Ash Wednesday, too. This night would afford Levi ample opportunity to navigate through the maze that was laden with traps and dead ends.

Moving discreetly away from the gathering, he glided stealthily down the dimly lit hallway until he found the stairwell that led to the lower level. He had been down here before and felt the presence of the demons who had been summoned here by Prinz and the other masters. His heart beat like the rapid staccato of a clock that was wound too tight. Finding a small room, dropping to his knees and touching his forehead to the cold, hard cement floor, he began to chant his request in a language unknown to himself.

He thought he knew what he was requesting, but only the traitorous beings that controlled his tongue knew. They knew that he was giving up on them and their pride would not allow it. Their eerie, hyena-like howls echoed and reverberated within Levi. He was being betrayed by the ones who had been betrayed by the best.

The worst.

By the time Levi slipped back into the main room, it was nearly midnight and the cavernous room was filled with hooded figures and with others who were unclothed. Sacrifices were made and out of the residue of the bodies, dots of ashes were smudged on foreheads in a mockery of Ash Wednesday. Just when it seemed that Levi would dodge repercussions for the absence of Karkass, he was surrounded by hooded figures who ushered him into Prinz's presence.

"Levi," Prinz intoned, "you have asked to increase your powers and your request has been granted."

The already shaken young man began to tremble. He knew the price that he would have to pay to increase powers would not be pleasant and he tried to call on what powers he did have. Remembering the proper protocol, Levi bowed as he brought his steepled fingers to his lips. "Thank you."

He was immediately grabbed roughly by strong hands. His garments were stripped from him and within seconds, he was slammed onto a cross that had been laying on the floor nearby. He was quickly fastened to the cross face down with ropes that tightly bound his arms, legs, and torso. Abruptly, the cross was stood up on end and he felt the blood rush to his head. *I'm going to die!* Just when he thought it could not get worse, the chanting got louder and more intense, following the rhythm of the drumming. He felt the white-hot touch of malevolent hands and other body parts touching and invading his body until everything went black.

Not knowing if he was experiencing reality or not, the surrealistic surroundings started to become clear. His father and grandfather were on either side of him dispassionately looking at the carrier of the birthright, the one who bore the family legacy. Relieved that he was still alive, Levi began to stir. Painfully.

"Arise, my son," his grandfather spoke with a flat tone of voice. "You have been presumptuous because of your desperation. Never again dishonor our family in such a manner."

Levi's lips parted and he tried to speak through swollen lips, but nothing came out. He watched his father and grandfather turn their backs and walk away. Their footsteps echoed down the hall.

Ted and Barbara Berryman had been keeping a constant vigil in the ICU department, they took turns going home to shower and attend to urgent domestic or business responsibilities. Sympathetic nurses allowed them more than the posted ten minutes allowed each hour whenever they were not directly attending to Max's medical needs.

It had been nearly four days and Max was still under sedation to keep him from thrashing around while the swelling went down in his brain and spinal column. His pale face was broken and bruised, swollen and nearly unrecognizable to his parents. Barbara wept and Ted paced. They kept asking the nurses when Max would be conscious again. They desperately wanted to find out how much damage the injuries caused. Would he be okay? Would he be mentally deficient in any way? Would he be paralyzed? Would he live? Lord God, would he live?

As the days wore on, fewer people came to the waiting room. Life went on for the rest of the world. Pastor Spalding, however, was there once or twice a day. Talking and praying, bringing a snack or a meal, the pastor ministered to his flock. He loved the so-called black sheep as much as he loved the white sheep.

Barbara wiped her tears and tried to make herself presentable when the neurologist entered the room with a nurse right behind him carrying the patient's chart. He nodded briefly at Ted and Barbara and then went about checking Max, muttering and grunting as he proceeded. Opening Max's eyelids one at a time and flashing a penlight into them, he said something about "equal and reactive" to the nurse and she dutifully noted it in his chart. He checked the reflexes of the ankles and knees, one wrist and one elbow. When he appeared to be finished, Barbara blurted out, "Doctor, how is he? When will he be conscious again?"

He gently held his hand up to quiet her. "I know you want to be able to communicate with your son, but right now we have to make sure that his brain doesn't swell. That could cause areas of ischemia, er, places in the brain that don't get enough oxygen. It could cause seizures or convulsions or do other damage; so, for the time being we're going to keep him sedated. His pupil reactions look good, but that doesn't mean that there can't be other issues. He's still in a tough spot, but he's young and he's strong. Most people would not have survived those injuries. God must want him around."

Both Ted and Barbara thanked the doctor as he turned and continued his rounds. They were not exactly sure if they received good news or not, but for now, at least they knew that his pupil reaction was good and they thanked God for that tiny ray of hope.

Pastor Spalding was in the waiting room when they returned to "their" corner to resume their prolonged vigil. "What's the word?"

Ted shook his hand. "Well, the neurologist was just in there and he said that his pupils were reacting right."

"Wonderful!"

"But he wants to keep him sedated to keep his brain from swelling and not getting enough oxygen as I understand it."

"That makes sense."

"But I can't stand the suspense!" Barbara blurted. "I just want to know that he's going to be okay. Why would God let this happen to him?" She looked at Pastor Spalding with a look that only a desperate mother could give. And when she did, he felt a pang in his heart as he remembered the prayer that he and

Jason had prayed for God to do whatever it took to bring Max back to God.

Pastor Spalding prayed quickly, *Oh, Lord, what do I say here? I don't want to hurt them any more than they are already hurting.* He sensed that he needed to have a difficult conversation with them. Clearing his throat, he asked, "Can we sit down and talk about that?"

"Sure." Ted and Barbara looked expectantly at their pastor. They trusted him.

"I'm sorry. This might be a tough conversation but it may give you some insight into why Max is in there right now."

"Go ahead," Ted replied. "I think I have an idea but we want to hear what you have to say."

"Let's pray first." Pastor Spalding led them in a brief prayer asking God for clarity and discernment, wisdom and discretion. He looked them in the eyes and then asked, "Have you ever prayed that God would do whatever it took to get your son's attention?"

They both nodded gravely.

"I've been praying that way for Max as well. In fact, I prayed that way on Sunday, just about the time he was in the accident. I'm not saying our prayers caused this accident, but it may well be the means that God is going to use to redeem his life."

That got a double-take from both of them.

"Do you know what your son does when he's not at work? I mean, who his friends are? What they do?"

"Frankly, pastor, we've been wondering the same thing and that's why we've been praying that way. We raised him in the church and he was baptized at the same time Nathan was." That thought gave Ted a jolt. "Wow, both of them were in serious wrecks so close together! I mean, they were friends and hung out. Max doesn't talk about much. He's just been so sullen and angry, especially since Nathan died."

"He doesn't talk to us much at all," Barbara interjected. "He comes home late or just spends time in his room. And, well, they did a test to see if he was impaired and some kind of pain killer showed up. He doesn't have a prescription for pain killers." Her bewildered reaction revealed her level of denial about her son's problems.

"Please," Ted said, "feel free to be honest. Frankly, we don't have anything to lose here and if he pulls through, we want to be able to help him."

"Well, I don't know about the prescription drugs, but I suspect that if he's using them, it's for emotional pain rather than physical pain. When he's been in church, he's been kind of aggressive and angry toward certain people."

"What do you mean? Who?" Barbara demanded with alarm as if she could not imagine her sweet son being capable of such actions.

"Well, it seems that after Nathan was killed, Jason Miller decided to stop hanging out with Max and his friends. He quit his job at the dealership and Max has been harassing and threatening him."

"Max wouldn't do that!" Barbara protested.

"Now, Barbara, let Pastor Spalding talk. He's not going to make stuff up. Jason did quit his job at the dealership." Turning to Pastor Spalding he nodded.

"I'm sorry. This is difficult. And this might sound far-fetched, but it seems that Max has gotten caught up with some kind of a group that might be a cult. Jason told me some things that line up with other things I've heard from some credible people in our community."

Ted and Barbara sat back in disbelief, mouths agape. They knew Max had problems; but a cult? "What kind of cult? In our county? I don't believe it. How could everyone not know about it?" Again, Barbara was in denial mode. The she-bear was rising up in her.

"Ted. Barbara. Max seems to have gotten mixed up with some people who try to lure young people into their group by making them do something illegal or immoral. Apparently, on the night that Nathan died, Max was trying to get Jason and Nathan to participate in one of those initiations. Jason left, but Nathan went with Max. I'm not privileged to tell you anything else. It's likely that Max was lured in himself, maybe as early as high school."

There was silence for several minutes while Ted and Barbara searched through their memories.

Finally, Ted spoke up. "You know, Max was never a great student, but he was a decent kid until he started hanging out with Levi Blevins in high school. I don't know what ever happened to Levi. I think his family moved out of the area." He heaved a great sigh and continued, "I'd always hoped to turn the business over to Max someday, but he doesn't seem interested."

There was another long and awkward silence before Ted continued processing the new information and adding it to the collection of memories he had of Max. Looking at a spot on the floor between his feet, Ted spoke in barely audible tones. "I, I haven't been a great father. I mean, I should have spent more time with the boy. I should have paid attention. I was so focused on building the business. For him. For me." He stopped, leaned forward with his elbows on his knees and buried his face in his hands.

"Ted, we all have regrets as parents. But you still have time to invest in your son's life. When he recovers from this, I know a good counselor who can help him if he's willing. This may just be the tool that God is using to get his attention and turn him around."

19

Friday, February 23

The snow had been cleared from the roads, but it had not completely melted. Some patches of brown lawn were beginning to show through, but where the drifts had piled up, the snow was still a foot deep. Abigail's thoughts drifted across the road. She wondered how Buster and the mares were doing. She really wondered how Lee was doing and when they might have a chance to visit again.

Breaking from her reveries, Abigail stoked the fire as usual in the early morning, building it up enough that it would still be going when she got home later that day. Her day was short again with just Carrie Sue and Amy. Breakfast was her usual and she packed a light lunch before heading out to her truck.

Starting the truck and dialing the defroster fan to high, Abigail talked out loud, "Lord, one of these days, I'd really like to have a garage or a car port. Scraping windows is a pain." *Oh, Lord, do You ever get tired of all my complaining?* A short while later, she was backing out of her parking spot and heading down the driveway. *I don't have to worry about Max for a while. Lord, please have mercy on that young man! Please redeem his life from destruction.*

Carrie Sue pulled in just before Abigail did and she was waiting in her car until they could enter the church together. They fell into their routine of small talk while Abigail got the CD music playing and they settled into their respective chairs in the inner office.

"So, tell me what's been going on? How did you handle all the ritual stuff from the last week?"

"Great, I mean, I felt restless and all. I was awake at three o'clock in the morning a lot, but I guess that's part of the deal. I prayed and then I fell back asleep."

"Excellent!" Abigail was excited about Carrie Sue's progress and was anticipating full integration soon.

"I guess the only tough thing was Mom. She kept bugging me and sometimes I felt triggered, but we prayed over any buzz words that she might have said."

"Good job. Any references to roses?"

"As a matter of fact, she did mention it again. I know she was fishing and was probably frustrated because Rosebud is already integrated," Carrie Sue said with a mischievous giggle.

"I love it! Let's pray and ask the Lord where we need to go today."

When the prayer was finished, Carrie Sue looked up and said, "I think we need to work with the pseudo-cores and the original Carrie Sue."

Abigail caught the tension in Carrie Sue and remarked, "You don't like that idea, do you?"

"Well, I just know that the more we get done, the closer we get to the day I have to integrate and it feels like I'm going to lose you."

"I know it feels that way, but it won't be that way."

"I just have a lot of doubts. I don't know if I believe. It's like I've got to see it to believe it. Ya know?"

"You've trusted God through all the steps so far. He won't let you down. Trust is a tough thing for all of us. Think of the blind man that Jesus healed. He put the mud on his eyes and told him to wash in the pool and then he would see. What if he would have stood there and said that he wanted proof that he would see before he washed the mud off? He had to believe to see; not see to believe."

"Okay," Carrie Sue said slowly and sighed. "Let's get it done. Who do we start with? Never mind. Lord, please bring out whoever we need to start with."

They were silent for a moment and then the original Carrie Sue came forward as the host Carrie Sue slid to the background. She was getting less and less shy and looked Abigail in the eyes and said, "Hi."

"It's good to see you again. How are you doing?"

"I'm fine, I mean, I'm getting more used to some things and I kinda feel a little bit older every day."

"That's the way it should be. Are you feeling a little more comfortable with the idea of growing up?"

"Well, I still am not sure that I can do it, but like you told my host, I have to believe to see."

"You are paying attention. I'm proud of you. What about the pseudo cores? How are they doing?

"I think that's what we need to take care of today. They were supposed to protect me and keep people from finding me, but you and Jesus kinda busted them. They're tired and want to go in and I want them to come back into me."

"That's fantastic. Let's pray and ask the Lord to make sure that there's no residual emotional pain or demon hanging with them and then go from there."

"Okay."

Abigail prayed and both the original Carrie Sue and Abigail felt that there was no reason to keep them from praying for integration.

"I feel better, like I'm taking up more space or something. I know that sounds crazy, but that's the best way I can describe it."

They talked for a little while longer and then she went back to her internal position and the host came back out.

"Okay, my friend, another big step. How are you doing with it?"

"I'm fine. Really, I am. I don't feel threatened by it as much. And besides, I know it'll benefit all of us."

They closed out the session with some preemptive prayers for the coming week – the first and the third of the month with the third also being a full moon.

Abigail went upstairs to see if Pastor Spalding was available for a minute. Ginny was there and greeted her in her usual energetic manner.

"Hi, Ginny. How are the kids?"

"Oh, you know kids; always something going on. What can I do for you?" Ginny was very sociable, but she was also aware of time constraints of other people.

"Is Pastor Spalding available for about two minutes by any chance?"

"You came at a good time, I think he's just finishing his lunch. Let me check." She bustled over to Pastor Spalding's door and rapped lightly before poking her head inside. "Abigail Steele is here and is wondering if you had two minutes for her."

"Of course, of course. Send her in."

Abigail heard the exchange and walked slowly over to his door. Pastor Spalding came around his desk with a broad smile and indicated that she should take a seat in one of the chairs. "Come in. Have a seat."

"I don't want to take up your time. I really just wanted to ask you if you know how Max is doing these days. And his parents, too, for that matter."

"Well, he's still alive," Pastor's face reflected the gravity of the situation. "They're keeping him sedated to keep his brain from swelling as I understand it." He paused, glimpsed down briefly as if he thought he might have been naughty, and then looked Abigail in the eyes.

"I don't know if I made a mistake or not, but Ted and Barbara were agonizing about why God would let this happen to their son. You know, the typical 'why' questions that we get when tragedy hits – anyway, we got into a discussion of Max's behavior and friends and, well, I told them that I had prayed that morning that God would do whatever it took to get that young man's attention."

"Whoa, how did they react?"

"They were a little shocked, but admitted that they had prayed that way, too. What really shocked them is our discussion about the probability that Max was mixed up with a cult."

"You don't mess around!"

"Well, that came out of the discussion about Max threatening some people lately."

"Hoo boy." Abigail was somewhat amused by her pastor's conundrum and could hardly keep from grinning because she could relate.

"I, um, well I told them that I knew someone who could help him if he was willing to get help." It was his turn to grin.

After they finished their conversation, Abigail excused herself and went back to her office by way of the kitchen to await Amy Bolton. It was not long before she heard the familiar footsteps coming into the office. As usual she had a mischievous grin on her face. Abigail never knew if it was because of some smart-alack prankster or some internal triumph.

"Hey there!"

"You look like you're in a good mood."

"Wait until you hear what happened!" She didn't wait for Abigail's response but launched into a colorful description of her encounter with Levi. "You should have seen the look on his face! He was expecting that little girl and he got Michael instead!"

Abigail reached across the space between them and high-fived Amy. "What little girl?" She had caught the reference to a specific child personality and knew that it was significant. It was also predictable that Levi would have tried to pull out a programmed part that he knew.

Amy hesitated and became more serious, "Um, well, it's a little girl whose name starts with an F." It was obvious that she did not want to say the name.

"I see that you're uncomfortable about this, but don't you think it's time to discuss your first name and all the programming and stuff that goes with it?"

Amy heaved a sigh, pressed her lips together tightly and then nodded in agreement.

"Let's open with prayer, then, and ask the Lord to bring out the one who needs to be here today." Abigail did so and before she was finished, she noticed a shift in Amy's posture from the triumphant adult to a cowering child.

Peering at Abigail, the young girl briefly looked her in the eyes and quickly looked down again.

"Hi, I'm Abigail. You're safe here. Can you tell me your name?"

A big-eyed fearful expression came over the girl's face followed by vigorous shaking of her head.

"I'm sorry, I don't want to scare you. Can you tell me what would happen if someone said your name?"

Again, a vigorous head shake.

"Let me ask you this, then, because I don't want you to get in trouble. If I say it and you just blink your eyes three times for y-e-s or two times for n-o, then you aren't saying it and won't get in trouble. Do you think that would work?"

The little girl looked relieved and blinked three times. She had a crushing burden that she had borne all of her young life and could see no way out of it.

"I know that Levi, that mean guy, came to your house a couple days ago to hurt you. He is loyal to the bad guys and to Satan but I belong to the real Jesus. I have an idea that he said something or did something maybe with his hands that made you come out." Abigail paused and was rewarded with three blinks.

"I'm so glad that Michael and the other protectors tricked Levi and kept you and the others safe." Abigail saw the nod of agreement and continued. "Do you know the other ones inside?"

The little one shook her head.

"Can you talk?"

Three blinks.

"Are you afraid to talk?"

Three blinks.

"Do you get in trouble if you write?"

Two blinks.

"I think I know a way to keep you from getting in trouble and get you all fixed up and into a place inside where you can't get called out again and you'll be safe. I know that Michael and the other protectors would be happy about that. Can I tell you and let you think? Or do you have to check with someone who's over you?"

"Look, lady, I don't know who you think you are, but you can't just con a little kid. I know what you want!" A hostile, older personality switched in and sat in an aggressive posture glaring at Abigail.

"Hello," Abigail said pleasantly. "You must be her protector."

"What's it to you?"

"Well, I happen to hate it when little girls have to face bullies like Levi."

"Just what do you think you can do about it?"

"I was just about to explain that to her when you showed up. I am trying not to insult anyone by going over their heads. That's why I asked if I needed to check with anyone who might be over her."

"Well, that's me."

"Thank you for showing up. Let me ask you the same question. Do you have to check with someone in order to make a decision about this little girl?"

"I can make my own decisions. I don't check with anyone." She was clearly agitated.

"Okay, then. If the two of you have the same name, why did she show up for Levi and not you?"

"Who told you that we have the same name?" she exploded. "Who are you, lady?" Fear drove her anger.

"I got the message from the Holy Spirit. It's called a word of knowledge. It happens."

The personality did not know how to handle Abigail and her uncanny knowledge. *What else does she know?*

"You know how Levi and his guys know things that they shouldn't. They have counterfeit gifts of the Holy Spirit's gifts. They get knowledge from demons and I get mine from God. And God usually lets me know stuff like that for your benefit, not for mine."

"Whatever."

"I think that if you are willing, we can keep you and the little one safe from Levi and his buddies. I was just about to tell the little one about that when you stepped in. Are you interested? You really have nothing to lose but a couple of minutes."

"Fine." She slouched down in the chair and crossed her arms and legs.

"Thanks. I suspect that your name, that Amy's first name that begins with the sixth letter of the alphabet, is highly attached to programming and double meanings that bring a lot of pain and fear whenever it's spoken," she paused and looked for confirmation.

"Yeah, something like that."

"Are you interested in getting free from that?"

Sighing, she reluctantly nodded.

"I haven't been given a full down load from God, so I'm going to ask you to either say or write your name down." Abigail pulled an extra ink pen and a note pad from her desk drawer and handed it to the personality.

She wrote one letter, looked as if she would crumple the paper up, but after glancing at Abigail, she finished the word and handed it back with a what-have-I-done-to-myself expression.

F-U-C-H-S-Y-A was written on the paper. "I won't say it out loud, but that's normally a pretty name, like a dark pink, rose-colored flower."

"Yeah, well, some people pronounce the first part like, um," she was not quite sure how close she could get without reprisals, "like the CH is a K instead of being like the SH sound."

"Ah, I get it. And the Y-A is slang for YOU."

"You got it." She applauded with a mock cheer.

"So, your name is an invitation for them to rape you. Or, more likely the little one."

"You are really racking up the points."

Again, Abigail ignored the sarcasm. "Would you like to break the programming and assignments off of the two of you?"

"Oh, just like that? Sure. Snap your magic fingers and make it go away."

"I'll take that as a yes," Abigail countered looking her carefully in the eyes. When there were no further retorts, she took that as a go-ahead and launched into a prayer that covered assignments and bogus covenants, strongholds and demons. When she was finished, she waited for a response.

"Okay, I gotta admit that was good. Thanks. And sorry for giving you such a rough time."

"No problem. You've never met anyone who didn't want something. We can do one more thing that will guarantee that you and the little one will never be pulled out again."

Abigail went into an explanation of integration. The two Fuchsyas were tired, had no more emotional or spiritual baggage, and so they consented to integrate. When that was finished, Amy was in executive control.

"Wow again."

"Praise God! Now I really understand why you never used your first name. Can I try it now and see what happens?"

"Uh, sure, I think."

"Okay," Abigail pronounced her name with the soft sound. "Fuchsya Amy Bolton, how's that?"

"You know, it's really okay. I think I felt something rumbling really deep inside, but it's not like the shuddering I usually get. I'm a little queasy, but I was that way before I got here."

They celebrated and talked for a short while, made an appointment for the following Friday and then went their separate ways. Amy went home to get ready for work at The Pizza Palace and Abigail stopped at the grocery store on her way home.

When Abigail entered her front door, she noticed the light flashing on the phone. She picked it up and played the message. "Hi, Abigail, this is Lee Norris. I need to ask you a favor. Can you call me when you get a minute? Thanks." He left his number and she heard the click.

Hmm. I wonder what that's all about. Abigail put her groceries on the kitchen table, returned to the front porch for an armload of wood, stoked up the fire, got it going again and then sat down by the phone. *I'm as giddy as a teenager! Lord, what's the matter with me?* Pressing the buttons, Abigail got up and paced in the living room until Lee picked up.

"Hello."

"Hi, I got your message. What's up?"

"My daughter has a long weekend coming up next week and she wondered if there was any way I could come up and meet her."

"That's nice."

"Yes, it is. She usually spends her free time with her mom, so I'm kind of surprised that she wants to see me. So, I told her that I would see if I could find someone to horse-sit for a couple of days."

"I'd be glad to do that. Just let me know the routine and which days."

"If you're not busy tomorrow, why don't you let me pick you up and I'll show you."

"What time?"

"I'm getting out of my rising-with-the-sun routine lately. I usually get there around nine. Is that okay?"

"Works for me."

"Great. I'm looking forward to seeing you."

"Me, too. It's been too long. Bye."

Sunrise was just past six-thirty these days, but Abigail had not been getting up with the sunrise on those cloudy mornings either. This morning, however, she did not go back to sleep after adding logs to the fire. Her mind began to replay the phone conversation with Lee yesterday. She liked the timbre of his voice and his Montana accent. She did not want to get her hopes up. But. Sigh. But.

Meanwhile, in town, Lee stirred at the sound of traffic not too far from his front door. *I can't wait to build my house and get out of town. Lord, give me patience! I am not a city boy.* He pressed the button on the side of the coffee maker and soon the aroma of coffee filled the tiny kitchen and he began to revive. Taking a steaming mug with him into the bathroom, he showered and shaved. He wanted to look presentable for his time with Abigail.

Finishing her Saturday chores, putting together some burritos for later, Abigail was pulling on her boots when she heard Lee's toot. Thrusting her arms into her coat, she gathered up her gloves and stocking cap. The weather report said that it might snow some more and the clouds confirmed it. Closing the front door behind her, Abigail carefully walked down the steps and headed toward Lee's truck.

Walking briskly toward her, Lee called out a cheery, "Good morning!"

"It is a good morning. How are you today?"

"Great. Ready?" He approached her and extended his elbow. She took it and he walked her to his truck, opened the door and closed it gently behind her once she was settled.

Very much aware of the gentlemanly gestures, Abigail breathed, "Lord, this feels like a date."

They were getting more comfortable with each other, but they were both relieved when they arrived at Lee's barn and had something else to occupy their attention. Working side by side seemed like a natural fit. It was as comfortable as if they had been a team for a while. Opening the side door, Lee held it for Abigail.

They were immediately greeted by a chorus of nickers and whinnies from all five horses. Abigail made a beeline for Buster. After listening to all his grievances punctuated by snorts and stamps of his feet, Abigail replied as if she had understood every nuance. "I know, Buster, I miss you, too. This is just best for all of us. We can't argue with God, you know. Besides, you are in a nice, warm barn with four pretty ladies."

Lee smiled as he observed the two of them. He noted the contrast between this horse-loving, woods-stomping, gun-toting woman and the one who left him for "a much more civilized lifestyle." His musings were interrupted by Abigail's comments.

"You keep making improvements here," Abigail observed. "I like the way you have it organized."

"Thanks. Hey, let me show you how to turn the water on. I usually keep it off to lower the risk of a frozen pipe. They're insulated and I buried them an extra foot deep. There's nothing worse than plumbing problems, especially in the winter. It's extra work, but I like to drain the hoses each time so they don't freeze and burst."

"I like the way you think."

Lee proceeded to show her where the water shut off valve was. He hooked up the hose, flipped the switch, and began to fill the water troughs for the horses. "I'll fill them up before I leave, that way, you might not even need to fill them up at all. But just in case they're extra thirsty, I'd better show you. While they're filling, let me show you where the sweet feed is."

Lee led the way to another chest freezer that had been abandoned on the property. He had cleaned it up and used it to keep the rodents and other critters from stealing morsels of grain. Filling a five gallon bucket half full of feed, pouring some into each horse's bucket, he talked soothingly to each of his mares as well as to Buster as he went.

"One of these days, I'm going to use the hay mow for hay, but for now, I'm storing it down here." Lee threw two bales onto his cart and rolled them closer to the horses. Reaching into his pocket, he withdrew his knife and deftly slit the baling twine. "I give them about a quarter of a bale twice a day. If I'm not going to be here, I give them a big third to half all at once."

"It won't be a problem for me to come down morning and evening. I actually miss doing that every day. This will be a pleasure."

They continued to talk and banter about horses and the weather. Before long, it was time for Lee to bring Abigail back home. He was disappointed that it was too cold and muddy to take a walk. The snow clouds were already sending warning flakes swirling.

"Hey, I made some burritos earlier. Want to join me for lunch?"

"I'd love to." Lee was profoundly grateful to be able to spend more time with Abigail.

"And maybe we can talk about some of the things that you wanted to ask me about."

"I'd like that."

The first thing Abigail did when they were settled in the house was to turn on the oven. She busied herself with stoking up the fire and putting final touches on the dining room table as their meal finished heating. Salsa and tortilla chips, sour cream and guacamole made it look like a fiesta. At least for Abigail. She was accustomed to simple meals most of the time. It was nice to have companionship and the excuse to make a meal into a special event.

Lee was hovering in the doorway between the living room and the kitchen. "Anything I can do to help?"

"No, just bring your appetite."

"Done. Now what?"

"Have a seat and I'll bring the burritos in. They should be just about right."

Abigail asked Lee to ask a blessing on their meal. Afterwards she served up the steaming burritos. They talked easily about the horses and the weather and then Lee asked her about her work and how she got started working with Satanic Ritual Abuse survivors.

"Well, that's kind of a long story, but I'll give you the Reader's Digest version for now. I was raised in a pretty good family. We went to church and all, but there were issues. My father was raised by a mean, angry man as I understand it and my mother was severely abused as a kid, too. They got married young and vowed to do better than their parents did. I think they really did. But, maybe because of my personality, I didn't do so well with their strictness and with Dad's anger. Because of Mom's background, she wasn't very nurturing. I turned into a bit of a perfectionist and had some OCD tendencies as well – both fear-driven things. And I had a lot of depression. In fact, I ended up in the looney bin because of it before the boys came along. I had two miscarriages and that kind of put me over the edge. And about that time one of my brothers was killed in an accident and a year later one of my cousins died of cancer."

"Oh, wow. I would never have guessed."

"Well, there weren't very many Christian counselors back then even if my parents would have recognized that I was hurting so deeply. Even when Darryl and I were married, there weren't many around. Besides, I thought I could just gut it out and pull myself up by the bootstraps."

"I'm so sorry."

"Thanks. But, I'm good now. It took a couple of decades, but I got through it and my last counselor must have recognized something in me by the grace of God. She asked me when I was going to start working with people."

"What did you tell her?"

"I told her that I'd pray about it. I was real sure that I wouldn't hear a word from God. But, go figure, about six months later, the Holy Spirit clearly told me to start a group for depressed women. So, I got space in the local library, put an ad in the paper, and women started coming out of the woodwork. Eventually, some of them asked me if I prayed with people one-on-one. I started doing that and then I decided that I needed to get more education. I found a rinky-dink little Bible college and seminary and started taking classes."

"But how did you start with SRA's?"

"They were some of the most depressed people around. They showed up at the meetings and I started working with them. I had no idea about the depth of dysfunction some of those women experienced. I had no idea about multiple personalities either. I told the very first one that I didn't know what I was doing, so if she would be my 'guinea pig' I wouldn't charge her. Well, I don't charge anyone anyway, but some like to make a contribution."

They began to clear the table while Lee asked more direct questions. They moved into the kitchen where Abigail started filling the sink and washing the dishes. Suddenly, she was aware that Lee was standing close behind her. He boldly put his hands on the edge of the counter on either side of her. Slowly turning around, Abigail looked up into Lee's smiling face.

"I like you. I really like you, Abigail Steele." Lee's voice was low and just above a whisper.

Abigail was clueless. "I like you, too."

"I mean, I really, really like you," Lee repeated his declaration as Abigail looked into his warm, brown eyes.

It seemed like slow motion to Abigail as Lee bent and gently kissed Abigail on the lips. She could feel the quiver of his lips and felt the flutter of her heart in her chest. Lee stood tall again and Abigail turned around to finish the dishes.

"Let me help you with the dishes and then I need to get some things lined up for the trip. I fly out Thursday and will be back sometime on Monday, the fifth. I should get home before the weather gets too bad."

"No problem. I'm looking forward to taking care of the horses... and seeing you when you get back."

On day eight after conception, the single-celled orb had doubled many times. Looking like a miniature soccer ball with dozens of miniscule six-sided sections on the surface, it was implanted into the wall of Amy's uterus which had been prepared for this moment, having received a message through a sophisticated hormonal communication system. Human chorionic gonadotropin levels were beginning to rise and soon Amy would become aware of the presence of a new life that was being knit together in her womb. But for now, Amy was oblivious.

Ted and Barbara Berryman were listening intently to the neurologist. "We'll begin to ease off on the sedative and see how he reacts. If he gets combative, we'll have to put him back under. We can't take any chances that he'll damage the spinal cord. The latest tests show that the swelling has gone down significantly."

"Oh, that's wonderful." Barbara finally exhaled.

"He's young and that's in his favor. We need to test his motor and sensory responses and we'll hope that his brain recovers as well."

"When will you do this, doctor?" Ted asked.

"I'm going to do that right now. You folks wait here and I'll let you know when we're finished."

Ted and Barbara had been practically living in the ICU waiting room for days now. The next few minutes were some of the longest ones there. The quality of the rest of Max's life depended on the findings that would be revealed soon. Indeed, the quality of the rest of their own lives depended on it as well.

After interminable minutes, the neurologist came out of the ICU with a smile on his face. "Max is coming around. He's able to feel sensations fairly normally – pin prick, pressure, and the like – and he's able to move both of his legs."

"Praise the Lord!" Barbara exclaimed.

"Now, he still has a long row to hoe, but this is very encouraging. We can begin to make arrangements for him to be transferred to Saint Joseph's. I'd prefer to send him to a neurosurgeon with lots of experience with cases like this. From there he can be transferred to a rehab facility that specializes in spinal injuries."

"Thank you, doctor," Ted replied extending his hand to shake the doctor's hand.

"I'll write the orders to get the transfer done and he should be on his way on Monday. A medical flight would be the safest for him. The nurse will let you know the details as soon as she knows. Meanwhile, go visit your son."

Ted and Barbara hastened into the ICU and assumed their customary places on either side of the bed. Max was wan and drawn, but he had never looked better to his parents.

His voice was husky and slurred, but he managed to say, "Hi, Mom. Hi, Dad."

It became clear that Max did not remember anything about the accident. They answered his questions and told him about all the people that were praying for him.

"Pastor Spalding has been here every day praying with us and for you."

Max turned his head from his father, sighed softly, and closed his eyes.

"What's the matter, son?"

"I don't know. It's just a waste of time. I'm just a waste of time." Max's words were slurred as he drifted off to sleep for a few minutes.

With each passing day, Max was becoming more alert and more aware of his painful wounds. He wasn't allowed to move or change positions without the assistance of a nurse. Each time it was an exercise in pain. He would break out into a cold sweat and curse at the nurses even when they reminded him that it was necessary to keep him from getting bed sores. Max was not a good patient and the staff was glad that he would be leaving soon.

20

Sunday, February 25

The majority of the community was waking up and going about their Sunday morning routines. There was a minority within the community that was just going to bed after yet another night of revelry. Little known and even less celebrated were the Ember Days. Taken from Zechariah eight verse nineteen where the prophet records, *"Thus says the Lord of hosts, 'The fast of the fourth, the fast of the fifth, the fast of the seventh, and the fast of the tenth months will become joy, gladness, and cheerful feasts for the house of Judah; so love truth and peace.'"*

The fasts were adopted and formalized to four series of Wednesdays, Fridays, and Saturdays which are celebrated in the four seasons of the year: Michaelmas Embertide was in September, Advent Embertide was in the winter, Lenten Embertide was in the spring, and Whit Embertide was in the summer. Embertides were dedicated times of prayer and fasting. It was all the better for the Satanists that the Judeo-Christian Church paid little attention to these holy days. They believed that it gave them a spiritual advantage.

And so, the cold Sunday morning appeared to be just like any other Sunday in February with a dusting of snow. And yet, the heavenly places were filled with activity that was unseen and unheard by the majority of the wingless earth-bound beings.

Abigail slid into the pew and sat down next to Cindy and Gary. They exchanged greetings and hugs.

"Where's Lee today?"

"He'll be here late," Gary replied. "He called and said that he overslept."

Within a minute, Lee did show up and rather than taking his usual place on the other side of Gary, he came down the side aisle and sat down next to Abigail. Neither one of them noticed the smiles and winks Gary and Cindy exchanged.

The congregation worshipped together and then sat down as Pastor Spalding sprang out of his chair and headed toward the pulpit.

"Good morning everyone," his voice boomed across the auditorium. "I've got some good news about Max Berryman. He's awake and moving his legs." He paused until the clapping and choruses of "praise the Lord" and "hallelujah" died down. "He'll transfer to a different hospital where they'll operate on his spine and then he'll be heading to a rehab facility after that. Keep the Berrymans in your prayers because this is going to be a long recovery period. It's miraculous that he survived all his injuries.

"And speaking of miracles, today I want to talk to you about miracles; the things that come immediately and suddenly. I'll be preaching out of the Gospels, so bear with me. I want to start in the Gospel of Luke. Luke was a physician and he recorded many of Jesus' miracles." Pastor Spalding went on to describe some of the miracles that Jesus performed – raising the dead, healing diseases, deafness, blindness, and more.

"Folks, did you ever wonder how long those sick and afflicted people waited for a miracle? We read that immediately they regained their sight or immediately the leprosy left him or immediately her hemorrhage stopped. We read that immediately the scales fell off of

Saul's eyes. How many times did something happen suddenly? Suddenly the Holy Spirit showed up at Pentecost. Suddenly an angel shows up and executes a jail break."

Pastor Spalding continued to recite other miracles and healings. "Are you waiting for a miracle? It doesn't matter if you're waiting for a big miracle – like Max Berryman's complete healing – or something a bit smaller, I want to challenge you to dig a little deeper into the context of the Scriptures. I contend that all of the suddenly and immediately miracles and moves of God were preceded by prayerful waiting. The disciples waited in the upper room and devoted themselves to prayer until the sudden appearance of the Holy Spirit. Paul and Silas waited and praised the Lord in jail until the angel suddenly came. The blind men sat by the pool or the temple gate or the side of the road day after day until Jesus suddenly entered their world.

"Come down for prayer if you want someone to pray with you for a sudden breakthrough. Feel free to come for any other need." He nodded to the worship leader and soon the worship team was back on the stage playing soft music while members of the prayer team came down to pray with several people. The rest of the people began to shuffle down the aisles to retrieve their children or to head home. Abigail and Lee walked together and when they got to the foyer, Pastor Spalding motioned for them to come over.

"Abigail, I have a favor to ask you. I'm going to visit Max this afternoon and pray with him and his folks before they transfer him. Any chance you're free to come along?"

That caught her by surprise, but she managed to stammer, "Sure. What time?"

"I was thinking that two o'clock would give us time to have dinner and get up there before shift change. It gets hectic then."

"That works for me. I'll meet you there."

Lee and Abigail turned and walked out of the front doors and down the steps to the parking lot.

"Hey, do you want to come over for supper tonight? I've got some leftover burritos.

"I'd love to. I'll be across the road taking care of the horses anyway. What time?"

"How about five? I'll be back home by then."

"Perfect. I'll be there. I'd be curious to see Max's face when he sees you walk into his room after all he's done to you. Are you sure you'll be safe? Do you want me to come along in case of trouble?"

"I'll be fine. No weapon formed against me will prosper."

At precisely two o'clock, Abigail was in the ICU waiting room. Pastor Spalding entered a few minutes later and strode over to her. "Max's parents have also prayed a whatever-it-takes prayer for Max. If you're ready, I'll check with his nurse to see if we can go in."

"Let's do it."

Soon Pastor Spalding was beckoning to Abigail from the ICU doorway. She entered and saw that Max was awake and talking with his parents. Ted and Barbara looked expectantly as they approached the bed. Max, however, scowled.

Pastor Spalding walked over to Ted and shook his hand and then extended his hand to Max. Max took it but did not look Pastor Spalding in the face. "Max, it's so good to see you coming around. We just want to pray for you before you transfer to St. Joseph's for your surgery. Is that all right?"

"You don't have to bother. You'd just be wasting your breath. I'm beyond hope."

"Now, why do you say that?"

Max looked nervously at his parents and then back to Pastor Spalding. He avoided looking at Abigail. "I just am. I've done too many awful things already. I can't be saved."

"That's not true."

"You don't know what I've done."

"We have a pretty good idea, Max, and it's not too late to change and get out. Your parents and I have all been praying that God would do whatever it takes. It might just be that this accident is what it takes to get you free and right with God."

Max was alarmed by the pastor's candid words that suggested that he and maybe his parents knew more than he thought they did. It had to be that woman! His eyes shifted uneasily between his parents' faces and Pastor Spalding's and Abigail's trying to read them.

"Why is she here?" Max demanded.

"She knows what it takes to get someone out of their commitments to a cult," Pastor Spalding said.

Abigail stepped forward and looked Max squarely in the eyes. "Max, you're not beyond hope. You know that I work to get people free. You can be too."

"You're crazy. You don't know what you're talking about." Max was getting agitated and the nurse started to drift over to Max's area.

Lowering her voice and moving close to Max's head, Abigail said, "Max, I think that someone promised you something that every teenaged guy wants. You took the bait and they have been holding it over your head ever since. But they lied. You have *not* sold your soul to the devil no matter what they say. There is a way out. Not easy, but doable."

Max wanted to believe her and settled down. The nurse drifted back to her charts.

"And, I want you to know that I have forgiven you for everything you've ever done to me."

Max was pierced to his heart by her words. *How can this woman forgive me after all I've done to her?*

His parents were baffled by the conversation but remained quiet.

Pastor Spalding spoke up, "Max, can we pray for you now? You have surgery and a lot of mending to do. We can pray about the other stuff later when you're back on your feet."

Max nodded his reluctant consent. The four of them joined hands around his bed and took turns praying for Max's quick healing and for the skill of the surgeons, for effective rehabilitation and for a quick return home. Abigail and Pastor Spalding slipped out leaving Max with his parents.

"Well, what do you think?"

"I think Max has a lot to think about and maybe he got a little shot of hope today. I sure hope he'll come for ministry. If he does, I think it would be a good idea for us to do it together."

"I'd love it. I learn so much from you. And so do the others in the ministerial alliance. They're looking forward to our meeting a week from tomorrow. Some of them have invited other pastors that they know."

"God is definitely at work in our community."

They parted ways at the main door of the hospital. Abigail headed home, excited about sharing the evening with Lee. She was beginning to allow herself to move on. Darryl would have wanted her to. *But is this the man?*

Lee was eagerly anticipating spending time with Abigail as well. He was asking the same questions. *Is this the right woman? Would Lisa accept her?* It had been a decade since her mother left him. He stopped the questions and went about the business of taking care of the horses. He loved the smells of the barn – the horses and the hay, the weathered wood and the oils that had been spilled over the decades. Stepping out of the barn, Lee's eyes studied the space that he had cleared for the house he was planning on building. *Maybe I need to make it bigger than just the simple bachelor's pad. Just in case.*

It was not long before Abigail heard his toot. She went to the front door and opened it.

"You want me to grab an armload of logs?"

"Yeah, thanks. I meant to fill up the log holder but I never got around to it yesterday."

Lee picked up an armload of split wood from the stack of wood and brought it onto the front porch. "I'll fill it up for you if supper isn't quite ready."

"Well, that would be nice. I'll have supper ready in about fifteen minutes."

Before long, they were sitting at the big dining room table again. Abigail put their place settings on the eastern side of the table so they could watch the sunset.

"I would love to have seen Max's face when you walked into his room."

"He was definitely uncomfortable, but I was able to let him know that he is not doomed and that there is a way out. I also let him know that I forgave him for what he did."

"How could you not just strangle the guy after all he's done to you?"

"God's grace. Max got caught up in something way bigger than himself. I think his parents have a lot more questions now."

"No doubt."

They continued to talk about Max and the other Satanists and then moved on to Lee's visit with his daughter. They discussed the horses and how they looked forward to spring with plans for gardens and building projects, livestock and chickens. Too soon they parted ways. Thinking similar thoughts but not verbalizing them, feeling similar emotions but not expressing them.

Lee's early Thursday afternoon flight was pleasant enough even with a short layover in Dallas before he boarded the flight to Colorado. He took one bag with him that fit in the overhead bin. Moving past the last of the security stations, he began to look for Lisa. *What did she look like now? She was always dying her hair.*

Lisa saw him first and ran toward him excitedly crying out, "Dad!"

He set his bag down and buried her in his embrace. "I missed you, Sweet." He put his calloused hands on her shoulders, backed up half a step and looked at her smiling face. "You're all grown up." There was a mist in his eyes and a slight warble in his voice.

"Come on, Dad, I'm in short-term parking."

They walked briskly through the crowds talking as they went. She described her college classes to him. He told her about the property he purchased and the plans for building a house in the spring. She told him about her newest boyfriend. He told her nothing about the woman that he really, really liked.

It was March first. Abigail was at the barn about an hour before sundown taking care of Lee's horses. She spoke to them as if they understood every word she said. "Well, ladies and Buster, it's another ritual day. Saturday is the third of the month and a full moon. Yet another ritual day. Oh, yeah, let's not forget Purim on Sunday. Never mind that, the good news is that we've made it through February and spring is just around the corner. You'll be enjoying your pasture again really soon." Abigail kept her thoughts to herself about having her work cut out for her with Carrie Sue and Amy tomorrow.

Making one last check around the barn, securing the door, she got back into her truck. Bouncing down the lane toward the highway, Abigail thought about all the things that she needed to do yet tonight. *Bills... writing projects... finishing the book that Cindy lent me... ah, so much to do, so little time and energy.*

"So, Dad, tell me about your new place."

"Well, I'm living in a tiny apartment in a tiny town, but I bought some land out in the country and I'm going to build a house. I'll be about half an hour from Gary and Cindy's place and about the same from your Grandpa and Grandma McVeigh. It has a big old barn on it which is housing my five horses."

"Five? I thought you only brought four with you. And what about Bullet?"

"Whoa, one thing at a time." Lee paused briefly and sighed. Lisa had grown up with the dog. "I'm sorry, Bullet didn't make it. His kidneys failed and he wasn't eating anymore. I had to put him down."

"Aw." Lisa felt bad for her father. "How old was he? I forgot."

"Almost as old as you."

"I guess it was time, but it's always so sad." There was silence between them before Lisa picked up the thread of the previous conversation. "So, tell me more about your horses and the new one."

"I did take four of ours – Misty, Sparkles, Lady, and Sassy, but the lady that lives across the road from me sold me her gelding."

"Why?"

"Long story, but mainly it's to keep the horse safe."

"Safe from what?"

"Like I said, it's a long story. The lady is Cindy's best friend from church and she was kind enough to board my mares until I got the fences up a couple of months ago."

"What's her name?"

"Abigail."

Lisa began to giggle. "You like her, don't you?"

"You're reading me like a book, kiddo."

"So...?"

"So what?"

"So, are you an item?"

Lee was getting nervous about this conversation that he did not intend to have with Lisa. He cleared his throat, "Well, we're not exactly an item, I suppose. We're just friends."

"Da-ad!"

"Okay, we're very early into this friendship. I am beginning to really like her, but I'm just not sure."

"Is she a Christian? Is she smart? Does she love animals? Does she love to be outdoors? Is she pretty? Can she cook? Does she have a good sense of humor?"

"Yes. Yes. Yes. She's all of those things and more."

"Come on, Dad. I can tell you're smitten."

"Smitten?"

"Smitten. You light up when you talk about her."

"Okay, maybe you've got me there. I would like to court her to see if she's part of God's plan for me. I thought I had that with your mother and I just don't want to get burned again. Abigail has been through so much that I don't want to hurt her either."

"Dad, don't go by your relationship with Mom. I love her to death, but I don't think anyone could have made her happy. She's still not happy."

"So, you're okay with me courting Abigail?"

"I heard from a reliable source that it's not good for a man to be alone, Dad." She grinned impishly at him. "I can't wait to meet her."

Abigail heard the rain pelting the window early Friday morning. "This is the day that You have made and I will rejoice and be glad in it, Lord." Abigail threw off her covers and stoked up the fire. She added more logs to the fire and more water to the pot that sat on top of it to supply some humidity. She decided to eat breakfast after she took care of the horses.

Donning her work jacket and hat, gloves and boots, she went out to her truck. It was such a short distance between the barn and her front door, but the way their driveways were arranged, it was nearly a mile to the barn. She was greeted by nickers and stamping hoofs. They were restless and bored in the barn.

"Pretty soon. Maybe when Lee gets back he'll let you out again." She quickly finished feeding them and headed out the door. She needed to get to work.

Carrie Sue was right on time as usual and looked better every week. Her posture conveyed her new-found assertiveness with shoulders back and head held high. She looked people in the eye more often, too.

"How are you doing today? You look great."

"Thanks. I feel pretty good, like I'm being more comfortable in my own skin if that makes any sense."

"Yes, it does. Let's get at it and open with prayer."

Their sessions were following a familiar pattern – check for triggers, check the internal world, do some preventive prayers for upcoming rituals. Host Carrie Sue reported that Original Carrie Sue, was participating in life more often. They were communicating regularly and developing a fondness for each other.

"How many characters do you sense are still inside your system besides your executive committee?"

"Not many that I can find, but that doesn't mean they're not hiding."

"It just seems like you are getting really close to full integration. What do you think?"

"I think you're right."

"Just don't forget that even when we think they're all in, there will still likely be some stragglers. I don't know why, but that seems to be the pattern for all my SRA survivors."

"I know. Maybe I'll be an exception. Maybe I'll be your first."

"How is your mother reacting to you these days?"

"I think she's mostly confused. I mean, she keeps switching into Dorkas and trying to intimidate me, but when it doesn't work or when I offer to pray for her, she goes into a fit and disappears, leaving Mom. Or, some part of Mom that I can only pity. I sure hope that she'll want to get healed one of these days."

"Me too."

Before long, their session was finished. Abigail took a short break and when she came back to her office, Amy was waiting for her.

"Hey there," Abigail greeted Amy.

"Hey," Amy gave a less enthusiastic reply.

"What's wrong?"

"I don't know. I haven't been feeling well lately. It's kind of weird. I'm queasy in the morning, but by afternoon I'm usually okay again. I've been like this for almost a week. I don't think I'm coming down with the flu and I don't think it's anything I'm eating. Maybe someone's trying to poison me."

"Why don't we open with prayer and ask if anyone knows anything about it?"

"Good idea."

By the conclusion of the prayer, another personality was present. She appeared to be young and nervous.

"Hi, I'm Abigail. Do you know anything about Amy's queasiness?"

The personality nodded but remained silent.

"What can you tell me?"

"This is what happens when they put a baby in me."

"You're pregnant?" Abigail tried hard not to show her shock. She did not expect this.

"Uh huh."

"How many times have you been pregnant?"

"I don't remember. Lots."

Abigail searched her memory and realized that Amy could well have been impregnated when she was abducted about three weeks ago and taken to the ritual at the Presbyterian church. Doing a quick calculation, she believed that the baby would be due in December. She also realized that since Amy had no children, all the pregnancies probably ended at rituals as well. "I'm so sorry they treated you like that. Is it your job to be there when they take the baby?"

"No."

"Do you know whose job it is?"

"There's another girl. They make me give the baby to her."

"Is she the only one, or is there one for every time they put a baby in you?"

Like so many others, this one was not forthcoming with information. Who knew whether or not divulging the information would be used against them? Their general policy was to answer a direct question with an indirect or vague answer. "Well, um, there's a bunch of different ones."

Abigail was afraid of that and she was not sure what that meant or how they made the exchange. Perhaps it was a description of switching from one personality to the other. This one's job was to carry the baby. The other parts' job was to deliver the baby.

"Is she or any of the others nearby? Can you see or sense them?"

"No, I don't think it's time yet."

"Are you comfortable with telling me your name? It would help me keep everyone apart."

"Gester. They said it's because I make them laugh. They think it's funny when they put a baby in me."

"Would it be all right if we talk about finding a way to keep all of you safe?"

"Yeah."

"Is there someone whose job it is to be in charge of all of you? Like maybe a protector?"

"Yeah."

"Do you think she would come out and talk to me?"

A subtle shift indicated that another personality had surfaced. She, too, seemed young and vulnerable with a mix of resignation and hopelessness. "How do you think you'll be able to keep anyone safe from them?"

"That's what we need to talk about. Have you been able to see some of what has been going on lately?"

"Some."

"Like when Levi tried to access Fuchsya?"

"Yeah, that was cool."

"We need to ask the real Jesus to give us a strategy to keep everyone, including the baby, safe."

The personality was open to dialogue and desperate to try anything. After Abigail explained some of the dynamics of healing and integration, the OB/GYN sector was on board and they prayed a comprehensive prayer for healing, deliverance, and integration for the whole group.

The host Amy surfaced. "Oh, wow! Oh no, I think I'm going to ralph my socks."

"Huh?"

"Toss my cookies! Barf!"

Abigail smiled gently at Amy's predicament. "Sorry about that. Looks like someone gets to be pregnant."

"Gee, thanks." Amy was actually quite pleased until a disturbing thought raced through her mind. "So, I'm carrying some master's baby?"

"Unless you know of some other sexual encounter."

"I'm not sure I want anything to do with it. I want it out of me. I don't want anything of them inside of me." Amy reacted strongly as she thought about which one of the men might have impregnated her.

"I'm not sure I'd feel any differently, but what is the alternative?"

"Get an abortion? Pray for a miscarriage?"

"Amy, I do know what a miscarriage feels like under the best of circumstances and how I beat myself up for it. I was mad at my body for betraying me. And I've worked with a lot of ladies who had abortions. They were pretty miserable afterwards."

"It sounds like another lose-lose situation."

"It does if we think that there are only two possible solutions. Let's reframe it. If we truly believe that God is the author of life and that He knits babies together in their mothers' wombs, then we have to believe that the

Satanists haven't slipped this one past Him. Your baby is here for God's higher purposes. Can you think of anything that those Satanists would hate more than knowing that your baby will follow in your footsteps and serve your God instead of theirs?

A wry grin formed and Amy replied, "I like the way you're thinking. I still need to have love for this baby."

"Let's ask God to give you the maternal love that you need."

They prayed and afterward Amy reported feeling a little more positively about the baby. After praying for protection from the upcoming rituals, they set their next appointment and parted ways.

Prinz was startled by the sudden appearance of Xerxes in his own home. Trying hard to cover up his lapse of attentiveness, Prinz immediately greeted him with a bow of obeisance. "Welcome. How may I serve you?"

Xerxes, the high-level master over several regions, eyed him with malevolence and silence. Prinz became increasingly apprehensive in the oppressive hush. He was unaccustomed to being on the receiving end of this kind of treatment.

With a voice that rumbled, Xerxes thundered, "You are failing to keep your region dedicated to its purpose. You're losing territory. You're losing people. What do you have to say for yourself? Look at you! You're not half the man you were a year ago!"

"I have not encountered this in all my years. I will rededicate myself to regaining all of this region for our master and king."

"How will you do that with fewer reinforcements?"

"We will take out that woman."

"Ha! You blame all your woes on a mere woman?"

"She has unusual powers, my lord."

"She is a daughter of Eve. She is a dust puppet. She is clay. A woman!" He spat out the words with all the disgust and venom that he could muster.

"She has special protection." Prinz was referring to the angelic host that encamped around her property and accompanied her whenever she drove to town. "Urdang's troops cannot penetrate like they once did."

"Pshaw! We'll see!" Xerxes got close to Prinz and breathed his foul breath on him. "Let's go pay a visit to this woman."

Prinz began to shake internally. Even his demons quaked in the presence of the superior powers. He felt the impending doom and knew that it was just a matter of time before he would be devoured just like he had devoured so many before him. Dutifully he followed Xerxes to the German engineered vehicle that befitted a congressman. Xerxes remained silent as he drove and followed the directions Prinz gave him.

The weather had been fair for several days with no precipitation in the forecast, but just as they turned onto York Creek Road, the winds increased enough that it caused the solid vehicle to be blown about in the lane. When they crested the final hill, they were pelted with hail stones the size of golf balls. The windshield sustained several chips and the hood looked like Swiss cheese with hundreds of indentations.

Prinz felt a strong sense of foreboding. Xerxes appeared to be calm as he called on his minions to keep them safe on this mission. Urdang and his comrades watched the clash from their assigned positions and attempted to assist the company that came with Prinz and Xerxes.

Xerxes did not know that the mighty hosts of God, His angels, were performing His word and obeying His voice by creating this custom-made hail storm. Taking ice from the storehouse of heaven, laying it down on the pavement, His sovereignty was ruling over all.

Cursing and calling upon his powers, Xerxes lost control over the vehicle. It fishtailed down the hill. He could not counter the swaying rear end by steering into the spin. When the vehicle made a full revolution, he gave up, took his hands off the steering wheel, and let out another string of curses. The vehicle spun in slow-motion gyrations past Abigail's property and just beyond York Creek where it slowed down, stopped rotating, and finally gripped clear pavement facing the correct direction in the lane. No wind. No hail. No ice.

Xerxes did not want to admit that Prinz was right; that he had encountered a superior force. Pride cometh before a fall. The stunned man sat there in the stopped car until he was brought back to the current situation by the honking of a car behind him in the road. *How did he get through without...?*

21

Monday, March 5

Abigail awoke to a clear but cold morning. She was excited because today the monthly Ministerial Alliance meeting would be held at Pastor Dennis Walsh's little charismatic church. It was located in Elmwood, an unincorporated township near the eastern border of the county. After her morning routine, she spent some extra time in prayer.

Several cars were already in the gravel parking lot by the time Abigail arrived. Recognizing Pastor Spalding's vehicle, she was once again grateful for his support and encouragement. Entering the main door, following the sound of the men's voices, Abigail soon joined the small gathering of clergy. Pastor Dennis Walsh greeted her warmly and offered her some coffee.

"Thanks, I love the smell, but I don't drink it."

"Hot tea then?"

"Perfect!" Soon she was sipping on a steaming cup of tea and listening to the conversations around her. As others joined the group, introductions were made. Pastor Walsh had invited Richard Morris, pastor of a non-denominational church in Pines which was located on the opposite end of the county. Pastor Morris was a hulk of a man and towered above Abigail. Her hand disappeared into his calloused but gentle paw. He explained that he was bi-vocational, that is, he was a farmer when he was not preaching.

Don Wilmore was a Baptist pastor. His church was near the southern border of the county on route 1950.

Pastor Spalding had been talking to him at a recent convention and he expressed his interest in not only the meeting, but the subject of the meeting.

Mike Griffin invited George Bordman, a fellow Presbyterian minister. He was from Hawville to the north. Abigail remembered travelling through the little town when she went to The Iron Skillet for the Thanksgiving event. In fact, her friends, Ken and Paula Archer, attended his church. Rev. Bordman was older with a distinctive voice. It was as if it had been strained and had a bit of a high pitch to it.

Abigail was surprised to see that Paul Overton had invited Rev. Benjamin Morgan from the Kingston UMC since he did not seem to think that there was a problem in the county when he was at the last meeting. She had driven past the Kingston church many times and had seen his name on the sign out front. He was a friendly man with a quick smile.

The fifth new person was Robert Warrens. He hailed from Bluebrook, another rural town that was barely a dot on the county map. It was located in the northwestern corner of the county on the same road as the lodge. His little storefront church started out as a Bible study that out grew his living room. He was just as tall as his friend, Richard Morris, and had asked if he could come to the meeting. He was concerned by the evidence of increased cult activity in his area.

There were nine pastors present plus Abigail. *Oh, Lord, You're up to something here.*

Once everyone was present, Pastor Walsh called the meeting to order. The informal agreement was that the host pastor would chair the meeting. "Gentlemen and Abigail, the ladies have prepared a very nice lunch for us today. Let's not keep them waiting." He led the way to the table and as soon as everyone was settled, he asked a blessing on the food.

After the ladies cleared the lunch table and brought out the desserts, they retreated to the kitchen. Pastor Walsh then got the attention of the group, welcomed the newcomers, and brought them up to speed on the concerns that had been the topic at their February meeting. "I think that after last month, they haven't dared to use my church again, at least, we've found no evidence. Does anyone have anything to report?"

Pastor Spalding spoke up. "Things seem to have quieted down at my church. At least, the ones that we know are active in the cult have been more subdued. One of them was in an accident and is in the hospital. I have to admit that I was a bit shook up about this one because he threatened a young man in church who quit the cult. The two of us prayed that morning that God would get his attention somehow and stop him. Looks like He did. We're praying that he'll be transformed even though he thinks he's a lost cause."

"I'm not sure what all I should say," Robert Warrens began, "but I drive past that old lodge a lot. It's not too far down the road from my place. There's always been a lot of activity around there and it's usually in the middle of the night. They try to conceal their cars and trucks, but with the leaves off the trees, I can spot them when I come around the curve coming off my three to eleven shift. Something's fishy about that place. I can feel it."

"That's not surprising," Abigail stated, "the upper level lodge members are essentially Satan worshipers.

It would be a perfect place to have their meetings and prepare for rituals."

"And now that I think about it, I've got this strange lady that comes once in a while. She was widowed a few months back. I met her husband one time and he sent shivers down my spine. Anyway, sometimes she's this pious saint and sometimes she's just plain nuts."

"Do you remember her name?" Abigail queried.

"I believe it starts with a W. I'll think of it in a minute." He pursed his lips and looked at the ceiling.

"Wagner?"

"Yes, that's it! Wagner. How did you know?"

"It sounds like the mother of one of my Satanic Ritual Abuse clients."

"She rants about her son not coming home."

"That would be Billy. He's probably been sacrificed by the cult." Abigail did not want to get into the whole story of Billy's attacks on her and his abandoned car that was found on Lee's property.

"So, she's one of them?"

"I'm afraid so."

"In my church?"

"It makes sense when you understand that the Satanist's goal is to rise as high as they can in both God's kingdom and Satan's. There will be wolves in sheep's clothing; tares among the wheat."

Solemn nods indicated that the men were beginning to understand that their county was infiltrated by more than a gang of teenaged hoodlums that would outgrow their adolescent pranks.

"If you don't mind my interrupting," Richard Morris injected, "I've got a lot of acreage that I farm and I ride my horses and four-wheeler all over the place, even onto neighboring property. Recently I came across what I thought was a campfire. Someone was real careful to try to conceal it, but I got a stick and sifted through the ashes. I'm beginning to wonder if those bone-shaped sticks that I tried to convince myself were sticks might have really been bones."

George Bordman spoke up, "Ever since Mike told me about the peculiar things that had been happening at his church, I've been looking more closely around my church. I found candle wax in the carpet around the baptismal font and the communion table, too. I just figured it was from some wedding or something, but I'm beginning to be suspicious – God forgive me - of some of my 'frozen chosen' elders."

"I have a lady that comes to my church," Don Wilmore added. "She sounds a bit like your Wagner lady – nice one week and angry the next. I'm a bit intimidated by her because she's taller than I am and sometimes I see something in her eye that looks downright evil. Actually, it's hard to look her in the eye because she's wall-eyed and she keeps switching the eye she uses."

"I don't suppose her name is Sherry?" Abigail asked.

"Yes, how did you know?"

"She was sent in to be my client with the assignment to destroy me."

"How did you handle that?"

"I told her that I knew that it was her assignment and she had two choices: she could leave because she would not succeed or, if she wanted to leave the cult, I would help her get deprogrammed."

"What happened?"

"One of her personalities pulled a knife on me, reamed me a new one, and left. I haven't seen her since. I don't know if she went underground or if they killed her off because she failed her assignment. I have a knife collection," Abigail added casually. "But that's a story I'll save for another time."

Abigail heard gasps from several of the clergymen who had not been prepared for conversations like this. She noted Pastor Spalding's sympathetic smile. He was where they were, not all that long ago. They continued to discuss particulars and generalities regarding the problem of Satanism in their county.

Dennis Walsh looked at his watch, "Speaking of time, it's almost time for us to close this meeting. I think that it has become evident that there is a problem. The question is, what is the most effective way that we can battle it? Abigail, what suggestions do you have?"

"I think that we all know that prayer and fasting is definitely number one on the list. It would be helpful for each of us to document in writing or with cameras some of the things we see or suspect, including names of people. We also have to recognize that it will take a county-wide effort to eradicate or transform them." They nodded in agreement.

"And we can't each be sitting on the side of the lake with a fishing pole. We need to collectively man the nets. I noticed something about the locations of the churches that are represented here. Look at the county map on the wall. There are five main roads that lead in and out of our county. Each has one of your churches on it plus several right in the heart of the county. If we think of your churches as being at the gateways to the county and pray accordingly, we might find some interesting results."

"You're right!" Pastor Spalding affirmed.

Pastor Walsh was astonished. "I just put that map up last week for our outreach program!"

"I think that was a God thing," Richard Morris said.

"Amen," came from several of the men.

"One other thought," Abigail added. "I know that it's hard to have people come to inter-denominational events, but if you men start to prep your congregations about the idea, we can move toward a county-wide prayer summit after we start with a county-wide food drive or school supply drive or something that's kind of neutral. Maybe we can have a booth at the county fair or something."

After that, they took turns praying for their county and asked for God's direction and for more like-minded pastors and leaders. They set their April the second meeting at Paul Overton's Methodist church on the southern edge of Hillsdale. Soon the church and eventually the parking lot emptied.

There was a flurry of activity in the spiritual realm that day. Shrieks reverberated throughout the atmosphere as dark spirits dodged the ribbons of incense that rose up toward the bowls reserved for this region. Winged messengers danced their celestial dances as they eyed the brims of the bowls filled with the prayers of the saints. Indeed, they had been privileged to carry answers back to earth already. It did not matter how large or small the answer was to these dedicated worshippers who rejoiced and laughed with the Most

High God at the raging of the leaders of nations and states and counties who counseled together to devise vain things.

Xerxes, the congressman, sat thoughtfully in the chambers of the nation's capital. His car was in the body shop being repaired. He was in a foul mood and he still had no explanation for his experience that day with Prinz. His mission was to destroy the Great Power and make life difficult for His followers.

He consistently voted for abortion-promoting bills and for the legalization of marijuana, for eliminating or taxing charitable corporations, especially churches and ministries. He voted to reduce the military and open the borders, to thwart independent oil production and promote solar power and global warming agendas. He promoted the increase of welfare programs, free college education, and increased taxes on those with jobs.

He supported the U.N.'s Sustainable Development agenda and wanted to weaken and destroy this nation. His agenda could be described as foreshadowing of the kings described in Revelation who have one purpose – to give their power and authority and kingdoms to the beast. Vanity of vanities, all is vanity!

It was fairly calm that week for Abigail but she always kept a wary eye on the calendar. Next week would be intense once again with the thirteenth and the Ides of March on the fifteenth. Several times she came in and found the message light flashing on the answering machine. The first call was from a referral by Rev. Griffin. They set a ten o'clock appointment for Friday.

Abigail got a number of hang up calls. Three times a threatening voice rasped, "Beware the Ides of March" and hung up after a malevolent laugh. Each threat was countered with her declaration that no weapon formed against her would prosper. *Humph! The Ides of March was remembered as a day of treachery because of the back-stabbing of a treacherous friend. They should be a lot more concerned about that than me!*

She and Cindy managed to meet for lunch at the little café. This was a special treat and they had a good gab-fest and prayer time about the Ides of March threats. She caught her up on family news from a rare call by her father. He was a proud father and grandfather. She loved him deeply, but he was difficult to talk to. He was a man of few words which made it awkward. They each communicated better face-to-face.

Thursday was stormy, but Friday dawned clear and crisp with just a hint of spring in the air. "Lord, I can't wait!" She was excited when she noticed the crocuses nudging their way to the surface.

Vicki Clayton arrived at the church just as Abigail pulled up. They introduced themselves and Vicki filled out the paperwork while Abigail set up the CD player before they began their session. Abigail took the time to tell Vicki about the impact of verbal assaults, and especially of vows.

Vicki began her story with a bang. "I caught my husband in bed with one of my friends. In my own bed!" Vicki was livid.

"Ouch! That's a stab in the back," Abigail remarked. "I'm so sorry. When did this happen?"

"It's been about a year. Actually, next week, it'll be exactly one year. March fifteenth. I'll never forget that day. I'll never forget what he did to me. What he's still doing to me. I'll never forgive them!"

Abigail had expected that it had been a more recent offense by the intensity of the emotions. Obviously, Vicki had kept all the pain circulating for a year and the wound had never healed. "Tell me what you hope to get from our ministry time."

Vicki was not expecting that. "I, um, well, I don't know exactly. Rev. Griffin told me that you could help me get through this." Vicki paused, thought for a few moments, and then gushed. "I guess what I really want is to be able to put this behind me and have some kind of peace so I can move on in life. I want my daughters back. I want justice. I mean, he married the traitor and they have custody of my girls. I don't have visitation unless it's supervised and I'm the one paying child support! How fair is that?" Vicki's face was red and her jaw was jutted out.

"I can help you. This is all very fixable. How old are your daughters?"

"Eleven and fourteen."

"Okay. How about if we set the legal stuff aside for right now and focus for a little bit on the anger and the other emotions?" Getting the nod from Vicki, Abigail resumed, "Can you tell me about that March fifteenth?"

"Sure. We have, we *had* a business. She worked for us. I was out running errands earlier that day but I forgot something so I had to come back to the office. The machinist said that Alan had gone up to the house. Heather wasn't around either, but that wasn't unusual. So, I went up to the house and figured that I'd join him for a quick lunch. I went straight to my bedroom to use the bathroom. They... grrrrhh... they were..."

"Do you remember what you were thinking and feeling at the time?"

"I was shocked! Angry! I, I couldn't believe what I was seeing. I thought I had a good marriage."

"Then what?"

"I grabbed the little lamp off my dresser and threw it at them. That's why I lost custody of the girls. It hit the wall but the stupid cord snapped around and put a teeny, tiny cut in his cheating forehead and a lousy drop of blood came out. So, he called the police and *I* was charged with assault. Eew! It's so unfair!" Her face was red again.

"Emotions?"

"Betrayed. Ambushed."

"Rejected?"

"Big time!"

"On a scale of zero to ten, which of the emotions rate a nine or ten?"

Vicki thought a moment and then replied, "Probably all of them. Actually, rejection and anger are more like a twenty."

"That's pretty intense. I know that this event calls for some intense emotions, but let's ask God to take us to the root of *this* kind of rejection and anger."

"Uh, okay," Vicki was cooperative even though this kind of counseling was totally foreign to her. Her last counselor was Rogerian and she was used to him rephrasing everything she said and repeating it back to her. She got to vent a lot, but it was not helpful.

"Lord, would You stir in Vicki's mind and brain and bring her to the source of this kind of extreme anger and rejection?"

Vicki's head remained bowed and her eyes were closed. Her fists were clenched.

"What's the first thought that came into your mind? Let me know, even if it doesn't seem to have anything to do with this issue."

"Okay, this is weird. I'm thinking about what my mom told me about my conception."

"Go on."

"She said that she didn't want any more kids, but Dad did. According to her, I was conceived because he raped her. What does that have to do with anything?"

"Everything. This is the taproot of your rejection and anger issues. Think about it a minute. What were the emotions that were swirling all around you when you were conceived and while you were in the womb?"

"Anger. Resentment. From both of them."

"And do you think that your mother might have had any feelings of rejection toward the baby that she didn't particularly want?"

"Oh, wow. I never made that connection."

"God did. That's why He brought that thought to your mind today. Emotions are chemically based and they cross over the placental barrier. So, all the feelings that were coursing through your mother's system crossed over to yours. The enemy took full advantage of that just like a roaring lion goes after the weak and helpless ones."

Vicki let out a deep sigh. "So, what can do we do about this? I mean, it's history. I was born."

"I noticed that your birthday is December fifteenth."

Vicki was curious. "Why is that relevant?"

"Do the math. If you were conceived nine months prior, that would put it right around March fifteenth – the Ides of March. A day of betrayal."

Vicki almost fell out of her chair. She was speechless as she processed the implications of the timing.

"Let's pray now about your conception and womb experience and ask God to demolish strongholds and get rid of tormenting spirits. I find that if any emotion is above a ten, it's probably demon-fueled, if you know what I mean."

"Yeah, I think I'm catching on."

They bowed in prayer again and when they were finished, Vicki's countenance was brighter and she seemed more peaceful. "I feel lighter," she reported.

"Excellent. Now let's take care of a couple of vows that you made. Remember that you bound your soul with several strong oaths and you need to intentionally renounce what you had announced earlier."

"What did I say?"

Abigail referred to her notes. "I'll never forget the date. I'll never forget what he did. I'll never forgive." Abigail reviewed the consequences of embracing the vows and spoke to Vicki about the principles of forgiveness.

"I want to do that. I need to do that."

Abigail smiled and said, "After you."

Vicki awkwardly prayed, "God, I'm sorry for making all those vows. I renounce them. I don't want them anymore. Please forgive me. And I forgive Alan and Heather for their... for their betrayal and for everything they're still doing. In Jesus' name, amen."

Abigail prayed in agreement with her and when she finished, she looked at the tears of relief flowing down

Vicki's peaceful face. Abigail ended the session with a prayer of blessing and then they set up an appointment for the following Friday.

Carrie Sue's session was focused on the upcoming rituals as well as touching base with the original Carrie Sue. She was making steady progress as she continued to peek in on her life. Host Carrie Sue was consulting with her more and more.

Amy Bolton's session also focused on the following week's rituals. Head Warden appraised Abigail of the internal tensions but was satisfied that Apollyon's level was still secure even though he described it as a volcano that was about to erupt. Abigail managed to remain composed when Head Warden made a rueful comment about it not being right that the guys had to experience morning sickness.

Lee was waiting expectantly at the barn. Abigail had been making it a habit to join him most evenings as he took care of the horses. It was the last thing he did after working all day on the lengthy list of projects that he wanted to finish before the construction crews arrived in a few weeks.

Their visits were becoming much less awkward and there was an endless stream of subjects that they talked about. They shared meals together. Sometimes Abigail put a picnic lunch together and they ate perched on bales of hay in the barn. More often, Lee was a guest at Abigail's dining room table.

"My daughter said that she'd like to come and meet you some day."

"I'd like that."

"She's a lot more interested in connecting with me than she has been in a long time. She said that after her school year is finished she'd like to come out to see the farm and visit with her grandparents and her cousins."

"Very cool. Change of subject." Abigail knew that men sometimes needed an alert to get out of one box and get into another one. "When are you going to put the horses out in the pasture?"

"Probably next week some time. I think they're calling for another snow storm Monday or Tuesday. I want to wait to see how that goes."

"Well, let me know. I love to watch them kick their heels up when they get free."

22

Sunday, March 11

People were getting accustomed to seeing Abigail and Lee sitting together with Gary and Cindy. There were some speculations and rumors but mostly they were pleased to see a fresh sparkle return to Abigail's eyes. Gary and Cindy were especially pleased. Today, the couple arrived together because, after he took care of all the horses, Lee picked Abigail up at her house. They planned to spend the afternoon together.

Pastor Spalding had wrestled with his message ever since the Ministerial Alliance meeting on Monday. He wanted to address the spiritual battle that was being waged for their county without being blunt. Since the Ides of March was coming up this week, he decided to preach on betrayal.

"I'll be focusing on Second Corinthians seven this morning," Pastor Spalding beamed at his congregation. "Turn there now and let's see what the Bible says about godly sorrow and worldly sorrow."

He used Judas Iscariot and Peter as his examples. He had them turn to critical verses in the gospels to make his points about them before concluding. "Judas and Peter both betrayed Jesus. The biggest difference in the two men was their relationship with Jesus. They both walked with Jesus the entire three years of His ministry. They both witnessed the miracles. And yet, Peter truly loved Jesus while Judas had a different agenda. Even though Judas realized his mistake at the end and threw the money back at the Pharisees, he went out and hanged himself. Peter realized his mistake and he went out and wept bitterly. Judas died and Peter was restored.

"Look at Second Corinthians seven verse ten again. *'For the sorrow that is according to the will of God produces a repentance without regret, leading to salvation; but the sorrow of the world produces death.'* That word sorrow means grief over sin or repulsion of sin."

Stepping down from the platform, Pastor Spalding finished with his appeal. "Folks, some of us were like Peter. We grieved over our sin. We were repulsed by it, humbly came to God and were restored to a right relationship with Jesus. There are countless others who have a different agenda. Some agendas are downright diabolical. Others are ordinary self-centered agendas. If you need to repent for anything today, please come down and get right with God. Live without regret for both time and eternity."

Pastor Spalding looked into the balcony as he said this. He was met with Sheriff Bynum's unmistakably angry glare.

The storm hit hard on Monday. March was definitely coming in like a lion. The roads were a mess but Lee managed to make it out to the horses with only a few skids. The snow was heavy and creaked as he made his way to the barn. He finished taking care of the horses and called Abigail.

There was no answer. If she was in the house she would have picked up. *Hmm. Surely, she's not out in this mess.* He turned toward her place just to check up on her. Pulling into her driveway, Lee let out a hearty laugh. Abigail was rolling her second large snowball down the front lawn!

"Hey," he yelled out the passenger window.

"Did you come to help?"

"Absolutely."

By the time Lee parked his truck next to Abigail's and came down the front lawn, Abigail had positioned the second snowball next to the first one and was rolling a smaller one to join the other two.

"Want some help putting them up?"

"No, this is going to be a swimmer. I just need some branches for his arms and then I need to make a couple of shark fins."

"Shark fins?"

"Yeah, you remember that cartoon with Calvin and his stuffed animal?"

"That was a while ago."

"Still funny. Warped, but funny."

Lee found some suitable branches for arms, a couple of dark stones for eyes, and then waited as Abigail put the final touches on the shark fins that she formed out of the snow. She made it look as if the snowman was swimming for his life in front of a school of sharks.

Stepping back and admiring her work, she smiled and said, "Perfect!"

Lee just shook his head in amusement at the playful side of this serious woman.

"My boys got me started on doing crazy snowmen. They loved that cartoon and their father loved to come home to their creations. Ahem! Our creations."

Tuesday was the thirteenth. The Satanists tirelessly pursued their occult agenda – the Luciferian agenda. Local and regional rituals were packed with orgies and futile attempts to satisfy insatiable appetites for power. Lasting into the wee hours of the morning, pumped up by an infusion of energy from their demons, they went about their day as if they had gotten a full night's sleep.

The surgery to stabilize Max Berryman's spine was successful. He had fractures of the seventh and eighth thoracic vertebrae causing minimal compression on the spinal cord. However, it was just enough pressure that it gave him minor altered sensations and some trouble with motor movements in his legs.

After recovering from the successful surgery, Max was sent to a large rehabilitation facility in Atlanta that specialized in the treatment of spinal cord injuries. He was making great progress according to his physical and occupational therapists. However, he remained sullen, agitated, and depressed – especially after a visit from Dr. Bacchus. Ted and Barbara made weekly trips to the out-of-state hospital. They tried to cheer him up, but to no avail. He was a tormented young man.

The Ides of March. Abigail continued to receive raspy-voiced threats. Each one was countered with Scriptural declarations. *"The Lord is my light and my salvation; whom shall I fear? The Lord is the defense of my life; who shall I dread. Though a host encamp against me, my heart will not fear."* She let Lee listen to one of them before she deleted it.

"You should save that. Someone could probably figure out whose voice that is someday. Besides, that's part of the documentation that you ought to keep. Just in case there's an honest official somewhere."

"You're right. I won't delete them anymore." She had four of them saved by the time she received several more messages Wednesday. She could hear clicking from the answering machine all night long.

Without Max's imminent presence, Abigail had let her guard down somewhat. She knew that Ranson was still in the picture, but after the encounter in the grocery store, he had not resurfaced. They could still send any one of their people to harass her at any time. "Lord, they're threatening some kind of a stab in the back, some kind of betrayal. I have to assume that would come from a trusted friend, not a known enemy. I pray for favor and no misunderstandings, offenses, or jealousies in any of my relationships. Especially Carrie Sue and Amy," she hastily added.

She knew from experience that personalities could turn on her; especially if they were programmed. One of her survivors had a false host who mirrored the Christian host in a survivor that she had been working with for a long time. Something did not seem right and yet the false non-Christian host functioned and spoke just like the Christian host. It took several weeks, but the Lord finally showed her the ruse. After confronting the false host personality and deprogramming her, she was integrated. Working with these survivors was an intense mental and spiritual challenge.

Abigail retired that night thinking that the Ides of March threats were much ado about nothing. However, she was not privy to the titanic clashes in the heavens. Curse after curse was thwarted by the Lord of hosts who judged that the curses were without a cause. They fell harmlessly to the ground, dissolving in the protective blood of Jesus the Christ. The reproaches, however, brought a sting to those who had sent them. Their wisdom was decreased as their fury increased with each boomeranged spiel.

An item that would never reach the public media was the disappearance of another young girl whose tortured body would never be found. Beware! The Ides of March.

Ever since the incident with Carrion, Zorroz had been sensing the displeasure of those in power above him: Daggett, Prinz, and even Xerxes. His wife and two daughters were at the ritual. He was placed in a double-bind that would change his life forever: Your wife or your youngest daughter. The treachery of the treacherous would not be forgotten. Zorroz renewed his vows to rise in power.

Sheriff Bynum would have to move again. They would have to change their church affiliation to keep meddlesome Sunday school teachers from asking too many questions. Their other daughter was being home schooled, but curious neighbors might notice that their five-year-old was not playing with her sister anymore.

Vicki Clayton was looking forward to her counseling session. She had not felt this good in a year. Abigail was pleased to see the spring in her step and the smile on the face that was drawn and bitter the last time she entered her office.

"Good morning."

"Yes, it is. I just want to thank you for last week. I almost cancelled my appointment because I just feel so much better."

"I'm glad you didn't because I think we need to pray about your legal matters."

"I'd like that but I'm not sure what can be done."

"Tell me about the charges."

"They're ridiculous!" Vicki started to turn red. "His lawyer is claiming that because I committed a violent act and caused a physical injury that left a permanent disfiguring scar, that it's a felony. And I'd be a danger to the girls." Vicki was flushed and the veins were obvious on her forehead. "Alan and Heather claim that I threatened to kill them."

"Did you?"

"No, er, well I don't remember exactly everything I said. I suppose I could have said something like that. But I never would."

"Of course not."

"So how do we pray about this mess?" Vicki did not sound very hopeful.

"Let's look at Psalm eighty-two and I'll explain some of the principles as I read through it. *'God takes His stand in His own congregation'*, or council and *'He judges in the midst of the rulers'*. It seems as if He's displeased with the rulers of the lower courts and He reams them out. *How long will you judge unjustly and show partiality to the wicked?* God is Judge of all. He's the Judge and God of all. I won't go into all the other Scripture verses that support this heavenly council, but that's where we want to take your appeal... not just to the throne of grace like we usually do."

"Okay."

"We believe that the accusations against you are unjust so we need to take your complaint to His higher court. You are not the defendant. You are the plaintiff and Jesus Christ is your advocate."

"Ah-h." Vicki was catching on.

"I'll pray first and you can pray in agreement."

"Let's do it!" Vicki bowed her head, closed her eyes, and folded her hands.

"Holy Judge and God of all, we are coming to Your court today asking You to open Vicki Clayton's case. We ask that You'd listen to all the arguments of her advocate, Jesus Christ, and call forth every defendant that has lied, exaggerated, or unjustly used anything that was said or done by her. You alone look on the heart. We ask that You'd move on the celestial and human agents that are involved in her case and render a quick and fair ruling according to the righteousness and justice that are the foundations of Your throne. We further ask that You'd keep this case open so that any future complaints may be filed if necessary. We specifically ask that You would cause all unjust charges against Vicki to be dropped, that You would reinstate free access to her daughters, and that You would cancel the child support decree and recompense her for all the child support that she has been compelled to pay in the past. And as Vicki prays in agreement, we ask that You would declare that it is finished!"

"I agree. God, I agree. Please let me get my girls back, amen."

"What are you sensing?"

"Hope. I'm actually feeling some hope. I think that no matter what is going on right now, I can move on with my life. Thank you so much!"

"Let me pray a prayer of blessing over you and then let's play this by ear. If you think you need another session, give me a call. But either way, let me know what happens with your girls."

"I will."

They closed and after a hug, Abigail went to the kitchen to eat her lunch. Carrie Sue was waiting for Abigail when she got back from her break.

"Hello, how's it going?"

"Pretty good. We made it through the thirteenth and the Ides of March. I noticed some restlessness, but it was really no big deal. Mom didn't even bug us. At least not as much as usual."

"Excellent! Let's open with prayer and see where the Lord wants us to go today."

"I'm not getting anything. Are you?" This was a bit unusual for Carrie Sue.

"Hm. Yes, actually the Lord has just reminded me of something that I was thinking about the other day: mirror alters."

"Mirror alters. What are they?"

"That's what I call them, anyway. I've found that there are alters that mirror other alters, especially some of the critical ones, like the host. They're not exactly like pseudo-alters who try to mimic another part, they just mirror them and it's hard to tell them apart."

"What do you mean?"

"I mean that there might be a non-Christian host who could slip in and mirror what a Christian host – you – would say or do. And they're good enough that they are hard to detect even by you or the others."

"Do you think I have one?"

"I'm not sure. I haven't sensed anything, but that doesn't mean there isn't one. Why don't we ask God to, um, smudge up any mirrors so that there wouldn't be a clear reflection. We'll ask Him to confirm or deny if there are any around."

Abigail intently observed Carrie Sue while they prayed. There was an almost imperceptible shift that she noticed.

Carrie Sue looked up and immediately said, "I'm sure that there's nothing to the mirror thing."

"Spoken like a true mirror," Abigail countered.

"Well, well," a flustered Carrie Sue sputtered. "I'm not a mirror, I'm the same host Carrie Sue that you've always talked to."

"Not exactly. Sometimes you have slipped in."

"Okay, so what? So, I'm the other host. I can do her job just as well as she can. Even better sometimes because I don't have all that religious baggage to carry. What difference does it make?"

"The difference is that she has a genuine relationship with God and you do not. You're programmed and demonized."

"I can pray and read the Bible and sing in church."

"Yes, but just going through the motions doesn't work. You need to be healed, too." Abigail could see that she was not getting anywhere with this one. "Would you mind if I speak with the other host?"

"No. I think I like being in charge for now. Don't worry, we'll be in church on Sunday. We'll sit right next to you and your friends." With that, Carrie Sue got up and left a stunned Abigail sitting alone.

Oh, that went well! Abigail's sarcasm rose up. "Lord, did I do something wrong? Please don't let Carrie Sue be harmed by this mirror image thing." She sat and thought about everything that was said. She thought about how familiar the mirror seemed. *She must have slipped in other times and I didn't catch it.* Remembering some previous interactions with Carrie Sue, Abigail began to realize that the mirror personality was a good explanation for Carrie Sue's baffling responses. "Okay, Lord, I refuse to feel guilty. I will trust Your timing on working this out."

Abigail got to take a longer break than she normally did so she got her grocery shopping finished. She also stopped at the gas station and topped off her tank. Surveying the lot, she noticed that the maroon truck on the other side of the island was the same distinctive pickup truck that had parked next to hers at the grocery. *Oh, Lord, is this another tail?* The windows were deeply tinted making it difficult to determine if someone was in it or not. She finished her transaction and pulled away, looping around at the far end of the parking lot where she waited.

A man came out of the gas station and as he entered the maroon truck, Abigail saw the braided hair. The man hurriedly put his truck in gear and darted onto the road as if he were either pursuing or being pursued. He did not appear to notice Abigail parked at the end of the lot. Once he was gone, Abigail headed the other direction and returned to the church for her session with Amy.

Stopping at the office, Abigail asked Ginny, "Hey, lady. Do you think Pastor Spalding has a minute?"

"I'm sure he does, just let me check." Ginny bustled the few feet to the doorway, rapped lightly, and spoke to Pastor Spalding. Turning around and giving Abigail a broad smile, she waved Abigail in and held the door open for her.

"Hello. Come in, come in."

"I only have a minute, but I just wanted to get a little extra prayer cover."

"Sure, sure, what's going on?"

"I might be getting a little paranoid, but whenever someone parks next to me at two consecutive places, I think I might be getting tailed again. The man that got into the maroon pickup truck at the gas station had a long braid down his back and was built a lot like the guy that showed up on the huge horse several times. He's probably the guy that poisoned Dude and maybe the one who left the dead dog down by the gate and I think he might be the neighbor that has the ritual site."

"Whoa, slow down." Pastor Spalding's eyebrows were half way up his forehead. "That *is* something to pray about. And I'll keep an eye on the property here to see if any strange vehicles are hanging around. We'll pray that it was just a coincidence, but if it wasn't, we'll still keep praying for your safety."

"Thanks."

Amy Bolton was a few minutes early today. There was little banter because she was feeling an urgency. After opening in prayer, she blurted, "Mayor contacted me and he says that he's done. I'll let him tell you more, but he basically said that the lower levels were going bonkers this week and were taking it out on his people."

"Okay, is he ready to talk?"

"I'm here."

"What's going on?"

"Can you do that privacy bubble thing?"

"Sure. Lord, would You please put us in a privacy bubble so that no one knows what we discuss."

"Thanks," the nervous personality said. "Okay, so you know that Joktan's guys have tunnels and secret passages that go up through our little town. They've been really hopped up since Apollyon's level six has been sealed up. Judas' level five has been taking it out on everyone, and especially since the Ides of March is his big day – being a traitor and all."

"That would make sense. How can I help you?"

"I'm thinking that I want to close down the whole town and just let everyone integrate."

"With all the fires we've had to put out, we've never dealt with all the stuff that your people are carrying."

"Yeah, I know. But if we could get all those babies and toddlers taken care of in a couple of minutes, why can't we do the same for all the others? I've had lots of secret meetings and everyone is on board."

"Let's do it." Abigail prayed the comprehensive prayer for healing and deliverance and then checked back with Mayor.

"It's a lot lighter now."

"Let's ask the Lord to integrate anyone that's ready and then see if there are any holdouts for any reason." They prayed again.

"There's a couple of them that haven't integrated. They're some tough looking teenagers and they're not very happy."

"Is one of them willing to be a spokesperson for the group?"

"I'll see."

"What do you want, lady?"

"Just want to talk and ask you some questions if you don't mind."

"What about?"

"You seem to be displeased about what just went down or maybe you guys have always been unhappy." Abigail's observation came across as an inquiry.

"Both."

"Can you tell me more?"

"We're ticked and we don't want to go anywhere until we make our cousin pay."

Abigail continued to pump them for more specifics. She affirmed their right to be outraged about everything that the cousin was permitted to do and then turned the conversation to a discussion about anger and forgiveness. "What do you think?"

"We're not ready."

"That's fine. But I am concerned about your safety inside the system. I mean, right now, with most of the town evacuated, you guys are the only targets left for the subterranean guys."

"We can take care of ourselves."

"I believe that you are resourceful, but you're really outnumbered. You'll be constantly on the run. Would you consider maybe moving into Head Warden's area if he's okay with that or maybe we can ask the true Lord Jesus to bring you to a safe place?"

They conferred and the spokesperson said that they'd be okay with moving into Head Warden's area. It was arranged and they went into the prison area where Head Warden's guards gave them a brief tour and then got them settled into their own quarters.

"I think that makes this a ghost town," Mayor quipped. "Can I go in now?"

Abigail prayed for his integration and then Amy resurfaced.

"It's a lot quieter in here! I like it."

"Let's pray for one more thing," Abigail had another idea that she assumed had come from the Lord. "Let's ask God to level the town and preserve anyone that might have been left behind."

"Good idea; then Joktan's people can't sneak up on anyone anymore. We'll know where their tunnels are."

Once again, they prayed.

"Wow! It was like there was a massive earthquake and everything was leveled. Then it all went up in smoke and there's nothing left but a bare field."

The man with the long braid did not like his current assignment. He had better things to do than follow that woman around. He had heard the rumors, seen the evidence, and was not anxious to be the next one to have to visit Dr. Bacchus because of an injury. Bad things have been happening to those who tangled with that woman. And he preferred to use the longer back road to get home rather than drive past her place today. There was something eerie about it that made him shudder and sent shivers up his spine.

23

Saturday, March 17, St. Patrick's Day

"Is this the O'Steele residence?" Cindy giggled.

"Close enough. What's up?"

"Oh, not much, but Gary and I decided we wanted to throw a spontaneous St. Patrick's Day and last-Sunday-of-winter party tomorrow after church. Can you come? We've invited Mr. O'Norris, too."

"Of course."

"Of course you can come, or of course I invited Lee?"

"Both. And, yes, I'll be there. What can I bring?"

"Just your appetite for corned beef with all of the trimmings."

"Yum! I'll be there." They chatted a bit longer and Abigail mentioned the "coincidence" that the man with the braid in the maroon truck parked next to her twice yesterday. They prayed for added protection.

Abigail checked the time. Lee finally decided that today was the day to let the horses go back into the pasture. He would be picking Abigail up any time now so she went to the back room to get her boots and coat on. She paused a moment and looked through the mostly glass door with the two side light windows next to it, scanning the empty pasture and the fields beyond it. Closing the back door, crossing the deck, descending the steps, she turned the corner of the house just as Lee tooted his horn.

"Good morning," Lee greeted her as she climbed into his truck.

"Top of the morning to ye," Abigail shot back with a silly grin.

"Oh, that's right. You must have gotten a call from Cindy O'McCord."

"Yep. Can't wait. It's been too long since we've all gotten together."

"I agree."

They quickly agreed on a plan for taking the five horses down to the pasture. Lee had already repaired the cut fence line and had walked it again yesterday just to be sure that there were no problems. Abigail led Buster, holding his halter close to his jaw for more control. Lee took Sassy and Lady. They walked the high-stepping, tail-switching horses through the gate and then slipped the halters off. All three horses took off running, kicking up their heels and tossing their heads. Buster was the first to drop to his knees and attempt to roll in the field.

Lee and Abigail watched with delight as the magnificent animals vented their pent-up energy on the turf. Finally, they closed the gate and returned to the barn to free Misty and Sparkles. Abigail took Sparkles while Lee took Misty because she was more high strung. Returning to the barn after their show, Lee remarked that he now had a lot of manure to haul out of the barn.

"I'd be glad to help. I could use a workout myself."

"I won't refuse help."

Lee fired up the tractor and brought the bucket close to the first two stalls. Abigail started on one and Lee started on the other. They talked. They stopped for lunch. They worked in a companionable silence. They held hands as they walked down to the pasture to check on the horses before Lee took Abigail back home.

Cindy had decorated the house with shamrocks and green balloons. The atmosphere was festive and the food was delicious. Grandpa and Grandma McVeigh were included as well. Traci and Bryan were excused from the table after dinner and the adults continued their conversations.

"So, Lee," Grandpa McVeigh addressed Lee, "how are the plans for your new place going?"

"It looks like the contractor can get in there next week and start the foundation on the house. I've been getting the other buildings in order but there's still so much work to do."

"You let me know if there's anything I can help with. I'm still handy with a tractor, you know."

"Thanks, I might just do that. I want to fence more land so I can get some heifers in here before too long."

"What breed?"

"Not sure if I want to go with Black Angus or Herefords this time."

They continued to discuss the pros and cons of the different breeds as well as a host of other things. Finally, the McVeigh's announced that they needed to head for home. They made the rounds to get hugs and kisses from everyone before they left. All too soon, the pleasant afternoon slipped away. Lee and Abigail said their good-byes as well and left together.

"What do ya think?" Gary asked.

"I think it's just a matter of time," Cindy answered with a contented smile as they high-fived and kissed.

Monday dawned bright and clear. Abigail was excited. It was the last day of winter. The days and nights were almost equal. Six a.m. to six p.m. Just the smell of the balmy spring-like air and the sight of the crocuses, the swelling of the buds on the trees and bushes made her excited. She was itching to rototill the garden. She couldn't wait to mow lawns again, to tend the grape vines and orchard. Each year was more productive than the last. This year she wanted to raise chickens and maybe start beekeeping now that the pasture was not occupied. Maybe, just maybe, the Lord would let her have a horse again someday.

She and Jan Milner were going to have that cup of tea today at four. They kept promising each other that they would get together for a cup of tea all winter but it never happened. This was the last day of winter and they were going to do it! Jan reminded Abigail of her grandmother. She would serve it from her fine bone china tea set that was fit for the most elegant of ladies. Abigail would not be able to resist drinking tea with her pinky up.

Abigail meandered through her day restlessly finishing small projects and trying to decide what she ought to do before the nice weather compelled her to abandon inside tasks. She saved the deep cleaning to rid the house of the inevitable dust and ash from the wood stove until she was sure that she was finished with it for the season.

At three forty-five, Abigail went to the back room to don her old boots. She was going to walk down her driveway and hike up Earl's Jeep trail that ran parallel to the road. She was not going to drive her truck to go just over a quarter mile.

Slipping out the back door, she frowned again at the accumulation of smudges that were apparent with the sun streaming through. *I'll have to clean these windows one of these days.* Walther was on her hip as usual and she was careful to lock the door, hooking the keys on her belt loop by the carabiner in a practiced move.

Jan's large black and white cat meowed his greeting and rubbed against her shin as she waited for the door to open.

"Come in! Come in!" Jan opened the door and stepped aside to let Abigail in. The two friends hugged briefly while Earl ambled over to take her coat.

"Do you believe that we waited until the last day of winter to get our cup of tea?"

"Well, between Earl's doctor visits and my doctor visits and the kids and the grandkids..." Jan did not finish her thought. The truth was that Earl's heart was a worry and Jan's arthritis was painful and debilitating.

The whistle of the tea kettle stirred Jan to action. "Have a seat and I'll join you in a minute."

Earl went back to the adjacent living room where he would eavesdrop and inject his comments into their conversations or he would simply just sit there and enjoy his coffee.

After settling down, Jan gave a contented sigh. "It's just so good to see you again."

"Yeah. I miss our tea times and I'm sorry I didn't make it more of a priority."

"That's a two-way street. But we're here today." She raised her steaming cup with the delicate flower pattern as if she were giving a toast. "To friendship."

"To friendship," Abigail echoed and raised her cup as well.

"To friendship." Earl lifted his bulky red, white, and blue coffee mug bringing a smile to the ladies.

"So, tell us about your beau."

"Beau?"

"Or do you have two of them?"

"Two?"

"You asked us to keep an eye on you and we couldn't help but noticing that there's a dark blue truck and a white truck that keep going up and down your driveway. Nearly every day."

"I still have twenty-twenty vision, you know," Earl contributed from the living room. It was followed by a deep laugh.

"Twenty-twenty-five," Jan corrected him.

"I can still hit a bull's eye at five hundred yards!" the former World War II veteran sharp-shooter protested.

Blushing and sighing, Abigail joined their laughter. "His name is Lee and he owns both of them. He's the guy that bought that property across the road from us."

"Oh. He's been busy."

"One of these days, I'll bring him up here to meet you. He's my friend Cindy's husband's cousin who just moved from Montana." Abigail was beginning to feel like a teenager being interrogated by her parents.

"How old is he? Does he have kids? Widower or divorced?"

"Okay, Dad, slow down," Abigail laughed at his protectiveness. He and Jan were not quite old enough to be her parents, but they made a good big brother and big sister. "He's going to be forty-eight. Three years and three weeks older than me. His daughter, Lisa, is in college and lives in Colorado, I think. His wife left him for someone else, but I don't know the details. Anything else?"

"Is he a Christian?"

"Yes, yes. We met at church and he's a Spirit-filled Christian."

"Good, good. That's the most important thing."

"It kind of helps that he's good looking," Abigail teased back.

Jan looked at her friend, "Abigail, you have a sparkle in your eyes that wasn't there before. I'm happy for you. I hope that it's the Lord's will for you and Lee to be together."

"Thanks. I think I agree. I have to admit that I've struggled with feeling like I'm abandoning Darryl and the boys. But I know that they would want me to move on. I know that if the roles were reversed, I'd want that for them."

They chatted comfortably sipping tea all along. Abigail finally announced that she needed to head back up to the house and leave them to get their supper ready. Besides, Lee was going to join her for supper when he was finished with his day across the road.

"I'll watch you all the way home," Earl announced.

"You don't have to; I've got Walther with me."

"No. I'm going to make sure you get home all right." There was no dissuading the man.

Abigail hurried down the Jeep trail, cut across the front lawn and passed by the north side of her house on her way to the back door. She did not know that about the same time that she left Earl and Jan's home, the man with the large horse and the braided hair rode out of his concealment and nudged his horse to a position from which he could clearly see the back door of the house on the hill.

His powers communicated her whereabouts to him. He waited to fulfill his assignment. He was not afraid of legal consequences. He was guaranteed by human agents that nothing would happen to him. He casually pulled his rifle from the saddle scabbard and readied it for his mission.

The sunlight gave him a clear view of the back of the house. What he was not counting on was that he was also clearly highlighted by the sunlight and was easily seen by a vigilant man with twenty-twenty-five vision.

"Jan!" Earl hissed into the door that he opened a crack. "Bring me my 30.06 with the scope! Now!"

Jan knew not to ask any questions. Ignoring the stiffness and pain in her old joints, limping to the gun safe, punching in the code, spinning the handle and opening the door, Jan located the rifle and pulled it out. Locating the ammunition, she took three out of the box and hurried to place them in Earl's outstretched hand.

Flipping the cap off of the scope and efficiently loading the cartridges, Earl brought the rifle up to his cheek just as the man at the end of Abigail's property did the same. Abigail was mounting the steps when the first shot rang out. Another one followed a split second later.

Lee heard the double shots and knew that they had come from the other side of the road. Leaping into his truck, he peeled down his driveway, barely watching for traffic and headed for Abigail's house. He had a feeling. "Lord, no! Oh, Lord. Please don't let anything happen to Abigail!" He prayed desperately.

Seeing no one in front, leaving the truck running, Lee sprinted in a crouch around the back as he pulled his handgun. His heart sank when he saw Abigail curled in a fetal position on the deck surrounded by the glass that had been blown out of the door.

Counseling related E-Books by this author

I am a Cutter, Please Help Me
Yo Soy un Cortador Ayudana Por Favor
Emotional Abuse and Verbal Assaults through Lies, Vows, Curses, and Judgments
Battling Anorexia, Bulimia, Binge Eating, Health Food Obsession
Panic and Anxiety Attacks
Heaven or Hell – Have I Lost My Salvation?
Mad at God, Self, and Others
Dissociative Identity Disorder
What's in Your Family Tree? Battling Generational Curses and Familial Spirits
Spiritual Gifts – Discovering Your Spiritual Gifts
Seeing, Hearing, Sensing God through His Brokenhearted Children

Fiction E-Books series by this author:

Ritual Abuse – Autumn
Ritual Abuse – Winter
Ritual Abuse – Spring
Ritual Abuse – Summer

Watch for paperback editions of the above titles.

Made in the USA
Las Vegas, NV
11 September 2024